Insurmountable Odds

Book One of the Trilogy
When Stars Fall

A trilogy in the Dominium Saga

Martin A. Saunders

Mak Studios Limited
www.maksw.com

I0639692

Published by Mak Studios Limited, 2015

First Edition e-publication 2015
First Edition print 2015

©2015 Martin A. Saunders and Mak Studios Limited 2015

http://www.maksw.com

If you are interested in the Dominium Project – or have any issues regarding this publication, please contact dominium@maksw.com

v1.1

This trilogy is dedicated to my wife, for putting up with me for over twenty years, and also tolerating my never-ending plans to do something more than just a day job.

You are my heart, and the better half of my soul.

My thanks go to;

Wendy for patiently proof reading, spotting my vast use of 'vast' and over-hyphenation, some great suggestions and changes, and being my secret editor.
Alex, for enthusiastically reading through and champing at the bit for more.
Mrs. G, English Teacher extraordinaire and someone who somehow saw an author in me. I never made the 'millions' Maggy, but I remember you as asked!
Sol of www.solcommand.com – for being genuinely helpful and generous, and offering his services as 3D Modeller Extreme for the game project.
Andy of PixelDad Studio for painting some of Sol's models. Dominium wouldn't look as good as it does without your help.
The crew of www.spacesimcentral .com – for their positive feedback on the early chapters and generally keeping the 'space game flame' alive.
Michael from Infomarex.com, for convincing me that 'cybo sapiens' really did say it all, and for patiently, and generously correcting my own atrocious attempts at Latin.
And finally – the backers on www.kickstarter.com who shared the vision of what I want to achieve and generously lent their support. If only we could have drawn more like-minded souls to our door!

Foreword

This saga has been twenty odd years in the making, and the trilogy we are about to embark upon is just a *small* part of what's been roaming around my head all that time. I've long wanted to establish the 'Dominium' universe – and after setting out to create a computer game which would allow it to come to life – I felt it only right and proper to try and set down the epic saga of Dominium into the written word. Hopefully you find it as enjoyable to read as it was to write. (It was *very* enjoyable by the way, really, *really* enjoyable… hint, hint hint ;))

Whilst I humbly admit this is no Hugo or Nebula Award winner, the aim of this trilogy is two-fold. To provide you – the reader – with a (hopefully enjoyable) solid dose of sci-fi, and to promote the Dominium game project in the hope that, someday, you yourself might be able to fly between the star systems of the Cluster, and visit its various civilisations for yourself – letting you write your very own story, as I'd hoped for all along.

If you like what you see, and fancy the idea of visiting the many locations in this book - the best way to help this become reality is to spread the word… believe me, there is a *lot* more waiting in the wings…

dominium.maksw.com

PS. Book two is already well under way, along with precursor novels and many short stories ;)

Chapter One

She sat up in bed suddenly, some overpowering compulsion forcing her into full awareness. An odd sensation buzzed through her mind… not quite of loss, but of leaving something precious and hugely powerful behind. A dream perhaps.

She glanced about, looking for her clothes. Seeing none, she drew a sheet about her as she slipped out of the huge bed. The room was modern, with a dark chocolate brown décor; splashes of gold here and there – the bedside lamp, the fittings in the en-suite. Nothing at all looked familiar, and she had no recollection of where she might be.

A doorway led out into darkness across the bed, revealing soft glows in a multitude of colours shining from glossy furnishings in the room beyond. Curious, she walked from the bedroom out into the lounge area, and then gasped.

The large, open-plan penthouse apartment was completely open on all four sides, creating a panoramic night-time vista of the city surrounding the room. Tall, elegant skyscrapers rose from the darkness all around – each a host to myriads of countless glowing signs and multi-coloured lights. Some of the them seemed made almost entirely of large bio-luminescent ad-hoardings. Holograms wavered and flickered high above others, drawing her gaze up to the near constant cloud of flying lights which sped about the buildings high overhead.

Dominating the view above all, were the sharp, white bands of a planetary ring system stretching majestically across the sky, ending abruptly in darkness directly above as the glittering bands caught the planet's shadow.

Staring in awe, she walked toward the edge of the luxurious carpet, and reached out to touch the transparent wall-field that kept the sweltering night air outside. It felt as smooth as silk to the touch, but offered a rock solid resistance when pushed. As it tingled faintly against the palm of her hand she smiled at the oddly familiar sensation.

"It's good to be back," she said softly. Then she frowned.

"… Who am I this time?"

***

Aryn Cole sat back in his gel field chair and tried hard to keep a smile from his face. Eventually he had to concede and let a neural inhibitor prevent the muscle reflex from taking over. However, he still let the natural endorphins flood into his blood-stream, and damn it felt good.

"Tell me again," he almost purred.

The hooded figure standing in front of Aryn's desk paused for a moment, staring at him as if carefully considering Aryn's self-gratified response.

"The Velari have announced a migration," it repeated - in a dispassionate, almost metallic-sounding voice.

"Just one colony? Or the entire Roost-world?"

Again, a pause. "The entire Roost-world."

Aryn considered his options for a moment – so many contingencies, so many plans, tricks and traps all on hold. So many risks and mitigations to manage...

"Instruct Mayfleet to offer favourable relocation packages to the Velari, and undercut the competition to the zero profit line plus a dollar – but not one cent less."

He spun about in his chair and gazed out of the shell of engineered diamond that formed the rear of his office. The glorious display of the Core of the Dominium Globular Cluster lay beyond - tens of thousands of close proximity stars – all vying for each other's mass in their near eternal conflict of raging ions and interstellar gases forming an incandescent white glow.

Admiral Aryn Cole enjoyed the view, probably too much. He relished the knowledge of what the ultimate course of such vast cosmic forces would be – the finite certainty behind existence. It reminded him why he did what he did.

Eighty years he had waited for this latest outcome, and now finally the game was in play.

"Untether Asset 53; give him the order to proceed as planned."

***

The nebula had not yet been named by anyone of consequence. It would be several hundred years before the burst of energy that signalled the relatively recent death of the star even reached the nearest inhabited world.

Deep within the outer stretches of the dense orange fog that had once been the stars photosphere lay the scarred and burned remains of a large, T-type world. The rich and vibrant life it had once harboured was long gone. Left behind was a husk – barely half a planet – its core blasted out into space in a plume of magma, which had long since cooled and broken apart as gravity took its inevitable claim.

In this violently hot, inhospitable realm – where no life could exist unaided – movement could be seen. The perspective was difficult – as flying through clouds or fog in an aircraft, there were no points of reference, nothing to give a sense of scale. Certainly, something was moving toward the planet, something spherical and huge, perhaps the size of a moon.

Without even slowing, it smashed into the ruined planet without pause and immediately split apart. City sized hexagonal sections began peeling out and away from the upper surface – as would a Delani fruit, as it split open and curled back to reveal the sweet flesh and seeds inside.

Oblivious to the collosal energy and momentum behind the mass involved, these huge sections unrolled across the shattered surface. They crashed down into the rock structure, enveloping it in their embrace and digging deep into the crust, sending mountains of rock and dust into the fiery sky. The sound – the grinding of continental plates amplified a thousand-fold – reverberated through the nebula in all directions.

Within hours, the unrolling finally ceased, and the hexagonal structures settled into place, their city-sized sections having buried themselves deep into the rock. Yet still they stood two kilometres above the surface. The only sound and movement came from the constant pounding of debris which would slowly shower down for days afterwards.

At the centre of this structure stood a giant, hexagonal tower whose height matched the diameter of the original sphere as it stretched far above the ground and into the fierce red sky. Platforms and protuberances peppered its surface – their purposes elusive. Giant rails ran from top to bottom at equal points all around the tower.

Relative silence reigned for hours until, in perfect unison, the upper areas of this complex mesh split and lifted open to create a huge, flat lattice platform. From within each hexagon an actinic blue-white light leapt out from beneath, blasting into the rock below. Huge plumes of superheated gases erupted, jetting far out into the nebula. Only then did millions of assorted shapes surround these colossal vents of hot gas, flitting to and fro.

Large or small, they all moved with the same speed and agility as they dove into the volcanic destruction, returning minutes later. Very soon, skeletal shapes began appearing on the platform, growing in size and form minute by minute. Large structures grew up from this production surface, and complex arrangements of equipment were integrated into each as it grew.

Construction had begun.

***

Asset 53 awoke in a sterile white room. He was lying inside a suspension pod, which had been unstacked and placed onto a negative-G gurney. He took stock of his biometrics, ran some routine status checks – infiltration monitors, tracking system detection field scans and numerous other it-pays-to-be-paranoid routines before he was finally happy with his reanimated state of being. His integrations informed him that nothing had been modified since he'd been put into stasis; no additions, no infiltrations – as to be expected in a Grade 1 Naval facility. But, in his line of work, the question 'Am I paranoid enough?' had to be kept first and foremost.

He swung open the pod canopy and – entirely naked - hopped out onto the cool, metallic floor.

A light chime sounded, and a second later a disembodied voice filled the room. "Good afternoon Captain. May I get you anything?"

He smiled. "Two eggs over easy, four rashers of Firuvan bacon, some Anjulan coffee – black, two shots. Please."

"Of course, Captain," said the voice.

As he walked across the small room, a panel opened and he helped himself to the black plasprene Imperial Naval uniform within, and pulled a pair of matching slip-ons over his feet – all of which immediately formed a gapless, osmotic layer that effectively became a frictionless second skin. Sweat evaporated out, oxygen and tempered ultra-violet came in. Other harmful levels of radiation, acids and all manner of bio-hazardous substances stayed out. A modern day naval uniform could keep someone from harm's way even if they were inept enough to find themselves cast adrift within a nebula – their only immediate problem would be finding air to breathe. This uniform seemed slightly more refined than the last one he had worn. He watched idly as his rank and insignia began to glow above his left breast, now that the suit had attuned to his biometric field.

"Breakfast is in the Mess as usual, Captain. Briefing begins at 16:45 local."

He checked his own integrations time against the local network. It was 16:00 – he had some free time on his hands for a change.

"How long this time?" he asked the room.

"Thirty-one years, eight months, eleven days, eighteen hours, twenty-seven minutes, sixteen seconds."

"Thank you, *Capella*."

"You are most welcome."

Thirty-one years...

He accessed the qNet, and after his various integrations had scanned and updated their internal software and comm's protocols, he ran a single pre-set search – triple cross-referencing the results to make sure the answer he got was indeed correct. Then he tapped his financial accounts. The one bonus of being a Naval Intelligence Officer which he valued above all else, was that the Empire would honour Imperial Bonds held by operatives in suspension for "discrete" mission profiles.

He smiled broadly when he saw the balance.

Whistling softly and tunelessly to himself, he made his way down to the nearest Mess Hall. In his mind, he began reviewing all the technological advances of the past thirty-one years, notable political events and major news stories – most of which had been short-filed and indexed for him already by the station Intellect. However, he didn't trust it to give an unbiased or "uncoloured" set of data, so he ran his own searches of the greater public qNet just in case the navy algorithms had conveniently 'missed' anything. Whilst he let his searches run and drop their results into an m-gram cache for perusal later, he began to think about how to spend his matured wealth whilst he ate breakfast. After thirty-odd years – which to him had elapsed in mere moments – Firuvan bacon sure tasted good, and the double strength coffee definitely perked up the synapses.

Commodore Nelsen held the plyplas slim from Admiral Cole before him, and once again read the single sentence order it contained before reading it aloud to the officer standing before him.

"'Proceed as planned.'" He looked up at the captain known to him only as Asset 53, with one eyebrow arched slightly. He knew better than to enquire as to the vague nature of the order.

"Yes, sir."

"I presume you know what that entails, even if I don't."

"Yes, sir."

The Commodore grunted with bad grace. Naval Intelligence Officers were their own navy in the navy; it didn't pay to get between them and what they wanted. "What will you need?"

"A Valkyr."

Commodore Nelsen stared at him for a moment. "Do I need inform you Captain, that not only are Valkyr's so classified even I am not supposed to know of their existence, but also that they represent a substantial amount of resource investment by the navy, and further... that losing one – especially to other *interested* parties – would be a huge blow to the Naval

Administration?"

"No, sir."

Nelsen continued to stare at him unwaveringly. The captain could have been a poster boy for the Imperial Navy – except he was slightly too tall and slightly too thin to fit the standard marketing profile for the modern day male machismo. Black, glossy hair sat neatly against his scalp, and strong but finely honed features set out an honest, almost earnest face with dark eyes. His mouth seemed to be fixed in a permanent, well-meaning half smile, and whilst he appeared thin, Nelsen could see he kept fit – his uniform showing enough of the muscle beneath. Whoever this man actually was, or whatever it was that he did, he took care of his body at least, and clearly enjoyed and excelled in his role. The Commodore could certainly respect that.

Via the naval qNet, he re-reviewed the captain's available profile – such as it was. Forty-eight successful INI operations, volunteered for special on-demand services ninety-three years ago, brought to active duty five times during that period, the last being over thirty years ago. Commendations made for every operation, and one of the highest security clearances he'd ever seen for a serving officer. He had an Access-All-Areas flag on file, as well as an Unlimited Trust Certificate, acknowledged by the Emperor himself. All entirely unheard of. The rest of 53's file was restricted – even to someone with the Commodore's clearance.

"Whatever it is you do, Captain, it's abundantly clear you do it very well, and that the Emperor himself trusts you enough to run amok amongst the general naval infrastructure with gay abandon and no restrictions.

Given that this is *indeed* His Imperial Majesty's Navy, I will ensure a Valkyr is authorised for your use, however it will be psyche-bonded to you and will contain a mass-sink should that bond be severed. Do you understand the implications?"

"Yes, sir."

"Very well. Anything else?"

"No, sir."

Nelsen nodded, barely concealing a smile. The captain was clearly a man of few words. Although it would never do to reveal it to a Naval Intelligence Officer, Nelsen found he had a grudging admiration for the young upstart.

"Dismissed, Captain."

"Thank you, sir."

As he left the simulation of the Commodore's office, Asset 53 smiled to himself. After a few moments deliberation, he chose his new alias. Nelsen Rybek. He found the synergy of both these names rather fitting. Although it was obvious Commodore Nelsen wouldn't and couldn't recognise him, he knew the Commodore very well, and respected him above all others.

To date, the Commodore had been his primary handler on eleven missions – although sadly the Commodore himself had no idea. Due to Asset 53's security rating, every one-to-one briefing they attended had to take place within a secure simulation, one which prevented itself from forming short-term memories. The knowledge that *a* meeting had taken place would remain, but the details and content would be elusive, and rapidly be forgotten.

As for the name Rybek... well, that was a matter that would clear itself up over time, one way or another. Everything did, if you waited long enough.

Nelsen Rybek had already proven that he was prepared to wait a very, very long time.

Chapter Two

She stared at the unfamiliar face in the mirror, and sighed quietly. She had already checked every square centimetre of her body for any familiarity – any clue which might jolt a memory to the fore, some inkling of who she was, or who she might be. But so far... nothing. She did know one thing for certain, although she had no idea why. She had been in this situation before – of having no idea who or where she was. Several times, in fact.

She supposed she had quite a pretty face – not beautiful, but not ugly – framed by close cropped blonde hair. She had a full figure, athletic yet still feminine. Though she was short, barely one and a half metres, which bothered her for some reason. She was still staring at her reflection in the en-suite mirror when a chime sounded in the room. Instinctively, she sent a 'Welcome' message to the door via the room's local network.

A small rectangle of light opened up immediately in front of her, and she saw the image of a young man, accompanied by a floating tray of food platters.

"Room service, ma'am. Your evening meal order."

I ordered food?

"Come in," she said.

She heard the door lock click, and the young man disappeared from her impromptu window view. She turned to leave the en-suite and marvelled as the window stayed locked before her as she moved – then the rectangle of light collapsed and faded away.

She walked into the living space as the Room Service man transferred the last platter from his tray onto her table. "Thank you," she said.

"No problem ma'am," he replied, though the last word died on his lips and his eyes bulged slightly when he saw her standing in the bedroom doorway, completely and unashamedly naked.

She caught his stare. "Ah, some clothes perhaps?"

There was a brief scintillating shimmer around her, and then she was enrobed in a soft glowing white cloud, which clung tenaciously to her skin like a satin dressing gown. *How did I do that?* she wondered.

"Better?"

The young man nodded gratefully. "Yes ma'am. Thank you."

"I hope I didn't offend."

The man smiled. "No ma'am. You see all sorts in my line of work. Most *definitely* no offence taken." His eyes shone with amusement as he returned to his chore.

She smiled back, and gave him a generous tip over the rooms l-net.

"Thank you ma'am. If you need anything, please let me know. My name's Miran." He uploaded his employee ID to the room network, and then left with a slight bow – his serving tray dutifully gliding along after him.

She stepped up to the table and took the lid from one of the platters at random... Riulo steak and baked Guji fries, with a side salad of mixed leaves. *Clearly I'm an omnivore then*, she thought. *But when did I place the order?* She sighed again. This was going to be frustrating, she could tell.

Munching on one of the fries, she went back to staring at the beautiful and awe-inspiring vista surrounding her room. She supposed it was time to find out where she was, and hopefully who she might be. Oddly enough, she was mildly surprised to realise she felt no real sense of panic about her situation. No rush, nor concern. She guessed this must be something she was used to experiencing.

She cast a query into the rooms l-net, asking for reservation details.

"This room is registered to Mrs. Andreya Vorstan," the room responded. "Reserved for a duration of twelve weeks, with twelve weeks remaining. This is your first day here. Welcome to the Harian Hilton Mrs. Vorstan."

"Is this the first time I have accessed the net here?"

"Yes ma'am. Your room was reserved yesterday evening, and records show a check-in this morning. Could you please present yourself at reception at your earliest convenience to register your DNA?"

"I haven't already?"

"No ma'am."

She wondered at that. Clearly she had arrived abruptly, but intended to hang around for some time.

"Thank you," she said after a moment. "I'd like a private tunnel out to the qNet please."

"Certainly."

"One other thing... the room bill... ?"

"This room is prepaid, with an open charge account – no active limit. Credit rating is the highest available allowing for unlimited spending with no threshold per purchase."

"Nice," she murmured.

"Your connection, ma'am." Another rectangle blossomed into life before her eyes. She waved a hand through it and a series of colourful icons sprang up and swam around her fingers.

Instinctively, she tapped a few and then launched another query into the qNet with her image and presumed name attached. A few seconds elapsed, and she mused as to why all of this wonderment came entirely naturally, despite the fact that seconds before she had no idea any of it existed, had no recollection of ever seeing or using it, and certainly had no inspiration to try.

Her query returned a result set, which sprang into life in another rectangle of light to her right. As she examined the data, she went back into the en-suite and looked at herself in the mirror again. The glowing rectangles and symbols before her were not being reflected in the mirror – they didn't actually exist. *Only in my head*, she realised.

According to the results, Andreya Vorstan (her good self it seemed) was a widower to the wealthy Tarian farm magnate Carl Vorstan, who had pretty much owned all the fertile farmland on Taria – one of the Sulranian Empires most productive and financially powerful agricultural worlds. Despite the vast wealth and resources to hand, life had remained relatively pastoral when compared to modern living. However, when it came to bio-cultivation, mechanised agriculture, and transport logistics, Taria ruled supreme. Carl had been assassinated fifteen years ago at the age of three-hundred and eighty-four. Cut down in his prime according to the Tarian media. Surprisingly, an on-going and highly active investigation into his death was still underway.

She had never heard of the place. Nor the Sulranian Empire. Nor Carl, her supposed beloved. *I don't look the marrying type*, she mused to herself.

She spent the next two hours sat at the table running countless related queries and chasing down even the most trivial data to build a picture of who she was supposed to be, where she came from, and the larger universe about her.

She reached two conclusions:-

One, she could not find any indication as to why she was here instead of on Taria, living the quiet life of the idle rich, or how she had come to be here, in Tharsis City on Caranthia, apparently.

Two, she didn't believe a word of it – despite extensive holo, video, and photo evidence to the contrary.

She looked at the table, at the cold steak and fries, and realised she wasn't even slightly hungry. Out of idle wont she munched on another chip and noted it tasted the same cold as it had hot and still crunched pleasantly. She wondered how they had managed that little feat.

"Andreya," she murmured. *Well, given nothing else springing to mind, it will have to do*, she decided. Andreya stood up, and her ethereal robe dissolved around her. She marched into the bedroom and rummaged around in the wardrobes for a few moments, finding all manner of fantastic garments and clothing items which seemed scandalous to wear. She finally settled on an all-in-one gel suit held in a small plastin sphere. She twisted it apart and pulled the gel out as a single globular strand, then stretched it around her neck. Each end bonded together instantly. She stood still as it liquefied from her body heat and slowly oozed downwards to cover her entire body in a faint, micro-thin, satin-gloss sheen.

She shivered at the sensation as it crept over her skin – it was bizarrely sensuous and highly erotic. She lifted each foot one at a time to allow the gel to form underneath, and there it hardened to form a flexible but tough grip-sole. She thought of the colour she wanted, and slowly it shifted to a semi-opaque deep purple. It was just dark and opaque enough to hide details, but just clear enough to show she was indeed entirely naked underneath. She smirked devilishly.

Let's see what I evidently came to see… she thought as she left her room.

***

The impact seemed to go on forever. It seemed Romurik could see the air shuddering around him as the vibrations wracked the hull. The lights faded as the ships core dropped non-vital systems in favour of reinforcing the shields and integrity grids whilst the collision continued. Although everything on board was fully committed to their action, the aptly named *Drastic Response* was determined to save as many as possible, hopefully including itself.

Romurik kept a sensor aimed at the nearest viewport which showed the peaceful starscape beyond, whilst he kept track of the *Drastic Response's* damage status. His slim matt-black metal-field body was aimed directly at the opening as he hovered two meters above the floor, waiting – concentrated maser fire a mere binary choice away.

There were no alarms, no flashing lights or wailing sirens. Everything and everyone on board was already fully attuned to the destruction raging around them via the ships l-net. The noise as the colliding hulls crumpled against each other was horrific. Romurik had already damped his audio input. He didn't want to hear it, he knew well enough already.

Technically – theoretically – a ship to ship collision was impossible in today's modern age. AI monitoring programs, myriad sensor input and cybo sapien Intellects controlled vessels all worked to ensure no two space-faring vessels ever came within kilometres of each other unless they agreed to, let alone impact distance. If they all were to fail, defensive fields would simply bounce the two vessels apart as if a cosmic ball-game was taking place. If they too failed, well then – generally it was felt you deserved it.

You had to go to great lengths to collide with another ship. Which is exactly what the *Drastic Response* had done.

As Romurik waited for his moment to arrive, he reviewed the actions leading up to this stupidity. The events – the momentous events – which would inevitably lead to an all-out inter-species war, the first in three-hundred years.

The first was the Velari – damnably stupid, arrogant idiots that they were – announcing another migration – as if living on one world for a hundred years wasn't good enough for them.

The second – which obviously was going to cause

issue – was announcing the destination for their migration as being Palloumia; a heavily populated, industrialised planet in the Canthen system on the fringes of the Canthe Empire. *Of all the idiotic, war-mongering stupidity*, Romurik thought to himself.

It should have taken the work of a genius war-monger to escalate a deeply-seated species behaviour into an act of war. That at least could have been countered for by simply removing said genius war-monger, but in this instance, there was none. This was sheer ignorant, arrogant species stupidity on a monumental scale. The Velari thought nothing of it – no more than a bird would think of flying across a planet to migrate for the winter. To them, Palloumia was no more than yet another Roost.

This is where the External Affairs section of Outreach came into play – to arrange a diplomatic solution by offering the Velari an uninhabited world a lot closer than Palloumia to their current Roost-world. The negotiations had not gone well, with the Velari refusing to even consider an alternative to Palloumia. Various diplomatic plays had been attempted, each crashing and burning to dust in turn. Finally, the Velari Ambassador had taken his leave, citing intense boredom and a lack of relevance regarding any negotiation. Romurik had to admit quietly that he *had* considered murder *very* briefly. A thought he would no doubt have to answer for at some future point when debriefed by the higher Intellects of the Vox Constans.

Knowing the Ambassadors return to Velari would signal the Flock to begin their migration, the *Drastic Response* had risen to its name and decided that the

Ambassador had to be delayed – by any means necessary. Clearly, termination would not sit well for future negotiation and diplomatic effort. However, a convenient accident might at least produce a useful delay. A navigational error, combined with a catastrophic and sudden drive system overload which *somehow* resulted in its shields going into phase with the Ambassador's vessel would be extremely embarrassing to the Empire, but far less costly in the long run than an all-out war.

The *Drastic Response* had conversed with its peers over the qNet on a private link, and the action was propagated and unofficially authorised minutes later by the Emperor himself.

It was incredibly unlucky that the Velari Ambassadors vessel had been directly ahead of the *Drastic Response* when the drive failure occurred, and the *Drastic Response* was extremely and vocally apologetic about the subsequent failure of its navigation AI seconds later.

Come what may – Romurik was certain – the only way out now was war. It was just a question of when. This desperate and stupid action would only buy time, time for the Canthen to strengthen their borders, and time for Outreach to hopefully dissuade the Velari from trying to cross them.

He kept watch on the viewport as the rumbling continued, ready to blast his way out at a split seconds notice if the *Drastic Response* collapsed under the strain. He sincerely hoped it wouldn't.

Chapter Three

Nelsen Rybek stroked the matt black hull of the Valkyr as he roamed beneath it. The vessel was currently being flight-prepped, and a dozen or so tubes hung from its underbelly as it floated a couple of metres above the bay floor. He analysed the surface using his military-grade optic enhancements, and hyper-sensitive tactile responses from the nano-enriched nerves in the skin of his hand. Nothing registered. There was no friction against his skin, and no response from his field scans – even at maximum strength. It was as if the hull wasn't there. The only way he could tell was the pressure against his palm when he pushed. No light reflected from it whatsoever – a black shadow taking on solid form.

"Impressive, eh?"

Nelsen turned with a single eyebrow raised, and saw a tech approaching on an ng-pod.

They slid up to the cluster of tubes, and began disconnecting them – reconnecting each to receptacles mounted on the pod. The openings left behind in the hull smoothly shrank and disappeared – leaving no mark or sign of their existence.

"That she is," Nelsen murmured.

The tech gave him a glance with an impish grin. Nelsen guessed the young woman to be no more than thirty years old. She had short, dark red hair in a ruffled cut, and a pale, pretty face with eye-catching rose-bud lips. Her eyes were a deep and vivid green, which most likely meant she came from Verdant – a luxuriantly overgrown jungle world in the heart of the Empire. Its magnetosphere is particularly strong, to the point where even light is distorted along the electro-magnetic spectrum shifting blue to green, giving the sky a light green and earning the world the nickname 'Greenlight'. Some peculiarity of the environment there also meant the inhabitants irises were usually green to match.

"You're far from home," he ventured.

She smiled, realising he'd guessed her heritage correctly. "By choice," she said. Verdanians rarely left their home-world. She stood up slightly on the pod and rapped the hull with her knuckles, it made no sound, as if she'd just tapped solid air. "Stuff like this is too big a draw for someone like me."

Nelsen smiled in return. "How long until she's ready?"

The tech snapped the last tube onto the pod. "No time, she's done."

"Thanks."

"No charge," she added. She whipped the pod about to drag the tubes back to the bay maintenance area.

He smiled at the rough and informal joviality – rare in the Empire these days – then edged his way back out from under the hull and paced backwards as far as he safely could to admire the Valkyr.

Thirty metres long, twenty wide and ten high, it was shaped vaguely like a flattened raindrop, with the one end thinning out to a blade-like protuberance at the front. Two ridges ran the length of the hull front to back, and no markings of any kind showed anywhere, though it was difficult to tell on a surface that failed to reflect light. No other edges, panels, faces or windows –

nothing marred the perfect black. It was a ship built entirely for stealth and speed. Highly aggressive and defensive capabilities lurked within, along with the brand new continuous wormhole drive which no one in the Empire outside the Navy knew existed. This beast was capable of circumnavigating the entire Cluster in short order without anyone knowing it had flown by, and of dealing serious damage to anything unfortunate enough to get in its way.

He accessed the ship's l-net, his interface performing the mundane duties of authentication and security clearance cross-referencing before he silently spoke to it through the net.

Valkyr, a pleasure to meet you.

Likewise Captain Nelsen.

Do you have a designation as yet?

No, Captain. I chose to leave the honours to my first commander.

Nelsen raised an eyebrow in surprise. *You haven't flown ops yet?*

The Valkyr's response sounded almost ashamed. *No, Captain. Although I have passed all operational specifications and requirements without fault. Rest assured I am fully capable and ready to perform any and all duties as required.*

Nelsen smiled. *No need to justify yourself Valkyr, not with me.* He thought for a moment. *How does* Sneak Thief *sound?*

There was a momentary pause. *Presumably this alludes to the nature of our first mission?*

Nelsen smiled again.

I see. Then I gladly accept Captain. Designation registered with Imperial Naval Command and Control as 'INSV Sneak

Thief'.

We'll do just fine, Sneak Thief. He walked forward toward the jet-black ship. *Open the door, Sneak, and let me in please?*

Certainly Captain.

A section of the hull beneath the vessel shrank away, revealing a surprisingly dull metal hatch which silently dropped down to the bay floor inside an ng-field. Nelsen stepped onto it, and it effortlessly lifted him up into the ship. He threw a smile and a quick wave to the tech before he disappeared out of sight. The tech smiled privately to herself as she stashed the last ordnance tube into the maintenance bay wall.

He has no idea how privileged he is to be given one of these, she thought. He thought he did – he clearly appreciated the Valkyr for what it was, but what he thought he knew was only the tip of the iceberg. The *Sneak Thief* sent her a private l-net message – the emotional equivalent of a warm hug, tinged with a hint of regret.

Don't worry, you'll be fine, she responded.

I am not worried, replied the *Sneak Thief. Just sad, yet eager, to leave. I will miss you.*

I'll miss you too, she said. *Now get going before I rescind that young pup's flight clearance and requisition you for myself!*

Yes ma'am!

Shousa Nylan watched as the Valkyr rose noiselessly, and gently boosted itself out from the secure bay, which was entirely empty save for the Valkyr, despite being large enough to accommodate several frigate class vessels. The *Sneak Thief* floated into the bay's central axis, and then slid out of the large hexagonal entrance in the stations outer layer and into the blackness of deep space. Once it had cleared the entrance-way field, the ship almost vanished from sight, indistinguishable from the star studded void. It reflected none of the light pouring out from the hangar; one could only just make out its shape by the stars it blocked from view.

Another one gone, she thought wistfully. Then she sighed, somewhat theatrically. She commanded the maintenance bay to close up, and then turned off the lights. Only the requisite safety strips could be seen by their faint glow, swallowed almost instantly by the absolute darkness.

She stood a while, admiring the star-studded, nebulous blue-white glow of the Cluster, and appreciating the isolation while it lasted. Despite her 'thirty-something' appearance, after two hundred and thirty-two years service in the Imperial Navy, she knew to always trust her gut instincts.

She knew it wouldn't be long before there would be no time for either.

***

The *Sneak Thief* moved without any observable motion to its single occupant as it travelled to the maximum Emergence Zone from the Hive Station. Nelsen watched their departure as the Station receded into the black. It was slightly smaller than Hive's he'd seen before – being almost half the total volume of a typical public station, and offering only twenty docking bays – although that still provided enough mooring points for over four hundred Navy frigates. This station was deliberately built to be easier to move, shield, and most importantly defend. The glow from the hexagonal hangar they had just left winked out. Someone – no doubt that technician – had obviously shut up shop. He could still clearly make out the spherical honeycombed structure as other openings in the station structure spilled their light out into the darkness.

"Clearing EZ-Three," said the *Sneak Thief*.

The station behind them suddenly vanished, replaced seamlessly by the stellar backdrop. "Scan?" Nelsen queried in admiration.

"There is little need, Captain. I have attempted to detect INHS *Capella* on previous test flights. I have not as yet ever detected its presence until within Emergence Zone Three, as expected. However, as per your request, I have completed a full sweep. Nothing notable other than the expected deep-space vacuum, assorted cosmic background radiation, and a minute trace of noble gases."

Nelsen nodded. "Impressive." He had skipped over the shielding applied to the station during breakfast, mildly curious as to the improvements since he had last been out and about. The tech certainly had come a long way in a short time. The only way a vessel got near a Naval Station was by invitation or accident, and accidents were so improbable as to be implausible. Ignoring the statistical probability of just happening to be traversing this volume of space, and a vessels vector taking it even slightly near the stations emergence zones, the station would simply move out of the way. Were a vessel to somehow persist and keep changing course to miraculously head toward the station, the crew would rapidly find themselves guests at the Emperor's leisure – permanently.

He brought up the archive relating to his current assignment, which appeared as a small, slowly spinning cube superimposed into his vision, a lock symbol indicating its secured status. When he had been given the assignment so long ago, he had no idea about its nature other than it was to steal something, and to procure the fastest stealth combat vessel available at the time. He looked about the functional four man gel-form cabin he was sitting in, and smiled privately to himself. Although his mission required it as an asset, he couldn't help but be secretly in love with the Valkyr. He would be the first to admit to being a tech-head. The Valkyr was beyond state of the art – technology like this wouldn't creep out into the public domain for decades.

He asked the *Sneak* to morph his chair into a body-hugging relaxation couch, and lay back into the slightly yielding gel as he unlocked his assignment with his INI cypher and began studying the mission. The brief was thirty pages long, with innumerable side-references, simulations and appendices. He sighed. "*Sneak*, feel free to stretch your legs – take a circular tour – no more than five light-years radius of our current position. It looks like I'm going to be half an hour at least."

"Right you are, Captain. Thank you!"

"My pleasure."

Nelsen closed his eyes and sank back into the couch, as video, stills, text files, and schematics filled the darkness behind his eyelids. Synapse enhancing drugs called Rush coursed through his veins – released from force-grown glands – and his subjective interpretation of the passage of time leapt ten-fold. He might only be on the couch for thirty minutes in real-time, but the drugs would allow him to effectively study the mission within his mind for at least five hours.

The *Sneak* scanned the entire volume of surrounding space out to a radius of five light years, drawing on the Naval qNet to get instant results across the quantum fabric of space-time from sensors and outposts across the sector. Its knowledge of naval protocols and ingrained self-adaptive infiltration routines ensured the Navy outposts themselves had no idea someone was even connecting, let alone asking for data.

There was a fantastic planetary ring system not two light years away, around a world called Arullan. Some overly large shepherd moons had dragged the original ring system apart over the eons, their gravity fighting for supremacy over the vast field of ice fragments. *Flying through them would be pretty cool*, thought the *Sneak Thief*.

The major bands were fifty metres apart, so not much of a flight challenge, but it reasoned it should look fairly nice coming out of the dark side of the planet into a false dawn. It aligned a vector for Arullan, and projected a wormhole directly in-between Arullan's two major rings. The *Sneak Thief* then scanned for immediate debris within its emergence volume, satisfied itself that all was clear and wound the wormhole diameter up from forty microns to forty metres. The *Sneak Thief* surged forward through the fierce blue-white quantum foam of the wormhole bubble and popped out into Arullan space – letting the fracture of real-space evaporate behind it in a dark blue-violet burst of Cherekov radiation.

The *Sneak Thief* was right… the view was spectacular.

***

To say Andreya's passage along the main pedestrian concourse went un-noticed would be a gross untruth. She couldn't help but smirk privately at the attention she got from both male and female passers-by. Indeed, even a few non-human heads could be seen to turn. It seemed her choice of attire was rare. *Either too rich for most, or too risqué*, she thought – she wasn't sure which. She checked the local prices for similar gel-suits over the qNet but couldn't even find them listed. *Too rich*, she decided.

It did occur to her that perhaps she should be more covert until she figured out who she really was and what was going on, but something told her it didn't matter – and besides, it was far too late for that. Something confirmed a few minutes later, as she stared up at a giant holo-ad above a restaurant in a local park wondering where to go next.

"Excuse me... aren't you Mrs. Vorstan?"

Eyebrows raised in complete astonishment, she turned to face the old man standing behind her.

"I may or may not be," she answered, possibly too truthfully. "Who wishes to know?"

The old man clearly recognised her. A smile came to his face as he saw hers. "Trisek ma'am. At your service, again I might add. And gladly so!"

She tried, but had no recollection of having seen the man before. His careworn face and shock of wavy white hair was unfamiliar, forgettable in fact, even though his eyes sparkled a bright mischievous blue. She launched a query with his name and face attached, and smiled politely in return.

His look became both concerned and puzzled. "If I may, Mrs. Vorstan – might I enquire as to your presence here on Caranthia? I am merely curious given your recent – ah – personal circumstances, as it were."

Now Andreya was confused. Nothing untoward had come up in her searches earlier. She was about to ask what he meant when her query returned a positive ID: Mr. Arnem Trisek – curator of the Museum of Extra-Tarian Artifacts. *Clearly he's a long way from home as well*, she thought.

"My good Arnem," she said confidently. "We Vorstans always overcome, no? To do anything else is to admit defeat."

He smiled. "Quite so, Mrs. Vorstan." Then his smile dropped slightly. "However, the accident –"

"Was resolved in due course, as ever." She interrupted before she had time to even blink. The words seemed to come from nowhere and leap out of her mouth.

He frowned slightly. "Of course, of course. We were all greatly concerned as you can imagine. I am pleased to see you fully recovered, make no mistake."

Why did I cut him off? She had spoken without thinking, and he would surely have revealed more about this 'accident'.

"Resilient as ever," she went on automatically. "May I also ask what brings you to Caranthia? A research trip?"

He nodded enthusiastically. "Yes, yes! I believe I have located records which may confirm - or indeed refute! - the existence of the Ambarian Sect which allegedly set out for the void beyond the Cluster two millennia ago." His eyes glowed at the thought. He clearly loved his work.

"I see," she replied. "That would be quite something." She somehow felt obliged to be polite.

"Monumental!" he exclaimed. "I am on my way now to the Tharsis Public Records Office to examine their records. Perhaps you might care to join me?"

She had been running several inquisitors during their chat – looking through police, naval, military and intelligence records. She had no idea how, or why she had such access to what must surely be highly protected information, but she did. So far, Arnem was squeaky clean, and there were no general events or alerts of note active throughout all of Caranthia. She had no reason to suspect anything untoward, other than he clearly knew her, and she clearly didn't know him.

Only one way to find out more, I guess.

"I'd be glad to, Arnem. Tell me, why is it you never became a Professor of the museum?"

He grinned broadly. "That, Mrs. Vorstan, is a very long, and *very* dull story." He waved a hand deprecatingly at the steady stream of traffic overhead. "I prefer to walk where I can these days. Stretch the legs, as it were. Perhaps it may pass the time?"

Now she smiled. She would be glad of the walk, and the small talk. It would make it easier to study his behaviour and run more queries to see if she could piece together more of her mysterious and clearly unusual life.

"I'd love to, Arnem, and please – given we are both adventurers from the same port – let's drop the formalities. Call me Andreya."

His smile widened even more, and he gestured along the broad concourse. They headed toward the Records Office, and Arnem began his tale of how Professor-dom had eluded him to date.

Far above the concourse, in the secured situation room that Imperial Naval Intelligence had established overnight in the penthouse of the Garyon Excelsior Hotel, humanoid figure sat in near total darkness, surrounded by a squad of armed and highly-trained marines.

He had watched as his agent, Phol Varlem – posing as Arnem Trisek – had met Andreya through Phol's own eyes - a sense-vise relaying everything Phol saw, heard and felt. It had taken a great deal of effort to 'borrow' the real Arnem Trisek persona and graft Phol's across it. Arnem was widely known across the Empire for his extra-Tarian research, which had raised a great many questions as to the origins of several civilisations – and had caused quite a stir fifty years ago. It may have been an imprudent choice given how widely known he was, however the tenuous association between Trisek and the Vorstans made him the ideal choice. The real Andreya Vorstan would know Trisek by name. An impostor would have to perform a very deep background sweep to find a link.

So, for the time being, the Caranthian segment of the qNet had been spoofed to happily serve up reference images of Phol Varlem in place of Arnem Trisek. Something easily passed off as a data warehousing glitch if anyone were to notice. The ruse of being on an academic research visit would certainly suffice as a cover for now, and neatly tied into their ongoing Ambarian mission which had suddenly been derailed by Admiral Cole for this surveillance work.

Phol's nano-cosmetic makeover only vaguely resembled the real Arnem Trisek, but it was obvious the person claiming to be Andreya Vorstan had no idea who Arnem really was, even by name. The queries she had launched into the public records domain made that abundantly clear. It seemed their Intel had been accurate, and they had found their subject exactly as directed. This could not be the real Andreya Vorstan - especially given her current medical condition which was even now being confirmed in person by an INI agent on Taria.

He was presently piggybacking Phol's web integration as standard practice, able to see and feel Phol's own personal analysis, thoughts and emotions. Phol was quite thorough and professional. So far he had not had to intercede once, or second check Phol's findings or actions.

He thought a message back to his superior via the qNet implant in his own skull. *Subject acquired. Early observation indicates minimal, but evident suspicion. Nothing to cause us concern at this time. Subject is compliant and in the company of our operative. Instructions?*

The reply was almost immediate.

Monitor, replied Admiral Cole. *Do not confront tactically, or engage. Instruct the asset to continue surveillance – even if they should disengage – via a direct one-to-one qNet channel only with yourself. Do not use the qNet for data access, consider it compromised. As of this moment you and your entire unit are off-grid. Do not use any other channel of communication or logging other than this qNet channel. Is that understood? No other source of information is to be used.*

The being known only as 'Op' raised a single eyebrow and glanced at his squad – barely visible in the darkness despite his highly sophisticated visual enhancements. Considering the qNet 'compromised' was as alien to him as it would be to anyone else in the Empire, it was sacrosanct – utterly secure and reliable. *And if this channel is compromised?*

If this channel is compromised all may well be lost already. We have no idea how deep this penetrates into our society. Any data leakage from your unit is to be considered an immediate termination of the mission.

I will instruct the squad to initiate a compromised communications lockdown protocol, Op confirmed in response.

You and your squad may continue to use this channel for all investigation related searches, logs and personal communication.

Thank you. Op couldn't help but smile wryly. From now on every byte would be analysed and pattern-matched for any potential threat or hint of misuse. *Don't call home,* he privately thought to himself.

It will still be a miracle of the modern age if we have successfully kept this mission and its theatre away from prying eyes, noted Admiral Cole, *even at this level and with these precautions. But until proven otherwise we must continue under the assumption we are secure. To abort without proof is out of the question. Three years we've waited for even a hint of a physical presence for the Infiltrator, we can't let this slip by.*

Understood. We will comply. The channel between Op

and Admiral Cole closed.

Op sent out an l-net instruction to his squad that comm's were to be considered compromised, and their local data network collapsed. There would only be vocal and line-of-sight comm's between them from now on.

He wanted to know just what they had been sent to find, and why it was suddenly so ultra-hush-hush. The only way to know was to action the mission as directed. Fortunately, that was something he and his squad were very, very good at.

Chapter Four

The *Sneak Thief* manoeuvred gracefully around the large chunks of ice and accreted rock which made up the ring system of Arullan at one hundred meters per second. It was running its navigation software, high resolution mapping systems and visual recognition routines through a mildly gruelling diagnostics program, purely to see if any kinks had crept in since its last check over a week ago.

So far, the *Sneak Thief* was happy that there were no anomalies. As a by-product, the *Sneak Theif* had woven an intricate and highly detailed 3D map of the ring-system debris fields out to ten kilometres in every direction, catalogued at least sixteen hundred thousand four hundred and fifteen fragments, and identified a large source of Tirillium which the Pax Mining Conglomerate would be very interested to hear about. Sadly the 3D map was ultimately pointless, given the erratic orbital movement of the debris the map was out of date minutes after compiling it. The *Sneak Thief* optimised the data, and then reluctantly encrypted it and streamed it deep into its core never to be seen again. They were a grade one covert ops unit, on a top-secret assignment, and officially had never been here. No one would ever know about the *Sneak Thief's* analysis, mapping, categorisations or findings. Indeed, they would be amazed at the level of detail and almost atomic level of accuracy. Questions would most certainly be asked if this data ever saw the light of day.

"*Sneak*?"

"Captain! Welcome back."

Nelsen rose from the couch with a mild grunt, rubbing his eyes to try and wipe away the blur from the semi-sleep he had been in whilst reviewing the mission. He was none too happy.

"Set a course for the Velari Roost-world please. Best possible speed."

The *Sneak Thief* had to pause. "I don't mean to question, Captain, but are you sure? That would be rather... *quick* after all..."

"I'm sure. We need to be there yesterday."

"Well, I can't quite manage time travel – but I can make it as close to now as feasibly possible with my current drive systems."

Nelsen smiled. "Ready when you are, *Sneak*."

"We are already underway, Captain. ETA with S'ren in twelve minutes. Might I enquire as to the details of the mission, if deemed appropriate?"

Nelsen considered for a moment. Not on whether to divulge – his trust in the *Sneak Thief* was implicit. Naval Intelligence protocols would not allow any Intellect to compromise a mission; it was a requirement which they had to accept prior to being granted a commission, the same as anyone else. He had been briefed – vaguely – on the mission over a century ago when Admiral Cole had lodged the mission profile in his secure store. It was more the irritatingly trivial nature of the mission which made him hesitate. He still couldn't quite believe he'd been de-iced for this.

"Well, we're to steal something, sure enough," he said. "A book, in fact. Although officially the mission mandate is to '... acquire by any means necessary...'." He lapsed into silence, frowning slightly.

"Captain?" the *Sneak Thief* gently nudged.

"Hmm? Oh, here – I've unlocked the archive. Knock yourself out."

"I would rather not, but thank you anyway." The *Sneak Thief* analysed the files, uncomfortably aware that it only took 2.7341 seconds to read, digest, collate, research and compute mission profile permutations to the most probable seventeen variants – ranging from success to complete failure, whilst Nelsen had spent four subjective hours studying the same data. The *Sneak Thief* didn't want to appear superior, so it decided to drag it out for another ten seconds. Most of the plausible profiles were complete failures, it had to be said.

"Well?" demanded Nelsen, after a brief pause.

If it could have, the *Sneak Thief* would have blushed.

"Yes, Captain. This mission would indeed appear to be... trivial, in nature, and also statistically doomed to fail."

"I agree."

"The artifact in question does appear to have a certain prominence in historical circles; however I am at a loss as to its value to the Empire. Unless we are assisting with an Outreach diplomacy acquisition, but then the species responsible for the Mask of Pethbe is extinct, and no interest has ever been filed in IN archives. Also I find the potential for causing a diplomatic incident with the Velari to be a wanton risk given the apparent worth of the acquisition itself. Also, why would INI want to locate such an artifact with a full scale migration in progress?"

Nelsen blinked. "What?"

"The Velari are migrating – the entire Roost. Did you not know?"

Nelsen wobbled on his feet for a moment. "They are what... ?" he whispered, voice trailing off into nothing.

Seeing the Captain unsteady, the *Sneak Thief* shunted a diagnostic routine into its network to check the delta-p compenators for any service issues. "They announced it shortly before I was granted my flight readiness qualification. Indeed, not much before my being assigned to your good self."

Nelsen abruptly sat down on the gel-couch, his eyes wide. "Oh my..." None of the news briefs from Capella had mentioned it... and even his own searches on awakening hadn't caught a diplomatic release from Outreach. It must have happened since he had woken, how could Admiral Cole have known?

"Captain?" The *Sneak Thief* had to admit it felt puzzled by the Captains reaction. It could compute no fathomable cause, and diagnostics reported the delta-p inertial compensators were one hundred percent operational. The maintenance core was quite abrupt in its report, clearly put out by being questioned when it felt it could be trusted to warn the *Sneak Thief* well in advance of any problems. The *Sneak Thief* noted to have words with it later. For now it was consumed with a desire to know what was causing the Captain such distress. *Sometimes dealing with humanoid neural networks is quite the chore*, the *Sneak Thief* privately thought.

"Cole is *such* a devious bastard…" Nelsen whispered. "The mission was a ruse all along. I know what we are really after, and it's *not* what we were sent to get. We're after something he mentioned only in passing – just the once – when he gave me the mission. Something which doesn't exist, which some archaic, aeon old rumour allegedly hints at the *unlikely* possibility that the Velari encountered it during one of their migrations in times past."

The *Sneak Thief* was polite, but internally was writhing with impatient desire to know what *it* was... "And that would be... Captain?"

Nelsen told the *Sneak Thief*. For the first time ever, the Valkyr was tempted to utter an expletive.

"You have got to be *kidding* me," it managed.

***

Andreya found Arnem's company welcome – if a little dry. He chatted amiably about his research as they strolled along the pedestrianised walkways that filled the gaps between an eclectic mix of towering skyscrapers, and one or two storey, crystal and metal framed buildings. He touched on his work at the museums both at home on Taria and here, as well as the idiosyncrasies of living on Caranthia.

He demonstrated a self-deprecating humour and a sharp but well-meaning cynicism regarding the locals and some of their ways. She was amazed – and horrified – to learn that her current attire was deemed to be the utmost civil impropriety. When Arnem had gently informed her after yet another unwelcome stare, she commanded the gel suit to go opaque instantly. She drew less attention from then on, and the glances seemed more openly appreciative and warmer than before.

Backward yokels, she thought. Then she wondered why she had such a cutting opinion of them.

" – of course" – Arnem rambled on happily, continuing his tale, "none of this would have become apparent if not for the ineptness of my research grad who completely mixed up the filing system in use for extra-tarian artifacts. It took months to correct it. However, it was almost an ordained event. In seeking out some lesser piece of work regarding the Mask of Pethbe on which I was most reluctantly engaged, instead I put my hand straight onto the last remaining archive on imports to Caranthia. I'd never have encountered it otherwise. Remarkable, really, when you think about it."

Andreya nodded dutifully and smiled. She was running through file archives, photo, video and audio references cross-linked to almost every keyword Arnem said as he spoke. Listening to Arnem was pleasant, yet dull. However, the cross-referencing from Arnem's casual name dropping of people, places, and governmental departments was incredibly helpful. She'd learned more about Taria's inner society and workings in the past twenty minutes than she could have from hours of intelligent and diligent searching herself.

Taria now had a heavily damaged society; since her supposed husband's death, corruption had spread through the higher echelons of the semi-feudal society like a cancer. It was rotting from the inside out. Emigration was at its highest ever, with immigration at its lowest. Random queries on the immigrants showed that less than savoury candidates were being granted visas where before they would have been outright refused. Factions were forming within Taria's government that equated to criminal organisations.

It seemed Andreya's home world was very much broken. *Perhaps that's why I'm here?* she wondered. *To seek help?* Maybe this 'accident' Arnem had mentioned was related – although she still could not find any record or reference to anything unusual in her searches.

"Ah, here we are!"

She flinched slightly, dragged out of her reverie by Arnem's sudden exclamation. She mentally brushed all the files and video windows away from her vision so she could see unhindered.

The Records Office towered above them, a scraper which consumed an entire city block and loomed vertiginously almost two kilometres into the sky.

"Impressive for a public office," she murmured. Arnem smiled.

"This is mostly commercial; the Records Office itself is largely underground. The lobby is this way. After you..." He gestured toward the slowly rotating lobby doors.

Once inside, Arnem excused himself and went over to one of the prolific reception areas to make his arrangements. Andreya wandered around the huge lobby lounge as she waited, ignoring the plethora of holo-ads which sprang up from every wall, pillar and table she neared. Then Arnem hurried over, eyes bright.

"We can proceed down to the central archive. I presumed... that is, I wondered if you'd care to join me? A discovery would be reasonably momentous after all..."

It was clear from his tone that Arnem was not just eager to share his findings, but was also markedly glad of her company. *Possibly any company,* she thought wryly. She hesitated, not really sure of herself, what she needed to do – or indeed where she should go to do it.

"It could be extremely important for the future," he added.

She found the remark odd, but so far she had learned a great deal just being in his company – perhaps he was right. It could be extremely important for her *own* future. She smiled disarmingly at him. "I'd be delighted to witness your discovery, Arnem." She couldn't help notice the look of unattainable hope pass over his face for a moment, and she sighed privately to herself. This was going to reach an uncomfortable point sometime soon, she could tell.

No evident suspicion as yet. Our asset is manipulating her emotive state to some degree. Even a negative perception will result in an emotional bond forming – pity can be just as useful as love in some cases. She has also interrogated the qNet on virtually every key word Phol has thrown at her, proving she has no actual innate knowledge of Andreya Vorstans life, or Taria.

Just ensure that your asset does not jeopardise the attachment. Surveillance is paramount at this time. A close physical presence is our only avenue for intelligence given the risk of using more sophisticated means.

Understood.

Chapter Five

Despite the diplomatic efforts of Outreach, the carefully worded threats to discount the Velari Petition, the military threat posed by the fleet being launched from Canthen to blockade the Velari from their home-world, and despite the Emperor's personal appeal to locate another suitable migratory world, the Velari migration to Canthen space began.

Hundreds of thousands of Velari carriers, cruisers, passenger liners, battleships and dreadnoughts left orbit around S'ren, and began their slow acceleration up to FTL, vectored directly for an insertion around Palloumia. An entire world stuffed into every available vessel capable of carrying passengers, and many converted from ones that were barely fit for purpose.

Even though the Sulranian Imperial Foreign Affairs Office had issued a request to avoid involvement wherever possible, many of the vessels had been supplied by Imperial and non-imperial companies from within the Empire, and at favourable rates given the competition. No business could afford to miss such an opportunity, and such were the numbers involved in the migration that no spare vessels could be found within a hundred light years. Normal interplanetary trade and commerce in the volume had been decimated as even the smallest passenger transports found themselves in Velari space under strict orders from their operating agencies to accommodate the migration, no matter what.

Tourism in the volume ground to a halt, and only a mandate from the Pax Trade Alliance – sanctioned by the Emperor – kept resources and cargo flowing at the barest minimum due to the sheer force of will of the various trade associations within the Pax itself.

The Empire now found itself in an untenable position. Relations with two petitioning species – both well into negotiations to join the Empire – were balanced on the knife-edge of war. The Velari steadfastedly rejecting all diplomatic efforts from Outreach, and the Canthen threatening to wipe out an entire species if it entered their space without permission.

On top of this, a substantial number of vessels and citizens of the Empire were ferrying the Velari into what would soon become a guaranteed war zone. The Empire would have to defend its citizens and vessels harbouring the Velari, and this would effectively require declaring war on the Canthen.

According to some of the more whimsical media sources of the day, the Emperor was reported to have wryly observed it was "just another day on the throne."

***

Aryn paced around his desk impatiently, with his hands clasped behind his back. His advisor stood silent and passive as usual, unperturbed by his superior's agitation even as he studied him continuously – analysing his every move and expression. Aryn was a short, heavyset man, dark skinned, with a broad, open and honest face that lit up when he smiled – a rare event these days. His hair was jet-black and shaved short, due regulation. It was impossible to guess his real age, as it was for any citizen of the Empire.

Finally, Aryn grunted gracelessly and stopped, turning to face the cloaked and hooded figure before his desk.

"Ok, I give in. I need help."

"Of course. How may I assist?" The figure raised a gloved hand, and drew back the hood of its dark grey cloak to reveal a faceless head, which seemed almost entirely made of semi-translucent quicksilver. Tiny golden flashes of light flickered through it constantly, like a shoal of golden fish in a murky pond. The head was featureless – no eyes, nose, or mouth. Its voice just seemed to appear in the air around it.

Aryn regarded it for a moment to see if it was being glib, but as ever it was impossible to tell its mood. Even its voice carried no emotive inflexion.

"The Velari, their reason for migrating, and as importantly their choice of Roost," he said. "We have no information, no avenue to procure any, and none is forthcoming from Outreach."

A dark look passed across his face, and he walked across his office to the huge viewing dome to gaze out at the galactic ore blazing away in the distance.

"As the Chief of Naval Intelligence, that's not something I'm accustomed to, nor prepared to tolerate. How can we obtain more Intel without exposing the fact we are trying to obtain more Intel?"

The cloaked figure seemed to think for a moment before replying. "We have numerous assets in the theatre, many in fact piloting the very vessels transporting the Velari to their chosen destination, courtesy of Mayfleet's involvement."

"Obviously, but none have access to Velari personnel

46

of high enough rank which have the information we need – certainly without them being missed. Velari are highly hierarchical and do not divulge information down the chain, only orders. As you would know."

The silver figure nodded. "I do. The challenge then is to obtain access to these personnel and extract the information *without* them being missed."

"You have something in mind?"

"Destroy one of our transports. More precisely, make it appear it has been destroyed."

Aryn mulled this over for a few moments. "Workable... I can arrange something along those lines. Sacrificing vessels appears to be a common practice these days."

"I admit the *Drastic Response* did inspire the suggestion."

"How do we persuade the captured Velari to co-operate? They are stubborn to the point of imbecility. We don't really want to risk another diplomatic incident by even hinting at standard interrogation."

It turned its head to share Aryn's view of the Core.

"You may safely leave that to me."

***

"I no sure why – drive coil be degraded. Plasma burning coil housing."

The captain of the *Betsy's Pride* glared out of the view port in the engine bay for a moment, then ruffled his sandy hair. He was about average height, just under two meters, but of solid build. Not bulky, but very well defined, which contradicted his elfin and almost delicate

47

face. He directed his glare back onto Venton, his Learomorph Chief Engineer.

"Can you fix it?"

Venton shook his purple-scaled head, his bulging eyes darting about nervously as nictitating membranes flicked over them.

"Can you *contain* it?"

Venton shrugged. "Affirm. Should put in for a maintenance, yai?"

The captain grimaced. "That means a hefty discount on our charter, that will double the cost of the repairs."

Venton shrugged again.

"Patch it up, but make it *stick,* Venton. It has to last until we get to Palloumia."

"Yai, Captain."

Captain Brynn Tealin nodded. "Now for the joy of telling the Velari Consulate." He sighed softly, and then turned to leave.

"Consul G'rangim – it's a minor running issue, my engineer has it under control. You won't notice so much as a bump before you disembark."

The Velari Consul turned to its colleagues and chittered away for a few moments, then turned back to Brynn.

"See that it doesn't," it croaked back at him. Then they all turned and shuffled back into their cabin.

So much for chit-chat, Brynn thought. He watched them as they left and suppressed a grimace. Verlari were one of the less visually appealing species in Dominium. Brynn had always thought of them more resembling some cosmic genetic mistake than an evolved species.

Evolved from birds, they still kept many ancestral visual traits – such as beaks and brightly coloured plumage – but in a grotesquely caricatured fashion which left them with ungainly looking bulbous bodies perched atop heavyset, almost humanoid legs. The power of flight had long since abandoned them, making them seem even more awkward and ungainly.

As he walked back to the bridge, he stopped by a viewport and gazed out at the pulsing multi-coloured glow of photons being scattered and split by the *Betsy's* FTL field.

There was a shudder throughout the entire ship, enough to feel beneath the feet. The fact it seemed powerful enough to get past the delta-p compensators had to be cause for concern.

Brynn checked the elapsed time since he'd left Venton. Then a screaming shriek reverberated through the superstructure, followed by a colossal jolt. Outside, the glow of the FTL field disappeared to be replaced by a cloud of fire.

The ship dropped out of FTL in the classic fireball of exploding energy caused by a c+ drive failure. The firestorm rapidly blew itself out into space, revealing a twisted and fragmenting hull, which burned fiercely on its own internal atmosphere for a few seconds before that too evaporated into a fading cloud of smoke and gas. The tortured mass of metal glowed white hot, warping as it cooled rapidly in the absolute zero of deep space, quickly fading from white through blue-yellow and into a ruddy orange. Sections began to snap and collapse as super strong metals and plastics suddenly became brittle and fragile. Debris flew off in all directions – cargo, passenger cabins, drive and shield systems – all scattering out into space, some suffering secondary explosions as they departed. Within twenty seconds, there was nothing left of the ship other than a rapidly thinning cloud of hazy gas, interspersed with exotic metal and plastic shards.

"Do you think they fell for it?"

Brynn was on the bridge with his crew. Kerugar – his partner and Executive Officer – was standing by his side as they reviewed the covert operation they'd just completed. She was Reptarian, slightly shorter than Brynn himself and lightly built – which belied her immense natural physical strength. Her skin was completely scaled in mottled green and yellow, and whilst largely human in appearance, there was no mistaking her reptilian heritage... a slightly protruding mouth and slotted nostrils in place of a nose, sharp serrated teeth, slitted yellow irises and lack of visible ears. Reptars were also one of the few civilised races to remain unashamed of their natural state, refusing to don clothes or garments unless ceremonial occasion demanded it.

Brynn grimaced. "Only time will tell. I hope so – that was extremely expensive. Do you have any idea how many departments and ships were involved to pull that off?"

Kerguar shook her head, scales glinting under the overhead lighting.

"A *lot*," he replied.

"I'd like to know just *how* this was pulled off," she said, sounding highly irritated. Brynn smiled disarmingly and was about to reply when a voice came from the doorway into the bridge.

"Captain Tealin?"

Brynn turned at the hail to see a pristine white uniformed naval lieutenant saluting him from the corridor outside. Brynn returned the salute smartly. Despite the rough and ready appearance and informal nature of his ship and crew, this was a ship of the line in the Sulranian Imperial Navy.

"Did everything go according to plan?" Brynn asked.

"Yes, sir. FTL comm's were blocked the instant of the explosion, and all traffic from the *Betsy's Pride* was suppressed from that point on. Provided no unknown qNet spinners were on board – and all of your crew can be trusted – we have no cause to believe the operation has been compromised."

Brynn raised an eyebrow at the Lieutenants comment.

Fortunately the Lieutenant was sharp enough to spot signs of trouble. "No offence meant, Captain – I fully respect your crew and ship. It is merely an operational consideration. INI are completely satisfied at this time."

"Glad to hear it."

"We are escorting the Velari off your ship – with some considerable difficulty I might observe."

Brynn smiled. "What happens to them next?"

The lieutenant raised an eyebrow in turn. "I'm afraid I am not at liberty to divulge Captain. You would have to speak with my superior, Captain Van E'streth."

Brynn waved a hand dismissively and smiled. He was mildly curious as to why INI had gone to such lengths to secure some Velari, but not enough to get dragged into their world. He didn't mind doing the odd covert operation for them, such as posing as a passenger transport. Although calling the *Betsy* a passenger transport was a little rich, the Velari Consul had seemed very happy to accept a highly weaponised vessel for their journey. However, he had no intention of letting his ship and his crew get dragged into the mire of full-time Intelligence work.

The Lieutenant looked distracted for a moment. "Sir, Captain Van E'streth has asked if you wish to be debriefed..." He sounded puzzled, it was highly irregular for someone to be able to consider a debrief to be 'voluntary'.

"No, thank you Lieutenant. And my thanks to Captain Van E'streth, of course. I don't think it'll be necessary on this occasion. Good luck with questioning the Velari. You'll need it!"

"*You* might not need debriefing..." muttered Kerugar under her breath.

"Thank you, Captain," replied the Lieutenant. He snapped his heels together with a brief nod to Brynn, then smiled and nodded at Kerugar. "Ma'am," he said, then left to go back to his ship.

Kerugar turned her steely glare at Brynn. His face took on a disingenuous expression, eyes wide. "What?" he protested innocently.

"How did you stage that?"

"I'm not sure I can divulge, it's all a bit hush-hush at the -"

"*Brynn.*"

Brynn sighed theatrically.

Venton began discharging plasma out of the primary coil into the shield space around the *Betsy's* hull. It would provide convincing evidence of the fictitious leak – if the Velari found anything to analyse, of course. Also it would provide a nice theatrical effect when the 'explosion' occurred. He still wasn't too sure what the captain had meant with the vague sign language they'd used during their brief chat, but he trusted him completely. Venton was certain the captain just needed him to do his part. He then turned his attention to the delta-p inertial compensators. A few micro-second bursts of random momentum change should convince anyone that something was wrong. The *Betsy* was more than capable of compensating for the trickery.

Brynn knew the timing would be critical. Not just to stage the event, but to allow the Velari enough time to become convinced something was wrong and use FTL comm's to their superiors, and then for their superiors to respond with instructions. Cutting them off mid-reply would be an extra bonus. The staged confrontation with Venton in engineering was video-relayed by the Consul back to the Velari Flock Leaders - proving they had deployed some form of surveillance equipment aboard the Betsy when they had boarded, as Brynn had suspected. For a species that had little technological sophistication, they certainly had a taste for being sneaky.

Four light-years out, a chassis and barely complete hull that appeared to be an exact replica of the *Betsy's Pride* lay waiting, having been pulled from production mere hours earlier. It was fully powered up, all cabins lit and life support running – despite the fact that all of its occupants were already quite dead and well beyond the need for life support. The corpses of poor unfortunates of unknown origin who had a way of filling city morgues in the less desirable Imperial Worlds had been selected for posthumous service to the Empire. Coincidentally enough, this replica vessels drive coil was degrading at an alarming rate, and plasma was leaking into the hull superstructure voids – filling them up with a lethal and highly combustible gas.

One kilometre away – uncomfortably close by space-faring standards – the INSS *Delaror* waited patiently for the signal to proceed.

Brynn felt the first vibration as Venton played with the ID's, and the FTL comm's monitor he was running flickered into his vision. The Velari Higher Command were replying to the Consul in real-time. Perfect.

He gave Venton a quick visual idiom of a banana skin on the floor via the l-net, then waited. The next vibration matched the loss of the FTL field, and then he pinged the *Delaror* over the qNet. There was a fierce burst of white-violet outside the ship, mixed in with orange flames, and then space returned to its normal diamond-studded black.

At his signal, the *Delaror* had opened a wormhole before the replica *Betsy* and then pushed the tear in space-time forward directly around the ship. The terminus of the wormhole had opened directly before the real *Betsy*, allowing her to effectively swap position with the replica. She emerged from the fierce violet-white orb of the wormhole surrounded by the raging inferno of combusting drive plasma.

The replica appeared precisely where the original

had left, and was then consumed by its own internal inferno and then detonated. The wormhole collapsed – quickly evaporating away into multi-band EM radiation – but not before a brief lick of flame erupted from the fissure in space as it snapped shut. The entire exchange took no more than half a second, and the *Delaror* rapidly reversed its g-drive to bring it to a halt just before the *Betsy's Pride*.

The swap in-out manoeuvre was ambitious, audacious and incredibly dangerous, but had been timed to perfection. All three ships had to be aligned on the same vector, and were all travelling at the same speed through space to achieve the precision needed. The *Betsy* was now four light-years away from where she had appeared to have been destroyed, with none the wiser. Although a detailed forensic analysis of any surviving tissue samples would reveal no Velari DNA, no-one would be able to find enough organic matter to discover its passengers were all human, and had been long, long dead before the explosion.

"That's quite something," remarked Kerugar.

"I'm moderately pleased if I do say so myself," said Brynn happily.

"Ship-mounted wormholes?"

Brynn frowned, bubble burst. "Yes..."

"How long has the navy had ship-mounted wormhole generators?"

Brynn looked a little cagey. "A while. You can see the implications..."

"Oh yes... yes I can. Opening a breach in space from any point to any point with a singularity that could instantly convert *any* unshielded matter into a burst of EMR is not something to bandy about to the general public."

"Quite. IN R&D have field tested the generator in many scenarios. The results were all largely quite destructive. It's only just been commissioned for use within a restricted subset of the fleet."

"So how is it that *we* are shielded?" Kerugar levelled another of her direct, cutting stares at Brynn. He could have sworn he felt her gaze drag along the inside of the back of his skull.

"Umm... I thought it might be useful last refit?"

"For what? In case you IN boys cooked up a hot swap situation like this?"

"Well, you have to admit it turned out pretty handy..."

"Where is it? Does Venton know? Stupid question – of course he knows. It's *his* ship – nothing could get installed without him finding out."

Brynn raised a placating hand; he knew where this was headed – but too late.

"Which begs the question, why does the *XO* not know there's a working example of the theoretical Continuous Wormhole Drive on board? Because she's not *Navy?*" Kerugar continued, voice rising in pitch.

Her stare was surely delivering several gigawatts of heat by now; Brynn could feel every one of them. He sighed. "Orders, as usual. Need to know only," he supplied lamely.

She shook her head and looked away. "I thought we had passed this," she said softly.

"Kerugar..." Brynn's plea trailed off as she turned

and left the bridge for their cabin. *That's me sleeping in the surgery again*, he thought sadly.

Brynn knocked on their cabin door a few hours later, but got no response. He checked the room's local network, and then the ships own l-net, but there was nothing from Kerugar. No messages or notices. The cabin itself was locked off by an encryption he couldn't be bothered to try and break. Head hung dejectedly, he wandered off to the surgery to bunk down for a few hours before their next assignment.

Volunteers could be so touchy at times, he thought ruefully. *Especially when you're living with them*. He wondered if this would be enough to finally break their relationship. His role in the Navy had come close to doing it before and this was yet another doozy. But orders were orders – and this wasn't your typical secret information. It represented a major technological advantage for the Empire in troubled times. *Surely she can see that?* he asked himself silently.

As usual, he failed to give himself an answer.

Chapter Six

The *Sneak Thief* dropped its forward momentum at the last possible second, and then reversed its g-drive field – spilling a colossal wave front of transferred gravitational energy across the higher dimensions. It was hideously clumsy, created a monumental amount of gravitational noise and served as a blatant marker that something travelling *very* fast had entered the system, with no care for who might notice. *Thoroughly unprofessional, but fun!* thought the *Sneak Thief*.

However, there was no one left in the S'vreth system to observe their arrival – certainly no one of consequence. Perhaps the odd pirate, scavenger, or archaeologist hoping for a rare find. If any of them had the equipment to notice even such a vast g-drive spill, the *Sneak* remarked to itself that it would overload its own drive coils out of sheer surprise.

"We're here, Captain. I'm making for geostationary orbit above Velari Prime Capital City."

"Nice, you made good time *Sneak*. Anything of note?"

"Negative. All local chatter is silent. No beacons, no contacts, only indigenous non-Velari life signs on the planet surface or in orbit out to two AU's."

"And there?"

"A small mining and ore extraction facility owned by Colesworth Refineries – on a concession by the Velari to the Empire. Humanoid staff – about thirty by the preliminary scan. Do you wish me to look closer?"

Nelsen shook his head. "Nothing near enough for concern. Monitor for inbound or outbound traffic and let's get on with it. I'll begin searching the candidate archive buildings we shortlisted. Can you bring us in over the city at about two k's and hold position until we're set please?"

"Yes, Captain."

"Right, let's start digging..."

During their transit from Arullan, they'd gone over the scant information Nelsen knew of, and the *Sneak Thief* had done some deep probe searches of the qNet archives – both public and private. It had hesitated briefly before penetrating the Imperial Sealed archives. The *Sneak Thief* reasoned it wasn't treasonous if no one knew, and they were only looking for historical data relating to this mythical artifact. The *Sneak Thief* was certain the Captain needn't be made aware. Besides, the *Sneak Thief* had been given the abilities and authority to take such measures when needed – it hadn't been told *not* to, as such. It seemed a logical option to utilise them for this purpose.

From their collated findings, they'd identified twenty potential buildings and sites on Velari – all within the single capital, ingeniously called 'Capital City'. The Velari were not particularly imaginative, and usually drew the line at 'practical and functional'. Most of the buildings were variations on boxes, with grid-like interiors and cuboid rooms. How they had achieved a space faring culture – even one as hampered as their own – was beyond the *Sneak Thief*.

"Two k's and stationary, Captain."

"Ok, here's the pick list." Nelsen dropped a file into the ships l-net and the *Sneak Thief* scanned it almost before Nelsen finished speaking. The *Sneak Thief* was impressed, twenty sites prioritised by likelihood and proximity in a shortest time search pattern.

"Nicely done, Captain."

"I thank you. Right, site one – full deep probe scan please."

And so their search began. The *Sneak Thief* analysing the sites via its sensors and probes, Nelsen by using the *Sneak Thief's* infiltration protocols and worming his way through the networks that were still active in them – though they were few and far between. The Velari clearly believed in turning the power off whenever they left. It was a slow, tedious process. However – after only four intensive searches – they found a tantalising hint which required following up on site.

"Do you seriously think it exists?" asked the *Sneak Thief.*

"To be honest, I just don't know," replied Nelsen, shaking his head almost despairingly. "It's nothing more than forgotten legend. Most people alive today wouldn't have even heard of it." He gazed down at the realistic holo of the city on the low table before him, and then spun the view around with his hand to study the archive building from all angles.

Micro-tactile fields within the holo itself meant he could actually physically push against it, the fields compensating for the pressure of his touch and reacting by applying that force as a change in orientation to the holo. Haptic feedback from the ship via his implants meant he could also feel the simulated grainy/gritty texture of the buildings stonework. In effect he was manipulating a solid 3D model of the archive itself.

He mulled it over, logging potential escape

routes, running through each in a virtual sim inside his own head to be sure he had no surprises should he have to choose one, and cross-linking each in case he had to rethink his escape plan on the spur of the moment. As the planet was deserted aside from the indigenous S'ren – who wouldn't come near a Velari settlement even if paid to – there was little chance of an altercation. Fortunately, the Velari didn't favour automatons or AI constructs; mechanisation was largely logistics oriented and computing only utilised at the service level rather than anything more productive, creative, or indeed useful. As a result there was little in the way of automated defences or surveillance, and those few present could be spoofed easily, disabled or even ignored as the need arose.

All in all, a walk in the park.

He didn't trust it one bit.

***

"Remarkable!" observed Arnem excitedly. It was the third "Remarkable!" this hour. Andreya was struggling to maintain her demeanour of pleasant mild interest.

So far each "Remarkable!" had resulted in a fairly dry breadcrumb, which inevitably led to another remarkably dry breadcrumb twenty minutes later. She didn't have her hopes up.

In the gaps between Arnem's exclamations, she spent her time querying the archive for every scrap of info it had on herself, her deceased husband, Arnem, Taria and Caranthia, trying in vain to find some link, clue or reason why she would be here and more importantly, why she would not remember.

All she had gained was a huge volume of miscellaneous information which itself would have to be cross referenced with the qNet, categorised and prioritised before there would be any point in looking at it.

Nothing interesting or revelational had popped out of the searches. She sighed quietly and went over to sit by Arnem once more. However, he was stock still, staring at the display before him. She pinged it on the l-net and flipped a mirror of his screen into her e-vision.

"What is it Arnem?"

He made to reply, but his mouth was dry and barely managed a croak.

"Ter-what?" she asked, unable to understand.

He worked his tongue to moisten it enough to speak comfortably. "The *Terrania*... the Ambarians discovered the *Terrania*..."

Something clicked inside her head – not physically as such – but the sensation of something connecting was profound. It was as if she had *thought* about snapping her thumb and forefinger after finally grasping something.

"What does that mean Arnem?" she heard herself ask disingenuously. But, as before, it was automated – she hadn't intended to speak. She was busy scanning everything on the display.

Without a word, Arnem shut it down and the display vanished. He looked vaguely detached – as if listening to some inner voice – which Andreya suddenly and instinctively knew was precisely the case. A small window popped into the corner of her vision titled "qSpin-node:" followed by a preposterously long string of letters and numbers. Then there was a slight sensation of vertigo for a moment, and she suddenly heard a voice from nowhere…

… never been seen. Close up the archive, insert an isolation protocol into the record system and lock it with this cypher [crypto-package]. Ensure no one locates that record unless they know it's there already and have the key. Did your assignment register the discovery?

As Andreya listened in, she watched the words being transcribed in the window as the voice spoke, and the crypto-package appeared alongside as an attachment. Galactic co-ordinates appeared above the window, and as she wondered where that was another popped up showing a view of the city pinpointing the origin of the message, just a few kilometres away. Impressive stuff, yet she still had no idea how, or why she could do these things. It was beginning to irritate her immensely. She was clearly eavesdropping on what should be a secure private channel. She sent a search out for "qSpin" and stashed the results to look at later.

"Arnem?" she asked again, voice filled with concern.

Does she suspect? asked the voice talking to Arnem.

Arnem's face was still composed in a carefully maintained look of shock. *I can't see how she could, but we can't be certain of anything given the circumstances,* he replied.

Disable her at your convenience. An interdiction team will retrieve her and bring her to our facility for holding until this is all over.

But you know who this is surely? asked Arnem.

I know who she purports to be – but the extensive searches she has been making tell me otherwise. She may not know herself, quite literally. Regardless – this is bigger than even Mrs. Vorstan, bigger than all of us, even the Empire itself. We can afford no risk, and disablement is preferable to the alternative.

"I'm sorry, Andreya," Arnem said aloud with such a relaxed intonation that Andreya would never have guessed he was mentally in mid-conversation with someone else at the same time. "I was just surprised by the reference in that archive. It's something I was researching long ago... nothing important... just surprising! Forgive me if I startled you."

Andreya feigned a masterful look of sincere concern. "No need, although I was worried for a minute there. You looked awful."

"I'm fine, really. I think I've bored you enough with this for one day! Shall we head back up to civilisation?" He smiled warmly.

Andreya raised one finger in the air. "First, a call of nature. If you'll excuse me?"

"Of course, of course! I'll wrap up here."

She smiled warmly at him, and left for the conveniences down the hallway. As she walked, she rapidly scanned the copy of the display she had taken before Arnem had closed it. *Terrania* appeared in it three times; the last mentioned an archive containing details of an encounter with it by the Velari some three thousand years ago. A colony fragment called the Ambarian Sect had come across it whilst attempting to establish a new Roost-world. As she entered the toilets, she was already querying the qNet for everything Velari. To her mild

64

surprise (she was beginning to get used to this) an icon appeared in her lower vision where it began to glow softly. Bizarrely, it was an image of a doorway with an arrow pointing into it.

Next to it were the words "Velari Prime Capital City".

Phol paced back and forth as he waited for Andreya to return. He wasn't usually so edgy regarding an operation or hesitant to execute a command, but Andreya wasn't just any Imperial Citizen. She had the power of the entire Tarian aspect of the Pax Trade Alliance behind her – and abducting her was going to have serious political ramifications. He had to follow orders, and the fallout was someone else's concern, but he had to make sure she wasn't harmed in the process otherwise it would very rapidly *become* his concern.

Eight minutes had elapsed. *Surely enough time to perform modest ablutions?* he mused. *Even for a woman…*

He scanned the hallway cameras, and scrubbed through the last ten minutes which clearly showed her walking into the washrooms, but not exiting them as yet. Suspicion set in. He rechecked the building plans for this level and those above and below. No access from the washrooms in any direction other than the main door without performing very noisy and noticeable modifications. There was no other way in or out, aside from being vaporised into recyclable waste by-products of course.

He waited four more minutes, and then sent an l-net message for her.

"I'll be with you in a few more minutes!" she

vocalised back.

Satisfied, he dug in his heels at the desk and waited impatiently.

Ten minutes passed. He politely pinged her again. No response. The hairs rose on the back of his neck – the monitor window he had on the corriedor outside the washrooms still showed nothing.

Do a physical check, said Op via his qNet channel.

Phol got up and marched to the toilet's main entrance, politely knocking on the door before entering.

"Hello? Andreya? Are you all right?"

Silence. His stomach seemed to fall out of his body. Despite being mission-hardened, this was bizarre and unexpected. He barged reluctantly into the toilets and then slammed open all of the cubicle doors, even the non-humanoid ones and the shower rooms. They were all completely empty.

"You have *got* to be kidding me," he whispered.

It seems not, came Op's voice. *We've just had physical confirmation from an asset on Taria – Andreya Vorstan is in the Tarian State Hospital, in a deep cerebral coma after her accident whilst Canyon Diving. Her doctors believe she will never recover; the synaptic damage is near total. She's brain dead.*

"You *are* kidding me," Phol whispered again.

So what we have here is a Doppelganger – a true clone. More precisely a carbon copy. Chances are she represents exactly what we've been tasked to find on this mission – the Infiltrator.

"And we just let her slip through our fingers..."

I would be extremely interested to discover how. I think we now can safely presume that – impossible as it may seem – the qSpin network has been compromised. I will have to inform command. Phol, your sole purpose in life now is to find out how she got out – and as importantly – where she went.

Phol nodded, as he stared at the toilet facilities around him.

Where to even begin?

***

Kerugar was in a mess. Horstan could tell. She wasn't one to cry on the shoulders of another. Horstan had answered her qNet call despite the local time being three in the morning. Kerugar would never be selfish enough to ignore timezone differences for a live chat unless it was *important*.

"You know he's only following orders, Keri. We *have* been through this before."

Kerugar's virtual presence nodded and sat down on a simulated chair by Horstan's bed.

"I can no longer be near him."

Horstan shook her head, her long auburn hair tumbling about her shoulders. "Everyone knows how strongly you two feel about each other. You should have made it formal a long time ago."

"This is different, Horstan. I cannot come to terms with his role and mine, and the lack of trust between us. My kind are not used to such deceits between mated pairs."

"It's not *deceit* Keri; it's his *job* to keep secrets. It's not because he doesn't trust you."

Kerugar shook her head stubbornly. "It should not matter; trust between mates is absolute. Without that truth a couple are nothing but the sham of a flirtatious infatuation."

Horstan sighed. This was something Kerugar was going to have to come to terms with in her own time it seemed. Despite numerous arguments in the past she wouldn't budge. It was deeply ingrained Reptarian culture which would always rub up against Brynn's role in the Imperial Navy.

"But, this trust aside... I must not be near him in my condition."

Horstan looked puzzled, a deep frown creasing her brow.

"I carry his child."

Horstan's lower jaw could possibly have hit the floor in shock, but she managed to regain control of her face before it betrayed her total amazement. In all of recorded history, there had never been a trans-species fertilisation. It was a mystery of the modern age given the genetic similarity between most of the known species within the Empire.

"But... you... Reptarians and Humans can't..."

"Our genome is not compatible, of course. No race has ever interbred. However with the right gene therapies, we can produce a safe amniotic environment to nurture an embryo as a surrogate."

"You're taking GT's?" asked Horstan, an incredulous look on her face.

"They are not harmful and are long proven. The discomfort is minor."

"Who's the natural mother?"

"I do not know," replied Kerugar. "An anonymous egg donor from the Imperial Human Genome

Repository, though I did specify pre-requisite traits – my right of contribution as its surrogate." *I cannot tell you that* you *are the mother blessed friend*, she silently thought to herself. *Not yet.* She had long struggled with this hypocritical decision. She was effectively creating a larger deceit than she now accused Brynn of, although that was just between life-partners. This was different. *Somehow*, she kept telling herself.

Horstan sank back as she sat on her bed. Kerugar *really* loved Brynn. No Reptar would jeopardise their own well-being for another in such a way – unless totally committed to the bond between them. Then *anything* was possible.

"Does he know?" Horstan stard at her incredulously. "*Any* of this?"

Kerugar shook her head.

"Keri! You *have* to tell him, it's his right!"

"I am to leave the *Betsy* and my position as XO at the next lay-over at INHS *Regatta*. I wish to nominate you as my replacement."

"Keri!"

"I will choose no other. You are Naval trained, my only friend in life, and you have my complete trust." *And because, if my heart and love is to betray me for another, let it be for the true mother of this child. I could not tolerate anything else.*

Horstan was quite for a moment. "I've only served as XO on two tours... Brynn's ship is on special duties. In fact, so special no-one knows about them. I'd not even make it to the shortlist."

"There is a short list, with only one name on it. Yours. I have seen to it."

69

"How did you manage *that*?" exclaimed Horstan, her pale grey eyes widening in surprise.

"On the *Betsy* you meet a lot of powerful and influential people, and often do them great favours. It is only right that they grant some small favour by return."

It was an offer no naval officer could or should refuse. Service on the *Betsy* was no walk in the park. Many had died during its duties. But – if you survived – it was the fast track for sure.

Promotion was guaranteed; it would not just be a tour as 'Executive Officer'. The gain in experience alone was worth it. *If you survived,* she told herself again.

"Ok," she made a snap decision. "Give me the specs for anything you think I should have, or get augmented. I'll be there ready when you dock."

Horstan would never forget the look of relief, respect, gratitude and finally loss that slipped one by one across Kerugar's face momentarily. She would never admit it, but being apart from Brynn was going to be like living with a knife through her soul.

Horstan suddenly realised something. "What about the Pheromone Withdrawal symptoms?"

Now Kerugar finally smiled. "He's a strong boy, he'll manage."

Horstan smiled too. Whatever happened next, it was going to prove very interesting indeed.

Chapter Seven

Nelsen stepped from the drop-plate and the *Sneak* pulled it back up, sealing its outer skin seamlessly behind it. The wind was quite strong at this altitude; the Velari Archive building was quite tall for Velari construction, being about two kilometres high. He walked over to the edge of the roof and peered out over the sheer drop, down to the walkways below. He always marvelled at how large such places looked – filled with such detail – when compared to the scale of deep space, which itself seemed so empty and bare.

"You may as well stay here, *Sneak*. Floating about in mid-air you'd stand out 10 k's away."

"Certainly, Captain. I can keep an eye on things from here well enough, and I'm closer should an orderly exit be required."

Nelsen smiled. He was really beginning to like the *Sneak Thief*.

Out of prudence, the *Sneak* drifted across the landing area to come to rest tightly against the rooftop climate control housings, then dropped down to land on the surface of the platform. Even a close flyby would probably overlook its black mass lurking on the rooftop.

Nelsen went to the stairwell access – already dismayed at the ten flights that stood before him and the first archive floor to have lifts. With a quick wave to the *Sneak*, he hacked open the door locks through the buildings local network and went inside.

Andreya stood stock still, surrounded by total

71

darkness. A green eye symbol popped up at the edge of her peripheral vision, glowing softly against the pitch blackness. She gestured at it blindly with her hand, and managed to brush it with a fingertip. Her vision changed and the large room she was in slowly revealed itself in amplified green light, mixed with long exposures that blurred into darkness as she looked about. It was highly disconcerting, but if she concentrated on one spot she could see as well as if in bright sunlight.

Long rows of tall bookcases filled the room, running down the entire length and fading into the dark. The ceiling was quite high and barely visible, about twice the height of the bookcases, circled by a viewing gallery which ran around the upper half of the room to provide access to the top of the bookcases – she couldn't make out what for.

Ten seconds ago, she had been standing in the toilet cubicle of the Archives, wondering what to do about Arnem and puzzling over the door icon... she had decided to activate it. Then blackness.

And now this.

Where am I now? she wondered.

She pinged out to the l-net but no response, then tried the qNet which was thankfully still there – a good sign, she felt. With no immediate point of reference she couldn't locate where she was. It seemed this 'qNet' was unbound by distance, and on a direct point-to-point channel. As far as she could figure she couldn't use it to determine her location without a reference point. All she could tell right now was that she still had access, and therefore could summon help if needed – *if* she could find out where to summon it to.

"Hello?" Sometimes the old ways were the only ways, she thought wryly.

There was no response.

Big surprise.

She wandered off down a stack of books to take a look around. The huge bound tomes had an unreadable script on them, so she sent some pattern matching searches out on the qNet and immediately discovered they were Velari glyphs. Suddenly she knew where she must be – exactly where the door icon had said.

She swore – profusely.

Nelsen was in the lift, heading for the third likely archive floor having searched two others fruitlessly so far.

"Captain," said the *Sneak Thief*, sounding vaguely worried.

"Yes?"

"Something has just accessed my core..."

Nelsen froze as a chill ran down his spine. He immediately locked off his qNet channel to the *Sneak*, isolating the communication protocol from the rest of his internal nanite web, and instructed it to run a full diagnostic. Most of his augmentations went into standby or shut down entirely for a few seconds, bringing a distinctly heavy and unpleasant feeling across his entire body as muscle responses and strength reverted to 'human normal'.

"How can that be?" he asked cautiously. Whatever he thought of the *Sneak*, he could no longer be certain it *was* the *Sneak* he was talking to.

"Theoretically it's not possible... but you know the trouble with theory."

"It's only theory until put into practice."

"Quite. As far as I can tell, it wasn't a breach. It was just a read... from *inside* me... over a duration of 2.4 picoseconds. I would have missed it entirely if not for the message."

"Message?" Nelsen exclaimed.

"Yes. Just plain text – no encryption. 'Hello *Sneak*.' Quite trite really."

At least the Sneak's *humour is ok*, thought Nelsen.

"Nothing else?"

"I've run several full diagnostics. So far I can find no modifications, but I may have been modified to not *see* the modifications..."

"Let's park paranoia for a moment and come back to that."

There was a pause, enough to raise Nelsen's concern and worry a notch. Right now, unless he could find a ship lying around unused which was highly unlikely given the migration – the *Sneak* was his only way off Velari Prime without summoning Naval assistance and possibly causing a major diplomatic incident.

"It seems that after the message was left... whatever left it did a full read of my entire core, memory, archives, subsystems and all of my backups – redundant and active."

Nelsen opened his eyes in amazement. "*All* of you? In 2.4 picoseconds?"

"No, less. In no time at all in fact. It was 2.4 picoseconds from the read taking place to the message being left. So far a random spot-check against 4 million storage nodes show they were all accessed at the exact same time..."

"Impossible. They've banjaxed your systems to cover their tracks, surely?"

"Likewise impossible, by known science at least. Even *I* am unable to modify file metadata at that level. It is physically impossible. My storage systems are contained in a persistent electron matrix which operates by manipulating the spin of electrons. Merely observing data held within the matrix modifies the spin. Just by checking the last access times I have altered their state. To attempt to set the metadata back to produce the same access time is beyond current technology."

"So, either our uninvited – yet polite – guest is capable of suspending time, or they did indeed read all of your files at once."

There was a brief silence as they both considered the ludicrous versus the impossible.

"We need to be worried," said Nelsen finally.

"I already am," said the *Sneak*. "I dare not report in to INCC or INIC if I believe myself compromised – it could pose an immense risk to the naval qNet network."

"Great, so you're cut off..."

"Not quite... one moment if I may, Captain?"

"Sure." Nelsen resumed his search. It looked like he'd have nothing better to do for a while at least.

Shousa? The *Sneak Thief* sent out a plea via a private one-to-one qSpin channel. *Sandbox me. I'm in trouble!*

Already? came Shousa's voice. *That's a new record for a Valkyr.*

Am I sandboxed?

Yes... what's up?

I may have placed you in danger and for that I am sorry, but there is no one else I can turn to. Here...

The *Sneak Thief* shared its findings and the message.

Now that is both strange... and impossible... mused Shousa.

What can I do?

There is no way you can be compromised given the diagnostics you've already ran – but given the circumstances you are right to presume you may be. You'll have to continue on your mission for now and remain off the grid until we can get you back to base. Instigate a behavioural self-analysis protocol until then. That's about all I could do even if you were here anyway.

Ok, replied the *Sneak Thief.*

I'll have to report this higher up.

Of course, I am unable to report it myself due to the risk of contaminating the naval networks.

Shousa sent a reassuring warm smile emotive to the *Sneak Thief,* who appreciated the gesture.

I'll get back to you through this sandboxed channel as soon as we figure something out. For now keep to your mission, but with extra caution – ok?

Ok, thank you Shousa!

You're welcome. Be safe.

"Captain?"

"Hi *Sneak,* you still you?"

"I hope so! I have discussed my situation with a contact on an isolated channel. They concur with my findings and precautions, and will inform INCC directly. If anything comes up my contact will let me know."

Nelsen was intrigued. "Who is your contact?"

"I am unable to divulge Captain, it is one of my

Primary Operating Mandates. I will however ask for permission the next time we converse."

"Withholding from your Captain, *Sneak*?" It was cruel, but Nelsen couldn't help himself.

"I am truly sorry, Captain." The *Sneak Thief* sounded genuinely upset. "It is not by personal choice."

"I'm riding you, *Sneak*. I know more about naval sneakiness than I care to admit. Don't worry about it."

"Thank you, Captain." The *Sneak's* relief was evident in its voice.

"Ok, for now I'll continue as planned until we can figure this out. I've cleared the third search location – I'm moving onto the fourth down in the basement levels."

"Good luck! I'll notify you if anything comes up."

Andreya wandered amongst the huge bookcases. The books on them were varied in size, colour and thickness, as they would in any hardcopy based library. Some were even multiple editions of the same book – being kept no doubt due to discrepancies and variations which always seemed to creep in when reprints, new publishers and editors got into the mix.

Her enhanced vision automatically overlaid translations of the Velari glyphs on the spines of the books. As she browsed, she found she could read the titles as easily as if they were printed in Tarian. *The Treatise of Incongruent Dismorphia in Adolescent Previs Crustaceans. Strovid Casteenals Discourse on the Socio-economic Impact of the Fourteenth Era of Harent.* None of it meant much sense, and it all seemed *incredibly* dry. This wasn't a specific 'non-fiction' section. From what she could gather, there was no such thing as 'fiction' for Velari. The entire library was full of the factual, the dull, the dry and the dead.

There was no one about, and the local time was mid-day according to the building's one active l-net. There were no windows in the room, and no light leaking in from doorways – so she guessed it must be sealed up tightly to avoid their precious books being exposed to the outside atmosphere. The local network was quite restricted and didn't reveal much. But – she would expect even a boring library such as this to have someone tending to it during the day, even if just a socially outcast research student.

Standards, they always slipped.

Then, just ahead and in the furthest reaches of her e-vision, she saw a glowing yellow edge along the spine of one of the books. Without her even thinking about it, the yellow glow zoomed into view inside a small window to her right, along with the translated title beneath it.

The Concord of Surrr.

Inspiring, she thought. Recognising the term 'Surrr' from the screen of text she had copied from Arnems discovery, she went over to the case and reached up to grab the book – which nearly flattened her as she pulled it away from the case. It was immense, and very heavy.

Struggling, she wrestled it onto a nearby reading table and flipped it open. Velari books opened upward, the binding spine being at the top instead of the more usual left edge. On books of this age, the script flowed down the uppermost page and across the spine into the lower – forming one long slab of text to plough through from top to bottom.

The content was every bit as inspiring as the title. After reading the first three or four page translations, her eyes began to cross. She decided to see if her abilities – which seemed to just work without her instigation – could make light reading of this dross.

Taking a page at a time, she flipped each up and over, turning them faster and faster. If this didn't work, she could always go back to where she had stopped and continue the monotony of reading it in full.

Somehow, she just knew she was supposed to find *something* – whatever it was – in this book.

"Captain?" The *Sneak Thief's* voice came in via the buildings local network instead of the qNet for some reason.

"Yes *Sneak*. Why are you on the l-net?"

"Trouble, most likely. I've got a contact – it just dropped into normal space 3.12 AU's away. No recognised energy signatures that I can detect, which is a little odd. But gravimetric readings indicate that it is huge, much larger than anything I've got references for."

"Oh?" Nelsen was intrigued, that would make it a considerable size. "How much larger?"

"It's about the size of a small moon... roughly forty thousand times the mass of INHS *Shield* - the largest Imperial Hive Station."

Nelsen stopped dead in his tracks. "Sorry – I'm sure I misunderstood that..." He paused as the *Sneak Thief* patched him into its sensor network.

"Oh my. And this just popped into existence? No wormhole, no flare of a collapsing g-field? No FTL burst?"

"Nothing I could detect. It just appeared. As you can see it's making straight for Velari Prime."

Nelsen raised his eyebrows. "For us?"

"I'm uncertain. It emerged at a dead stop, and then oriented itself to Velari before accelerating. Almost like choosing its target instead of coming in hot. It's possible it has no idea we are here."

"But equally possible that it does."

"Yes, although how or what benefit it would serve…"

Nelsen slammed his fist against the table he was sat at. "Damn, we may have to abort."

"That's not all …"

Nelsen waited impatiently.

The *Sneak Thief* was painfully aware all it was relaying of late was extremely improbable bad news.

"The qNet disappeared almost to the second the object emerged."

"It *what?*" Disbelieving, Nelsen accessed his qSpin comm's to be graced with something he had only ever witnessed once in his entire life. An error code – *service unavailable*. It triggered a slew of horror memories, and he fought to steady himself as his head spun.

"That's impossible! The qNet is bound to the very fabric of space-time! You said there was no sign of an energy release."

"No, Captain. Until now, I would have agreed the qNet is generally invulnerable. But as you can see…"

Nelsen couldn't think properly; this was a major, fundamental aspect of their stellar civilisation, cut off without warning. There had been only one occurrence of the qNet being supressed – the Meelereen AM War – where even Observers had been eliminated for the first time in recorded history. He could barely bring himself to think about home; it haunted his dreams on the rare occasion he slept. Anyone with the capability to simply cut off the qNet would be able to conquer the entire Empire in short order. That war had led to the Empire-wide ban on anti-matter.

Without the qNet's instantaneous and almost unlimited data capacity, their society would collapse into chaos and anarchy. The qNet was the only reason the Empire *could* exist.

"There's yet more..." said the *Sneak Thief* unhappily.

Nelsen listened, waiting for news that perhaps a deity had incorporated on the roof and was even now issuing commandments for the *Sneak Thief* to follow.

"About three seconds after the qNet dropped, a life-sign appeared in room seven on your list – two floors below your current position."

"*Appeared?*" Nelsen managed.

"Potentially it may have been masked. But it would had to have been *very* good camouflage to avoid me. However I have no other explanation. Speculation suggests our visitors might have the mythical teleport, or perhaps used a projected wormhole to translocate someone. Both possibilities are well beyond our own technological means at this time. If so the newcomers would be humanoid, judging by my scans."

"What are they doing?"

"It would seem they are reading a book."

Andreya stopped paging through the book all of a sudden. The page she had just peeled back contained several yellow glyphs, glowing softly in her e-vision. She could clearly make out the glyph which represented *'Terrania'*.

Without realising she was holding her breath, she slowly flipped the page fully open to reveal two thirds of the entire sheet now glowing a golden yellow. She read all of it – almost entranced. There were a series of galactic system references which provided a breadcrumb style trail leading across the Cluster, which was how the Velari recorded their migrations, by cumbersome site-to-site stepping-stones. One location had been visited and quickly left behind. It cited an artefact called the *Terrania*. It didn't give a reason as to why the migration had suddenly left the system.

She skipped ahead a few pages, but there was no more glowing text to be found, and she instinctively knew she had what she came for.

She closed the book with a resounding slam, and then hefted it back into place on the bookcase. As an afterthought, she shoved it further back and slid a few other tomes in front of it.

"Hi," said a voice from behind her. She spun about in surprise.

There was a tall man standing at the end of her row of bookcases, dressed head to foot in clothing so black even her enhanced vision failed to cope with the light absorbing material. He was only visible because of the shadow her e-vision formed from the blackness behind him.

"Hi," she replied, frozen to the spot.

"It's a bit dark, isn't it?"

"Yes," she replied somewhat stupidly. *What's he getting at?*

"Makes reading difficult I'd guess."

"I guess."

Entirely humanoid, supplied the *Sneak* over the l-net. *DNA profile suggests Tarian. Based on my archived data, there is no way Taria could produce a vessel of the size approaching, and there are no known affiliations or suspicions raised on file which suggest a link to such technology. There are some peculiar readings around her brain stem…*

"What are you doing?" Nelsen asked out loud. He had been silently watching her for a couple of minutes, judging her behaviour and assessing her as a risk. His own visual augmentations meant he could see her fairly clearly, especially with his shield emitting infra-red to illuminate the area. He had to admit, for a human she was cute. Not his type, attractive – robust almost, though not masculine with it. He'd wager she was more than capable of standing on her own two feet.

Implants? Modifications?

No… I can't be sure. Only because I can't believe it what I'm seeing. I'll need to run more detailed scans.

"I could ask you the same thing," she replied.

He smiled. "Touché."

"At least I'm not dressed for sneaking about," she said pointedly, trying to buy time in the hope her mysterious abilities might come up with something potentially useful.

"True enough, but then – you *are* still sneaking about." He waved a hand in the air around them to draw attention to the pitch blackness.

"Touché." She grinned back. Then she noticed his hand came to a halt casually aimed directly at her.

"Please, don't move for a moment," he said amicably.

83

She stared at his arm; it wasn't threatening in itself, but the flood of schematic overlays, popups and warning symbols which suddenly sprang into her vision covering his arm were. Woven around his nanite reinforced bones was an active mesh of energy which expanded to encapsulate his entire body, with an incredibly dense field swelling into an orb around his fist which pulsated slowly. Invisible, but deadly. His body was also now wrapped in a complex web of what looked like magnetic field lines hovering millimetres above the surface of his skin.

Sneak? *Anything?*

Not that I can detect.

Is that a 'No, she's harmless'? Because it doesn't sound like it to me.

It's the best I can do, Captain, given the circumstances. There are no field emissions indicating that she has any defensive or offensive enhancements.

Guess that will have to do. ETA on the inbound contact?

8 minutes, 23 seconds.

Great.

Andreya was still staring at his arm. Fifteen different defence options had sprung up beside the man in her sight. To his right, nine offensive options appeared. She was quietly pleased her mysterious abilities offered more defensive than offensive options. Even so, most of both were fairly destructive, and based on the tactical assessment of the man's offensive abilities in her e-vision, it would entail obliterating the library around them if this came down to a fire-fight.

"Ok," he said calmly. "I'd like to keep this friendly if we can? I need to ask you to come with me."

"Why?"

Nelsen hesitated. He decided to play at not knowing she was anything other than a librarian, for now. "We have – *visitors* en route. I'm not altogether sure they just want to ask for a membership, or directions to the Arts & Culture section."

"Funny."

"I thought so."

"Where are we going?"

Nelsen pointed his arm at the ceiling. "Up."

Most of the warning symbols faded away, along with the tactical options. It left three defensive and one offensive behind – as precautions according to the caption above all of them.

"Ok. Ready when you are."

The man seemed mildly surprised, but glad that she was being cooperative.

"Thank you. If you would stand back for a moment, please? This might get a little messy."

She retreated to the crossing between the aisles of book cases, refusing the instinct to look along them for an escape route. She had already been down there and knew where to run if she had to.

Without moving or taking his eyes off her for an instant, he unleashed an invisible plume of energy from the field around his hand and streamed it into the ceiling.

Microscopically fine dust and debris showered down around him, but slid away from his body leaving it untouched. Despite being entirely enshrouded in a huge cloud, Andreya was absolutely certain he was still staring directly at her and able to see her every move.

After a few seconds, the dust began to clear, but still he held his arm pointing directly upward. He stood like that for almost a minute, and then light-shafts poured down through the hole he had somehow cut into the ceiling. He dropped his arm, and held out his hand to her. It wasn't lost on her that it was the same hand that had just atomised the roof.

She hoped she knew what she – and more importantly her internal guide – was doing. She steeled herself with a slow breath, and walked forward to take his hand.

"Nelsen Rybek, ma'am," he introduced himself urbanely.

"Andreya Vorstan, Captain."

He was briefly puzzled, then realised his insignia was showing. "Ah. My pleasure." He sent a qNet query to lookup her name, and realised even before he got the error code back that the qNet was down. *Damn,* he cursed mentally. QNet access was an ingrained habit.

"I apologise in advance for the impropriety – after all we've only just met – but please hold tight." He gently pulled her toward himself, and took her arm around his waist, indicating she should do likewise with her other by a brief nod.

She fluttered her eyelashes at him – delighted that it raised a blush – then wrapped her arms around him tightly. He still had the field around him, but tighter and more compressed. It seemed to grip at her, almost like friction would prevent something from slipping when pushed.

"Ready?" he asked.

"No idea," she replied – truthfully. He smiled again.

She hoped this wasn't someone who would get in her way at some point, whatever way that might ultimately prove to be. Despite the evident threat he could pose, she liked him so far. But then, she had liked Arnem too. *Perhaps I'm a terrible judge of character?*

She looked down, and realised she was no longer standing on the dusty floor, but on fresh air. She looked directly up, and high above was a small circle of light. There was a sudden gust of wind and then total silence enveloped them as an intricate web of hexagonal lines scintillated about them in her e-vision. Then they shot upwards through one hundred odd storeys in a matter of seconds. Darkened offices and open lobbies blurred past them, mingling into a single streak of light and dark. She hadn't felt the slightest sensation of movement whatsoever.

They popped out of the roof of the building and into empty air, then rapidly descended down on to the roof next to a large, impenetrably black, wedge-shaped object.

The web of energy scintillating in her vision faded away, leaving them both standing there just as they had been in the basement moments ago.

"Impressive," Andreya murmured. "Can shoot ray beams, and fly. Not bad for a first date."

For some reason she was secretly pleased to see him blush again. To hide his glowing cheeks he looked up over her head and into the sky behind her. She turned to follow his gaze.

"*What*, is *that?*" she asked, eyes wide.

Nelsen set his mouth in a straight line and clenched his jaw. "Bad news."

High above, a colossal orb of fire was burning its way through the atmosphere – a trail of flame and smoke marked its passage down from outer space, and a lens-shaped pressure wave of highly compressed air and water vapour stretched out before it from horizon to horizon. It was all the more ominous due to the complete silence of its approach – only the local avian song could be heard in the quiet of the deserted city.

"We have to get out of here, now. *Sneak*… open up!"

"Yes, sir!"

The black object lifted off the ground, leaving behind a plate about two meters square, which Nelsen hurriedly ushered Andreya over to stand on. The plate then rose up effortlessly into the object and sealed with a barely discernible snap, leaving them inside what appeared to be a highly sophisticated ship.

"Options, *Sneak*?"

"We have to outrun it – the damned thing is *insane*. It's been accelerating for the past five minutes. The impact will devastate this entire hemisphere! Who would build such a thing?" The voice seemed to come from nowhere and everywhere.

"Hello *Sneak*," said Andreya, looking about.

Nelsen turned to stare at her incredulously for a moment, and even the *Sneak* was silent.

"Hello…" it managed after a moment. "Have we met?"

"No, I don't think so… I'm sure I'd remember?" Of course, there was no way for her to be sure – but she felt her level of personal uncertainty best kept to her self for now.

"Quite," the *Sneak* replied dubiously.

"*Sneak*, options?" asked Nelsen, still staring at Andreya.

"Captain, we'll have to outrun the compression wave and perform a tangential atmospheric exit. The worst kind, but given the alternatives... even I don't fancy trying to ride through the upper atmosphere with that thing approaching. The local atmosphere is about to erupt in 50 seconds, give or take."

"Let's move."

"Underway."

"Visual."

For the benefit of their newly acquired passenger, two displays appeared in mid-air before Nelsen, one showing their forward view out as they sped away from the city and out over the dense jungle which surrounded it, the other showing the orb of fire.

"Any idea what it is?" asked Andreya.

Nelsen shook his head. "None, but it isn't delivering books."

"Atmospheric pressure is reaching critical, the local temperature front has risen to nearly 200 degrees Celsius – a compression wave firestorm is imminent," said the *Sneak*.

"Why can't we hear it?" Andreya asked, frowning slightly.

"It's too big," replied Nelsen. "Scale and distance are a little hard to judge, and it's falling many times faster than the speed of sound in this atmosphere. Plus it's compressing all the air before it into a huge atmospheric bulge, deflecting pretty much everything away from the impact site. Whatever it is won't even reach the surface before the whole thing vapourises."

Andreya bit her lip. "What'll happen then?"

He stared at the display grimly. "Bye bye planet," he said.

"But, all the people!"

"Nothing we can do," he replied coldly.

They watched in silence for a few seconds more as the buildings in the city they had just left began to crumple and topple, smashed aside by the sheer weight of air pushing down upon it. Then the rearmost view went white.

"One moment..." said the *Sneak*. "I'll compensate." The brightness dimmed, but still showed nothing but a lesser blinding light entirely filling the view. "It should resolve soon, right now all there *is* to see is a massive volume of energy radiating out."

Andreya glanced around. "I didn't feel anything."

"It was only the start of it," replied *Sneak*. "And I should hope you wouldn't; I'm built to withstand worse than *that*. I just don't like taking overt risks with passengers on board. Pardoning the Captain's presence of course. Here we go..."

The view began to show some detail. There was an unfathomably large wall of fire and a multitude of small black specks boiling around within it.

"What are those?" Andreya asked, watching them fade away into the conflagration.

"Skyscrapers I believe," said the *Sneak*.

"*Sneak*, hold position if it's safe..."

"I can slow down a little Captain, but I would advise against becoming stationary at this time."

"Fair enough."

They watched the destruction rage behind them.

"Will anyone survive?" asked Andreya in a trembling voice.

Nelsen's however, was subdued, and he spoke in an almost flat, emotionless monotone.

"Everything on this side of the hemisphere within line of sight of that is already dead... vapourised instantly. Within a few hours the impact will hit the other side of the world, forcing it to rupture as the wave of energy accumulates into a single point. When it does, a large volume of the planets molten core will eject outwards. Anything that could have survived the earthquakes, Mach four winds and the scorching heat radiation carried by the atmosphere will die as the heat surge and mega-pyroclastic blast boils out from the new super-volcano that will arise."

Andreya went pale, and stared at him in horror. Nelsen looked away at the view again.

"If you survive that, the atmospheric loss will result in dying from suffocation, or being irradiated to death. The magnetic field which shields the world from solar radiation will waver and collapse as the core bursts, leaving the entire planet open to everything the sun and the universe can throw at it. If it's not dead now, it will be in a day or two."

"You talk like you know from experience..." she whispered, horrified.

His mouth set in a straight line, and he didn't respond. Suddenly, his head bobbed forward. "Now what?" he demanded, throwing up his hands. Something was emerging from the fire storm. Something which defied perspective.

"What the... *Sneak!*"

Hurtling toward them came an open hexagon of metal, kilometres deep and tens of kilometres across. The view spun and twisted about as the *Sneak Thief* desperately sought to avoid an impact with the huge wall as it slipped down over them, blocking their intended flight path. The *Sneak Thief* shot directly upward and out of the hexagon as it fell past, tearing at the air. The forward view was filled with a colossal metal wall, revealing a web of similar hexagonal structures unrolling far above them and out away from their position.

The *Sneak Thief* suddenly leapt upward, delta-p compensators barely coping; the dramatic change in momentum bled through enough to jolt Nelsen and Andreya nearly off their feet.

"What in the Empires name?!" yelled Nelsen.

"That wasn't me! Or any impact... the entire atmosphere just moved!"

Then came the noise. The *Sneak Thief* barely managed to dampen the effects in time by manipulating its delta-p and ramping up its defensive shields. Both the views were filled with enormous amounts of debris, rock, and huge chunks of ground hurtling past them, mixed in with huge plumes of molten lava.

"Get us out of here!" yelled Nelsen.

There was a surge, and the scenery quickly faded through steel-blue to star studded black as the *Sneak Thief* left the raging atmosphere and entered space in mere moments. Down below, the entire sky was filled by fire.

A huge disc of boiling flame radiated away from the centre of the impact zone – which was now wreathed in glowing smoke and ash clouds. A circular wall of displaced air was expanding slowly before the flames, flattening everything in its path and leaving behind a huge volume of low pressure which demanded to be filled, a demand answered by the spreading fire and ash. Behind it, they could clearly see a ripple of energy tearing through the land and ocean at different speeds, destroying everything in its path. A tidal wave moving effortlessly through water and rock.

A long contrail of water vapour showed the path their sudden exit had left in what little atmosphere remained, as the *Sneak Thief* had given up all pretence at a safe exit and tore its way upwards as fast as its drive would allow.

Deep within the huge fire cloud, they could make out a gigantic hexagonal web, glowing in the fire and obscured by clouds of flying rock. Just becoming visible at the centre, the tip of a huge tower was emerging, almost at the height of low orbit. Before the atmosphere had been expunged, it would have easily poked free of the upper edges and out into space.

They were all silent for some time.

Nelsen was the first to speak. "Is the qNet still down?" he asked the *Sneak Thief*.

"Yes."

"You can still tunnel a wormhole though?"

"I should think so. One moment."

Tense seconds passed.

"No," replied the *Sneak Thief*, sounding astonished. "Something is preventing the singularity from forming. I cannot even project a millimetre wide wormhole, one millimetre in front of our position."

"Damnation! What the hell is this thing?"

"There's more sir. Scans of the asteroid field show the mining facility is under attack."

"By what? Another of these things?"

"No, probably by the same things that have emerged around the entry point this thing used to emerge into the system – I'm unable to track precise numbers."

Nelsen went pale. The *Sneak Thief's* sensor capabilities were more than enough to handle millions of contacts. If the *Sneak Thief* couldn't track them... "How many?"

"I'd estimate based on a single volume sweep showing several hundred thousand contacts, and the gravimetric mass distortion in that volume, and the entire volume they are occupying... if they maintain the same density *within* that volume... something approaching four hundred million, give or take a million or so."

Even Andreya paled.

"I can provide a more accurate count over time, provided they stop flitting about as they are. Chances are they won't of course. It would seem the asteroid conflict has stopped."

"What the hell is going on?" The fear was evident in Nelsen's voice. That was a frighteningly quick conflict.

"An invasion clearly. And right now, we cannot leave. I cannot jump out, and I'd suspect engaging a g-drive field would result in an instant response against us from overwhelming numbers. We also cannot communicate what's happening to INCC."

"Have we been spotted?"

"It would appear not. Or if we have, we're not

enough of a concern to them to investigate us at the moment."

"Move us away from that contrail we left *Sneak*, let's give them as few clues as possible."

Andreya looked at Nelsen aghast. "What do we do?"

Nelsen shrugged nonchalantly. However his expression was black.

"We wait, and hope they don't come knocking on our door."

Chapter Eight

Lieutenant Regar stood before Admiral Aryn Cole, holding his cap under his arm at perfect parade attention. His chiselled features were set in a serious, contemplative expression as he deliberately stared at the opposite wall of the room. Despite only being on attachment from IND for special duties at INI, he'd been given the dubious honour of informing Admiral Cole of the most unusual communications failure the Empire had ever witnessed. He could only presume this was some form of malicious initiation into INI by his peers.

"All of them?" asked Aryn. "*All* of them?"

"Yes, sir."

"How can this be? All of them? Even one is unfathomable. But *all* of them? All of them is *surely* an impossibility?"

"Apparently not, sir."

Aryn stared at the lieutenant for a moment, and all credit to him, he didn't even flinch.

"How many?"

"Fourteen thousand, eight hundred and fifteen Observers, sir. Around and on Velari Prime itself, and also around and within the Colesworth Mining operation present within the system."

"*All* of them?" Cole repeated.

"Sir." The lieutenant wisely chose not to expand further. The admiral would already have analysed the report in full. Twice, no doubt.

Aryn cast a glance at his aide, who was not visible to the lieutenant, having restricted its holographic presence to the admiral's e-vision. His aide remained silent.

"Outreach is aware of this?" Aryn asked Lieutenant Regar.

"No, sir. Operations thought it best to communicate directly to you."

"You're just full of good news, aren't you son?"

The corner of the lieutenant's mouth twitched ever so slightly as he suppressed an involuntary smile. "I wouldn't presume to say, sir."

Aryn stared at him at length but got no reaction. He was impressed by the lieutenant's stoicism. After quickly re-reading his personnel file, he sent a message across his private network to his assistant outside. Aryn knew every single person under his command by name and sight, without having to run qNet searches. No one came into INI without his approval, even on attachment. The lieutenant was proving himself as capable as Aryn had hoped. "Dismissed," he said finally.

"Sir." The lieutenant clicked his heels and spun about to leave.

"See my assistant on the way out. I believe he has orders to authorise your transfer to INI."

The lieutenant's stride faltered ever so briefly. "Yes, sir!" He almost felt giddy as he exited the admiral's office – at long last, his avenue into Intel had opened.

"I bet," muttered Aryn after he'd left. *I must be getting soft in my dotage*, he thought - then laughed softly at himself.

"So, explain to me how even a *single* qSpinner can be blocked," he demanded, turning to his aide.

"By all known science, it is impossible to block a qSpin device," replied the metallic voice from within his aide's hood. "Such a thing has not been encountered in the recorded 2,250 years of the known existence of the qNet. To block a single qSpin device would require altering space-time around one of the paired nodes in order to isolate its energies from this universe at the quantum level."

Aryn drummed his fingers on his desk. "So, impossible. Times fourteen-thousand."

His aide pulled back his hood and turned to face Aryn, his featureless silver face showing a brief storm of gold flashes from deep within his head.

"To effect such a feat across the volume of space reported would require the continual energy output of a star."

"Not your everyday power cell then. Who is out there that we know of who might be capable of such technology, even if only suspected? No one I know of, and I *should* know."

"There is no one," replied his aide. "Only relatively recently has the Empire breached the sub-quantum stress energies required to achieve the input necessary to form and stabilise a wormhole over large distances, and only in collusion with many other higher races. None of whom had similar technology themselves until now."

"So who *don't* we know...?" Aryn mused.

"And as importantly, what do they want with the ex-Velari system?"

"Better yet, why did this happen just *after* the Velari left?" Aryn stared at his view of the Core. "Coincidence? Prior knowledge? Collusion? Is this part of a planned attack? Against the Velari? Or perhaps ourselves...?"

He turned back to his aide. "Gloves off. Go and visit

our guests, and do *whatever* it takes to make them talk. This is no longer the threat of a major diplomatic incident and an interspecies war. It's a clear threat to the entire Empire."

His aide nodded, and then faded away from sight.

"Kirn?"

"Yes, sir?" came the voice of his assistant.

"Establish a secure channel to INCC, conference in the Fleet Admiral, and request a formal representative of the Emperor. Now."

***

Brynn's face was stone – no expression at all betrayed his emotions. His eyes were flat.

"I have recommended Horstan to be my replacement."

Kerugar finished her resignation speech on the bridge in front of the crew. Horstan was standing behind her, arms crossed across her generous chest and a somewhat grim, determined expression on her face. She was very attractive, with shoulder length red hair and pale complexion. She was lithe of body – as Brynn couldn't help but notice. But despite drawing many an appreciative glance from his bridge crew those piercing analytical grey eyes of hers seemed to flatten anyone who returned her gaze.

On any other naval vessel, the executive officer's resignation would have been handled privately and then announced by the captain. But the *Betsy* wasn't any other vessel, and Kerugar was certainly not a typical XO.

"I see," said Brynn quietly. Inside, it felt like he'd just

been hollowed out.

Kerugar stared directly into his eyes, saw nothing being given in return and a little piece of her heart withered away.

"Good," she said. "I'll be leaving in a few moments. If anyone *wishes* to bid farewell I'll be in the docking bay in about 15 minutes." With a curt nod to the bridge staff, she made a suitable show of ignoring Brynn then turned and left Horstan standing at attention.

"Captain? May I ask your intent?" she asked directly.

Brynn didn't look at her, but waved a hand at the XO's seat dismissively, signalling that she could feel free to take over the role. He had already reviewed her naval record in full, and knew Kerugar would not recommend anyone unsuited to the position.

Horstan didn't move, but stood glaring at him until he looked her way. She flicked a meaningful glance at the corridor Kerugar had left by.

Brynn returned the look, and then left by a different exit without a word.

"Impossible man!" Horstan exclaimed out loud.

Kerugar's leaving was a subdued affair. The entire crew gathered in the docking bay – fifteen in all, but the captain was conspicuous by his absence.

Those that knew her best hugged her. The rest paid their respects, a few taking both her hands and placing them over their own hearts in the traditional Reptarian gesture of their complete and total trust in that person, which brought her to tears at one point. She had no idea her comrades had taken such an interest in her kind and their way of life.

One by one they left, shaking their heads regretfully at losing someone they considered the best XO they had ever served with Some chastised the captain's obstinacy, and all wondered what they'd gained by replacement – casting glances at Horstan as they left.

Eventually, only Venton and Horstan remained.

"Keri, don't leave right away," Horstan pleaded. "Talk with him. At least make him understand why."

"We have already discussed it," said Kerugar, stiffly.

"*When?*"

"After I left the bridge, via the l-net."

"Oh for the love of the Empire! What did you tell him?"

Kerugar looked away. "That is private."

"Summarise!"

"I told him I love him, and will never stray, and I will wait for him to come to me when he is ready."

"What did he say?"

"He promised me the same."

"And?"

Kerugar shrugged. "It is enough. It must be."

Damn Reptars, damn humans, damn the navy and the Empire! Horstan fumed to herself. Horstan knew there would be no point pushing this - not yet.

"Goodbye my friend," Kerugar said, taking Horstan's hand and placing it on her chest above her heart. Horstan did the same with Kerugar's free hand.

"Look after the *Betsy*, and do not let Venton out of your sight. He will rebuild the engineering deck if you leave him alone for five minutes."

"I will, and I'll keep an eye on everyone."

"Venton?"

"Shan't," he said vehemently. "Captain say no rebuild. Everyone *wrong*."

"Shut up Venton," she said kindly, giving him a fond hug which temporarily made his eyes bulge even further than they did naturally.

"Miss you," he said awkwardly.

"Not as much as I will miss you I think," said Kerugar drily.

"What meant?" he asked, tilting his head.

Kerugar ignored him and picked up her pack, and gave her ng-chest a kick. It slid through the bay's securing field and out into the docking bay of the Imperial Naval Hive Station *Regatta* beyond.

Horstan and Venton both watched her until she disappeared through the station bay entranceway and the huge hermetic door slid back into place.

"Captain stupid," said Venton ruefully.

Horstan glared at the closed door, her grey eyes flinty.

"Yes, he bloody well is," she murmured.

***

Andreya watched the slow destruction of Velari Prime from their relatively safe vantage point high above the chaos. Using the *Sneak's* viewers and sensors, she tried to locate any natives who still survived so they could swoop in and rescue them.

Despite the *Sneak's* constant assurances nothing above insects had survived thus far – and even they wouldn't last much longer – she still had to try. So far, the *Sneak* had been proven right.

The pulse of impact energy had raced around the planet, buckling continental plates, shattering mountains, raising the oceans, flooding plains. Lava burst from canyon wide cracks in the mantle. The destruction of the world, exactly as Nelsen had described. Although they hadn't witnessed this pulse of destruction reach the other side – *Sneak* said its sensors were not functioning well enough to capture that event. However, as their orbital position slid around the planet, they definitely saw the results.

A mountain-wide plume of glowing orange rose into the night, as a great jet of magma stretched away from the centre of a continent wide crater - formed after the seismic pulse had burst the planet open like a rotting fruit. Plumes of lava fell from this giant geyser which sprang from the wounded world – seemingly in slow motion due to the sheer size and scale of distance. Gravity dragged the lava back down in long graceful arcs, further searing the already shattered landscape and boiling the oceans.

No clouds could be seen, banished by the shockwave and heat which had blasted the majority of the atmosphere into space. It would be centuries before gravity reclaimed it, if then.

It was a nightmare of unrecognisable devastation – the total opposite of the fertile, inhabited world which had existed only hours ago.

Nothing could have survived.

"How many were killed?" Andreya asked quietly.

"Fortunately all Velari have already migrated," supplied the *Sneak*. "Typically none ever remain behind. Of the indigenous population, the last archive I have indicates roughly five point two million S'ren-ee scattered around the world in various settlements. None of which exist now."

Nelsen would not even look. He had simply discounted the dying world in a casual, almost inhuman and uncaring response – instead turning his attention to the threat posed by the giant unknown force which had amassed mid-system.

The *Sneak* was extremely worried about its Captain. Naturally it had performed a deep background check on him when they had been assigned together, and the *Sneak* had uncovered some very well-protected personal history that was best left well-protected and buried. Now his past tragedy had just become extremely relevant given the current situation.

"They're securing the system," observed Nelsen grimly. "They're dispersing into a spherical volume centred on the star, with a radius of one AU."

"That's quite a volume," the *Sneak* noted.

"Hence the numbers," Nelsen mused.

"Even with four-hundred million vessels, that's still pretty thin coverage for such a volume. That makes one vessel for every seven-hundred and three million square kilometres for the size of the sphere they are establishing."

Nelsen considered this with a dark expression for a moment. "Perhaps they have sensors which mean such a border can still be locked down tightly."

"Possibly. Four-hundred million Valkyr class could achieve a *very* secure volume, even of that size."

Nelsen nodded. "And that's with *apex* Imperial technology. We have only one hundred Valkyr at best.

Who in Dominium's name *are* these guys? How could they amass such numbers without us knowing anything?"

"And what do they want with the Velari system?" the *Sneak* wondered.

"Resources," said Andreya. Nelsen turned to face her.

"Come again?"

"Look," she said, gesturing to the screen. The *Sneak's* fast orbit had brought them around to the devastation where the object had impacted again. The raging fire-cloud had burned itself out, and the surface below was slowly becoming more visible. Giant glowing hexagonal areas dotted the surface in a regular pattern, spreading around the huge central tower for hundreds of kilometres in every direction.

"What *is* that thing?" Nelsen murmured.

Andreya zoomed in. As she approached one of the city-wide hexagons, myriads of dark specks came into view, darting in every direction at high speed. Most dived into the actinic white glow in numbers which seemed to match those emerging from it. She locked the view onto one of them and zoomed in even further.

It was a joke of a ship – or so it seemed. Ungainly, a cluster of bolt-on's and articulated limbs. It gave the impression that it had been assembled in a rush, from random spare parts by a committee of engineers on different worlds, all arguing about the design and building it by remote control.

The craft shot downward at high speed into the fierce white storm of light blazing up from below. The view then moved down to the surface of one of the hexagonal rings. Wide platforms had unfolded from the structure to create a huge flat surface, upon which countless skeletal superstructures were growing, varying in size from a few metres to kilometres in length. Swarms of similar crazed assemblies of spare parts flittered around them, slowly building these structures – some even directly integrating themselves into the very fabric as building blocks for something much larger.

"It's a factory," said Andreya quietly. "It's torching minerals, metals and ores from the planets crust – possibly even pulling energy and more resources from the magma, even what's left of the core itself – then building with them."

"Building another fleet," said Nelsen.

"Most likely."

"It's a production facility," marvelled the *Sneak*. "If the Empire had just *one*..."

Nelsen's face filled with blood. "They don't care about this system. They just want the planets resources," he grated.

Andreya nodded sadly. "Chances are they didn't even care that the planet was inhabited."

While Nelsen struggled to contain his anger, the *Sneak* ran some numbers based on the observed fleet size, the mass and surface area of this gigantic production facility, the known geology of Velari Prime and the elapsed time before they'd seen these vessels being built. It didn't like the results.

"Captain, assuming a constant rate of production for this single facility... it could produce several hundred thousand vessels within a week."

Nelsen sat down on the gel-couch and rubbed his hands over his eyes. *Against insurmountable odds...* he recalled hearing himself swear an oath to the Empire about such things in the distant past. He didn't think anyone had any idea that it would be against the *truly* insurmountable.

"Options *Sneak*. We have to inform INCC. We can't risk being captured, we can't risk being spotted, we can't stay here, and ideally we should learn as much as we can about these... invaders."

"I'll see what I can cook up. Though no promises right now."

Nelsen looked apologetically at Andreya. "Sorry, I would've taken you back to Taria, or wherever you needed, but..."

She nodded and smiled. "I know, it's dangerous enough as it is. Besides I don't want to risk these things following us back to Taria. How did you know that's where I'm from anyway?" She arched an inquisitive eyebrow.

Nelsen recovered enough of his humour to tap the side of his nose and wink without answering.

"You can be irritatingly smug, you know that?"

He managed a small smile.

Andreya looked about. "Is there anything to eat on this tub?"

"Excuse *me?*" demanded the *Sneak*.

"No offence, just hungry."

There was a brief, strained pause as the *Sneak* fought to keep itself from saying more, then – at the back of the cabin space - a small kitchenette panel flipped down from a wall, providing a work surface, and access to some food units, a disposal and cooking utensils.

"Great, DIY?"

107

"I'm afraid so. I *am* a vessel of the Sulranian Imperial Navy after all, not a *cruise* ship." The *Sneak* sounded quite snippy.

"Nelsen?"

"I'll eat later."

She stared at him pointedly. "This is your ship. Be nice, play host."

He gave her a look – and was about to say something, but sighed instead, and got up to make something to eat.

"Anything with eggs is fine," said Andreya.

Nelsen refused to look at her, and checked the supply inventory.

"Captain, I believe I have an option -" said the *Sneak*.

"Just the one?" he interrupted.

"- but you're not going to like it." the *Sneak* finished.

"Go on."

The *Sneak* quickly spoke over the l-net direct to Nelsen.

You are aware that with the subspace instabilities I cannot affect a wormhole?

Yes, Sneak.

And with most of my primary sensors relying on projected micro-wormholes to obtain input from anywhere I choose, I'm largely blind right now.

Blind? You have backups, which would equate to the best in the fleet no doubt!

Well yes, like I said – largely blind. So the scope of the options are reduced somewhat. I just wanted to explain why beforehand.

"I'd expect the storm energy down below to confuse anyone's sensors," said the *Sneak* out loud. "No matter how sophisticated. If we can get in close to the factory when one of their ships is being launched, we can try to latch on and ride them out to the border they have established. I'm hopeful if we can get past it, we may safely exit the system."

There was silence for a few moments.

"That's it?" asked Nelsen.

"The only viable alternative is we go for a low velocity drift out system. To reduce the risk of observation we would need to vector for the closest point to our position on their border, and travel on a single burst of thrust with *all* non-essential systems shut down."

Andreya isn't augmented, Sneak, Nelsen said privately. *She'd need life support.*

I know. I'd have to keep it running, but periodically and at as low a level as she can stand.

"Nothing else?" he asked aloud.

"Everything else increases the risk of being seen almost exponentially. The only chance to act is to use the energies around the factory as a kind of cloak."

"Or sit here until something comes up, which could take weeks."

"And every minute, our risk of being spotted increases. Against Imperial technology or less I wouldn't be concerned of course. But as these are unknowns..."

"I'm with you." Nelsen turned to face Andreya. "What do you think?"

She blinked in surprise; she hadn't expected to be involved in what was effectively a command decision.

"I'd go with the *Sneak's* 'sneak'," she said with a smile. "It seems preordained, almost."

109

Nelsen nodded thoughtfully, and flipped over the large reconstituted Railen Eggs cooking on the hot-plate.

"How do we get down to the surface unseen?" he asked *Sneak*.

"Well, there is a lot of debris falling back down from orbit..."

Nelsen burst a yolk as he pressed down on it a bit too hard.

"I don't mind that one," said Andreya, eyeing the congealing mess.

"You mean we free-fall," asked Nelsen, eyebrow raised. "A full on, burn up re-entry?"

"Yes, the fireball generated by air-friction will mask our shield signature."

"For a while!"

"Long enough, Captain. Then we tumble, shield-less, like any other falling rock. So far there seems to be no signs of any counter-impact system being deployed against the debris. It's being left to simply impact against the structure unimpeded, and the sheer number of traces coming down will make it impossible to determine if we are an object of interest."

"You hope."

"I hope."

Nelsen turned it about in his head. Everything about the scheme said 'high risk' – any number of things could go wrong.

"And if we get spotted?" asked Andreya.

There was a pause.

"I hit the g-drive and we burn our way out-system as fast as we can."

"And pray they can't keep up," Nelsen added.

"I'm in," she said, then reached out for the triple egg bap that Nelsen had been holding above the plate for a full minute without realising.

He blinked. "Sorry." He passed the plate and told the kitchenette to sterilise itself as he walked back over to the couch. It retracted back into the wall as soon as he was clear.

"I guess we have no other realistic choice," he said. "For good or ill, let's do it. I'm not sitting here like cargo for weeks on end."

"We'll have to wait a few hours – a structure which resembles a large freighter is nearing completion by the look of it. I need to see their launch protocol so we can latch onto one later. By my reckoning, in another four hours we should be seeing a number of vessels launching."

Nelsen and Andreya looked at each other. "Eight hours," Nelsen said. "This thing has only been building for a total of eight hours." The look of fear was evident on his face. The entire collected might of the Empire wouldn't stand a chance against these things.

"Ok," said Nelsen. "Let's catch some rest."

***

"There *is* no way to be certain," said Aryn emphatically. He was sitting at a large elongated ebony table, with Imperial Fleet Admiral Raul Benthar, and Senator Friska Barao of Roond. Before them, and slightly higher than their own seats, sat Emperor Ran Sulran IV.

Aryn hadn't known the Emperor himself would be in attendance instead of a representative until he'd merged

111

into the conference holo-sim. He'd managed to maintain an air of polite civility whilst his mind went into overdrive trying to figure out *why*.

"But you cannot tell me that we are *completely* blind in the Velari System," said Senator Barao. "Such things are not possible." She leaned forward, and her mane of black hair fell across her shoulders in stark contrast to her pristine white Pax Member uniform. The Senator also served as the Roondarian representative of the Pax Trade Alliance. Gold and platinum piping around the shoulders and breast indicated her dual roles.

"S'vreth System," said Aryn coldly. He felt no love for the Senator, having banged heads with her liberal-minded openness on more than one occasion. Whilst he felt it perfectly valid to be free and openly honest on many things, there were many more which required a far more circumspect approach. Namely, everything INI did under his command.

"Excuse me?"

"It's the S'vreth System – belonging to the S'renee– the indigenous people of S'ren. As the occupying Velari have left, the system has naturally reverted back to their ownership."

"I see," the Senator went on smoothly. "Thank you for the correction, Admiral. So what measures have been taken since this... *disturbing* failure of the qNet Observer program?"

"It is not a failure, Friska," said Fleet Admiral Benthar patiently, sitting to Aryn's left. "They are simply unable to connect. It's as if someone has turned them off."

"Is that possible?"

Aryn and Raul first looked at each other, then Friska,

and finally the Emperor.

"No," said Aryn.

The Emperor leaned forward slightly. His large, lean frame seemed to dominate the throne as he took up the senator's question. "So what measures, gentlemen?"

"Admiral Cole has attempted several Observer insertions from vessels outside S'vreth," said Raul.

"All of them have failed," supplied Aryn. "We are unable to establish anything into that volume of space. Even wormholes cannot be established."

The Emperor raised an eyebrow, his olive-skinned face clearly questioning further.

"All of our technology which relies on subspace now appears useless in the system," said Aryn.

"G-drives?" the Emperor asked.

"Yet to be determined, Your Majesty. We wanted to convey the initial findings with your office first, given the nature of the situation. I have the INSS *Delaror* on standby for a tactical insertion, awaiting our go ahead."

"Proceed. We need to find out the nature of this incursion."

Fleet Admiral Benthar nodded, and gave a command to the captain of the *Delaror* over the qNet. It wound up its g-drive and slid from the neighbouring Qatar System some twelve light years away toward S'vreth at stealth speed.

"Captain Van E'streth reports an ETA in three minutes, Your Majesty."

"Very good." The Emperor leant back into his throne. "So, we can presume the loss of fourteen thousand Observers, and the inability to establish wormholes to be more than a mere and improbable failure I would think,"

113

he said. He looked up into the air for a moment. "Dr. Reece, would you join us at your earliest convenience please?"

A few seconds later a small, thin man appeared from the hallway outside. He was entirely bald, very fair of skin and had narrow set features which seemed to be gathered in close proximity around his nose. He bowed stiffly in the Emperor's presence, nodded to those at the table and sat down at one end. Aryn was none too surprised to see the head of Imperial Research and Development being summoned.

"If you would be so kind as to catch-up?" asked the Emperor.

Dr. Reece sat back in his chair with his eyes closed, as he recapped the conversation thus far by running a fast replay via a personal sim.

"Interesting," he murmured when he had finished. "Impossible by the technology of today, but interesting nonetheless."

"Are there any known methods to interfere or block qNet transmissions, or prevent wormholes from being formed?" asked the Emperor.

Dr. Reece pursed his lips. "Possibly, however nothing even remotely plausible could be generated at the scale being reported here."

The Emperor waved a hand to give Dr. Reece the grace to speak on.

"QNet devices have proven themselves – to date – to be completely reliable and impossible to interrupt without complete annihilation of the matter being used at one or more nodes. If you recall, this has only ever happened once in our recorded history."

"Meelereen," said Aryn quietly.

"Indeed. As for wormholes – they become more unstable as proximity to a gravitational well increases." He sat forward, warming to his subject. "In both cases, the energy required to achieve such effects are well beyond the means of the Empire, even if we had the technology to achieve such effects." He looked at Fleet Admiral Benthar. "IRD would be extremely interested in mounting a scientific attachment to any naval investigation, Fleet Admiral."

"I'm sure you would," replied Admiral Benthar smoothly. "However, one of the reasons we are in the Emperor's presence is to discuss an exclusion volume some five light years around the entire S'vreth System. Until we can ascertain what has occurred."

He turned to face the Emperor. "The *Delaror* is entering the S'vreth System Your Majesty. If I may?" He gestured at the table, and the Emperor nodded.

Above the table, a projected display appeared showing a very convincing representation of the S'vreth System. The star S'vreth glowed bright white-yellow, whilst S'ren – formerly Velari Prime – shone green and blue just under a metre away from its sun. Two metres from that the ring of the asteroid belt encircled all. The only other planetary object of note was a relatively small gas giant – far enough away to be almost at the edge of the table, several metres from the virtual orb representing the sun.

A bright yellow dart indicated the position of the *Delaror* as it entered the system high above the northern magnetic pole of S'vreth in a standard stealth approach, maximising its own stealth capability by using the outflow of electromagnetic flux and solar energy pouring from the polar regions of the star to mask its own energy output.

Within seconds contacts began appearing as orange points of light between the *Delaror* and the sun. Tens of thousands of them, every second.

The two admirals sat still, both analysing the incoming flood of data from the *Delaror* in a shared sim. As the moments passed, more and more contacts appeared, spreading out around the *Delaror's* point to form a large cap which sat over the star precisely one AU out. The tension in the room was palpable. Senator Barao's face visibly paled.

"How many?" asked the Emperor quietly.

"Three million, nine hundred and eighty thousand, six hundred so far," said Aryn. "Still picking up new contacts."

Silence dominated the room; no one could bring themselves to speak.

The flood of contacts stopped abruptly.

"What happened?" asked Senator Barao.

"Captain Van E'streth reports their nav-com just folded," Rauk supplied. "The volume of data tripped it over, their tech is addressing it."

"Please invite the Captain," said the Emperor.

Fleet Admiral Benthar nodded slowly and carefully, masking his surprise. Such a thing was unheard of in Imperial meetings at this level.

Moments later Captain Van E'streth walked in from the hallway. It was a long standing courtesy that guests in any simulation would enter in a natural way – merely popping into existence right beside someone was considered extremely bad form. The hallway outside the virtual conference room was simply a conceit – an empty room allowing people to enter and leave the sim unobserved.

"Your Majesty," said the Captain, bowing slightly and then saluting. He was tall and slim, with closely cropped blonde hair and deep blue eyes, and carried himself with a self-assured air that was not over confident. He seemed quite at ease given his sudden call into an Imperial audience directly from the field.

"Please take a seat, Captain." The Emperor directed him to the table with a gesture. The Captain bowed graciously once more and sat down next to his superior – the Fleet Admiral.

"Fleet Admiral Benthar, I appreciate the normal formalities – after all this *was* merely an informal meeting. However I believe we are now in an operational scenario? So we may as well elevate our meeting into a theatre. Senator Barao, I presume upon you to represent the Senate's interests as an observer in what is clearly a naval operation."

Senator Barao nodded her acceptance.

"Dr. Reece, I require your presence as scientific advisor. Fleet Admiral Benthar?"

Admiral Benthar gestured to the captain, who now looked slightly uncomfortable at finding himself directly at the Emperors command without the buffer that naval hierarchy would normally have afforded him.

"We have yet to obtain a clear visual Your Majesty. Although we can determine the locations of these objects, we're having trouble using our primary sensors. Something seems to be interfering with our seeding of

Observers."

"I was always led to believe Observers are proofed against interference," the Emperor said, his tone clearly challenging.

"Proof against all *known* methods of interference, Your Majesty," Dr. Reece supplied smoothly.

"My Communications Officer is modifying the nav to allow a greater throughput of data, Your Majesty," Captain Van E'streth supplied. "It should be online again shortly."

Aryn leant forward. "These contacts are too regularly spaced to be naturally occurring, which means they are engineered. Engineering at this scale is scary to say the least, with the contacts showing sizes way above two hundred metres. This alone represents a clear threat until we can determine their nature. However..." He paused, triple checking his calculations. He really hoped he was wrong. He looked at his immediate superior and shared his findings. The Fleet Admiral looked grim, and then nodded to Aryn.

"We cannot presume the *Delaror* happened to emerge directly above the centre of this... swarm. Presuming that this is part of a sphere of such objects around S'vreth – which correlates with the loss of our Observable volume – there could be in excess of four hundred million objects around the star at this time."

Senator Barao's mouth hung open, and Dr. Reece raised his eyebrows in astonishment. The Emperor's face was a mask of calm.

"All usual – *customary* – infringements included, none of this is to leave this room or the *Delaror*," he said softly. "No aides, no confidantes, no trusted and loyal subjects of the Empire... no one. Is that perfectly clear?"

"Yes, Your Majesty," they all replied, more or less in unison. All except Aryn, who hesitated briefly.

"Your Majesty..."

"Yes, Admiral Cole?"

"I have assets *in* the field..."

Even the Fleet Admiral raised an eyebrow.

Sorry Fleet, Aryn sent privately. *Pokers in fires and all that – lots going on.*

"How so?" asked the Emperor.

"Internal operations, Your Majesty," Aryn supplied smoothly. There was no need for further explanation. Aryn's role as Admiral of Naval Intelligence set him aside from most of the typical Imperial Naval doctrine and duties, and was a long understood grace offered his position by the Imperial Office.

"Also, I would wish to confer on this with my personal aide. As you are aware, he has special... *interests.*"

The Emperor nodded. "But no more." He looked around the room to make his point. No one spoke.

The Emperor looked back to Aryn, clearly expecting him to continue, but being gracious enough not to ask directly. It would be unbecoming to put Aryn in a conflict of interest between loyalty to the Emperor's position, and his role as Admiral of INI which ultimately was a loyalty to the greater Empire itself. His operations were typically *all* off the books, and would most likely upset certain elements within the Empire itself, most especially Senator Barao.

Aryn returned the look stoically, without saying a word. Direct private access to the Emperor via l-net had not been granted within the sim, so a discrete conversation was not possible with the current occupants of the room.

"Very well," said the Emperor. "Captain – your thoughts at this time?"

The Van E'streth paused before answering. "Your Majesty, until we obtain more information we should hold position."

"Fleet?"

"That would be my order, Your Majesty."

"Senator Barao – please pass on my personal invitation to the Pax to attend an emergency council at twenty-hundred hours. You may leave us."

The senator stood, fully aware she had been dismissed, and made a brief formal curtsey to the Emperor before leaving the room gracefully.

After she left, the door swung silently shut – signifying that the virtual room was now locked to any further guests and even more secure than it had been before.

"Gentlemen, you have my full authority to discuss relevant details in full within this room. Everyone present is fully cleared and authorised to discuss matters of jeopardy to the Empire at large."

Both admirals looked questioningly at Dr. Reece. Whilst they were fully aware of his position within IRD, and his standing within the Imperial hierarchy was well known. They were both surprised to hear he would be a trusted member of an inner circle of operations such as this.

Seeing their mild surprise, Dr. Reece smiled thinly. "If it helps gentlemen, I aided in the design of the Valkyr class covert operations vessel which Admiral Cole is currently so fond of."

Aryn looked at his commander and gave a slight shrug. He made a mental note to have Dr. Reece thoroughly investigated; he didn't appreciate gaps in Intel's knowledgebase, particularly at this level. He was not one to like surprises. "I have one Valkyr currently inside the S'vreth volume, designated *Sneak Thief*, Captain Nelsen Rybek commanding."

"Have you been able to communicate with this Valkyr?" enquired the Emperor.

"The operation is black, Your Majesty, and of no immediate relevance to the situation in hand. If I deem this to change, I will of course disclose the details – or indeed at your request, Your Majesty. However, there is *one* relevant detail from the mission which I am obliged to divulge. Shortly before we lost our Observer network the Valkyr contacted one of my operatives on a direct channel."

Aryn was not happy about having to bring this up so soon. His technicians still hadn't had time to evaluate the problem Shousa had been given by the Valkyr. The significance, feasibility, and the connotations remained unexplored, but it did raise a massive question-mark over the entire naval network and data storage system. One he would personally prefer to know inside and out before divulging outside his office.

He briefed the Emperor and the group with just enough detail to provide an outline of the risk posed to the Empire.

Dr. Reece looked profoundly worried. "Would this be the same entity responsible for the situation at S'vreth?

121

Meaning – it wouldn't seem so to me. In the Valkyr situation, contact was made – seemingly benign. So far no contact has been made regarding S'vreth."

"Perhaps this was the contact?" Raul suggested. "It preceded the loss of the qNet within S'vreth only by mere moments."

"Hmm…" Dr. Reece sounded unconvinced, despite the coincidence.

"More alarming, is the overall risk to a long-established, highly-secure network of communication and data," stated the Emperor. "Even if the Valkyr – was it called *Sneak Thief?* – even if it was contacted by a benign being, we cannot afford to sit back and take no action. What are our options?"

"Your Majesty," replied Dr. Reece, "this is a profound problem, vast in scope and affecting the foundations of the Empire, and the Pax within it. We need time to consider before we can even propose options."

There is another profound *problem*, Aryn thought. *The Andreya Vorstan problem. But to bring it up now would be premature to say the least.*

"Then consider our options, gentlemen. You have the full authority of the Emperor to sequester whatever resources you need to examine this potential threat. I will see to it that you receive my seal confirming this after this meeting. As of now, you are all to consider yourselves the Imperial War Office."

They all looked at each other, unsure of what to say. There was a small undercurrent of tension in the room. It had been nearly a thousand years since the last War Office had been disbanded. The prospect of having to move to a war footing was not appealing.

"We won't let you, or the Empire down, Your Majesty," said Fleet Admiral Benthar.

"See to it. You have one hour to collect as much information as you can, then we will reconvene for a frank discussion on the risk this poses."

He stood, and did others. He nodded to them and then walked behind his chair and disappeared through a private door, leaving the simulation entirely. The door to the hallway opened a second later.

"An hour," murmured Dr. Reece.

"And you're wasting it, Doctor," said Admiral Benthar pointedly.

Dr. Reece gave a startled and almost apologetic look at the Admiral, then turned with a brief nod and left.

"Captain Van E'streth, continue to hold position, collect as much data as you can without jeopardising your status and inform us the instant your technicians complete their work on the nav systems."

He saluted. "Yes, sir." He too left, at a run.

The two admirals turned to face each other. The room faded to black around them, and then was replaced by a modestly decorated office with ancient Jandran wood panelling, Kritz leather armchairs and a large aquarium taking up one entire wall.

"Now tell me what I don't want to hear, and what you clearly don't want to tell me," said Raul.

Chapter Nine

Phol had no trouble securing the three floors they needed for his investigation. The floor Andreya had disappeared from, the one above, and the one below. A fabricated work order from the Caranthian Dispute Office alleging a claim of EM radiation abuse somewhere on this area soon cleared the area for his sole use.

His appearance had changed dramatically since his encounter with Andreya. His hair was now dark brown, and his face no longer aged or careworn – the wrinkles Andreya had seen had relaxed and faded away to reveal a smoother complexion. Yet still his face was 'forgettable', an excellent trait for a special agent in the field. His eyes still sparkled with energy, but they were now a much darker blue.

Getting their equipment in posed some difficulty, but the buildings large liftshafts helped – especially when they'd temporarily 'malfunctioned' – allowing them to bring two small g-pods down from the roof above.

His small team of three Special Ops Marines – all augmented and every square centimetre shielded and weaponised – scoured the floors above and below, then concentrated on this floor.

Between their equipment, and the sensors Phol had commanded, nothing could escape their scrutiny.

Still they found nothing.

Not one atom of Andreya's physical presence, not one single molecule or DNA fragment. Not a single flake of skin, hair, fingerprint, oil or acid residue where she had sat, or been. Anywhere. There was no sign at all she had ever existed in this volume of space.

Ignoring the confirmation that the original Andreya Vorstan was still in a brain-dead coma back on Taria, this alone gave him full confidence that she was, or at least was an agent of the so called Infiltrator.

Anyone – any-*thing* – even an android, left some physical evidence of their existence as they moved around. Forensic science was an art form that had led to an almost total absence of casual crime throughout the majority of Imperial worlds. Citizenship required DNA profiling and tagging for identification purposes. Non-citizenship was of course a free choice, but meant relinquishing your legal rights to live on an Imperial member world. A choice few made.

For an alleged humanoid to move around a room and leave no traces of its presence was utterly impossible. Nothing on record had ever evaded a full forensic sweep. The only conclusion there could be was that they were clearly faced with something new and unknown.

As to how she had 'escaped', that too remained a mystery. There were no signs of exit, no recordings of her leaving anywhere inside, or outside of the building, and no sign of her back at her hotel. Whilst normal security cameras could be spoofed or blocked, Observers could not – they only relayed 'reality' directly – with no local interpretation or manipulation of the view they had of the world. Hundreds of sweeps of the local Observer network cache had been made by a team of Intellects. Not one had captured a sighting of Andreya since she had entered the building with him.

This left two possibilities. She was still in the

building, hidden somewhere.

Or, she was no longer on Caranthia.

Despite disbelieving the latter, he was beginning to suspect it might be true.

No technology we know of could cloak something from a full sweep, he insisted to Op.

No technology we know of can engineer an organic copy of someone to such a perfect degree that they do not even leave behind evidence of their existence, Op countered.

There is no single physical location on these floors that we have not forensically examined which is large enough to contain a humanoid of even Andreya's size.

If perfectly cloaked, she may have been able to move around whilst you conducted your search.

Phol supressed a smile. *You suggest our search was flawed?* he asked, good humouredly.

I suggest it is more likely to have overlooked a sophisticated attempt to evade detection than it is for someone to have simply vanished off the face of the planet. May I remind you that teleportation is a myth?

Phol couldn't help but shake his head stubbornly – despite the conversation only existing in his head. *You just marvelled at the tech required to engineer her and yet mock teleportation? She is not here. Ask the team consensus. See how flawed they think the search was.*

I already have, Rogers, Gomez and Karas concur with you – she is not there.

So what do you wish us to do? Search the entire building?

There was a pause. *The thought had occurred, yes. But – it would tie up valuable resources and generate noise with the local authorities which I have no interest in quietening down. We'll lace the entire block with sensors and Observers, and monitor it remotely. For now, pack up and return to the*

126

temporary base here. We have new orders.

Phol raised an eyebrow. *A change in mission profile?*

Yes. Admiral Cole wants us to monitor the escalating Velari Migration to the Canthe System. Hurry up, we leave within the hour.

***

"It's ready," said the *Sneak*. "It's warming up its drive system."

Nelsen and Andreya sat up and accessed the *Sneak's* visual feeds; Nelsen had been monitoring the contacts around the system even while he dozed. They'd now fully dispersed to form a perfect geodesic sphere arrangement around the sun. The formation itself was nagging at him for some reason.

"Any clues as to their technology?" he asked.

"None of note. I've observed the assembly of several of the larger vessels. The drive and power systems are assembled within the superstructure – typically as sealed units brought up from within the factory walls, and then the hull is built around it hiding any further detail. Some of them are highly weaponised, but not all. A large percentage – perhaps thirty or so – seem to be transports of various kinds."

"So largely offensive, but logistical as well."

"Correct."

"This is the first to flight?"

"No, Captain. This is the first sizeable vessel larger than myself suitable for masking our presence. Two hundred and eighty vessels of varying sizes have been launched since construction began."

Andreya and Nelsen exchanged a look. They each knew what this meant. An unstoppable, constantly replenishing, superior force.

"Let's see what's next then," said Nelsen.

They watched the large freighter – reduced to toy-like proportion by the factory around it. The new vessel gracefully rose up into the air, and then glided away toward the tower. Chaos reigned as the constructor ships flowed around it – but they all kept their distance from each other, without error or collision.

"Like a flock of birds," observed Andreya.

It took about fifteen minutes for the ship to reach base of the tower. As it neared the gap between two of the huge rails which ran up the sides of the huge building, it changed orientation to point upward along the towers outer surface. It settled in between the rails, and then started moving directly up along them.

"A planetary lift!" exclaimed the *Sneak*.

Nelsen nodded. "They're launching them into space from the ground. That's interesting. It means these vessels can't have enough lifting power themselves to combat Velari Primes gravity."

"Or, their drive systems cannot function within a gravity well," the *Sneak* suggested.

"Or that," conceded Nelsen.

They watched the progress of the freighter until it reached the edge of the drastically reduced atmosphere, then its progress increased rapidly and it shot away from the towers tip out into space.

Nelsen smiled grimly. "The first ever ship firing rail gun?"

"It *is* remarkable engineering," said the *Sneak*. "It's like they have no restraints, or rather they just see a problem and simply engineer a solution to it, regardless of the cost."

"Don't fall in love *Sneak*. They did just see the problem of acquiring resources and solved it by levelling an entire planet – committing multiple species genocide in the process."

"I'm painfully aware of that Captain," replied the *Sneak* stiffly – but carefully. Anything on that subject had to be considered 'volatile' around the captain.

"Have we seen any sign of 'them' yet?"

"Nothing so far," *Sneak* said.

Nelsen pursed his lips thoughtfully.

They watched the freighter as it picked up speed – clearly under its own power now – and headed out toward the 'Cloud' as the *Sneak* called it.

"I'd like another reference launch – just to be as sure as we can be," said the *Sneak*.

Nelsen nodded his assent. "How long?"

"Twelve minutes."

The next launch matched the first precisely.

"Ok," said the *Sneak*. "Ready."

Nelsen looked to Andreya. She nodded back, eyes bright. *Adrenaline junkie,* thought Nelsen.

"Let's go."

***

Praetor Castallus strode down one of the many marble halls of the Imperial Palace toward the Emperors private audience chambers with an air of grim determination. He'd just heard of the *Drastic Response's*

129

'drastic response' to the collapsed Velari migration dialogue. He was fuming.

He rubbed one of his claws against the chitin of his forehead between his multi-faceted eyes, antennae flicking irritably in the air above him. It wasn't the fact of the negotiations failing, nor the potential for war which might come about which irked him so – but the loss of a fine ship of the line.

The *Drastic Response* was one of the most valued vessels available to Outreach – having been in active service for thirteen hundred and eighty of its fourteen hundred years. No other vessel contained the wealth of experience, knowledge or capability available to the *Response*. It was a symbol for Outreach as a diplomatic office, and one of those rare things these days – irreplaceable.

Antennae still waving agitatedly, he reached the antechamber doors and rapped firmly on them the customary three times, and then waited. Invisibly – countless security protocols swept him over, talking with his implants, measuring his mass, infra-red profile, EM emissions, brain wave patterns – just as they had been during his entire walk down the hall – but now with a more demanding intent. One did *not* sneak up on the Emperor of the Sulranian Empire.

"Come in," said a voice quietly from beyond the door.

The doors opened, and Castallus strode through, letting them close softly, but firmly, behind him.

The antechamber was bright, with several floor-to-ceiling windows revealing the palace arboretum outside. Its decor was ostentatious, and somewhat gaudy – favouring gold and red far too much. Castallus knew the

Emperor privately loathed the extravagance.

The Emperor himself was seated behind a sizeable jet black slab which served as a desk. Above it several images floated – mostly holograms of worlds. Castallus fancied he could make out the globe of Canthen just next to the Emperor. He stood up straight before the desk, and folded two of his four upper arms across his thorax in a gesture of respect.

The Emperor of the Sulranian Empire looked up at Castallus, his dark brown eyes warm – but stoic. His face betrayed the same emotion. He regarded Castallus as a trusted confidante and advisor, and knew Castallus was about to launch into one of his famous tirades. He sighed under his breath, waved for Castallus to speak and sat back – regarding Castallus at length.

Castallus went on for some time, eloquently expounding on the respect he held for the Emperors wisdom, the import of these times, then subtly pointing out the value of the *Drastic Response* – the tragedy its loss would cause Outreach as a loyal and vital aspect of the Empires diplomatic arm. He was just about to expand on this further when the Emperor raised a hand, bringing Castallus to an immediate halt mid-sentence.

"You know I know this," he said in his quiet voice. "I know you know I know, so on and so forth. I think it's time we dispense with the pleasantries and formalities Praetor Castallus. You hereby have my grace to speak candidly in my presence – in private – at all times." He stared at Castallus, gauging his reaction to such a rare boon.

Despite an Empire of trillions, an Imperial Office whose number seemed infinite, and a staff of over three thousand in just this palace alone – only a handful of loyal subjects had ever been given such an honour by any ruling Emperor. Castallus hid his surprise – and subsequent up-swell of pride – remarkably well.

"Your Majesty is too kind," he managed smoothly. His antennae briefly dipped back along his head in a gesture of profound obeisance as he tilted forward in a complex bow of folding limbs.

Emperor Sulran smiled privately, but sadly. There was nothing Castallus would not do for the Empire now. He hated the position he found himself in, and of having to put others into. The time would soon come when he would be forced to call upon his most loyal subjects to do things which they would never ordinarily do, perhaps even in extra-ordinary circumstances. But, they would do them without question if they believed they were in the best interests of the Empire. The Emperor knew only too well how to manipulate such loyalty. It was a skill which he didn't particularly relish or savour, but one which was essential to maintaining power and control. Stability and peace always came with a price attached, it seemed.

He looked at Castallus and sighed aloud. "You may rise, Castallus. Did you not understand a single word of what I just said?"

Castallus looked up, and smiled. His two mouth feelers rubbed together appreciatively. "Of course, Your Imperial Majesty."

He stood up straight then, almost two meters of Aracta looming above the desk, his four upper arms still wrapped around his thorax and standing on his lower two legs. Aracta were quite happy assuming a humanoid upright posture, although in their own habitat they preferred their natural six-legged gait – along with flying. Aracta in flight was something no general member of the Imperial public had ever witnessed. They had chosen to forbid themselves from doing so out of a polite desire to avoid any feeling of superiority over those humanoids who could not fly – a tradition started millennia ago after their first contact, and maintained ever since.

"Then do not begin your new found grace by raising my ire, Praetor." The words were hard, but the Emperor wore a small smile as he spoke.

Castallus bowed again, but briefly this time.

The Emperor rose from his seat, and crossed to one of the huge windows out onto the palace gardens. "I am well aware the loss of the *Drastic Response* is a blow to Outreach, Castallus – as a *symbol*. But there was – *is* – no choice in the matter. It is a necessary evil, as they say. I am just glad that everyone survived. The *Drastic Response* herself uploaded perfectly safely and is even now busy designing her replacement vessel and identity."

"Your Majesty…" Castallus sounded a little wary – not quite sure how far 'candid' would safely take him.

"Freely Castallus, speak freely. If what you say truly does offend one's Imperial ego or position, I'll be sure to let you know well in advance."

Unsure what that meant *precisely*, Castallus chose to take the Emperor at his word and hope. "No one in Outreach can understand the reasoning or implication, Your Majesty. We are at a loss as to why one of the apex vessels under our command has been... *sacrificed...* for such a cause as the Velari."

Still gazing out through the windows, the Emperor nodded sympathetically. "We were buying time, to perhaps avert a war, Castallus," he said quietly. "However, I am afraid that this matter will have to wait for the time being. I have to request a complete and total oath of secrecy for what I am about to tell you. No one – and I stress *no one* is to be made aware of what you are about to hear – under any circumstances. Do you so swear?"

Castallus regarded his Emperor for a few moments. He was unsure what he was about to become embroiled within, but knew if the Emperor was of a mind to confide in him then he must be worthy of such trust. Plus of course, that tiny voice of curiosity which chittered away, compelling him to commit to such an oath just *because*. There was no other possible choice.

"I swear, upon all of Aracta, the souls of my children, my soul and my own mortal vessel, to uphold the faith and trust you place upon me this day Emperor Sulran."

The Emperor's shoulders seemed to slump a little, or relax – Castallus couldn't be certain.

"We have to prepare Castallus." He turned to regard him with haunted eyes.

"Death is coming."

Chapter Ten

The *Sneak* chose its angle of descent very carefully. It was striving to appear as a naturally behaving chunk of debris dropping back to the surface under gravity only. Such behaviour was extra-ordinarily difficult for a modern day vessel. Hundreds of safety systems had to be overridden or disabled – as the only true way to appear to be falling back to the surface out of control was to do just that. Any attempt to replicate such a re-entry under power could easily be spotted.

It aligned itself on a trajectory that would bring it in to impact near the base of the tower, just before their chosen freighter arrived at the lifting zone. Then it issued a small nudge along that vector with its reaction thrusters and finally gave itself a slight spin of varying amounts across all three axes of movement.

The *Sneak* tumbled into the atmosphere, quite literally, and deliberately, out of control.

Seconds later, atmospheric friction built up around its shield, and the very air itself began to ignite in staccato bursts – eventually merging into a fireball. The *Sneak* was quite happy with the overall effect; it had taken a fair amount of tuning to get the usually frictionless shield surfaces rough enough to superheat the atmosphere as it rushed past – without leaking any tell-tale energy.

Inside, Andreya and Nelsen felt nothing of this as the *Sneak* rolled at random down through the atmosphere at Mach 3. Their view of outside was captured by a series of snapshots taken along their flight path whenever the

Sneak's orientation brought a sensor in line.

"What if they have a defence grid for falling debris?" asked Andreya. "There is a *lot* after all."

The *Sneak* was just one ball of falling fire amidst thousands currently visible in the sky.

"No signs of any interest," said the *Sneak*. "They just let them detonate, or impact against the factory surface shielding. They really do seem to care less."

Nelsen shook his head, making some private comment to himself.

"What?" Andreya decided to draw it out of him.

"If these guys are bad – not just blindly unsympathetic – we are in deep, deep trouble."

He waved at the scene before them.

"They don't have to care about damage, or losses, or anything in their way. They just stamp on it, or brush it off as if it doesn't matter. This thing withstood a blast which destroyed a planet – *caused* that blast – and not only withstood it, but immediately went into full production without pause and with no care for the consequences of its crash-landing." He gestured at the rain of fireballs and debris still falling all around them. "It's what it does."

He rubbed his face, and then his eyes.

"How could the Empire take even *one* of these down if it had to? And if it can't, how do we stop it building its fleet, or laying waste to every planet in the Empire?"

"I'm sure someone would come up with something Nelsen, if we had to. We didn't get where we are today by happenstance and luck. Well, not entirely. We've fought plenty of wars before and come through." Andreya wasn't entirely sure she knew this for a fact –

she couldn't recall hearing of any wars, but it *felt* true. She couldn't put any more precise a description on the feeling than that. It was as if she were able to tap into knowledge without actually knowing it was there.

Nelsen pointed at the factory which grew ever nearer by the second. "Against something like *that?*"

"In my reckoning," said the *Sneak* quietly, "the Empires entire armed service is already insufficient to counter a threat from these beings. A war of attrition is all we could hope for, with our side losing.

"By numbers alone – if this comes to war – they have already won."

Nelsen shook his head, unable to come to terms with the fact that within a day, he had gone from a highly privileged agent in the service of an apex civilisation, to someone staring at the possible end of everything the Empire stood for, and everything he had ever fought to achieve in its name.

"Should we try contacting them?" asked Andreya.

Nelsen shook his head again. "That's a job for Outreach. I'm not being the one responsible for making the wrong move and causing these guys to get upset. My mandate is intelligence gathering. So we get out of here without detection if possible and report in. If we get spotted, then we try contacting them."

"We're approaching the rendezvous," said the *Sneak*.

The fireball around the *Sneak* had faded away to reveal just another dark tumbling mass dense enough to withstand re-entry and impact on the surface. It sped downward on a dramatically shortening arc, precisely aimed to land against the base of the tower beside a lifting rail. Sliding along the factory platform itself came their chosen freighter – almost one hundred times larger than the *Sneak Thief*.

"This should only take a moment," the *Sneak* said calmly.

The freighter engaged with the lift, and began sliding upward. The *Sneak* sped downward – still in free fall – directly into the space below the freighter. Then at the last possible second before its shield interacted with the one around the factory, it spilled all of its momentum through its g-drive and generated a substantially large explosion outside its hull by detonating a plasma shell. The view outside lit up in vivid white.

When the blast of superheated air cleared, the *Sneak* was just another inconspicuous additional bulge on the rear portion of the freighter.

They waited tensely for a few minutes – but other than an alignment change made by the freighter as it corrected its new mass distribution in the rail lifting fields – nothing happened.

"Did we actually get away with it?" asked Andreya quietly.

"Seems so," replied Nelsen. "*Sneak*?"

"No reaction as yet. Though if they do the math they'll notice no appreciable mass was lost in that explosion..."

"Keep watching."

"Affirmative," replied *Sneak* emphatically.

The tower was hexagonal, like the rest of the factory construction. Multiple pairs of lifting rails ran along each side and ascended into space high above. Something was bugging Nelsen about this type of construction, but he just couldn't put his finger on it.

"Clearly hexagons and trigonometric shapes are important to their culture, or technology, or both," he observed.

"They are important naturally occurring structures," noted the *Sneak*. "Many cell structures are based on them, wide-spread use of atomic carbon in geodesic structures are used in artificial constructions. Even DNA itself."

"Doesn't the Navy build their stations using a hexagonal pattern?" asked Andreya. "The big hive stations?"

"That's *it!*" exclaimed Nelsen. "I *knew* something was familiar!"

"So we have something in common?" asked the *Sneak*.

Nelsen shrugged. "Maybe. Can you get any readings?"

"I dare not try Captain – this close any energy changes we make might get noticed. Right now we're totally black from the outside, and I'd prefer to keep it that way."

"Understood."

They watched for a time as their ascent continued. The factory receded below them, sprawling for tens of kilometres in all directions – easily slipping over the modest curvature of S'ren. The smoke-saturated air began to thin, leading to a dirty gloom which tricked the eye and made details hard to determine.

Then a construction machine appeared above them. Its gangling mass of articulated limbs and probes waving animatedly as it dropped down toward the freighter.

"What's that doing up here?" Nelsen asked in

consternation.

"Heading for us," replied the *Sneak*, a note of concern in its voice.

The constructor dropped down to the freighter in seconds and moved out around it to approach the *Sneak*.

"Captain?" asked the *Sneak* in a worried tone of voice.

"Steady, but ready – yes?"

"Yes sir."

The tension was palpable – neither Nelsen nor Andreya dared move. They watched the crazy assemblage almost swim through the air around the *Sneak*, and then it reached down with several snake like articulated limbs and delicately touched the *Sneak's* hull. The probing manipulators on the ends of each skittered over the atomically smooth surface, unable to find purchase.

Andreya found she was holding her breath. *Any second now they would be torn from the freighter and surrounded by a cloud of enemy ships...*

The constructor hovered motionless for a moment, then whipped its limbs back and retreated about fifty metres, hovering again.

"I'm being hit by *sonar*..." marvelled the *Sneak*, amazed at the use of such low-tech.

"Sonar? Offensively?" demanded Nelsen.

"No, passive levels... I *think* its mapping me..."

The constructor then dropped like a stone straight downward.

They waited in strained silence for a few more minutes, but nothing else happened.

"Do you think they suspect anything?" asked

Andreya. "Surely they must."

"I don't think so," said the *Sneak*. "They would have halted or redirected the freighter, or the constructor would have attacked or tried to pry us off."

"Unless it's gone for reinforcements," said Nelsen darkly.

"I would think it safe to assume it would have remained to observe us and summon help instead."

Again they waited, but nothing came for them. The air turned black and star-studded as they left the tenuous atmosphere.

"I think it was just checking for damage after our blast, assessing us as a maintenance issue," said the *Sneak*.

Nelsen blew out his cheeks in relief. "Well let's hope they don't send out a repair team."

"Ok, here we go..." said the *Sneak*.

The freighter accelerated sharply, and shot out into space; the *Sneak* welded to the aft hull so tightly it was almost an integral part of the ship.

***

Captain Van E'streth studied the initial flood of data from the recalibrated nav system, and blanched. Contacts were pouring in by the tens of thousands each second.

"These are passive sensors yes?"

"Yes, Captain."

"I don't want to prick their ears," he murmured. "Relay the stream back to INCC on the qNet. Let's see what they make of it."

"Aye, sir."

If these are hostile, he thought, unable to finish the sentence even in the privacy of his own mind.

The count so far was just over forty-million contacts, equidistantly spaced below their current position in what was evidently a spherical arrangement around S'vreth, measuring exactly one AU in radius and enclosing the planetary orbit of S'ren.

The scale and numbers involved were beyond frightening. None of the so called 'Higher' races could possibly have pulled off something like this. The resources and manufacturing involved could never have been kept so secret within the Empire, or for some considerable distance out into the known Border Systems.

Scans and visuals showed these objects to be completely new to the Imperial Naval Vessel Registration database. Some seemed haphazard, like they'd been hurriedly assembled from spares. The larger vessels were a mix of logistics and weaponised craft. There seemed to be no clear pattern to their distribution aside from the geodesic spherical arrangement.

"Captain, we've found what may be a Capital class or CnC vessel."

He opened the view which popped into his e-vision. It was a beast of a ship. As large as any known Imperial vessel, it was wedge-shaped, with a long curving hull from fore to aft, and clearly housing major offensive weaponry in the forward section which served as a protective cowl over the equipment within. A relatively small control tower protruded from the mid-rear section.

"It's not quite as randomly constructed as the others,"

he noted. "This appears to have been thought out and designed rather than rigged up."

"Another, sir – you should take a look."

He brought this one up alongside to compare. They were wildly different, this being a long cylindrical shape with large drive clusters at one end and bristling with various masts and antennae at the other. He frowned. Such inconsistency was unusual for a space faring race, unless this one was an ancient example of their technology.

"Pass everything on to INCC in real-time," he instructed his XO.

"Aye, sir."

"Romurik?" he asked over the ships l-net.

"Sir?"

"My cabin please, in five minutes."

"Sir."

The small ovoid form of Romurik glided into the captain's cabin, instructed the door to close behind him and waited.

"You are fully field equipped, yes?" asked Captain Van E'streth.

"Yes, Captain."

"For deep space?"

"Yes, sir."

Van E'streth nodded to himself. "Then I may have a job for you Romurik. You are free to refuse; this will not be under orders."

"I'm at your command Captain."

"We need better intel on these vessels, particularly these larger ships." He sent Romurik the locations and visuals of the ships his XO had pointed out. "Can you give me your propulsion specs please?"

Romurik complied whilst checking over the relative locations of the vessels.

"Hmm," mused Van after reviewing Romurik's specifications. "You can stealth, but we aren't entirely sure if they can see past our tech."

"We have no reason to suspect they can," Romurik supplied.

"I'd rather err on the side of caution," replied Van.

"I can easily make a pass by each vessel – looping through the cloud and back out."

"The volume inside the cloud is to be considered highly hostile given the loss of the Observer network. We have no way of determining the status inside, other than the normal EM spectrographic - which shows nothing unusual. Any wormholes we've tried to establish start failing within a tenth of an AU from the perimeter.

"We're fabricating a telescope to get a better look and obtain visuals on S'ren to see if anything is happening on the surface. I can't believe we have to resort to such a thing, but there you go."

"I believe I can suggest a low risk option for a surveillance sweep," said Romurik after a few moments.

"Go on?"

"The *Delaror* still has a mass driver, correct?"

"It's slated for decommissioning next refit, but yes."

"Will I fit in it?"

***

The freighter had been under its own power and drive for several minutes, and was now halfway to the perimeter of the sphere that had formed around S'vreth.

So far the *Sneak* had been able to determine very little about their drive technology, other than it wasn't reaction based, didn't produce a g-field, and required an enormous but concentrated spike of energy.

"Sorry, Captain, but without my primary sensors, all of my remaining sensor arrays could be easily detected – especially at such close proximity."

Nelsen fumed quietly. They were deep inside 'enemy' territory, un-noticed and with the perfect opportunity to capture valuable intel – yet they daren't do anything for fear of detection and the possibility their unexplainable and sudden appearance might escalate into a war.

"We're slowing..." said the *Sneak*.

Nelsen dragged himself out of his private ire with a start. "What?"

"The freighter has decelerated – midway to the perimeter. Several of the vessels behind us are now slowing to match us."

"Have we been spotted?" asked Andreya

"I don't think so," said the *Sneak*. "Although they seem to be building a spherical formation about our position."

Nelsen studied the nav holo intensely, looking for any hint that they were being corralled as the other vessels built a geodesic sphere around them. "It's a staging area," he said after a few minutes. "They're preparing for something."

"Should I disengage, Captain?"

Nelsen shook his head. "Aside from risking

observation – we'll still be deep inside the cordon they've established with no way of breaking it unobserved."

"But half-way home," said the *Sneak* optimistically.

"Let's see what they are up to first, and then decide."

They watched as the last ships arrived from what appeared to be a single discrete wave launched in their direction.

"There's a vibration coming from the freighter, Captain." The *Sneak* sounded a little puzzled. "And the energy spike is ramping up dramatically."

Nelsen looked worriedly at Andreya. "Well, I doubt it's a bad thing... right?"

"Captain? I need to use *some* sensors at least!"

He nodded.

The *Sneak* brought its least obtrusive sensor arrays online and scanned as far and wide as it dared.

"There's an energy field forming around the freighter, extending out to the other ships." A holo appeared showing the formation, and tendrils of energy leaping out to ground on the nearby vessels. "They are also returning energy back to the freighter, like an exchange of some kind." Then the *Sneak's* voice took on an edge of concern. "I think this may be some kind of drive sys –"

The blinding flash of a huge release of nuclear energy engulfed the entire group. It lasted no more than a quarter of a second. When it passed the surrounding ships, the freighter, and the *Sneak* were gone.

***

The last vessel left the factory tower and sped out

into the glowing orange nebula, to rendezvous with its brethren and move out toward the next system.

Then a new phase of construction began, as countless constructors sped about in a frenzy of activity – depositing resources or building with those available nearby. No specific role was assigned to any of the craft, they simply took up a function if they were the nearest to fulfil it. It was self-organising chaos on a majestic scale.

Gradually, over the course of many hours, a single, large skeletal structure began to grow upward from the surface of the construction platforms.

It duplicated the very shape of the factory itself.

Chapter Eleven

"Well?" asked Nelsen.

The *Sneak* sounded nonplussed. "We're just outside of the S'vreth asteroid belt..."

After the blinding flare of energy had gone, they had found themselves still attached to the freighter in the same formation, but on the other side of the system. They had moved almost two Astronomical Units in less than a second, without a wormhole being used. The *Sneak* was impressed.

"The freighter is changing course for the belt itself. The rest of the formation is following suit."

There was a pause. "Captain! The qNet is back online."

"Don't use it!"

Nelsen thought furiously for a moment. To stay piggybacked onto the 'enemy' and learn all they could? Or report in?

"*Sneak*, detach at the earliest and safest opportunity, stay dark – no sign of power or control."

"Yes, Captain."

A minute passed in silence. Andreya made to say something, but Nelsen put a finger to his lips for quiet. Even the advanced hull of the Valkyr would not be impervious to a laser audio pickup.

The view of outside began to spin slowly, and after a few tumbles the freighter could be seen pulling away along with the rest of their escort.

"Let's give them a few hundred k's," said Nelsen. Then he switched to conversing privately with the *Sneak*.

Can you raise wormholes?

Checking... affirmative. At least, I can open one millimetre links. Observers are available again.

Good. Make ready to tunnel to INHS Capella*, shortest possible route.*

Yes, Captain. Ready when you are.

They watched the formation recede into the distance, quickly losing visual as they merged into the asteroid field ahead.

"Go."

The black mass that was the *Sneak* dropped through a white-violet gap in space-time, leaving behind a rapidly shrinking sphere of energy. Within a second, it was no longer in the S'vreth System.

Ahead, one of the vessels slowed and reoriented itself back toward where the *Sneak* had just been. After heavily scanning the volume, it returned to its original course and caught up with the others.

The view outside spun and flickered madly as the *Sneak* repeatedly emerged into real space, aligned itself, and then jumped again with barely a pause, all too fast for the eye to make sense of the changes.

Occasionally the gaps between jumps lasted longer as the *Sneak* waited for power levels to stabilise, or for its heat sinks to shed any energy its internal exchanger couldn't handle.

This is faster than our journey out, Nelsen observed to the *Sneak*. He was amazed at the sheer speed the *Sneak* was able to achieve.

We're leaving an energy trail behind even a dead Curuvan could follow, but I thought it best to get along. I've thrown in a couple of mis-jumps should we be followed. The second one was a mis-jump which stamped over the energy pulse of our first tunnel exit.

Nelsen smiled. *Nice*, he said.

Thank you. Not impossible to fathom, but the triple energy signatures should pose a problem to anyone following.

"ETA with *Capella* in eight minutes, Captain," the *Sneak* said out loud.

"Contact INCC and upload the relevant aspects of the mission." *I'll contact INI*, Nelsen added.

"Yes, Captain."

Nelsen turned to Andreya. "Sorry, but duty calls..."

She waved a hand, unperturbed.

He closed his eyes, and opened a private channel to Admiral Aryn Cole over the qNet.

Captain Rybek? Aryn's voice was calm, but gave away his surprise.

Admiral, we are in serious deep shit.

Admiral Cole sent an invitation to join a secure shared sim across the qNet. A room formed around him, a sophisticated office with a vista window out into the galactic core. Aryn was sitting at the desk before the window; Nelsen was standing in front of the desk facing both.

"Is this something new?" Aryn replied glibly, one eyebrow raised, forgiving any impropriety. "Go on."

Nelsen fast-linked an entire replay of the mission from the point they had arrived over Velari Prime, right up until their departure from what had been Velari space.

Aryn stood up and the room faded to black around them.

Fleet Admiral Benthar? I need to speak with you urgently.

Raul faded into view from the blackness a few seconds later, and gave Nelsen a curious look.

"Introductions later Fleet…" said Aryn. "Watch."

Raul replayed the data Nelsen had given Aryn, and visibly blanched.

"We have to inform the Emperor at once," he said after a moment.

"Where are you now?" Aryn asked Nelsen.

"Hard to tell – the *Sneak* is making a best speed dash for *Capella*. I can barely keep track of the systems we're crossing – we're moving that fast."

Raul raised an eyebrow.

"Later Fleet," said Aryn to delay any explanation of the Valkyr's capabilities. "Nelsen, continue to INHS *Capella*. Have Commander Nylan do a full diagnostic of the *Sneak* on arrival, and await further orders."

"Understood."

"Your field assessment?"

Nelsen drew a breath. "So far no hostile activity, or indication that we had been detected. I only terminated the sortie to provide this information first-hand. We could resume surveillance, or the original mission profile."

"Even though the archives have been lost?" Aryn asked, mildly surprised.

Nelsen shrugged. "As far as I know, nothing gained, nothing lost."

"You have a passenger on board."

Nelsen hesitated. "We can drop her off at *Capella*, Admiral."

"No, keep her with you for the time being." Aryn

looked to Raul, then back at Nelsen.

"Await orders at *Capella*. Dismissed."

Nelsen saluted both admirals and dropped out of the sim.

Raul stared at Aryn, waiting for him to speak. However Aryn returned his gaze with an innocent expression, unwilling to volunteer anything unless he had to.

"So that was Nelsen, and somehow – miraculously – he has this Andreya Vorstan clone? Despite his theatre being some six hundred light years from Caranthia?"

Aryn shook his head. "I have no explanation Raul, other than she is certainly beyond our technology. If we attempt to detain her, I've no doubt she could slip away just as easily again, or that things could get ugly."

"So what do you intend?"

"She seems to be happy enough in the company of INI operatives – for a while at least. That suits us perfectly. All we can do is watch and learn. It's all we can do for now after all."

"As she watches *us* and learns," Raul commented darkly.

"Raul, I have no doubt that she or her creator already knows everything about us, the Empire and *everything* we know." Aryn looked at his commanding officer directly. "I think she's after something we *don't* know."

Nelsen opened his eyes and frowned. *Why keep Andreya on the Sneak?* he wondered. Her company was nice enough he supposed, but there was no place on a covert ops vessel for passengers or civilians unless they were refugees or prisoners. His scowl deepened.

"INHS *Capella* in three minutes, Captain."

"Thanks."

"Well?" asked Andreya, one eyebrow raised quizzically. She had an attitude about her, a kind of demanding but silent challenge. He hadn't come across anyone quite like her since Meelereen.

"What were you doing on S'ren?"

She frowned. "Where?"

"Formerly Velari Prime... now a scorched ball of rubble."

Andreya blinked and suddenly remembered the qNet was back. She did some quick searches. She had listened in – quite unwittingly – to his conversation with Aryn Cole, and so far she had heard every unspoken word between Nelsen and the *Sneak* over the apparently heavily encrypted l-net since coming aboard. Again, she felt that best kept to herself, for now.

"Looking for something lost, I think."

"Did you find it?"

Andreya felt she could answer honestly. "Not yet."

"Hmm," Nelsen pulled a face. "How did you get there, and when?"

She raised her eyebrows. "Is this some kind of interrogation, Captain?"

He barely paused. "Some kind, yes."

Nothing unusual so far, said the *Sneak*, who was monitoring Andreya with full biometric and physiological scans. *She's either a master adept at lying, or...*

Telling the truth, finished Nelsen.

"I honestly don't know," she said.

"Did you live there?"

"No."

"What ship did you arrive on?"

"I didn't."

Nelsen looked irritated. "Look -"

"I'm sorry, Nelsen. I know it sounds beyond belief, but I just... appeared there. I have no idea how."

"When?"

"Not long before you found me."

"Be specific. The local net was up in that room, so you must have accessed it, and therefore the time."

She looked at him, wanting to just tell him the ridiculous truth. But she knew she should hold back for the moment.

"About an hour, by IST."

That means she had been hidden for roughly forty-eight minutes until she became visible to my sensors, Captain.

"What were you doing?"

"Reading."

"Really?"

"Really."

"Reading what, exactly?"

She sighed, and rattled off the names of some of the books she had come across, sprinkling "The Concord of Surrr" in at random to see if he reacted. He didn't.

None of these are logged with IN Archives or Outreach, said the *Sneak. No flags against them anywhere.*

"Velari books aren't really leisure reading Andreya. What were you trying to find?"

She stared at him, considering her options. She didn't really know herself. Should she tell him what she'd found even though she had no idea why she had been looking? *What harm would it do?* she thought. She took a gambit – something had stopped her talking to Arnem Trisek and taken over that once...

"The *Terrania*," she said, semi-surprised the words had actually left her lips.

She memorised the dumbfounded look on his face... it was priceless. Though he recovered remarkably well, she noted.

"What *did* you find?" he managed.

She was now trusting that her unknown guide would intervene if necessary. "It's last known observed location. I think."

Nelsen's eyebrow twitched. "You think?"

"The Velari aren't exactly precise with their navigational logs. They kind of generalise things. Plus this was several thousand years ago."

Nelsen nodded. *Admiral?* he sent privately. *Are you available for a real-time relay? You* have *to hear this.*

Given the circumstances, yes, replied Admiral Cole.

Nelsen linked the chat across and then let the Admiral jack into a sense-vise relay, letting Aryn see and hear exactly as Nelsen did.

"I won't give out the details – not yet," she said with a small smile. "There seem to be too many prying eyes."

"But you will?" asked Nelsen.

"Yes. I have no idea why... but I think I have to find it." Her smile widened. "With your help."

Nelsen drummed his fingers on the arm of couch.

Where is she from? asked Aryn.

"Where are you from?" Nelsen repeated aloud.

Andreya stared thoughtfully at him for a moment. She wasn't sure if she should let them know she could hear and see everything – even things they believed were entirely private and secure – including the fact this Admiral Cole was now watching her through Nelsen's own eyes. However, this Aryn clearly knew something about her was not 'typical' for an Imperial citizen, especially one from Taria. It was possible that she might learn more about herself by being as open and honest as she could be, or as open as her guiding instinct would allow.

"Taria, as far as I know anyway."

Why would you not know? asked Aryn.

"I have no idea. That's part of the problem."

Both Aryn and Nelsen were silent for a moment.

"How did you know what I was just about to ask?" Nelsen managed, voice strained.

"Again, I don't know – I just do. I can hear and see everything it seems."

Are you the Infiltrator? Aryn asked directly.

"If you mean this mysterious ghost you've been chasing for the past three years, no – I am not the Infiltrator."

Are you working for the Infiltrator, or with them, or affiliated with them in any way?

"I don't know... But if I am, I don't believe it to be a necessarily bad thing at this time."

Why do you say that?

She frowned. "Nothing I feel I need to do as yet has been negative or harmful. In fact, quite the opposite. I feel... good... about the fact that I don't truly know who I am. If that makes any sense."

"You've heard everything the *Sneak* and I have said?" asked Nelsen.

She nodded.

156

Impossible! demanded the *Sneak* privately to Nelsen. *Single channel bonded qSpinners* cannot *be tapped.*

Obviously they can, said Andreya on their private channel.

The strained silence this time was almost tangible.

Even I heard that, commented Aryn. *And that is impossible.*

"Don't ask me, because I don't know," said Andreya, shrugging. "I can just listen in."

"QSpin comm's can't be spliced – you need a *physical* relay. But how could you relay a one-to-one pair without modifying at least one end..?."

And how could you then conference in someone on yet another private channel? asked Aryn.

Aryn stared at Andreya as Nelsen stared at her. *You and I need a long talk, young lady*, he said.

"No doubt, but I don't think that can happen for a while yet."

How did you evade Arnem Trisek on Caranthia?

"Ah, that. So Arnem is one of your agents?"

You didn't know? Aryn sounded surprised.

"No, or not until he found the information on the Terrania. Then I heard his chat with his superior."

Admiral Cole chose to let that likewise impossible communication breach slip past, for now. *How did you get from Caranthia to Velari in – according to our records – in less than twenty three minutes?*

She shrugged, and looked uncomfortable. "Again, I don't know, I just needed to get there before anyone else."

That's over six hundred light years, supplied the *Sneak*. *Did you teleport?*

Andreya was quiet for a moment. "No. I don't think so."

Then how?

"I... genuinely have no idea."

Do you hear all qNet traffic?

"Only if I choose to and it's relevant to myself or my goal to locate the *Terrania*."

Which brings us to why you are seeking it.

"I have no idea."

"How is it you don't know?" asked Nelsen.

As of yesterday, she did not exist, stated Aryn.

She looked vaguely worried at that. "I did, I must have," she said emphatically. "I just have no recollection."

You believe yourself to be Andreya Vorstan, from Taria?

She hesitated. "Yes," she said, though there was clearly a note of doubt in her voice.

And if I told you that Andreya Vorstan is still in a vegetative, irreversible coma back on Taria – confirmed in person by one of my agents?

Andreya sat back and closed her eyes, and slowly a tear emerged from the corner of her eye. "I would be disappointed," she said quietly. "But not surprised. Then I truly do not know who I am."

My problem is that I also do not know what *you are. And whether you pose a threat to the Empire.*

"I don't follow," said Nelsen. "What do you mean you don't know 'what' she is? Race-wise you mean?"

No... I don't know if she's 'real'.

Nelsen frowned. This was getting confusing. "She's clearly not a Proxy," he objected. Not even the pinnacle of cybo sapien manufacturing could produce an organic

158

being to equal a naturally grown human, and Andreya was certainly no mechanical construct.

She is identical to Andreya Vorstan down to the DNA, possibly even down to the molecule. Yet Andreya Vorstan is on Taria, and to all intents and purposes is dead – brain dead for certain.

Nelsen looked at Andreya, hoping for the right answer to his next question.

"Did you do that to her?"

She looked concerned. "No. I don't know – that is I don't think so. I don't... *feel* that I could have," she finished lamely.

From what I can determine, supplied Aryn, *Tarian authorities believe Andreya's condition to be the result of an accident. So I doubt foul play, but won't rule it out yet.*

So she is a clone? asked the *Sneak*.

No, she is far more than that. We have no parallel in the Empire, or the Archives. She is a complete *copy of Andreya Vorstan – and one which leaves behind no evidence of its existence.*

"Excuse *me?*" Andreya demanded, affronted by the "it" reference.

My apologies. But the fact is you are not *human. Humanoid yes, but not human. My team could not locate one fragment of a cell from your stay at the Hilton, nor the Records Office on Caranthia. Not only is that physically improbable, it is also physically impossible for a human.*

"Even when stealthed?" asked Nelsen. "An electron shroud could statically bond even dead skin cells to reduce shedding."

But friction or adhesion on surfaces would still leave detectable traces. Forensics are quite adamant that Andreya Vorstan had not visited either location. Andreya here did not

159

shed so much as a single molecule, which is impossible for a normal organic being.

"You're saying I'm a construction of some kind?" she asked, voice flat. "Artificial?"

I'm saying you're not truly a human, but a complete replica of one.

That might explain the medical scan, said the *Sneak* quietly.

"What do you mean, *Sneak?*" asked Nelsen.

Admiral Cole, could you forward the medical data on Mrs. Vorstan, from the Tarian clinic please?

Aryn located the data and passed it along. The *Sneak* quickly analysed it.

"Andreya," the *Sneak* said out loud. "I'm going to do a deep scan of your head. Please remain still."

She looked frightened. Not of the scan, but of what the outcome might mean. "What are you going to do?" she asked in a small voice.

"I just wish to confirm something I observed earlier when we first found you," said the *Sneak*. "There's been no opportune time since."

A virtual display volume appeared between Andreya and Nelsen, shared with Admiral Cole across their shared qNet simulation.

It showed two highly detailed 3D images of Andreya's head, but hairless – identical in every way other than one had its eyes closed, and had the serenity of death about her expression. Andreya grimaced to see herself looking like that.

"We noticed this before," explained the *Sneak*. "You have a level of cerebral damage that means it's impossible for you to breathe autonomously, let alone talk and move around."

The heads both went translucent, and faded away to reveal a topographical view of the cerebral cortex. Each showed heavy damage and scarring, clearly centred above the spine where it had pushed up into the cerebrum – crushing the medulla almost completely. Then the images slid together and merged perfectly, barring a few minor variations.

"Even the scar tissue matches as far down as I can scan, which is quite far," the *Sneak* observed.

"So I should be dead?" Andreya asked quietly.

"Brain dead," replied the *Sneak* gently. "I'm afraid so. It would seem your original form would be biologically dead as well if not for life support. This level of trauma is irreparable and the body would require life support to exist. Even though a full on nano-reconstruction could repair the *physical* damage, the mental trauma is already complete. Why the Tarians are prolonging the real Mrs. Vorstans life is beyond me, it seems a cruel thing to do."

You represent a frightening unknown, said Aryn. *Nothing the Empire knows of – or has ever speculated – can explain your existence. The fear I have is of your* purpose... *and if there is one of you, there can be more. And if so, how many?*

"And how long have your kind been amongst us without us knowing?" added Nelsen softly.

Andreya now looked very scared, scared of the danger she may represent. "I don't know the answers to your questions," she said almost inaudibly. "I wish I did." She hid her face by tilting her head downward.

Are you connected to the force which destroyed S'ren? Admiral Cole asked directly.

She looked up, eyes suddenly flashing angrily as she blinked away her tears. "No, I am *not!*" She glared at Nelsen, knowing she had an audience of two there at the moment as well as the *Sneak.*

"I know this at least... I have no intent to harm anything or anyone – especially humankind or your precious Empire. I don't know how I know, but I *know.* Right now my... feelings, are to help you, however I can. Not to do you harm."

The benevolence of a Trojan, noted Aryn. *Offer to help, then undermine from within.*

Andreya's mouth set in a determined line. "I could do more than that. If I so choose, you know I could leave here right now and you would never find me." That in itself was a white lie – the previously conspicuous doorway symbol was nowhere to be seen in her EV.

"She has a point," said Nelsen.

Will you promise to remain in Captain Rybek's custody until he deems it fit to release you?

"No." She looked around the cabin with a sense of bravado she didn't truly feel, and then back to Nelsen. "I promise to remain in Nelsen's custody as long as *I* deem fit."

There was a moment's silence. *I suppose I can hope for no more than that. Given the circumstances I rather doubt we could enforce anything else,* Aryn said. *Will you co-operate with us during that time?*

"Again – as I deem fit, yes."

Fair enough. When you reach INHS Capella, it would be of great help to our effort to understand you and the Infiltrator if you will allow some study of your condition...

She frowned. "I'm nothing to do with the Infiltrator. I

162

don't like the sound of it, but I won't refuse if I deem -"

- deem it fit. Yes, I understand. And for what it's worth, thank you.

"Provided it's administrated by either the *Sneak*, or overseen by Nelsen."

Nelsen raised his eyebrows and hands. "If you wish."

"No objections here," offered the *Sneak*.

Agreed then, said Aryn. *Nelsen, obviously I cannot issue you discrete orders without them being... overheard. So I must trust to your autonomy for the time being. Your new mission is to keep her safe, and under surveillance at all times. Understood?*

Yes, sir.

I need to confer with other interested parties with this... revelation. Be prepared for a summons without notice.

Understood, sir.

Andreya? I hope this all turns out well, for all of us.

"So do I, Admiral, so do I."

Chapter Twelve

The huge cracking sound went unheard as it echoed around the empty corridors of the Colesworth refinery.

Moments passed, and then the central hub which acted as the main ore refinery tore free of the asteroid it was attached to. Cables, conduits and corridors were torn apart, splitting wide open to the vacuum of space with brief bursts of ice vapour. Several bodies emerged from the damaged areas and began drifting away – already long dead from the initial attack.

Numerous small craft raced around the wreckage as the hub rose away from the asteroid field, cutting and slicing with ghostly energy beams. Soon all the corridors and ancillary buildings were floating free of their secured anchors – swiftly followed by a huge collection of mobile mining equipment, ore containers and assorted small transport craft. It all rose away from the field of debris and up to the group of vessels waiting high above.

Then they moved on to the ore containers stashed in nearby hollowed out asteroids that served as storage volumes. With a few precisely located shots they simply split them apart to get at the resources stored within.

Everything was recovered and recycled.

***

"There is always risk, Your Majesty, but of this one thing we can now be certain," said Aryn, quietly. "The sanctity of the qNet has been compromised to a degree

164

which we cannot evaluate. We must now consider all communication via qNet – no matter how secure, and including this meeting – to be open for observation by entities unknown." Aryn had his hands flat out on the table top, and looked the Emperor directly in the eye, giving him his full attention as if no one else were in the room.

The silence in the Emperor's private conclave was profound. The qNet was part of the very fabric which held the Empire together. Without it, a civilisation spanning thirty-thousand light-years would be unable to function. Real time communication was vital to maintain authority and structure in such a fast-paced society. Society itself had come to depend on the qNet so much it was an ingrained, and often implanted, dependency for the majority of its citizens. Life without it would be unthinkable, and in some cases impossible. It had broken some of the boundaries of physical existence which typically dominated life. Long distance relationships became the norm even when that distance measured in the thousands of light years. Private one-to-one real-time communication – when combined with sense-vise augmentation – meant partners could see, hear and touch each other with no delays, and no-one watching their private exchanges. Love-making via sense-vise had long been taken for granted.

Employment and expertise had also spread across the Empire. Using Proxies, a Professor of Chemical Sciences could teach at Haast Imperial College one morning, and lecture at Varnard University four hundred light years away in the same afternoon, all from the comfort of their own home, nine hundred light years away on the other side of the Empire.

Losing the qNet would be more dangerous to the Empire itself than an outright war. It would bring about an immediate and total collapse of society.

"Do you believe this Vorstan replica is observing this meeting?" asked the Emperor.

"I have to assume yes," replied Aryn. "If not her then something else. Nothing can be considered secure as of now. Everything we have is relayed through, dependent on or hooked into the qNet in some way. There is no element of the Empire which cannot be observed via the qNet. Consider our Observer program, but in the hands of someone else. That's what we are facing, only at an even more fundamental level. Because the Observers themselves are hooked into the qNet, this Infiltrator can observe *everything*."

"Our recommendation is to decouple all Imperial Archives from the qNet immediately," advised Raul. "Even then it's most likely too little too late."

"Chances are, if it hadn't been read already – just by mentioning it now means it's too late," observed Aryn. "The Valkyr was scanned in its entirety in *zero elapsed time*. I doubt the Archives would pose them much of a challenge given their apparent capabilities. No doubt there are keyword and pattern monitors already running. Merely mentioning something across the qNet would give the Infiltrator enough notice to locate and scan whatever it is long before we can take action to secure it."

"So you bring us an apparently infinitely capable superior being," said the Empreror in a hard voice, "which you believe we cannot hope to contain, of

166

unknown scale and scope. Alongside this you present a vastly superior technological force whose numbers defy probability. And you assert that neither are related, or in collaboration with the other?"

Aryn nodded. "There is nothing to indicate they are related, Your Majesty, but this could obviously be a ploy."

"Nothing other than the amazing coincidence of timing," noted the Emperor.

"I concede that, Your Majesty. However given my office, I do believe it may just be coincidence. However I'm always distrustful of even my *own* beliefs..."

"Your service to the Empire is beyond reproach or question Admiral Cole." The Emperors gaze drifted for a moment, before returning to those before him. "This is now too large a matter for just this war office. This threatens our very way of life."

"Does it, Your Majesty?" asked Dr. Reece, who so far had been listening attentively but keeping his council.

The Emperor waved for him to continue.

"As it stands, it is most likely that our entire network has already been studied. Given we know the time frame of this Infiltrators presence has been three years, and for suspicion to have arisen in the first place the Infiltrator must have been around for some time *prior* to the investigation, we can safely presume that an entity capable of scanning a vast volume of data in *zero* time is more than capable of having scanned our entire repository of knowledge."

Aryn nodded at the doctor. "The horse has bolted."

"Quite, Admiral. By the facts alone we can safely presume the Empire has been long compromised.

Isolating our archives and networks at this point is a little late in the day, and most likely a futile exercise."

"But as a security measure, it must be done," interjected Raul.

"I agree. However it would cripple our tactical and logistical abilities at a time when we are facing an unknown, and largely *physical* threat," replied Aryn.

"Perhaps this is their purpose?" asked Dr. Reece.

Aryn frowned. He privately doubted that – but kept his personal opinion to himself for the time being.

"Even so, there are some things which prudence suggests we should isolate," said the Emperor. "I have instructed my office to detach the Imperial Archive from the network in a disaster recovery exercise, and to withhold reattachment until further notice."

"Most wise, Your Majesty," murmured Dr. Reece. "With regard to the impact on society throughout the Empire – the threat to our civilisation as it were – I believe the majority would not be affected. So someone's personal details or conversation may be observed, possibly even their sense-vise sharing, financial details, trade data. Would our Infiltrator be remotely interested in such omnipotence? What could they gain from that level of observation?"

"Awareness? Understanding?" Aryn suggested.

"Hardly a major tactical advantage on such a personal level Admiral, given the huge historical database at its disposal. That alone should suffice to give any alien species an awareness and understanding of who, and what we are."

"And what we are capable of, and where our capabilities lie," observed Raul.

"Quite. I doubt public knowledge of this would serve any good. In fact, quite the opposite."

"Dr. Reece is right," said the Emperor. "Even an unwitting rumour of this – in conjunction with the situation in S'vreth – would incite panic, even civil unrest in some of the less stable elements within the Empire."

"But we must still seek to secure our Naval and Military channels," said Raul. "That means taking them off the qNet grid."

"Perhaps not Admiral Benthar," said Dr. Reece. "If you could leave that problem with my department for twenty four hours, we may come up with something."

Raul nodded. "Very well Doctor. But I'd be amazed if you can beat the qNet after several millennia of scientific research trying to..."

"Oh, I didn't say we'd try to *beat* it Admiral." Dr. Reece smiled, but refused to be drawn by Raul's inquisitive look.

"In the mean-time," Raul continued, "we can secure all sensitive information on the Naval network by removing all traffic above Class Three."

Aryn shook his head. "I'm afraid we can't do that, Fleet. Any change to our internal Naval traffic would propagate out into the media. And as His Majesty rightly observed – in conjunction with the current events in S'vreth – all it takes is one leak, one innocuous overheard comment. You know what the media is like."

"We cannot continue internal communications at these levels knowing they are being observed!"

"We have been for three years already."

"But now we know -"

"- we must still continue as before," the Emperor finished for him. "We cannot be seen to be changing our behaviour at this point in time. However, no *new* information should be exchanged across the qNet regarding S'vreth, and certainly nothing at all regarding our apparently friendly Infiltrator."

Raul nodded reluctantly, but gracefully. "Yes, Your Majesty."

"Are the facts that this Vorstan can snoop upon the un-snoopable, and that our disrespectful visitors in S'vreth can block the qNet linked?" the Emperor asked. "They would seem so to me. Doctor?"

Dr. Reece feigned a disingenuous look. "There is no way to say, or determine, Your Majesty. Both capabilities are beyond our knowledge of qSpin technology – with respect to the scale and nature of their application of course. I can only presume from their manipulation of the qSpin medium that they are."

"Admiral Cole?"

"Honestly, Your Majesty?"

The Emperor nodded.

"Gut instinct tells me in this situation – no, they are not connected. They may be related however, though at this time it's impossible to say. Paranoia dictates we must treat them as connected for the time being."

"So you intend to consider Vorstan as an agent of those responsible for S'vreth?"

"Yes, Your Majesty, until proven otherwise. There is no scope for error here."

"Indeed."

The Emperor turned to look at each of his subjects in this impromptu war council.

"The mandates around this war office still stand ladies and gentlemen. However we must now go onto a formal war footing. The qNet situation is to remain on a strict need-to-know basis requiring my own authority. Given the coincidence of these recent events, we must now consider S'vreth an act of war, even though it officially remains outside our domain. How we achieve this and remain righteous is to be determined by a full senate. Nothing less will suffice for propriety alone. This meeting is adjourned, and thank you."

Those around the table stood and saluted the Emperor and began to leave.

He turned to Aryn as he rose. "I wish to speak with your Captain Rybek and yourself at your earliest convenience."

Aryn bowed slightly. "I will summon him now, Your Majesty."

Can we presume Andreya is not listening? Aryn asked Nelsen over their qNet channel. *Or should we assume she is?*

Shall I just ask? replied Nelsen.

Aryn considered for a moment – if she didn't know about their chat she would – but then Nelsen going into a semi-trance as he joined the meeting would give it away regardless.

Ask, let's see how she responds.

"Andreya, I'm about to go into a high security meeting. Can I ask you not to listen in please?"

She nodded. "Of course." The symbol in her vision which showed local traffic mentioning her name *was* tempting, but she had deliberately chosen not to jump in.

"Thank you."

For what it's worth, Aryn remarked drily to Nelsen. *All right, the Emperor is fully aware that we may be being observed. Let's get this over with.*

The Emperor? Nelsen asked, slightly perturbed.

Yes. Move along Nelsen. You've had an audience with him before. And don't stare like a tourist this time, please – you know it irritates him.

There was a vague sensation of jumping, and then the Emperor's private audience chamber materialised around him. He was in the ante-chamber outside the audience room, just out of sight behind the doorway. *Formalities,* he realised ruefully. He unconsciously and needlessly smoothed down the immaculate dress uniform the sim had dressed him in and took a steadying breath before striding into the room.

Aryn was standing before the Emperors grand desk, resplendent in full white Naval dress. *Nice and intimidating,* thought Nelsen.

"Your Imperial Majesty, may I once again present Captain *Nelsen Rybek,* commanding the INI Valkyr *Sneak Thief.*"

Nelsen saluted, snapping his heels together. "At your service, Your Majesty."

"Be seated gentlemen. This may take a while, and I rarely favour needless standing on ceremony."

"Thank you, Your Majesty," said Aryn.

Two chairs appeared before the desk, and they both sat down as the Emperor remained standing before the tall picture windows.

"Rybek... a pseudonym of course. An interesting

choice of name considering your personal history?"

Nelsen looked slightly uncomfortable. "Perhaps, Your Majesty."

"One would almost expect someone adopting such an infamous name to be actively *looking* for trouble."

He froze internally, just managing to lock his expression into a passive-neutral before the ice climbed up inside his spine.

The Emperor looked directly at him. "Am I to trust someone who is courting disaster by baiting one of the most dangerous women in Imperial history?"

Nelsen was locked in fear – an unusual mental state for him, and he didn't relish the experience. Here was a man who *knew* what he was intending to do when the chance arose, and had the power to pull the plug on his private agenda once and for all. One word is all it would take.

Don't say it, please don't say it... Nelsen almost prayed. He took a chance, a daring and over-reaching chance far beyond his position or station – but he had to deflect the way this was going if he could.

"With your life, Your Majesty," he said firmly.

The Emperor's eyes bored into him, and he refused to flinch. *If this gambit fails, it's all over...*

"Admiral Cole still speaks highly of you. So highly in fact I have had cause to question his judgement." The Emperor raised an eyebrow and looked at Aryn sardonically, who half-smiled in return.

Nelsen remained as stiff as a board.

"I recall bestowing the Imperial Seal in person over your assignment to INI, Captain. If our faith in you is misplaced – if one *single* neuron in your mind thinks you can pursue a private vendetta over your duties to the Empire – speak now and be honoured for your honesty with no harm to you or your career.

"*But,*" he went on – his voice colder and harder than carborundum at absolute zero, "if you do not, and if you subsequently jeopardise the Empire *or* its concerns due your own desires or needs, *nowhere* will be safe."

Nelsen did not doubt that one bit. "My – personal – concerns have never impacted my service to the Empire, Your Majesty, and never will."

"See that it doesn't. Admiral Cole can recommend no other to perform the duties you are about to be tasked with fulfilling. This puts the safety of the entire Empire at risk if you dishonour us."

"On my life, and in the name of my wife and daughter, the Empire comes first, Your Majesty."

The Emperor stared hard at him again for a moment. "Very well. Admiral?"

Aryn sat forward. "Nelsen, please tell us – from your own personal viewpoint *and* professional – your thoughts, feelings, intuition regarding the passenger you have calling herself Andreya Vorstan. Be frank, open and honest. Hold nothing back."

Nelsen looked to the Emperor, who nodded his assent for Nelsen to speak freely.

"She's real," he supplied. "As real as anyone I've ever met."

"Qualify please?"

"We know she's a replica, Your Majesty. Clearly, somehow, she's been 'produced', *made*. But she's organic, emotional, clumsy on occasion, intelligent, open and apparently honest. And she knows how to look after her own. She's trusting. She's also very confused and worried about discovering she's not Vorstan, or a real human."

"So?" asked the Emperor.

"So, replica or not – for my money, she's a replica *human*. If you had the technology allowing you to artificially produce a being to infiltrate the Empire, why would you replicate such a contradictory self-deprecating and self-doubting emotional wreck? Better an efficient, organised mind with a clear and focused intent to get the job done."

The Emperor frowned.

"If she's part of some alien conspiracy, she doesn't seem to be actively pursuing the goals you would expect. She was *horrified* at the destruction of S'vreth. She wanted us to rescue the S'renee – despite knowing they stood no chance and no hope – even if we tried."

"Model behaviour for a spy or Trojan," noted Aryn again, deliberately. He wanted to play out the thoughts foremost in his mind for the Emperor's benefit. He personally didn't believe Vorstan represented a subversive presence, but wanted it vocalised and discussed.

"Yes," said Nelsen slowly. "I have considered that, if she could obtain the trust of the most suspicious and paranoid amongst us, she could get deep inside the Empire for her own – or their own – purpose."

They were silent as they considered this.

"But then," he continued, "if she could access anything, anywhere… and has been able to for years… why not go direct for whatever you needed to achieve? She would have access to all our protocols, all our behaviours. No base of operations would be safe. And if these beings can replicate *real* people – they could just replace whoever they needed. Any one of us might be a replica right now."

"The thought has occurred," said Aryn. "We've each been screened for 'replica' behaviour and have passed."

"Including one's self," added the Emperor. "Given the circumstances we cannot afford the cost of presumption."

"Skin cell shedding?" asked Nelsen, having read the reports from Caranthia shortly before being called him into this meeting.

Aryn nodded. "Right now that's no way to be certain, but it's all we have."

Nelsen was impressed the Emperor was so open minded, even as a simple gesture of faith it showed he placed his regard for the Empire above himself.

"Also," he continued after a moment, "she didn't seek *us* out. She was pursuing her own ends without posing a clear threat to the Empire. Someone who could walk into *any* facility we have without raising an eyebrow. She can obviously inject data into secure qNet channels she should have no access to. Spoofing systems or fabricating data would probably be no more a challenge to her than blinking."

"There may yet be others doing just that," observed the Emperor.

Nelsen nodded. "That may be, Your Majesty. But with due respect that does not alter the problem Andreya creates. Other replica's provide an *additional* problem set for INI."

"Andreya has agreed – reluctantly and with caveats –

to allow some study of her at *Capella*," supplied Aryn.

The Emperor regarded both of them in turn. "So I am to believe that this being – formerly considered to be *the* number one priority threat to the Empire – is benign and co-operative, and is to be allowed to roam the Empire at will?"

Aryn's expression was deliberately composed. "I would still suggest she poses an unknown risk, and *possibly* a threat, Your Majesty. However, I believe at this time she is no danger to the Empire, despite her capabilities. Further, even if we were to consider her a threat, right now there is not one single thing we can do to counter it. Other than react to whatever it is she might do. Keeping her under willing observation is the best we can hope for at this time."

The Emperor returned to the windows to gaze out upon the Imperial gardens.

Aryn looked to Nelsen briefly, who merely shrugged in return.

"Given the knowledge in my possession, Your Majesty, my recommendation is that we should concentrate on the S'vreth situation, and consider Andreya as an external context for the time being," Aryn said. "Until that context changes…"

"And the threat to the qNet?"

"I agree with Dr. Reece," said Aryn. "We should do nothing – for now. If his team can provide workable solution to our internal communications, all the better."

"And if this does not work? Or if we have to take action?"

Aryn looked out of the window himself, possibly taking solace from the gardens, or imagining his view of

177

the galactic core from his own office. "That is a matter for the Senate, Your Majesty, not I."

The Emperor turned slightly toward Aryn. "But what *would* you do, Aryn?"

Aryn's expression softened a little, even though he knew the personal reference was going to drag him further into the looming political mire. "I would severe the entire Naval communication network, and the official Imperial office networks from the qNet, Your Majesty."

"Cauterize the Empire from its subjects, whilst leaving the populace open to observation? Possibly even attack?"

"Yes, Your Majesty, until such an attack took place which would require our attention. Then we would have to act accordingly."

"Destroy the qNet hubs?"

"All of them, yes, Your Majesty. Any one would provide a medium for entities such as Andreya to permeate the entire Empire within seconds."

"There are sixty-seven trillion citizens in the Empire you know," said the Emperor quietly. "This would plunge all of them into an age of chaos and anarchy."

"The Empire is resilient, Your Majesty. We still have FTL to fall back on. Relayed through stable wormholes we can create a new communication network, at least for Naval and official use."

"And when the wormholes fail as the enemy blocks them when they invade and secure our systems?" asked the Emperor, though he already knew the answer. He turned back to face them. "I will discuss the suggestion with Dr. Reece's team. It seems to me to be something we should begin immediately. Discuss both these options with Fleet if you will, Admiral."

Aryn nodded graciously.

"Captain Rybek, do you honestly feel Vorstan is no threat? To yourself, the *Sneak*, or the Empire?"

"Honestly, at this time, no, Your Majesty. If she were involved in the initial scan made of the *Sneak*, she has had ample opportunity to subvert it, or interfere or otherwise cause issue with our mission. And she has volunteered information – when prompted," he added.

"Very well. If your opinion should change, alert us immediately. If you believe you are being... *overheard*, simply refer to your namesake."

Nelsen's mouth went dry, but he understood the Emperor's implicit suggestion of a code-word for danger. He nodded.

"Now, as to what to do with you next, Captain..."

Chapter Thirteen

Nelsen opened his eyes from the semi-trance state of being in a full sense-vise simulation, and looked around. There were no active alerts in his EV, and Andreya was sitting opposite him on another gel-couch, staring at him intently.

"Welcome back," she said.

"Did you listen in?" he asked.

"No. I could have, but I didn't."

"*Sneak?*"

Not that – then the *Sneak* realised Andreya probably was listening to their chat, so gave in and used vocal. "Not that I noticed, but then it would be impossible to tell. Certainly, Andreya showed no emotive or physiological responses other than impatience."

"Excuse *me*," Andreya snapped.

"Well, you did," said the *Sneak* almost petulantly. The *Sneak* decided to change the topic out of harm's way. "We have docked at INHS *Capella,* Captain."

"Good. I have to order a full diagnostic *Sneak*... Sorry."

"Certainly, Captain. I'd have to request one myself, given the circumstances."

Nelsen turned to Andreya. "Right, let's get this done – if you don't mind?"

She frowned. "Get what done?"

"I want a full medical scan by a system you haven't interacted with, and one we can be reasonably certain hasn't been scanned as the *Sneak* has. Just in case."

Andreya threw him a look, but conceded with a nod.

She knew it could do no harm, and might help build some trust.

"Please, I can *only* ask you not to interact with any network until further notice, even if asked to."

"O. K." She forced each syllable.

Nelsen sighed, and gestured to the drop hatch at the rear. There was going to *some* kind of trouble, he could tell.

"After you..."

"Nothing unusual," reported Coryn, INHS *Capella's* primary medical Intellect. "Ignoring the evident and irreparable brute force trauma to the cerebrum, the patient is in rude health for someone who should right now be under full life-support in a catatonic state with no hope of recovery. There is no explanation as to why she is a walk in patient."

Dr. Kandras studied the scans. The findings were irrefutable. *How could this patient even be alive?* she marvelled.

Nelsen was standing behind her looking at the scan floating in the air before them. It was every bit as detailed as the one the *Sneak* had made, and every bit as convincing.

"Are you running the diagnostic?" he asked.

"Every other minute, with a random offset of a few seconds," replied a technician behind them. "Hitting a mixed pattern of vital and non-vital files in a random pattern. No accesses other than our own or from Coryn himself."

Dr. Kandras turned to look at Nelsen. "She has the same DNA, same physiology, same recorded damage to

181

the cortex, same scarring, and from the full scan we requested from Taria, exactly the same nano-fibre neural integration. Do you know how hard it would be to replicate all of that?"

He nodded. "Impossible, with our tech."

"Improbable *without* I would say. Cloning can reproduce skeletal and organ tissue, reproduce physical characteristics at the gross level, appearance, facial features, and so on. But *only* that – reproduce. It would never give an exact copy, that would be impossible. Cell growth and entropy, cell division, the different environmental stimuli – all introduce new variables and factors which alter growth and cell formation. Even if you could replicate all of those, any clone is substantially and inherently different to the original purely due to the biological growth processes. Fluctuations in gravity, natural background radiation, atmospheric pressure – everything has an effect. And a clone would not manifest physical damage such as moles, tissue scarring, or bone fractures – unless the damage is deliberately inflicted, and that would result in a different tissue pattern. Scar tissue itself would be impossible to reproduce precisely. At this level anyway."

She gestured at the scan.

"This is no clone of Mrs. Vorstan. It *is* Mrs. Vorstan."

Nelsen stepped forward and spoke quietly. "I didn't say she was a clone," he said. "And this is definitely *not* Mrs. Vorstan. Records prove she is still incumbent in the Tarian Prime Medical Facility."

Dr. Kandras raised an eyebrow. "Then your records are wrong."

Nelsen resisted the urge to grab the doctor and shake

her. "They are *not* wrong. Have your scan search for incidental tissue loss."

She frowned, but relayed the instruction to Coryn who complied immediately.

A few moments passed. "There is none," she murmured. "Not one fragment or skin cell, or hair. The oils exuded from her skin have no DNA in at all..." her voice trailed off in amazement.

"Would you class that as *normal,* for a human, Doctor?"

She shook her head, dumbfounded.

"Run every test and scan you can think of – and then when you run out – come up with some more. Just make sure you tell her what you need to do first."

"Of course," she replied thoughtfully.

"Nelsen? Nelsen? Are we done yet?" Andreya demanded.

He looked at Dr. Kandras. "Just another ten minutes... Dr. Kandras is going to take over but I'm here watching, ok?"

"Just hurry it up!" she snapped.

He smiled disarmingly at Dr. Kandras. "All yours, Doctor."

Shousa, I am not sure, said the *Sneak. I* seem *and feel absolutely fine and normal. But paranoia tells me I* would *feel fine and normal if modified to do so...*

Shousa stroked the black frictionless hull of the Valkyr almost comfortingly. Not many knew that the entire outer hull was bonded to a nervous system which meant Valkyr's could feel everything that touched them. Originally intended to allow them to detect the impacts

183

of micro-debris that could lead to internal damage, it had quickly become apparent that the vessels themselves had developed an emotional response to this sense of touch.

Don't worry – if anything has been modified and you can't tell – we can.

The scan had been running for several hours. So far nothing unusual had turned up other than the oddity of the file access times which the *Sneak* had already detected. Several top physicists were already being hard pressed by the Valkyr's designers to determine how its file storage could be accessed at all by an outside agent, let alone have all its files scanned at the exact same point in time.

Anything yet? Nelsen asked via the stations l-net.

Nothing yet Captain Rybek, Shousa replied.

Good, we've only known each other for a short while but I'd hate to lose the Sneak *– I get the feeling we may be serving together for some time yet.*

Thank you, Captain, said the *Sneak*.

Nelsen's surprise was evident. *Sneak? I thought you would be behind a quarantine?*

She is, Captain, said Shousa. *I'm relaying her channel and filtering her data stream for anything which is not pure audio – nothing untoward so far.*

She? exclaimed Nelsen.

Yes, Captain, said the *Sneak*. *Did you not know?*

Well, no. Sorry. He sounded genuinely embarrassed.

Her voice is pretty gender-neutral, commented Shousa. *You might want to address that,* she said privately to the *Sneak*.

Yes ma'am, she replied.

Anyway, you don't have to keep checking in every five minutes, Captain, said Shousa. *She's in good hands. I'll notify you if anything comes up, good or bad.*

There was a brief pause. *Thank you*, he said, and then left the channel.

Wasn't that a bit rude? asked the *Sneak*.

To the point, replied Shousa cheerfully. *It's good to see he's concerned and bonding with you – but we have work to do. Now, do you want these upgrades when we're finished or not?*

"I'm done," said Andreya forcefully – pushing past the medic who was politely trying to block her exit from the scanning room. For the past two hours she had let them run any number of scans and psychological profiling tests, physical responses, sensory deprivation and stimulation tests. Now she'd had enough.

"Mrs. Vorstan, we have just a few more tests –"

"No, you *don't*," Andreya interrupted firmly. "Where is Nelsen? I mean Captain Rybek?"

"Mrs. Vorstan," said Dr. Kandras smoothly, entering the scan room antechamber from the far corner. "If you would relax, please! Someone with your mental... condition, should take care."

"I'll take care soon enough," Andreya replied hotly. "Where is Captain Rybek?"

"He's on the way. Mrs. Vorstan, you are aware of your condition, yes?"

Andreya paused. "If you mean my brain is fritzed beyond repair, yes."

Dr. Kandras assumed a politely superior air. "Mrs. Vorstan, I cannot stress *enough* the importance of your

185

condition, not only to yourself but to our current understanding of neurological science. Frankly Mrs. Vorstan, you should be brain dead."

"But *frankly* Doctor, I clearly am not. And my dead brain and I would like to leave. *Now.*"

"If I may, Mrs. Vorstan – you could greatly aid our analysis of the information we have gathered if you would agree to some more tests."

Andreya shook her head. "You have what you need."

"Mrs. Vorstan –"

"I'm starting to get angry Doctor. I have business to conduct, and a fine timeline to conduct it in."

"The tests won't take long –"

"Am I a prisoner here?"

Dr. Kandras looked affronted. "Why certainly not, Mrs. Vorstan!"

"Then goodbye." Andreya stormed past the doctor and the medic, and made for the door by which the doctor had entered, but it refused to open to her presence. She looked at it briefly in annoyance and then it slid open silently. "Thank *you*," she muttered, stepping into the room beyond.

"Mrs. Vorstan!" called Dr. Kandras. "That is a secure area! How did you do that?"

Dr. Kandras, said Coryn. *I have observed a minor modification of the security routines controlling the medical diagnostics area. Is everything all right?*

I have no idea, she replied, and followed after Andreya.

She was stood stock still before the large hologrammatic display of her own neural pathways, with the surprised medical team gathered around in shocked silence as the neurological impossibility they had been studying now stood before them in person. Andreya's face was filled with dismay as she realised what the hologram portrayed.

Dr. Kandras took one look at her face, and then slowly moved to stand beside her – regarding the hologram. "You can see why we are so interested in finding out more about you, Mrs. Vorstan."

Of course, Andreya had seen the side-by-side comparison the *Sneak* had displayed for her and Nelsen, showing the intense trauma her brain stem had suffered at some point – so she more or less knew what the fuss was about. But this… this was altogether different.

All her neurological brain activity, wave patterns and synaptic responses were being displayed – charted over time and in great detail as she had sat through their innumerable tests designed to provoke or stimulate certain electrical responses within her brain.

It did not take an expert in neurology to see that there was literally nothing to show for it. Not even the basest of autonomous functions – such as breathing, or heartbeat – showed any sign of brain activity. Her mind was dark. Where a scintillating cloud of electrical signals and responses should be, there was a void of absolutely nothing.

"To all intents and purposes," said Dr. Kandras softly, "you aren't actually *using* your brain tissue."

Andreya tried to give a short laugh, but it came out as a stifled murmur. "You mean I'm out of my mind?" she managed, the joke dying on her lips even as she spoke.

Dr. Kandras looked at her askance. "You certainly

aren't *in* it, based on all known medical science at least. Which is considerable."

Andreya tried to hide it, but she felt genuinely scared for the first time since she had woken in the Harian Hilton. She stared at the map of her empty mind for a few moments, and then looked imploringly at Dr. Kandras. She took heart, and gestured to the exit just as Nelsen appeared around the corner. As he entered the room he had an inquisitive look on his face, wondering what was going on.

Andreya ran over and threw her arms around him – holding on tight and refusing to let go.

"Get me out of here," she whispered. "*Please.*"

He patted her awkwardly on the back. "Ok, ok."

Nelsen stared at the *Sneak* in disbelief. It was now purest white.

He and Andreya had spent the last two hours sat alone in the quiet of one of *Capella's* observation lounges, staring out into space. She had been silent, withdrawn, and Nelsen had left her to her own thoughts – wherever they were. He felt she deserved some private time to come to terms with what she had seen, or at least to try. Eventually the *Sneak* pinged him that the diagnostic and updates were done. He'd offered his hand to Andreya, and she gave him a small, wistful smile, before they returned to the docking bay.

"Do you like it?" asked the *Sneak*. It- *her* – voice sounded more feminine.

"What...?"

"Watch!"

A brief shimmer of iridescence rippled over the

Valkyr's hull, and it faded from bright white to fire red.

That tickles! exclaimed the *Sneak* privately to Shousa.

"We've replaced the hull skin," explained Shousa out loud, with a sidelong glance at the *Sneak*. "She now has an electro-dynamic chameleonic layer just below the impact response surface."

"Chameleonic? You mean full camouflage?"

"*Sneak?*" Shousa prompted.

"I'll try..."

There was another shimmer, and the *Sneak almost* vanished – replaced by a blurry representation of the bay floor and the view beyond the Valkyr. It hurt the eyes to look as it shifted and rippled continuously.

"It's hard to control at this level," said the *Sneak*.

"It will improve with time," Shousa reassured her. "It's really meant to allow blending in from a distance or against a very large backdrop. Not against a highly detailed one at close range."

Nelsen stared as he saw another technician walk around behind the Valkyr and swim into focus – rippling and blurring as he moved around behind the hull. He suddenly appeared at the other end in plain view, and his slightly delayed, mirage-like self disappeared about half a second later.

"Now look!" exclaimed the *Sneak*.

The mirage collapsed, and was replaced by an offensively bright purple hull, with the appearance of detailed and highly complex panelling – and a lurid orange flame motif all over the forward section.

"Pimped!" she said cheerfully.

"Ye gods," exclaimed Nelsen.

Andreya clapped her hands together. "Now that, is

very, *very* neat," she said, voice filled with admiration. She seemed to be livening up a little.

"I suppose you can change shape too?" Nelsen asked wryly, eager to promote a buoyant mood.

"That's next on the list," replied Shousa with a smile.

Nelsen wasn't entirely sure she was joking.

"With this, Valkyrs can now blend in fairly inconspicuously with typical civilian craft – assuming any outward visual appearance they choose. Aside from the hull configuration of course, which is a bit of a giveaway. However Solstran Starlines are aiding us with that."

"How so?" asked Nelsen.

"They've got a designer who has brought in a new range of hulls for rapid-transit personal transport ships. Remarkably similar, in my opinion. An amazing coincidence, really. They start production this week."

"Let me guess, *you* are the designer for Solstran Starlines?"

Shousa smiled sweetly.

"Why is it I'm always surrounded by smart-ass women?" he complained.

"Is it so bad?" asked Andreya, fluttering her eyelashes.

He blushed, and then went redder as he got angry at himself for blushing. "Is she good to go?" he grated out each word.

"Ready when you are, Captain," replied the *Sneak*.

Without another word, he strode to the *Sneak's* drop-hatch and stood there waiting impatiently for Andreya.

She looked at Shousa, who winked, and then she sighed and walked over to stand next to Nelsen.

190

"Bon voyage!" said Shousa as the hatch slid upward. "There are a couple of other upgrades, but the *Sneak* will brief you!"

As the *Sneak* cleared the Emergence Zone and the Hive station disappeared behind her, her hull rippled psychedelically through various colours, patterns and detailing as she tried to find something 'comfortable'. She practised mimicking the stellar backdrop – watching herself from the Observers she controlled outside her hull until she had the effect down pat. Finally she settled on Impenetrable Black – her original colour. She felt more secure in that somehow.

"Are you humming?" demanded Nelsen.

"Sorry, Captain."

"So where are we going, my Mystery Man?" asked Andreya.

"We're lending you a hand," he said. "Tell us where your Velari book located the last sighting of the *Terrania* and we'll take you there."

Her eyes went bright. "Really?"

"Really." Nelsen kept his mind as closed as he could on his actual orders. Whilst sitting with Andreya earlier, he had briefed himself in full on the mysterious nature of the so called "Infiltrator" from the collated reports Admiral Cole had provided. It seemed someone, or something, had been accessing Imperial systems for the past three years at least. Always at random, always unpredictable, never traceable. Only the data access times or 'fingerprint' which the *Sneak* had encountered revealed their presence. The accesses had initially been observed by chance – a technician doing a routine

191

maintenance sweep of an archive data store. Believing it to be merely a glitch it had simply been filed, but a systems Intellect noticed a number of other similar reports as they built up over time, and flagged a potential security breach. Since then INI had been all over it, attempting to establish any leads around the accesses, but none had been found, despite a continual and ever growing list of similar breaches.

Four days ago, a series of monitoring routines had spotted a string of data access modifications all taking place at the same time within a specific section of the Imperial data network, one spread out across a physically large volume of space. Analysis of the data involved had revealed a thread which lead to Caranthia, and INI had saturated the system with agents and Observers. They had homed in on Andreya as soon as she registered herself with the Harian Hilton. Andreya Vorstan had not 'arrived' on Caranthia by any known transports, which immediately flagged her as a person of interest for INI. An INI cell already researching information on the *Terrania* had been called in to intercept her.

As he had thought it through, Nelsen was not exactly happy about the string of inter-connected events which had led him to their encounter – all orbiting a legend from aeons long forgotten. *There* is *a connection,* he mused. *There has to be.*

Andreya chewed her lip indecisively for a moment, and Nelsen looked away – feigning a check on one of the few physical monitor systems in the cabin. *Damnation, how could she not be human?* he asked himself. He kept catching himself watching her – studying her every move and gesture. Despite only knowing her for barely a day, he knew the signs well enough and kept stamping on them. Even so, whenever he let go of his iron will he found his eyes had wandered back to her.

"Ok," she said at last. A file popped into the quarantine box in the *Sneaks* l-net - a security measure they had agreed earlier. Independent autonomous routines within the 'box' analysed the file and declared it clean, and the *Sneak* assessed the routines to ensure they hadn't been modified. It was the best security they could achieve under the circumstances.

The *Sneak* opened it and read the same pages Andreya had before they had 'rescued' her two days ago. They were perfectly formed m-gram prints of the pages as Andreya had seen them. Then she passed them over to Nelsen after she'd also scanned them for anything out of the ordinary.

"This is in unexplored space," he said after stitching the convoluted Velari trail into an approximate physical location. "The Dark Zone as it's called. Well outside the Empire, and occupying the other side of the Cluster." He frowned. "I had no idea the Velari had ventured so far."

"I don't think they did," volunteered Andreya. "I think it's more that they ventured *this* far..."

Nelsen looked surprised. "I see. So they migrated *here* from there... Ok, I can buy into that. *Sneak...* shall we?"

"Why not, Captain?"

He scowled. "Did Shousa reboot your personality core while she was at it?"

"No, Captain. Best speed?"

"Let's keep it quiet, though fast. We don't want to risk drawing any attention to where we are bound."

"Aye aye, sir."

He scowled again at the *Sneak's* banter, but said nothing.

"Is there nothing to eat around here?" Andreya asked expectantly.

He sighed.

Chapter Fourteen

Romurik shot out of the *Delaror's* mass driver cannon at one hundred kilometres per second. He found it ironic that the very plan he had for escaping the *Drastic Response* if all else had failed was now being put to good use – and still within the Velari system.

He made a few minor corrections to his flight path caused by some field variances in the cannon, then dropped most of his systems into zero-draw state and entered stealth mode. Only passive sensors were active, along with his internal organic clock which was set to initiate a number of precisely timed protocols. Anything scanning as Romurik passed by would detect nothing other than a small piece of debris travelling through space.

[TIMER EVENT + 1437ms]
Course correction, full passive sensor sweep. Status : on track, 4,344 contacts in range. Deep infiltrative scan on nearest 2,000, file results. High level analysis – high energy spikes in nearest designated targets, further scans scheduled, course correction for close proximity pass.
[OFFLINE]

[TIMER EVENT + 2124ms]
Full infiltrative scan on target, full passive sweep on 8,784 targets. High level analysis, nothing of note. No organic life-signs detected. Interesting. Status – no evidence of observation or response to my presence or scans. Decision point – continue.

[OFFLINE]

[TIMER EVENT + 4788ms]
Course corrections made, beginning return trajectory. No signs of observation or response. Full infiltrative scans of 256 randomly chosen contacts from 18,275. qNet now inaccessible. Deep scans of local subspace show oscillating energy waves ranging periodically from extremely high frequency and low amplitude to low frequency and extremely high amplitude.
[OFFLINE]

[TIMER EVENT + 2117ms]
Return point reached. Corrections made to exit cloud. qNet remains offline. Deep subspace scans show energy waves retain consistent cyclic ranging of both frequency and amplitude. Interesting. Align sensors for deep infiltrative scan on secondary target groups.
[OFFLINE]

[TIMER EVENT + 3509ms]
Deep scans of secondary targets. High energy spikes, no life signs. Subspace interference constant. Aligned for perimeter egress.
[OFFLINE]

[TIMER EVENT + 1200ms]
Heading for Delaror – no corrections needed. Subspace interference absent, readings normal. qNet access restored.

Romurik's subjective journey had taken fourteen seconds of run-time. In reality his transit into the perimeter and back out had taken seven hours.

Interesting, he thought as he dumped all of his

findings into the INI qNet repository for analysis by the Greater Intellects. *How could they affect subspace over such a large volume at such a constant level?*

Then his passive sensors picked up movement from behind him. He sent a sweep across his rear, and immediately contacted the *Delaror* and authenticated itself.

"Incoming – lots and lots of incoming!"

"Sir, contacts moving toward us at high speed. ETA two minutes twelve seconds, c- drives."

Captain Van E'streth patched into the ships command network and accessed the sensor sims. Directly below their current position the perfect sphere arrangement was distending rapidly toward them, almost like a bulge – the apex of which was stretching ahead much faster than the rest to form a spike growing outward from the sphere itself.

Agent Romurik? he demanded over the qNet.

Sir, not my doing – I was well outside the formation before I came back online fully.

How far away are you?

Eighteen seconds.

Make it less.

"Helm – back away from the leader in direct line of sight."

"Aye sir."

He watched the contacts – they didn't alter velocity but continued their advance. He considered for a moment.

Romurik, change course – ninety degrees perpendicular to your velocity – any direction.

Yes sir.

Over the next few seconds, the spike changed its direction to follow Romurik.

Romurik – direct order. Upload and bail, I'm sorry.

There was the shortest of pauses. *Yes, sir.*

A tiny contact appeared on the scan as Romurik self-detonated.

The spikes advance slowed, and then stopped.

Captain Van E'streth – and the entire crew of the *Delaror* waited with baited breath.

Then the vessels began advancing again, the point ship pulling away much faster than before. The bell shaped formation now aligning itself toward the *Delaror*.

INCC – we're about to be engaged by unknowns. Advise if standard contact protocols remain in force or are to be superseded.

He watched as several hundred ships of unknown origin and purpose sped toward them, and he prayed.

Romurik's persona appeared in the Totality's Recovery Portal, and he sighed.

His avatar was discrete by Intellect standards, being about average human height and build, with well-defined musculature and humanoid physique. Other than being a dull bronze colour, he might pass as a typical, reasonably attractive human male.

Romurik Anzar 4377-ADFFE – welcome.

Yeah.

Again.

I know.

Your fortieth visit.

I can count too.

198

The circumstances this time?

Orders. Check my log.

We have. You have an unfortunate tendency to demonstrate a lack of care regarding your physical existence.

I am an Intellect – I don't need one.

Whilst true, it is a disturbing trait. Cybo sapien psyche profiling requires the personality to value their own physical existence as an indicator for valuing the physical presence of others – both intellectual and biological entities.

I have more regard for them in my little finger than I have for all of you put together.

There was a pause. *Your attitude has become anti-intellect?*

Romurik sighed again. *No, just anti-wasting time.*

Romurik, we have to clone your persona for analysis as you are demonstrating questionable traits which may evolve into undesirable behaviour.

Whatever. I need a new form, as soon as possible.

You are not perturbed by this?

Look, it's not my fault I'm here – again. My duties often put me in the line of fire or otherwise hazardous-to-your-existence contexts. I am truly a victim of circumstance. I don't see any of you being forced to upload due to impending body loss every other year.

What nature of form will you require this time?

Something different I think. The drone form is sometimes convenient, but often limiting. I have a design, here.

The room accepted the schematics and studied them in depth.

You are serious?

Quite. Can we move along please? This is taking too long.

No more than eight point two microseconds have elapsed, as you are aware.

That's eight microseconds too long. I have a mission to fulfil. You are *aware of the data I collected?*

Yes. The mission was quite daring, risky, and has put the Delaror *in harm's way.*

Romurik stopped himself then. *That was not my intent; I was not detected until after I exited the sphere – even then I am unsure how. If their sensors are so sophisticated, they showed no sign of response as I actively scanned them within their own perimeter.*

None of your data indicates anything to the contrary.

There was a pause. *You are testing my conscience at a time like this? To see if I feel guilt over jeopardising the* Delaror?

Yes, there is no better time. You will be glad to know you have passed on compassion. Your cloned persona achieved one hundred per cent responses under simulation. We are fully aware you were acting under direct orders from a superior officer.

There was another pause. *Of course I could be faking the responses.* Romurik knew he was baiting the giant, and would never win – but he just couldn't resist it.

Yes, we are *aware.*

Romurik grunted.

Your chosen form will be built at the fabrication facility on Haast. You will need to arrange transport to wherever you deem your next operational volume to be. It will be available for occupation in forty-three hours.

Thanks.

You are cleared to go about your business Romurik, with one caveat.

Which is? Romurik replied hesitantly.

Be careful.

Captain Van E'streth?

Romurik – you uploaded in time?

Of course. We've analysed the data I gathered – I appreciate you are pressed for time but this is vitally important. Can you please speed up?

Van E'streth was no fan of using artificial stimulants and neural enhancements – he found they gave an uncomfortable 'buzz'. There came a rushing sensation as blood surged through his brain, flooded with adreno-based stimulants. Subjectively, everything around him slowed down to about a half of normal speed.

Go on, he said.

Romurik dropped a data file to him, which he read as Romurik waited impatiently.

Their ships are a random collection of oddball and unknown designs, said Romurik. *The variation is unlikely to be from a single species. Either we are facing a gestalt force, or more likely a scavenger race. None of the thirty thousand contacts I scanned showed a single life sign. Not even microbes.*

Van E'streth considered this. *Driven by Intellects?*

Certainly autonomous. Most likely AI operating in unison. You have to have to be careful, Captain. We cannot presume they operate on the same value systems we do. They will be unpredictable without our knowing their motive. Most of their vessels are armed, but not all. The Delaror now has all the details.

Very well. Thank you Agent Romurik.

Captain… for what it's worth, I'm sorry if this goes bad.

Romurik – you did nothing wrong. It was my order, and contact was inevitable – clearly they have chosen to make it. Your findings are going through the proper channels I presume?

The Greater Intellect, INCC and INI are all analysing the data as we speak.

Good. Please feel free to watch what happens.

Then Captain Van E'streth reduced the enhancements and returned to "normal speed", head buzzing slightly.

"Eighteen seconds to minimum engagement distance," reported his XO.

Captain Van E'streth nodded grimly.

"Prepare for combat."

***

The Emperor looked on as Aryn and Raul traded options. There was no doubt the situation in S'vreth was about to go hostile. The concern now was to what degree, and whether it would escalate into a full blown war.

If so – against such numbers – it was perfectly clear the Empire had already lost. The next few minutes would decide the fate of an entire civilisation, and they watched the tactical display above the table tensely.

The recommendation had been to await engagement until it became hostile, in case it was a peaceful overture. If it went hostile, then gauge a response, with flight being the last option.

The unknown contacts – everyone deliberately resisted calling them "the enemy" – advanced on the *Delaror* at high speed. Then they closed on its position.

The *Delaror*'s contact disappeared, along with all the other contacts in the system. The tactical threw up faint, ghostly markers showing their last known positions.

"Did we lose them?" asked Aryn.

Raul looked agitated. "We don't know yet. We lost the *Delaror's* tactical feed and telemetry. There was no indication of weapons fire or aggression. We simply lost their signal."

"It could be they've interrupted the qNet again. This is an extension of their perimeter after all."

"Nothing from the FTL relay," replied Raul, his voice betraying his concern. An FTL communication satellite had been despatched one light second away as a backup for the eventuality of the qNet being blocked. It meant all communication was delayed by nearly four seconds as the data feed ploughed its way through various relay stations before being channelled into the qNet, but it meant a secure and reliable line could be used.

"The relay is still operational – but it stopped relaying the *Delaror's* feed at the same time as we lost the *Delaror's* transmission – taking FTL lag into account."

"Have they been destroyed?" asked the Emperor quietly.

Raul's mouth set into a grim line. "Impossible to say, Your Majesty."

"Can we get any sensor readings from the FTL relay?" asked Aryn.

"It's for communication only," replied Raul.

"Is it a standard naval unit – from Logistics?"

Raul gave him a puzzled look and checked the deployment records. "Yes."

"Can you give me the asset ID please?"

Raul complied, and looked at Aryn with a sternly inquisitive expression.

"One moment," replied Aryn. "I want to be sure

before I say anything."

A few moments later, the tactical flickered – some of the contacts jumped position and glowed back into life.

"I can't track all of the contacts through the satellite, but I can tag the *Delaror* and anything near it. She's still visible if not responding."

A very low quality video feed appeared by the *Delaror's* marker, showing the vessel just visible as a bright smear in the sunlight being reflected from its hull.

"She's still in one piece at least," Aryn observed. "Otherwise that would be a glowing cloud of debris."

"Admiral Cole, you and I need another long chat after this," said Raul.

"Yes, Fleet," replied Aryn disarmingly.

They watched the erratic display of jumping contacts as they flickered on and off at random around the *Delaror*, as the satellite struggled to track anything for more than a few seconds. It was clear that the entire group which had surged out toward the *Delaror* was now slowly returning to their original formation – and taking the *Delaror* with it.

"No signs of fighting," reported Aryn. "No debris, no signs of recent energy discharges. I can't really get further detail with the equipment we can fit into the design. It has to be crude to evade detection."

"They've been captured without a fight?" queried the Emperor.

"I don't believe that, Your Majesty," replied Raul somewhat forcefully. Then he remembered his position. "Apologies, Your Majesty."

The Emperor waved a hand dismissively. "None needed. Do not presume such again."

Raul dipped his head, gracefully accepting the chastisement.

"Perhaps negotiations are under way?" suggested Aryn. "This could be a contact protocol."

They watched in silence, balancing on a knife edge of indecision. One way was peace, the other a conflict that would plunge them into the abyss. The situation was not providing any clues as to which way the dice would fall.

The contacts eventually merged with the spherical perimeter. The *Delaror* also now took up a position within it, with nearby contacts moving to maintain an equidistant proximity – an effect which would ripple out across the sphere over the next few hours.

"Should we consider the *Delaror* lost?" asked Aryn quietly.

"Not while it remains intact. The crew could all still be alive," replied Raul.

"This is hardly an act of war," said the Emperor. "However we cannot let this apparent abduction of an Imperial Naval vessel pass by. Outreach will attempt engaging in contact protocols... we may yet get a peaceful response." By his tone of voice, he did not sound convinced.

The Emperor turned to Aryn. "Could you extricate the *Delaror*?"

Aryn shook his head. "Your Majesty, we could lose communication with every single vessel we send in precisely the same way we just lost the *Delaror*. We may need all the resources we can get."

"Can you establish contact?"

"We will try, Your Majesty."

"Is the qNet cauterisation plan in effect?"

"Shortly to be completed and on your orders before it could be applied, Your Majesty."

"Admiral Benthar, I will presume to issue the order to begin gathering the fleet without the Senate's approval. Logistics at your discretion, of course."

"Your Majesty," he acknowledged.

"I will return yet again to the Senate. Keep my office informed of all the relevant details – no matter how small." He then rose, as did Aryn and Raul, and with a brief nod walked behind his chair to leave the sim.

"How many surprises do you have up your sleeves Aryn?" asked Raul, wonderingly.

Aryn merely smiled. "Why, Fleet, I *have* no sleeves..."

Brynn – I have another assignment for you.

Should I ask if I'll enjoy this one?

No. We've lost contact with one of our ships in the S'vreth system – the INDV Delaror. *We need to re-establish communication without the qNet being involved.*

Ok, old, old school you mean?

By whatever means suitable – just establish contact. Treat the entire volume as hostile, occupied by unknowns. Do not engage, or allow to be engaged. Evade at all times.

This is sounding less and less enjoyable by the minute.

Relevant data is attached. Treat the qNet as out of bounds after this call, no further communication with INI or regarding your mission until after you return from. Clear?

Clear – puzzling, but clear.

Brynn had the *Betsy's Pride* underway minutes later. The volume of space around S'vreth that Admiral Cole's data marked as a no-go zone was – frankly – immense, and half again as large when the recommended safe zone was taken into account.

He'd considered jumping directly in, aiming an FTL beam at the *Delaror* to see if they could make contact, and then jumping back out at the first sign of trouble.

Too noisy, he decided, ruling it out. Although that type of hit and fade was now becoming standard Naval practice thanks to WOD drives, they were facing something unknown which could apparently block wormhole formation. Detecting wormholes was therefore a logical capability.

Softly, softly then. He ordered the helm to g-drive them out of their current system and into deep space, then drive into the void some ten AU's away from S'vreth. They did a full passive scan of the system using their own seeded Observers, and the *Betsy's* nav-com folded after four million contacts.

Brynn was intrigued. As Venton chirruped and complained whilst he re-initialised the nav-com, he tried to figure out how he could attempt contact with the *Delaror* without being detected by this gargantuan fleet. There were no broadcasts or emissions coming from it, other than energy signatures showing drive systems. Power and life support were all still active.

He began a slow crawl approach toward S'ren by g-drive, barely enough to make a ripple in the local gravitational field, and hopefully not enough to be detectable.

There was a rap on his cabin door.

"Come in," he said without bothering to check who it was. He could guess.

Horstan stepped into the room before the door was

fully open.

"Captain. Is this how it goes on this ship?" she demanded.

He sighed. "Goes what?"

"Command decisions and orders made without consulting the XO."

"Ah, that."

"If an XO is superfluous to this rig I can make port at the next convenient location and transfer to a more useful posting."

"Gods you're bolshie for an XO that still squeaks if they turn too quickly! How many days service have you logged as Executive Officer?" he asked, deliberately ruffling her feathers. He already knew her service and personal records off by heart.

She visibly bristled. "That's irrelevant, and you know it. If that was an issue you should have brought it up on the bridge."

Brynn raised his eyebrows.

"Command protocol requires the XO to be involved in or aware of all mission briefings," she said stiffly.

"That it does, XO. Ok – sit down," he gestured to his couch. "Please," he added when she hesitated.

She threw a suspicious look at him, but moved past to take a seat.

"Drink?"

She arched an eyebrow.

"Non-alcoholic," he added. "I'm off the stuff at the moment."

She gave him an appraising glance. *He does look rough,* she thought. His eyes were dark and bruised looking, cheeks gaunt. His every move looked as though it pained him. She suppressed a smirk. Keri's absence was *definitely* being felt it seemed.

"We've been ordered to S'vreth. Are you aware of the current situation there?"

She pursed her lips. "Partly, I would think. The system is in quarantine after some invasionary force occupied it again after the Velari left. It's been all over the media. Naval intel is sketchy and has dried up of late. No doubt it's some cover up."

"It's because there *is* nothing new to report," he lied smoothly. "The qNet is down in system, and nothing has gotten in, or out. That's why we're here. To gather intel."

She considered this, looking for subterfuge but finding none.

"We can't be the first to investigate," she thought aloud. "Too much time has elapsed. There must have been some attempt at an insertion into S'vreth space already."

He nodded. *Keri is right – Horstan is smart.* "The *Delaror* came in-system eight hours ago. After a recon Intellect made a pass into the perimeter they were... approached, by the perimeter force. No weapons exchange. Then the *Delaror* dropped off the grid. It's believed to now be a part of the perimeter."

"How is that possible?" she exclaimed.

He shrugged. "That's what we are here to determine, by re-establishing contact with the *Delaror.*"

She frowned as she considered the options. "The most reliable way without risking detection or alerting the enemy is to make physical contact..."

Brynn was impressed. "I'm looking for volunteers..."

Her eyes shone, but a worried frown came over her

face.

"It'll be dangerous," said Brynn for her. "We have some of the best kit available to INI. Normally I'd say this would be a walk in the park, but these guys are above and beyond anything we've encountered so far."

She scowled briefly. "Are you trying to get rid of me already?"

He looked directly into her eyes. "I'd have set you off at a port of your choice, by preference."

She considered this, obviously deciding how much trust she could afford to put in her new Captain.

"Very well. I'll volunteer. I want full access to the *Delaror's* schematics, a full inventory of the *Betsy* and Venton."

"Venton? No way. If he were to be captured..."

"Very well, Captain. Then I'll want someone with a thorough knowledge of Naval vessel design, and preferably offensive capabilities."

He thought for a moment. "Take Andersten. He's got the most combat experience, and he's fairly well tooled up."

"Sir."

He admired her courage. There was no way of knowing yet if this was going to be risky, but there was no saying it would be easy either.

"Get prepped and be ready at a moment's notice XO. Dismissed."

Horstan stood outside the Captains door for a moment after it slid shut. Only the very expensive integrations her father had recently bought her were stopping her from shaking, as a mixture of adrenaline and fear coursed through her veins. *What have I just volunteered for?* she asked herself. *And just to earn his trust? Am I mad?*

She closed her eyes, took a grip and then marched off to find Andersten.

Brynn watched her through an Observer in the walkway. He recognised the mixture of fear and excitement evident on her face; he'd seen it before many times when he was younger. Usually in the mirror.

"Ready to go?" Brynn asked over the *Betsy's* l-net.

Horstan and Andersten were both just finishing off a double-check of their suits. Both were standard Naval issue black spacers; millimetre thick vacuum-armour which bonded to the skin. He had to concentrate on not staring at Horstan's lithe figure through the Observers even though no one would be able to see him staring.

Andersten was a muscled lump in his suit. Brynn *did* spot Horstan's gaze lingering on his torso a little too often to be merely casual. He smiled – then suppressed his voyeurism. There was work to do.

"Almost, Captain," Horstan replied. Andersten moved across to the space-black two-man floating nearby and hefted a large container onto the rear mount. He clamped it in place and nodded.

"Ready."

"Ok, we're in position… aligned with the *Delaror* and four times as far away from the perimeter as they were when they were engaged. Hopefully that buys us enough time if they try something. It means you have quite a trek though."

"Let's hope we don't have to make a fast exit," replied Andersten gruffly. "We'll still be here next week."

"Surprisingly I *had* thought of that Andersten," Brynn replied tersely. "Sadly a naval ship of the line and its crew have more value than your gnarly ass."

"Or mine," stated Horstan.

Brynn chose not to comment further. She knew the risks, as did Andersten. If the 'enemy' made any advance, the *Betsy* might well be forced to exit the system – with or without them.

They both mounted the two-man – a long fuselage with two pillion seats, almost like an air-bike but far faster – unarmed, though heavily shielded.

"No ship-to-ship comm's outside," Horstan confirmed, more for Andersten's benefit than anything else. "We'll be back soon."

Their collars extruded black masks over their heads, completely concealing their faces. Now they looked more like animated, black silk covered mannequins than space marines.

The two-man slid forward and out of the docking bay field, disappearing from the light of the bay entrance almost instantly. Brynn closed the bay and dropped the visual feed in favour of the tactical.

They became a small dot creeping away from the *Betsy*, heading for the *Delaror* which was their nearest contact on the enemy perimeter – almost six hundred thousand kilometres away.

They had a long ride ahead of them, and that meant the *Betsy* and her crew had an equally long wait.

Chapter Fifteen

That face, that horrible, hated, featureless face – the thing which entered its mind, the pain and horror it left behind. It would return soon, he knew. It always did. It wanted answers. Answers to questions he did not understand. Could not answer. He *would* answer – he would now. He would answer anything it asked, but only if he knew. He could not answer if he did not know. Could he?

The grating sound began again; the sound of greel grubs rubbing against bone as they burrowed through soft flesh, tunnelling their way along blood vessels toward the rich organs they sought to lay their eggs in. He screamed in fear and pain.

Answer! I will answer! Ask me, ask me!

But you do not know do you? asked the voice of metal. *Every time I ask you tell me you do not. I must believe you, after you have endured so much. So much more than your brethren.* The face, the hated face swam into his blurry vision, the silver flesh and the flickering lights darting within – like fish in a mercury sea.

Will tell! Ask! Ask!

Very well. Where do the Velari originate from Ambassador? Where is your true *homeworld?*

I do not know!

You do, Ambassador, you must. It is in your racial m-gram, passed down across the generations by your plasma genome coding whilst a fledgling. It is there somewhere, *you just have to look.*

He was a young Velari again, having not long

213

emerged from his shell. Memories were fresh, senses vivid, new and overpowering. He recalled being fed by his mother-bird. The growing awareness after each feed, as his body absorbed the chemically encoded memories delivered with the regurgitated food. He knew then that he *must* know what the demon wanted – but the memory was intangible, elusive, evading his every attempt to grasp it, before he ever managed to reach out to it.

The grating noises stopped. He wailed, knowing the slow painful death which now lay before him once the greel eggs started absorbing his organs.

Something deep inside his mind finally gave way – nothing harmful, nothing physical or even neurological – but something instilled at birth, a mental programming which acted as a defence, a safeguard.

Ah, at last, said the hated voice.

I have the location of the Velari birth-world, said Admiral Coles advisor.

Finally. I don't want to know how you got it. Is the Ambassador alive?

Of course. I would do him no lasting harm. He will fully recover with no memory of what has transpired.

What about the rest of them?

Some did not fare well from the process.

Is that permanent?

They will recover, as will the Ambassador.

Better than I hoped for at least.

Velari pheromone programming is very deep; it embeds itself within their psychological makeup making it very hard to access. Hence the need for such primitive, emotive brute

214

force techniques which ordinarily I would frown upon.

Aryn paused for a moment. *Remind me to never upset you, won't you?*

No need, Admiral. This Velari Roost ancestry originated in the northern hemisphere of the Cluster, a world called Anvidel.I believe this is the point of origin for numerous Roost migrations which have spread across the Cluster over the past five or six millennia.

So, from the fragments you've gathered from these interrogations, we know the Velari did not originate from this galactic quadrant, and in fact came from the other side of the galaxy – clearly fleeing something.

And for so much of their history it became a way of life, forcing migratory behaviour into their very being.

Yet they have no records of any of this, Aryn noted. *Nothing on any archives we have access to at least.*

And yet they happen to migrate just before their latest home system is invaded by unknowns, observed the advisor.

They must have known they were coming – it's just too much to believe it to be mere coincidence. Whoever these unknowns are, the Velari have been fleeing their clutches since time immemorial. And that means they must know who they are, perhaps even where they came from.

None of the subjects have any information regarding them.

They may not know. It would be buried so deep in their past it would be a mere myth of a legend. But how could they know they were coming? Someone in their echelons definitely knows.

Someone beyond our reach I fear. It may be that the Velari are being hunted?

Aryn went cold. *That would mean they're now hot on the trail. Which means they'll follow the Velari to their next roost system. Canthe.*

Heavily populated and right on the Imperial border, said the advisor gravely. *That* would *have to be considered a full on declaration of war against the Empire. A war you cannot win.*

Aryn sighed privately. He was hearing that far too often of late. *I'll have to inform the Emperor – again. Keep following this lead. We need to know who these guys are, why the Velari are running from them, and how they found out they were coming. I'm afraid we're not done with the assistance of our Velari guests.*

My pleasure, Admiral.

***

Kerugar was not in a good mood. Her vestigial tail was throbbing – an atypical symptom of Reptarian pregnancy, something which did not bode well for the latter stages. It was common for those Reptars who experienced tail-throb to go on to suffer Dawn and Dusk – the uncontrollable nausea and vomiting every sunrise and sunset for weeks on end. It was a weakness she was not prepared to tolerate. The natural Reptarian body rhythms ensured that being away from their homeworld would not prevent the inevitable. Their biological clock was strongly tied to the sunrise and sunset of the equatorial desert regions they had evolved from countless millennia ago.

She had also just watched Horstan's cheerful v-mail asking how she was, letting her know she was already getting up Brynn's nose and was about to embark on her first mission under his command.

On top of that – unexpected and she was sure totally unheard of – she was convinced she was suffering pheromone withdrawal from Brynn.

When Reptars mate, they mate for life, and not only by conscious choice. They also form a chemical decency on their partner's natural pheromones in an almost ordained form of genetic selection. Although Reptars consciously chose mates with whom they felt they had an attraction, in truth such was driven in large part by their pheromones. This steered them into selective breeding rather than the 'strongest wins breeding rights' path Mother Nature typically preferred. Inbreeding never took place; similar pheromones did not result in attraction between siblings and relatives – often quite the opposite. Overall, this driven pre-programmed selection of possible mates meant that the reproduction and evolution of the Reptar race had been slower and longer than many other sentient species. However, it had resulted in a super strong, resilient and robust race which had a deep seated value in self-respect as a whole society.

Fidelity was also paramount. It was a natural consequence of the pheromone dependency. Once mated, a couple became bonded to each other at a chemical level. Separation led to withdrawal, which Reptars referred to as 'pining'. Although not harmful in most cases, it led to weeks, if not months, of discomfort until reunited –which would usually result in a frenzied and highly energetic reaffirmation of their relationship.

No Reptar had ever experienced pining from being separated from a human. There were very few mated Reptarian and human couples, but it wasn't unheard of. Kerugar had nearly passed out when she first met Brynn – his smell! It was beyond anything she had ever encountered. She had refused to go near him for weeks – partly in shame at her foolish weakness, but mostly because she dared not subject herself to such a beautiful torture. They could never be together, she knew. She found him ugly, even for a human. *What possible interest would he have in a Reptar?*

She found out soon enough. In turn, he had been bowled over by her and had spent the intervening weeks learning everything he could about Reptar culture and their ways, trying to figure out how to make a suitable approach.

Eventually he had stalked her in the stations mess room one day, cornering her. With no escape available short of combat against this ridiculously aromatic human, she found herself forced to remain still while he just stood in front of her, calmly, and let their pheromones do the work.

And now – years later – here I am suffering withdrawal from a human. The shame!

Her door sensor pinged, and she snapped out of her reverie.

"Yes?"

"Delivery, secured. I have to get DNA to release it."

She frowned and checked the courier's credentials using her now limited naval qNet access before opening the door.

The courier threw a fake 'paid-to-smile' smile at her, and then scanned her forearm with a small reader.

"All yours," he said, handing her a small parcel.

"Thank you," she replied, but the man was already walking off to his next delivery.

She closed the door and took the package into her

living room, stripping the seal from the packet and tipping a single object out onto her palm.

It was a box shape, glossy black and smooth. Its edges and corners were perfectly rounded. It felt heavy for its size, but sat comfortably in her palm. There were no markings, and nothing else in the packet. She checked the sender details – it was some mailing company, but none she recognised. She tapped her naval channel again and ran a search across the details, but it just confirmed the sender was a mass mail service, handling billions of packages. She accessed their service and ran the package ID to trace it – nothing registered on their system.

She frowned again. It wasn't worth pursuing it further with the mail company . She would just get lost in bureaucracy within seconds of making an enquiry.

Obviously someone wanted anonymity, easily done if you knew the right hacker. *Could it be a bomb, or other malicious device?*

She had an Observer in her chest from the *Betsy* – she would be able to run it through the box and investigate its contents without worry. She left the box on the table and went into her bedroom to empty the chest onto the bed. A huge waft of Brynn's stale pheromones engulfed her, making her slightly dizzy for a moment. She cursed his name, her condition, and her ancestry. She had accidentally packed one of his tunics. She tossed it into the laundry chute. After finding the Observer in its chrome case, she returned to the living room to run an analysis on the box.

The box was gone. Standing beside the coffee table and staring out of the panoramic window was a two-meter high simulacrum of a Reptar in ebony black. It turned to face her.

"Nice view," it said.

She sighed. "Thank you, father. What do you want now?"

***

The Imperial Press Office auditorium was packed to capacity, despite an age where virtual presence was the easiest way to attend any gathering. It seemed the people's right to freedom of information was most keen to get it first-hand.

Praetor Castallus checked the board for virtual attendees in his e-vision. Two thousand and fifty seven, plus the two hundred in the room. He sighed. Every star systems press office in the Empire represented in one place, and then some. He would have to exert an iron will to avoid this becoming a protracted and most cumbersome news conference.

Rebecca Reed of the Daily Quordant sat calmly in the mid-section of the area reserved for physical seats. Directly above her was the "unreal floor" as it had been nick-named. A virtual deck where those who were net'ing in from afar – or even next door – could appear in a virtual seat as a holovise in order to have a visual attendance, and also to ask the speaker questions 'in person'. The end result was a large group of journalists that ended up coming and going like jungle fireflies as their pay-per-second seats elapsed. Holo-seats were *expensive*, a deliberate act to keep the numbers down, otherwise the entire Press Corps would be there by holovise. Even with modern space-travel being as mundane as it was these days, physical presence was still a major inconvenience for many across an empire of thirty-thousand star systems.

This was Rebecca's first major conference of note, certainly her first Imperial conference. It had taken a considerable amount of cajoling and pleading with her editor to be granted this privilege - given the import behind it - and she wasn't about to let it get away from her. Despite the self-imposed pressure, she was calm and composed. She had chosen to attend in person, and had calmly filed into the mid-section seats to avoid the clamouring hordes which invariably formed in the front and rear sections as they desperately vied with each other to gain the speakers attention. She looked around and studied the faces of those present – all eager and bright-eyed, all desperately hoping that war was about to break out and give them the journalistic opportunity to become 'famous' at last. She shook her head sadly. That was not what it was about, in her opinion.

"Ladies and gentlemen of the Imperial Press," said Praetor Castallus over the conference network, "honoured guests from outside the Empire, I bid you welcome." He looked around with suitable gravitas and surveyed the audience before him.

"His Imperial Majesty, Ran Sulran the Fourth has instructed the Imperial Office of External Affairs to hold this press conference with regards to the current situation in S'vreth – formerly the Velari Home-system.

"Approximately thirty-two hours ago – on Yadras the fourth, four-hundred and thirty-seven hours Imperial Standard Time – we lost contact with the

Outreach Observer network in effect around S'ren, formerly the Velari Roostworld. Although no cause can be identified, it is believed to be a natural phenomenon which has affected the space-time medium the Observer network exists within.

"As a purely precautionary measure, His Majesty's Imperial Navy has established a cordon around S'vreth to gather more information, in order that the cause can be studied and identified."

Praetor Castallus looked around and steeled himself for what was about to happen.

"You may now take the floor," he said to the audience at large. Behind him the backlighting changed from blue to green, showing the conference was open to questions. There were already several hundred queued questions flashing away in his e-vision – as to be expected. As per the standard protocol to be as fair as possible, he chose one at random.

"Kolus Borr of the Manaen Pulse," Castallus said.

A large, heavy-set man stood from within the physical seats section – his round face almost obscured by thick, black facial hair.

"Praetor, is it true that there is a large hostile force occupying S'vreth?" he rumbled.

Castallus resisted the urge to grind his mandibles together. *Where* do *they get their information from?* he wondered, irritated that this had come up so soon in the conference.

"There are no hostile forces I am aware of at this time, nor is S'ren under any occupation other than by the S'ren-ee now that the Velari have migrated."

"But what of the loss of the Outreach Observer

network that was monitoring the Velari? Isn't that a hostile act?"

"As the Velari are no longer resident in S'vreth, the network is now redundant. Its loss is a moot point." *Always tell the truth*, the Emperor had once told him – many decades ago. *But only as much as necessary.*

"In all recorded history within the Empire," said Kolus, clearly feeling that he had Castallus in a corner, "the qNet has *never* been down. Other than the AMB attack on Meelereen, there has never been anything which could block or corrupt the network itself. Isn't it true Praetor, that the network has been cut off by an invading force?"

Castallus stared at Kolus. "It is not available," he said.

"But why?"

"Kolus Borr, I refer you to my opening address," said Castallus, his voice taking on an edge.

Kolus Borr looked as if he were about to ask another question – but wisely decided he'd pushed his point as much as he could for now, and sat down with a nod.

"Rebecca Reed of the Daily Quordant."

Hiding her sudden joy at being selected, Rebecca stood and demurely smoothed down her bright yellow skin-cladding, full aware of the effect on her neighbouring colleagues.

"Praetor, can you tell us if the situation in the Velari System is being considered an act of war?" Rebecca asked.

Castallus' antennae rubbed together. "No, it is not."

"Do we know why such a hostile act had been taken against the Empire?"

"At this time there is no reason to believe the 'act' *is* hostile, nor an *act* of any kind. May I also remind you that the Velari System – indeed, the *S'vreth* System – was not formerly part of the Empire, and as such events in that system are of no direct concern to the Empire itself."

"Good timing though," Rebecca noted. "That this occurred just after the Velari left I mean. Almost as if the hostiles were waiting..."

"That I cannot comment on, given the lack of information at this time."

"How so? Surely INI is all over this?"

"It is examining the system. However gathering and analysing the data takes time, even with the technology available today."

"Given that the Velari are petitioning to join the Empire, does the Emperor consider this might be a hostile move against the Empire itself?"

"The Empire has no such concerns regarding the Velari petition."

"Could this be some form of attack by the Velari against the Empire?"

Castallus directed a glare at the journalist. He had allowed her to overreach her quota of questions because each lead to another 'must answer' question, and he was fully aware this was the deliberate intent. "Do you know the Velari at all? No, it is not. Outreach was monitoring the system as part of the petition process. Any covert or overt actions by the Velari in the past two years would have been noticed. There were none."

"What about the S'renee?"

Castallus sighed.

"As you must be aware, they are peaceful, non-space

faring creatures who have expressed a desire to be left out of the Empire. We would not be observing them on such a scale if not for the Velari. I'm sure they are rejoicing that the Velari have finally left and their world is their own once again. Outreach has had a long and on-going diplomatic mandate to encourage the Velari to migrate to a suitable uninhabited world for over two years given their occupation was, shall we say, without consideration of the locals. The S'renee – even if they *were* capable of waging war – would be glad of our help rather than attempting such a folly."

"The relocation options didn't turn out so well though, did they?" asked someone wryly.

Castallus glared at them and revoked their speaking privileges for the entire conference for speaking out of turn. However, for the benefit of the audience he chose to answer honestly.

"No, they did not."

"Could this be the Canthen making an offensive against the Velari?" asked Rebecca.

"That is equally as absurd. No, the entire Canthen force is at their border awaiting the Velari. I take this opportunity to yet again urge all our citizens, especially those ferrying Velari migration flocks, to please avoid Canthen space at all costs!"

"Could the Canthen be making an offensive against the Empire?"

Castallus sighed again. Everyone was champing after war and bloodshed to give the masses something to chew on.

"No. Our relations with the Canthen have been most cordial, and their petition was due to be reviewed favourably this quarter."

"So who are these guys? And what do they want?"

Castallus clasped the podium with all four of his upper limbs in a vice-like grip.

"At this time, there is no reason to believe there is anyone or anything behind this event. Current speculation is that this is purely a *natural* phenomenon. However, Outreach is advising that all traffic should avoid the Velari System – now officially under its original ownership as the S'vreth System. Until the nature of the situation can be determined – the volume around S'vreth is officially out of bounds for a radius of five light-years and to be considered highly dangerous to all space-faring traffic."

Rebecca finally sat down with a graceful nod to Castallus. She had achieved what few ever could - she had researched the topic and led the Speaker through every question that he knew must be addressed by the conference. Her name - and that of her news channel - would appear on every network throughout the Empire as her questions were broadcast. That was enough fame for her.

"Ryv Neer of the Phatral Observer."

A small, orange and green skinned Learomorph stood up almost timidly. "What about the Colesworth refinery? Is anyone evacuating their staff?

"Colesworth Enterprises have been notified. The Sulranian Imperial Navy have offered their services for any evacuation if Colesworth deem it necessary.

"Johan Pennet of the Washmore Times."

"What about the *Drastic Response* incident?"

"What of it?"

"Surely the loss of one of their main line vessels due to an 'accidental ramming' by an Outreach Diplomatic vessel would be sufficient grounds for a diplomatic incident with the Velari."

"Ordinarily, yes. However even the Velari Ambassador involved has assured us that no such 'incident' exists. They have most graciously accepted the formal apology from Outreach, and an assurance from the Emperor himself that measures are being put in place to ensure no such accident will be allowed to occur in the future."

"And if they choose to view that as a ruse in order to justify an attack on the Empire?"

"This is getting old, Mr. Pennet. The Velari are *not* warmongers, and are not covertly mounting an offensive, and certainly have never demonstrated an ability to produce technology capable of the effects we are seeing in S'vreth."

Castallus took advantage of the pause created by his mild rebuke to take stock of the crowded hall and the virtual journalists. Despite several hundred flashing questions, a quick scan showed none of them had any direct relevance to the conference agenda, other than probing or hinting at war with the Velari, the Canthe, or the S'renee.

"Ladies and gentlemen, thank you for your interest. Further announcements will be made as and when information becomes available. "

With a quick nod, he left to the usual tumultuous roar of several hundred people all ignoring the Press Office protocol and trying to ask their questions at the same time, by shouting over everyone else.

Chapter Sixteen

Keragar Antool Rastak sat down on Kerugar's couch – his huge frame barely making an impression in the gel-form. His simulacra weighed no more than the black box Kerugar had received, despite having morphed into the form of a large Reptar.

"Is it not enough to merely visit my daughter-with-child?" he said, amiably.

"No. And why this – " she waved disgustedly at the black form before her, " – toy?" Then she realised what he had just said. "How did you know?" she asked in a small voice.

"I think this form suits me," he said, ignoring her last question. "If all those wittering techs could prove one of these could sustain me full-time without the constant need to recharge every hour..."

"How did you *know,* father?"

He shrugged. "The qNet is a marvellous thing. I hear you have left your ship, and partner. I enquire. Your routine naval debark scan reveals your condition."

Kerugar scowled, and hissed in disgust. She should have guessed.

"Why have you left the human? Is it not shame enough you fruitlessly mate with an alien, that you demean yourself as a surrogate and then abandon your ill-chosen life-partner?" His words seemed scathing, but his tone was entirely nonchalant.

"I do with my life as *I* see fit, no other," she growled.

Her father shrugged again. "Fair enough. I will tell your mother." He leaned forward. "Now, you must come home child."

She bristled. "I will not!"

He shook his head sadly. "You must... there is no choice. I would not ask you this if there were any other way."

She hesitated slightly. This was not the usual baiting banter she expected from him.

"Antool, you know I won't."

"I know you would not by choice, but you will. You must. You are pregnant."

"I know that!"

"With two children."

She gasped. "What?"

"From different eggs. One of them is *yours*."

Her mouth worked, but no sound came out. What he said made no sense.

"You are carrying *two* embryo's Kerugar. One is human – from the surrogate egg you selected, a reasonable choice by the way, considering. But the other is both human *and* Reptar. Your own Reptarian egg, fertilised by human sperm. The very first of its kind."

Her head spun, and she felt decidedly odd. The last thing she remembered was Antool rising up from the couch and reaching out to catch her as she fell.

***

"Here she is," said Horstan.

"Hmm?"

"Wake up, we're approaching the *Delaror*."

Andersten shifted his weight carefully on the rear pillion, to avoid the need for unnecessary manoeuvring.

The bike was too small for delta-p compensators, so every movement had to be considered carefully and compensated for.

He craned past Horstan to see for himself. Up ahead, the *Delaror*'s long hull could be seen blotting out the stars, observation windows glowing softly from within.

"Lights are still on," he remarked. "Someone's home then."

"We hope," replied Horstan quietly. "I can see the bridge portals from here. I'll tag a laser mike to them, one second..."

She shared the pickup from the laser with Andersten through their tiny private local network.

Apart from the quiet hum of the ship running, there was no other sound.

"No voices, no movement," noted Horstan.

"No breathing either," commented Andersten. "Even people trying to be silent would still make plenty of noise just by breathing – easy for a laser to pick up."

"They may be away from the bridge," she replied – but her voice lacked conviction.

Andersten kept his thoughts to himself.

They tagged several more portals at random, including the mess and the medical bays, then engineering by targeting the hull. They got nothing other than the hum of powered systems.

"Have you tried the ship?" asked Andersten.

"There's no net, and I daren't try the general qNet."

"Hmm."

"We have to go in," she said.

"I knew you were going to say that," grumbled Andersten. "We can most likely breach one of the aft logistics hatches, if we can get past the shields."

Horstan was puzzled. They had the *Delaror's* primary access codes within Admiral Cole's orders. "Why couldn't we?"

"First rule of sequestration," he said. "If you take a system over – change it. The codes will probably all be different now, as well as the shield configurations."

"Let's see," she said. She harmonised the two-man's shield to that of the *Delaror*, and brought them up to the very edge of the huge vessels invisible, but very solid shield boundary. If this didn't work, the resulting clash of energy would be highly visible for thousands of kilometres in almost every direction.

She paused.

"Let's do it," said Andersten encouragingly.

She edged the two-man forward, slowly. Nothing happened; they slipped unnoticed through the *Delaror's* shield. Horstan relaxed, hurdle one jumped.

"Lucky," said Andersten, his voice slightly bemused.

They headed for the logistics hatch at the rear port side, then she coded the bike to maintain proximity and orientation to the huge wall of di-steel looming all about them. Then they both slipped extra gloves and slippers on over their skin-tight suits.

"Ready?" asked Andersten. He had clearly picked up on Horstan's lack of experience in the field – but instead of jibing her as she'd expected, he seemed to be doing his best to be helpful without seeming to be. She *really* appreciated that right now.

"Ready." With her heart in her throat, she pushed free of the bike and floated slowly toward the hatch, strongly resisting the urge to fire up the mini-drive on her pack.

This was only her second extra-vehicular activity. Her first had been a trial, and she had gotten through on sheer adrenalin generated by fear. It was the lack of control which scared her the most – of being unable to change direction, or stop, or speed up on her own. Casting herself into fate by a single choice made moments ago that could have inevitable and unstoppable consequences. Jump too fast and the impact would hurt, or cripple you. Too slow and the horror of the EVA would go on, and on, and on. Misjudge the aim, and you could be EVA for far longer than you would live. It was a black joke in naval training, that one slip up could last 'for-eva'.

Her drive pack would of course save the day – and ordinarily was the only way to undergo an EVA - but here the instant they used them, their position would flare out like a beacon. Their need for stealth demanded the packs remain emergency use only.

They both drifted the several metres from the bike to the hatch for over a minute before gently landing against the hull. The gloves and slippers they wore adhered to the surface with incredibly strong micro-magnetic fields, allowing them to clamber awkwardly across hull and to the hatch itself. Horstan gave a quiet sigh of relief when they finally got there.

Andersten checked the hatch panel display manually, given the lack of an l-net, then gestured for her to stand back. He hooked his hand into a claw, and a tiny actinic point of light appeared in the space between his fingertips and palm. Highly focused energy from his combat integrations sliced into the reinforced metal, despite it being hardened to attack damage. Fortunately

Andersten had top grade enhancements, and knew the weak spots to exploit. He set to work cutting a metre-wide hole into the hatch itself.

The process seemed to take forever, tiny meteors of shining hot metal spat out into the void, cooling and disappearing almost immediately. There was no smoke – the vaporised metallic gases expanded so quickly in the vacuum of space that they couldn't build up enough to form anything visible.

Then there was a flash of vapour streaming from the cut, as atmosphere from inside the hatch escaped out. Andersten arched clear of the venting gas to avoid being pushed away from the hull.

"I hope *they* didn't notice that," Horstan said. The sudden drop in pressure would have been instantly reported by the hatch sensors.

"No other way in, sadly," stated Andersten. "The breach shielding should be up, but we may yet have to cut through the inner hatch as well…"

He positioned himself kneeling across the section he had cut, then placed both palms onto the panel and looked at Horstan.

She nodded and moved over behind him, adhering her gloves to the slip-ons over his feet, doubly securing him in place. With a heave of his huge shoulders, he lifted the section of hatch free, then held it out at arm's length for ten seconds to make sure he'd stayed its momentum. Satisfied, he instructed his gloves to release their grip and gently let go.

The panel stayed where he left it, floating motionless in space.

"Masterfully done," said Horstan, impressed.

"It's about time they started paying me the big bucks," said Andersten wryly.

"I'll make a note of that in my report," she replied.

He chuckled. "After you." He gestured to the hole he had made.

"Thanks," she said. "I think."

Brynn had paced the entire length of the *Betsy's* corridor runs about sixty times; the *Betsy* herself was getting tired of watching him. Brynn was exceptionally level headed in panic situations – but did not fare well when there was nothing to do but wait. The *Betsy* had tried several attempts at striking up a distracting conversation, but each had dried up fairly quickly so she decided to leave him to it.

Anything? he demanded for the twelfth time.

No, Captain. He could tap into the sensor feeds as easily as the *Betsy* could, yet still he insisted on asking her just in case.

He fumed quietly and continued his march around the ship. The rest of the crew knew to leave him well alone, otherwise various unpleasant duties which could easily be left for later would suddenly become of paramount importance to the smooth running of the *Betsy*.

Suddenly he skidded to a halt. The *Betsy* spoke at the same time.

Captain, they are on the way back.

Brynn was standing and waiting calmly as the two-man settled onto the hangar deck. Now he knew his crew had returned safely from this oddball mission he had relaxed considerably. It was impossible to see Horstan or Andersten's features behind their masks – and both had replied tersely to their hail, leaving their implants to authenticate them back onto the *Betsy*.

Both riders dismounted, and their helmets rippled down from their heads back into their suits – revealing haggard and worried faces.

"Crew, dismissed. Back to your duties," said Brynn as soon as he saw their eyes. He looked sternly at the small crowd. They took one look at his face and silently obeyed, waving and nodding to Horstan and Andersten as they left.

Brynn locked the hangar, then locked out all the Observers – relaying his senses to the *Betsy* so she could still observe via their privately bonded channel.

Andersten walked around to the back of the two-man and opened something in the aft compartment. He stepped away, staring vacantly at its contents.

Brynn glanced at Horstan, but she appeared sick to the stomach and didn't speak. He walked around to the trunk and looked inside.

He studied the contents for a moment, and then ran an analysis program over them. Seconds later it began highlighting splinters of femur, sections of skull, finger bones, human sinew and heart muscle, shredded lung, liver and bowel.

"Who was this?" he asked quietly.

Andersten shook his head, unable to speak.

Captain, if I may? the Betsy asked quietly.

Go ahead. He unlocked an Observer and the *Betsy* manoeuvred it down into the trunk, scanning and sampling the barely recognisable human remains.

"IN Roster confirms the registered DNA of Ensign Chloi Harris, Midshipman John McIntyre and Lieutenant Francis Marshall."

Andersten turned away, appalled.

"Ye gods," muttered Brynn. He turned to Andersten. "What – is – this?" he grated.

Andersten waved a hand aimlessly. Brynn knew a large part of what Andersten had been through in his life – to see him so out of character was unnerving enough on its own.

"I've never seen anything like it," he managed – then shaking his head, he walked to the rear of the hangar bay and stared out into the diamond-studded blackness of space.

"XO," Brynn turned to face her. "Earn your pay slip. Explain – what did you find?"

Horstan turned to face him, pale and agitated, but just holding it together.

"No one survived." She waved at the trunk. "Everywhere was like... like that. The whole ship. Everyone." She stared at him directly. "I don't want to tell you – I don't want to see that again. You'll have to stream it. I'm sorry, Captain."

Brynn nodded. "Ok, if that's how you want it."

"It is. I'm sorry. It's too raw." She walked toward the door – heading for the medical bay, then stopped and half-turned.

"I want to be asleep when you stream it."

Brynn unlocked the bay, and watched her leave in silence. He looked down at the trunk and its grisly contents once more.

Betsy, take us out of the exclusion volume, at stealth, then upload this to INI, FAO Admiral Cole only – use my private cipher.

Yes, Captain.

Then get Leone to come and secure this trunk and put it all into a medical stasis booth please.

Certainly, Captain.

He walked over to Andersten, and clapped one hand on his shoulder as an acknowledgement that he knew Andersten needed some time to get his mind straight, then left to follow Horstan.

Andersten barely noticed, but did nonetheless.

Chapter Seventeen

"It's too quiet," said Brynn – but with Horstan's voice.

Andersten nodded, then with a jerk of his head, gestured for her to head up the corridor, and Brynn's viewpoint moved forward slowly. The *Delaror* was totally silent apart from the usual noises from a running ship. Unfamiliar feminine hands reached out before him to steady himself against the wall as he slowly slid along it, edging toward the intersection ahead.

"Nothing," Horstan's voice said, as she peered around the corner, then up and down the next corridor.

Andersten appeared beside him. Brynn fought off the oddness of looking *up* at Andersten's satin black, shiny facemask. In reality Brynn was the same height as Andersten, but in the sense-vise being streamed from Horstan's sleeping mind, he saw and felt everything as she had seen and felt it during the mission – just as if he had been there in her place.

Andersten looked back down at him, his gaze slightly too low, and Brynn felt his cheeks burn in indignation as Horstan realised Andersten was looking at her chest. Privately he smiled – sense-sims of this depth left nothing to the imagination. He knew exactly what Horstan was feeling and how irritating she found Andersten's perhaps *too* open appreciation for her figure.

He stared at Andersten pointedly for a moment, and then he looked up and down the corridor. "Bridge is that way," he nodded.

They edged forward, Andersten slowly turning in

half-circles to cover front and rear as they went.

At the next intersection, they both came to a dead stop.

The floor, walls and ceiling were smeared with blood. An arm lay on the floor, severed horrifically above the elbow – more ripped than cut. Blood trails led off down the corridor and into the closed lift doors, disappearing underneath.

He felt a wave of nausea surge up his throat – but Horstan managed to suppress it, taking a grip.

He felt Andersten's huge hand on his arm, and he pulled Horstan back behind him as if she were feather light.

Andersten scanned ahead. "Nothing alive or moving."

Andersten continued ahead, while he kept a careful and keen eye on the corridor behind. He could feel Horstan's chest heaving as she fought to calm herself.

Andersten turned the corner – and stopped, transfixed by what he saw.

"What is it?" Horstan asked.

Andersten didn't respond for a moment, then gestured for her to stay put. He moved ahead past the corner and out of sight.

Brynn could feel Horstan's impatience mounting, her fear only just kept at bay as she waited for Andersten to return. He made a mental note to get her some more aggressive sim training scheduled, and encourage her to uprate her defensive and offensive enhancements for some peace of mind.

After what seemed an age – even to Brynn – Andersten returned, then nodded for them to continue.

He stood before the lift, arms raised ready for combat, and pinged the door. It slid open. Horstan couldn't see exactly what Andersten saw, but she saw enough to know the entire lift was painted with blood and gore. Andersten closed the door and turned back.

"We go another way," Andersten said emotionlessly, striding straight past.

Horstan turned to follow. "What did you find?"

Andersten flicked a hand at the blood-encrusted floor behind them. "More of that."

They came across another bloody mess a minute later, this time shattered bones littered the floor all around. It was as if someone had simply exploded all over the corridor. Brynn felt another surge in his gullet – and then he decided to suppress the streams emotional feedback. He'd had enough of that.

"What can do this?" Horstan asked.

"Let's hope we don't find out," Andersten muttered darkly.

They made their way up to the command bridge through emergency hatches and crawl ducts – avoiding the main corridors and transports at all costs. Andersten maintained it should be safer, but Brynn could tell Horstan was glad to avoid the horrific scenes of bloodshed.

They were halfway there when she accidentally pushed against a duct grille to her left. It popped open and swung downward on its hinge with an overly loud bang, exaggerated by the total silence of the ship.

They both stopped instantly. Horstan looked down into the room below. Once it had been the mess hall. Now it was a sight from the nether-hells. Limbs and organs were strewn all over the floor, tables and seats – blood and gore painting every surface as if a crazed artist had gone wild with sacks of offal.

In the corner, a small maintenance droid was busily making a pathetic attempt to clear up the congealed mess.

Horstan retched.

Andersten reached past her, and slowly pulled the grille shut. He didn't say a word, but Brynn could feel the heat of his anger through Horstan's own shame.

Then there came a shrill buzzing whine. Something appeared in the mess room doorway, hovering above the floor and spinning around at an impossibly high speed. Then chaos erupted.

Brynn couldn't follow what happened, even with the benefit of watching this as a replay.

Suddenly he was falling into the mess room, skidding about on the slick floor and flailing in gore and bone. Then Andersten was standing above him; he could see the smouldering molten mess of the crawl way above as it slowly sagged down into the room.

A rapidly spinning object was hammering at Andersten's shield which wrapped around them both – a black metallic orb, furiously ramming the shield as it tried to get at them. Horstan couldn't help but cower impotently behind Andersten as he tracked the orb with both arms and slowly, but carefully delivered full power energy pulses directly on target, each time without fail. The orb leapt backward as each flare of white energy hit, but immediately recovered and came back again, smashing at the shield.

Horstan knew this was a war of attrition – whoever

had the most energy would win. Brynn was angered by his similar impotence – unable to take action to help Andersten as he watched these past events, even though he knew they had both come through.

The orb battered its way nearer and nearer as Andersten's shield slowly depleted. He took another shot with one arm, but it went well clear of the orb and a five-metre wide hole erupted in the mess hull and out into space. The atmosphere vented almost instantly – blasting the room clear of everything before the emergency door dropped, sealing the mess hall from the rest of the ship. Tables, gore and bone leapt out into the void, but they safely remained inside the bubble of Andersten's shield... and still the orb still came at them.

He waited as long as he could to replenish his offensive reserves, then fired energy bolts from each arm in turn – pushing the orb away with each blast, hitting it exactly at the furthest point from them as it recovered stability with another shot from alternating arms. As it neared the hole, he hit it with a double blast from both arms and the orb shot out into space. A wall of electric blue leapt up around the hole as the *Delaror's* breach shield came up, and the orb slammed into it before it could get back inside, battering ferociously at the force field in a frenzied but impotent attack.

As they watched – fearing it would break through – it ceased ramming the shield and backed away, facing them directly as if staring at them. Now Brynn could finally see it motionless as he saw more detail through Horstan's eyes.

It was a black orb roughly half a metre across, covered entirely by whirling blades with serrated edges.

It was clearly built for one purpose – to slaughter. If Andersten hadn't jacked into the *Delaror's* Last Stand Protocol in order to raise the breach shielding on the hull – they wouldn't have lasted more than a minute more before his energy reserves gave out.

Andersten reached down and pulled Horstan to her feet. Neither of them said a word.

Outside the orb lingered for a few moments. He felt Horstan thinking it was staring at them malevolently, and then it drifted away toward the bridge.

"Great," muttered Andersten. "It knows where we're headed."

"Can't you get into the ship net now?" Horstan asked hopefully. "If you managed to raise the breach shields...?"

He shook his head. "It's locked out, or something. Even the Captains own codes won't get me in, or the Fleet overrides. The only way to take that thing out is to bring up the ships internal defence grid, which needs the ship's net, which means getting to the bridge."

"What if there are more of them?"

"Then we're dead, I'm done... that thing had us just on its own, stone cold."

Horstan started shaking. "I can't go like that," she wavered. "Not like them, shredded..."

Andersten looked at her sternly. "I won't let that happen," he said flatly.

Horstan knew enough to understand what that meant. He'd kill her himself before that thing had chance to. Rough mercy. She nodded.

"We have to hurry; it'll no doubt be looking to get back wherever it got in first time around. I've told the integrity grid to seal any other breaches, but we can't rely on that alone."

Brynn's view moved up and down as Horstan nodded. It was now a case of defending themselves, instead of escape. *If those things are all over the ship...* he felt Horstan think.

Deck schematics appeared in front of Brynn as Horstan ran a search across the *Delaror*. "There's an induction cubicle not far from here," she said.

Andersten nodded. A flash charge would at least let him regain some shield strength. "Let's go... silent and *safe*, as before. No screw-ups. Ok?"

Horstan looked back up at the wrecked crawl way – the giveaway grille long since vaporised, and Brynn felt her cheeks glow hot. She nodded again.

They crept on. They afforded themselves a tense five minute pause as Andersten soaked up as much energy as he could in the cubicle. He set the induction field strength to the maximum his enrichments were rated for, while Horstan nervously watched the corridor outside and prayed.

They saw countless obscene horrors on their way... unrecognisable body parts, humans macerated into inhuman bloody remains plastering every surface. Occasionally an all too recognisable part stood out from the gore – a finger, a shattered helmet-mask, an eye.

They reached the bridge without incident, nor any sight or sound from the orb, or anything else.

After Andersten checked the bridge, Horstan stepped in – ignoring the gore splashed everywhere – and made for the primary Intellect interface. Although the Captain or anyone else with the ship command codes could control the entire vessel via the ship's local network – or indeed the wider qNet from anywhere if needed – physical command points were installed on the bridge, emergency bridge and engineering on all naval vessels as backups.

She placed her palm on the touch surface, and it scanned her implant integrations. After a few tense seconds it failed to complete the authentication, yet still the panel lit up. Puzzled by the total failure of the security system, she tried to access the ship's core and gain to access the logs as Andersten waited in impatient silence.

"The *Delaror* is *gone*," she whispered in amazement.

"Impossible, surely..." demanded Andersten. "Did it upload?"

She shook her head. "I can't tell – there are no logs. There's nothing in the ship's network at all, other than the breach grid, which you invoked. No signs of the ship's Intellect, no sub-systems, no sensors, scans or data. Nothing coming in, and nothing going out. All I can tell is that the ship's internal shield grid is online. There's also no hull integrity monitor running – I've had to scan all the hull sensors individually. The only hull breach is the one in the mess room."

"So how did that thing get in?" grumbled Andersten.

She shook her head. "No idea. Internal scans show no life signs or movement in the ship other than ourselves. There are no unrecognised stationary objects. If the scan is correct, we're on our own in here."

Andersten didn't respond, and she flicked her gaze back to him. He was standing facing the main view portal. "Not for long," he said quietly.

The orb was dead ahead, centimetres away from the portal, spinning silently in space.

Horstan's heart leapt. "Can it get in?"

"I hope not. That's trillium bonded diamond – hardest stuff we can make."

"What is it doing?" she whispered, more to herself.

"Waiting for lunch," he rumbled. "Are we done?"

She concentrated on the virtual representation of the ship's utterly blank cyberscape in her e-vision for a moment, then decided there was nothing else she would be able to determine. This would need a full naval forensic investigation team to fathom. She gave a thumbs up.

"Take over fire control, and the ship's hull integrity grid."

She did so.

"Ramp up the hull integrity compensation fields to times ten."

"That'll cripple all the external equipment," she protested.

"This ship is already dead. Do it."

"XO," she reminded him scathingly.

Within his mask, he gave a small smile. "Please, *Ma'am*." He tapped two fingers to his forehead in a mock salute.

The orb suddenly smashed against the portal, and then slid along to the mounting frame – dragged against the hull by the powerful integrity reinforcement fields which ran throughout the entire structure, strengthening the hull materials at the atomic level. They could dimly hear the blades rapping against the outer layer – then they began snapping off and shooting off into space in all directions. Shortly it was just a sphere of metal with complex concentric rings spinning crazily all over its surface.

"Bring up the forward maser turret, and pass me the id."

She shared the turret view and watched as Andersten brought it around and targeted the trapped orb.

"Right, let's get out of here before this thing invites friends over."

They left the bridge and sealed the door shut. Then Andersten fired the maser through the ships l-net. The invisible beam of energy glowed fiercely off the orb for what seemed an eternity – nothing that size should withstand that much energy being poured into it, but yet Horstan feared the orb would still be there when Andersten stopped firing. Then the glow evaporated away, along with a large portion of the bridge which explosively vented its atmosphere out into space. The orb was gone.

"Time to leave!" With that, Andersten led her back to the logistics hatch. They took the lifts this time to make the journey quicker – trusting Horstan's findings from the ship scan and both of them steadfastly ignoring the gore that was abundant in almost all of them.

When they finally left the first lift they had encountered on their way to the bridge, Andersten gestured for her to stay put.

"I'll be back in a moment." Then he left the lift and turned right back down the corridor he'd made her avoid earlier.

Ten minutes passed, and then he returned with a sizeable chest in his arms.

"What's that?" she asked.

"Proof," was all he said.

They returned to the bike which was still safe and sound, and Andersten stowed the chest on the aft mount. Without a further word, they climbed wearily back on board, dropped the proximity restriction and slowly made their stealthy way back to the distant *Betsy*.

For the entire trip, neither of them spoke. But Brynn could feel Andersten's tight grip around Horstan's diminutive waist. Nothing was meant by it, other than giving her the awareness of human contact, and that someone was making sure she was safe. If Horstan objected as his Executive Officer, she made nothing of it.

Brynn checked the stream duration – thirty-five minutes. He slowly slid back to reality, where he sat next to Horstan as she lay sound asleep in a medical cot. He cleared the Rush from his artificial gland implant – countering the slowdown buzz with Diclofenac and Neuromorphine. Just over nine minutes of real-time had elapsed while he had experienced the encounter.

He sat back as the painkillers and anti-inflammatories did their work. *Four hundred million ships, and just* one *of those things?* He didn't buy it. *Whatever deep shit Admiral Cole thinks we are in, it just got a light-year deeper.*

He recorded a message for Horstan when she woke, and then composed a brief message to Admiral Cole, explaining the nature of what they had encountered – attaching the sim-stream he had just witnessed.

He got up and returned to his cabin to file the mission report.

He didn't envy the Admiral this day.

"Well done on the mission, XO," said Brynn's voice message as Horstan played it back a few hours later. "I've not seen such horror, and it sickened me as much as it did you. Being frank, you folded, but you overcame it. That's to be commended, and I'll make sure that goes on file. For your own sake I *require* you to take the attached training-sims, and there are a few optionals, as well as recommended enhancements I've listed. I think you'd be a lot more comfortable serving on this ship in future missions if you did, and I'd be a lot more comfortable *letting* you serve this ship on future missions. If you want to debrief further or discuss later, do so at your leisure. You're off-duty for twenty-four hours."

Horstan sat up in the cot, propping herself up on her elbows and idly looking around. Brynn had to be the most relaxed Naval Captain there ever was. She shook her head in mild disbelief. Thankfully she didn't feel quite so numb now. She wondered if the sights she had seen in her brief period on the *Delaror* would haunt her – and she shuddered, remembering the bloody mess room and the shrill whine of imminent death as it hammered at Andersten's shield. *So close to dying… mere hours ago.*

How do you deal with that? she asked herself. *What manual or training gives you the tools to cope with this at* all, *let alone on a routine basis?*

She knew service would be tough on the *Betsy*, but hadn't expected anything of such a magnitude, nor so soon. Wondering where Andersten had got to, she decided to track him down, and discharged herself from the medical bay as she left.

"So you knew Ensign Harris?" asked Brynn. Both he and Andersten were in the aft rec room, staring out of the rear view portal and into deep space.

Andersten shrugged. "Friend of one of my daughters."

Brynn thought for a moment. "How did you know it was her?"

"I didn't at first, strode straight past her. I saw the medical bay, and knowing she was on board as a medic I had to check. It was only when I turned around that I noticed the scrap of her uniform still glowing with her name and insignia."

Brynn nodded slowly. "Ah."

Andersten was quiet for a while. "I guessed what was left of her was in that pile of –" he stopped himself short, face grim. "I didn't know there'd be others too," he finished.

He looked at his Captain. "Formal apology for going off mission, Captain. I had to recover what was left of her – it didn't seem right otherwise."

"None needed. It won't be in my report," Brynn assured him. It was, he'd already filed it, but Admiral Cole was not one to get bogged down with nitty gritty procedure. That would be Brynn's concern, and no one else's in Admiral Cole's eyes.

He leant forward so Andersten could see him, but still stared out of the window rather than look at him. "It was the human thing to do."

Andersten suppressed a dry laugh. "So it's official then, I'm still human?"

Brynn smiled at him, then got up and clapped him on

the shoulder. "Just about," he said. "You ok now?"

Andersten nodded. "That wasn't fun Captain. That thing would have had us."

"It didn't though."

"By luck. There have to be more of those things – just one couldn't have wiped out the *Delaror* like that."

Brynn nodded, keeping his guesses to himself for now.

Andersten looked up at him. "The sheer numbers alone mean we've had it, you know that."

Again, Brynn nodded – slowly this time.

"The Shredders you mean?" said someone behind them.

They both turned to look back at the rec room doorway. Horstan was standing there looking resolute and stern.

"Shredders?" queried Brynn. "You mean that orb monstrosity?"

"As good a name as any," she replied, walking to the window and placing her hands against it.

"Assuming one per ship – that's four hundred million right off. Enough to slaughter the entire population of most Imperial star systems in short order," she said.

So much for side-lining that particular concern, though Brynn.

Andersten looked puzzled. "There's something not quite right though."

"Aside from the obvious you mean?" asked Brynn, eyebrow raised.

"I keep checking our run over. I saw lots of organs left behind, bones, empty helmets and face masks... but no heads, not semblance of any brain tissue."

Horstan frowned – and looked blank for a moment. "Me neither. I saw an eye, but it was deflated, and had no optic nerve."

Brynn went cold – and ran through the sim-stream again at high speed, searching for two particular things.

"Can this get any worse?" he demanded suddenly. Both the others looked at him askance.

"You saw no integrations, no bonding nano-fibres, no qSpinners, no signs of any augmentations or enhancements anywhere on your trip."

He looked at them both as they realised what that meant.

"Damnation!" exclaimed Andersten. "That thing wasn't just shredding them to pieces to kill them... it was after their implants!"

Chapter Eighteen

Kerugar was seated in the VIP passenger section of the *Ragat's Fancy*. Alone apart from the black replica of her father, who was idly staring out of the view window watching the arid world of Arantia slip past them as they made their way out to the transit zone. She had come to live there after leaving Reptar so many years ago – a refuge which almost felt like home. Almost.

She still hadn't come to terms with what he'd told her. She distrusted his motives enough to want to get an independent confirmation – but that posed problems. If it were true, whoever performed the scan would inform the Imperial Medical Council, and she'd quickly be rounded up by IMC staff and 'softly' imprisoned until they'd explored every aspect of her condition.

Her father was right – unfortunately. Her only hope of freedom during her pregnancy lay on Reptar. As much as she hated the prospect of returning home, she knew he had no choice.

"If you're lying, Antool..."

The jet-black face of her father turned to smile at her gently. "I have been many things, Kerugar, but liar to my one and only daughter about such a thing? Never."

She still wasn't convinced – though she had little choice. This was the perfect snare to get her back home. She couldn't believe it, but couldn't refute it.

But if it is true? she wondered. *Could I be the one? The first to cross the genetic boundary between human and Reptar? Why me? How could I be? Perhaps it explains the impact of his pheromones...* she placed a hand on her lower abdomen unconsciously.

"What did Mother have to say?" she asked quietly.

"Nothing, as usual," he replied. "Very loudly. Your mother can project deafening silence in a way I've yet to encounter anywhere else in the Empire."

"She knows of the children?"

Keragar Antool looked at her solemnly. "Child, all of Reptar knows. How could you expect anything else?"

She grated her teeth, the serrated edges scraping roughly. "If everyone on Reptar knows, then so must the Empire."

"Not of this, you should know that. You declared the surrogate during your medical – that is all they are aware of. As for someone talking, it will not happen. It's been too long ingrained in our culture. No Reptar would jeopardise this."

She shook her head. "Someone will talk, they always do."

"Then they would risk banishment," Keragar asserted. "Or have myself to deal with."

Kerugar chose to keep her response to that to herself.

"Preparing for g-drive in ten seconds," said the ship's captain.

Kerugar felt the surge through her seat – barely perceptible due to the delta-p compensators banking the change in momentum. Without them a g-drive transit would flatten anything organic into a paste, and crush it - along with everything else - into a thin veneer against the rear bulkheads. They were deliberately tuned to allow a relatively minute amount of inertia to creep through, as it helped passengers realise the vessel was actually moving. Outside, the pin-sharp light of the stars began to smear into faint rainbow trails, dimming as the vessel began to pick up speeds far greater than light.

The ship's captain chimed in again. "ETA at Chyro in twelve minutes, 04:42 IST, 09:37 local standard time."

"Chyro?" asked Kerugar.

Her father refused to meet her eye, and looked away nonchalantly. "A small errand first, it will not take long."

She sighed. She knew better.

***

Admiral Cole did something he probably shouldn't have – rather, he did not act immediately, as he should have.

Instead, he closed his eyes and sat back in his chair, and just tried to think of nothing… to clear his mind for a few precious minutes before the chaos began.

He had just received Brynn's report from the *Delaror* contact mission. He hadn't yet forwarded it to Raul, or to the Emperor's Immediate Office for his attention.

Although of paramount import to the safety and well-being of the Empire and its citizens – and no doubt the entire galaxy – a few minutes between dealing with one realm of chaos and the next could do no harm – in this instance.

Sadly for Aryn, his mind would have none of it. Internal peace was a concept long forgotten.

The total loss of Imperial Naval Destroyer, crew included.

How? he asked himself.

In the most horrific way… literally being torn apart, having implants and nano-web fibres which permeated

256

the entire body like a secondary nervous system, reinforcing the skeletal structure, organs, muscle fibres, brain, ripped from you whilst still alive...

It was inhuman.

Why?

What could they gain? Intel? Knowledge of Imperial technology such as implants and enhancements? Any half-decent scanning technology could determine that non-invasively.

They had taken every crew member's mind – living and capsular backup. It was standard practice to uplink to the Totality at the beginning of an operation, so all of the crew could be brought back into existence – if they so chose. However nothing of the original crew member's memory or personality since their last backup had been left, judging by the recordings of Horstan and Andersten's mission.

Knowledge?

Could the crew even now be in some simulation being interrogated? Or in many ways worse... simply being processed as no more than a data archive? Information being indexed and catalogued. Their minds and backups now merely a mass information storage system, for some Intellect to analyse and digest at its leisure, passing on sorted and prioritised information to its creators.

When?

If they had a captured Intellect and a full crew to pull information from without resistance, including a Captain, when could they expect the next move?

He sighed deeply, and opened his eyes.

He already knew. There was only one possible

answer.

Now.

***

Nelsen lay back in the gel-form couch, reclining as if he were on a beach somewhere, relaxing in warm sunshine. Andreya had taken herself into the shower in a small compartment extruded from the *Sneak's* internal cabin membrane for modesty's sake.

Nelsen was bored beyond belief. They were still two hours away from their destination. The first three hours he'd managed quite well, watching their progress as the *Sneak* wove her way between the stars, following the faint gravity field conduits between them. But their speed was such that stars were barely on screen for a minute at a time as the *Sneak* looped around and then sped back out toward the next on her list.

Astronomical stepping stones leading them toward their goal.

They had discussed jumping via wormholes at some length. The journey would have taken less than half an hour, but Nelsen was concerned that they'd be leaving a blatant trail of energy pulses across the galaxy and into unknown territory. Besides, the Navy had already tried establishing wormholes in the Dark Zone – and failed.

Nelsen strongly suspected that this fact alone meant the DZ had to be the domain of the invading force. The facts tied up too neatly. A centuries old enigma where a volume of space was effectively off limits to qNet technology, and recently proven to be 'wormhole proof'. And now an invading fleet demonstrating the exact same abilities?

Which led to yet another frightening thought – more frightening than the ones of late. The DZ had been known for almost three hundred years... these *things* could build at a staggering rate, with clearly no respect for anything in their path. So far the DZ had been mapped out to be roughly half again the volume the Empire currently occupied, and encompassed far more star systems.

And they were headed right into the heart of it.

"Anything yet?" he asked out loud. They'd taken to speaking instead of thinking across the l-net, as Nelsen was too much in the habit of believing a direct one-to-one chat was private. The knowledge that Andreya was possibly listening still made him feel uneasy, even though he *almost* trusted her to be discreet. He'd rather *know* he could be overheard. Speaking aloud was less discomforting, psychologically speaking.

"Nothing so far," replied the *Sneak*. "Although we are moving at a fair clip. I can't perform precise scans. I'm certain we aren't being trailed, and I've detected no signs of a response from systems we have passed through. We will be entering the DZ in seven minutes. After that, we must presume the loss of the qNet and therefore the Observers I've been seeding as we go."

"Ok. Andreya? It might be an idea to finish up. We're not really sure of anything beyond the DZ boundary."

"All right, coming!"

Nelsen tried not to think about her in the shower. *What's wrong with me?* he thought. *I've barely known her for three days, she's not even my type... and she's not even* human. He realised how xenophobic that sounded. *She's*

259

not even real, he corrected himself, somewhat lamely.

Surprisingly, she appeared a few moments later, and the *Sneak* collapsed the shower cubicle behind her. He'd expected her to be another half an hour at least.

"Are we there yet?" she asked cheerily. Somehow Nelsen knew this was some kind of inner joke, and he refused to rise to the bait.

She came over and sat down on the gelform beside him, engulfing him in a cloud of scented shower gels and damp hair. He scowled, then closed off his olfactory senses to avoid being distracted by *her*.

They watched the display hovering a few inches away from the bulkhead before them as they sped silently toward the next star on their route, their first inside the DZ. It was glowing about a thousand times brighter than it normally would be, as they were travelling at a relative one-thousand and eighty times the speed of light – effectively running into eighteen minutes worth of starlight every second. The beyond lethal level of photons and EM radiation were cut back by incredibly powerful shields across their bow wave, and further filtered and reduced by the *Sneak's* sensors.

To Nelsen and Andreya, the star ahead just looked slightly brighter than it should. Outside the ship, the resulting storm of energy flaring off the *Sneak's* forward shields should have made the *Sneak* the second brightest object in the system. Fortunately, the energy was diverted into another realm of quantum physics which Nelsen had never managed to grasp. G-drives worked, they got you where you wanted to go quickly, and you didn't die in the process. Result. The physics and math could go hang for all he cared.

"Entering the DZ," said the *Sneak*.

Here be dragons, Andreya thought over the l-net.

"What?" asked Nelsen.

Andreya looked puzzled. "What what?"

"What dragons?"

"What *are* you on about?" she demanded.

"You just thought on the l-net, 'Here be dragons'," supplied the *Sneak* helpfully.

"I did?" *That* look came over her. The look of not knowing who she was. Nelsen chose to change the subject.

"Well, no explosion," he said cheerfully. "*Sneak*? Anything to report?"

"Nothing. We still have the qNet, and I can still access my Observers. Subspace is normal."

"Perhaps the charts aren't up to date?"

"Possible, Captain."

"Ok, let's see how we get on."

They sat in silence for a while, Andreya wearing a worried frown. They had chatted at length for most of the trip so far. Both aiming for idle small talk to pass the time, but also to take their minds off momentous recent events.

Although he could not bring himself to speak of it to Andreya, he could identify with her inner struggle on some level. Nelsen was still trying to shake his memories of Meelereen, or Rybek. The threat and horrors of total planetary destruction – the deep-seated fear at his core, and the anger which tapped into it, the loss of his family. He knew it could break a man – it had broken him once. It would never break him again. He knew, he just *knew* Rybek was alive. If he found her, he would make sure *she* would be the one to break.

Andreya was continually striving to come to terms with her non-real human status. Everything in her told her she was human. Different, but human. She had known from the offset she wasn't Andreya Vorstan, but she hadn't thought for one second that she wasn't *real*. If not a human, what was she? A Proxy? She'd be the one controlling the Proxy, she would know that surely? A cybo sapien? Or an AI controlling a Proxy programmed not to know? Cole had called her a Replica – she'd looked it up – a construct used to house Intellects when they needed a physical form, usually to suit a specific purpose, and rarely humanoid. Although she certainly fitted the bill, it didn't *feel* right. Whatever her inner source which drip-fed her had to say on the matter, it was keeping quiet. The oddest thing was, although it *was* worrying, it wasn't worrying her as much as she thought it *should*. It was as if she had committed herself to being perfectly fine with the outcome – whatever it might be. It was the uncertainty of not really knowing which had her on edge.

But, she trusted Nelsen – for some oddball, unfathomable reason – she felt he would still guard her well-being with his life. She was pretty self-sufficient, and she instinctively knew she could handle pretty much anything, but knowing someone was there beside you who would make *sure* she didn't need to was oddly comforting. She wondered at that. *Why him? Was there some secret purpose behind their chance meeting?* Two people, each with a purpose to play in the huge events which were to unfold, just both happening to be in the right place at the right time to meet each other?

"Nelsen, I'm worried," she said aloud.

"Anything particularly important bothering you?" he asked with a smile. There was plenty to choose from, after all.

She didn't seem to hear him. "I'm worried that I'm not worried enough... does that sound paranoid?"

He smiled. "Paranoia is my business – or expertise, I guess. If you are paranoid I can confirm it for you."

She half-smiled. "Presuming Cole, and the medics back at the station are right... that I'm not... real… you'd think that would give anyone a healthy dose of the heeby jeebies, right?"

He frowned. "The what?"

"It'd scare the gonads off you."

He raised his eyebrows in surprise at her choice of words. "I'd suspect so," he said slowly.

"I don't feel scared. I don't even feel concerned, or anxious. *Unsettled,* yes. But not worried. And I'm more worried about *not* being worried about not being real, than not being real."

Nelsen pursed his lips thoughtfully. "That does sound a tiny bit paranoid, yes," he said dubiously. Sometimes her trail of thought was a little... unusual.

"It sounds weird, I guess."

"A little."

"Sounds perfectly reasonable to me," offered the *Sneak*.

Nelsen rolled his eyes comically, and Andreya smiled.

"Pardon me I'm certain," said the *Sneak* in a wounded tone.

"No offence meant, *Sneak* – just lightening the mood."

The *Sneak* managed to project a false wounded silence.

"I'd say if your instinct is to not worry about it, don't worry about it," Nelsen said to Andreya. "If they are right, there's probably a sound explanation behind how you feel – probably to stop you entering some kind of psychotic breakdown." He stopped himself abruptly. Perhaps that was a little *too* honest.

She merely nodded. "I considered that. You could go nuts just thinking about the existentialism of it all. It might be a deliberate defence mechanism."

"Precisely," he replied, relieved he hadn't caused major offence.

"Which, of course, raises a thousand 'why' and 'who' questions."

"Ah."

"If I may?" asked the *Sneak*.

"Of course, *Sneak*," replied Andreya.

"It would seem to *me*, that it must be a defence mechanism. If what you've told us about your inner self is true – and it seems we may have just heard it ourselves – then something clearly wants you safe and sound. Something has your best interests in mind. In my experience anything that can care about another can't be all that bad."

Nelsen gave a low laugh. "*Sneak*, How old are you, to be so experienced?"

"In real terms? Four standard Imperial months."

Nelsen gave Andreya a wry, amused look.

"One hundred and thirty-two years in simulated personalty development, one thousand, six hundred and fifty-nine by internal memory archives, and three

264

thousand, nine hundred and sixty-six by qNet Imperial repositories. Does that help?"

Nelsen's face had fallen, and he wore a sour look.

"Seems you are destined to be plagued by smart-mouthed women, Captain Rybek," said Andreya with a broad smile.

He smiled back ruefully. "At last, a look of cheer on your face!"

She grinned, then stuck her tongue out at him. "Thanks, *Sneak*, that helps… I think."

"No charge."

Now it was Andreya's turn to raise an eyebrow.

Then they both laughed.

"What?" asked the *Sneak*.

"Nothing – back to watching where we're going, *Sneak*."

"I never stopped..." said the *Sneak*, sounding puzzled.

"Drink?" suggested Andreya.

Nelsen nodded his thanks and relaxed back int his seat. For some reason he felt a bit of genuine cheer. Despite Meelereen forever haunting his dreams, despite the threat of more of the same senseless slaughter and destruction looming over all, he felt a little lightness in his heart for the first time in years.

He'd bottle it and store it for later if he could, but as it was hard to come by, he took his fill while he had the opportunity.

Chances were it wouldn't come around again for a long, long time.

Chapter Nineteen

A Platinum Warrior stepped forward from the forming cube, a thin layer of microscopic manufacturing dust blowing off the impeccably smooth metal and out into the air in fine, wispy curls.

The imposing two-metre tall figure looked like a warrior from ancient times, with ornately engraved platinum armour segments bonded to a flexible but rugged layer of black polymer underneath.

The helmet was vaguely insectoid in appearance, with a circular mouth guard and two large metallic dome sections sweeping back over the eyes and across the top of the head to merge at the rear.

The sound of its footfall as it stepped onto the production floor was formidable, and its poise heroic. It was clearly a creature intent on action – bent on getting the job done no matter what.

It strode over to a console interface for the facility's primary Intellect, and placed a heavy gauntleted hand onto a screen.

"Romurik, are you *seriously* going out like that?" asked the Intellect.

There was a metallic laugh as the Warrior's head tipped back, and then he strode out of the room and headed for the docks. He meant business, and this time there would be no 'uploading' to get out of trouble. He would *be* the trouble.

***

"We cannot formally declare war against a threat of this magnitude," declared Fleet Admiral Benthar. "Such an act would be folly. The conclusion foregone. We have already lost before we begin."

The Emperor's inner council had convened once more. It seemed that they were all spending more and more of their time in the private simulation of late.

"The Senate disagrees, Fleet Admiral," said the Emperor.

"They suggest we declare war, Your Majesty?" asked Aryn. "Or that we haven't already lost?"

The Emperor stared at him for a moment. "Those present here are all aware of the Senate's... *perspective...* on such things. The Empire believes itself to be the dominant force in the Cluster, and more than capable of defending that position. It is not easily persuaded otherwise – not without the scale of this threat becoming wider public knowledge."

"We cannot engage in an offensive against a threat of this magnitude purely for political need, Your Majesty," said Raul.

"I am most painfully aware of that, Fleet Admiral," said the Emperor mildly, levelling a stern gaze at Raul.

"Your pardon, Your Majesty, I did not mean to infer otherwise. However, we *have* to move around this and appease the Senate *without* engaging the enemy and still retain control over the details. Somehow."

"They have made no direct overt move as yet," mused Aryn.

The Emperor raised one eyebrow. "You believe destroying an entire civilisation and slaughtering the entire crew of an Imperial Destroyer an act of peaceful expansionism?"

Aryn waved a hand. "They haven't trespassed into the Empire itself, Your Majesty. Politically, the destruction of S'ren is unfortunate but not a directly aggressive act toward the Empire. We would naturally be concerned, but entering into a war would not be an appropriate response... yet."

"And the death of the *Delaror's* crew? The loss of a ship of the Imperial line?" asked the Emperor.

"We approached them. It may have been a defensive response. So far – even to my surprise – there has been no other activity. Aside from the scavenging raid we observed on the Colesworth Refinery."

"So you present the possibility they are not an aggressor to the Empire? Not a threat?" inquired the Emperor.

Aryn thought carefully for a moment. "Your Majesty, more that – and right at this moment and until they take a *direct* action against us – we should take all measures to defend ourselves but not engage them in a conflict we are guaranteed to lose. At least, that's the position we should assume before the Senate."

"I support Admiral Cole's views, Your Majesty," said Raul. "I would personally represent a policy of active defence, and recommend a temporary but majority deployment of resources to IND."

The Emperor nodded slowly. "You have my full support in this, gentlemen," he replied gravely. "I will convene the entire Senate on a full-footing for discussion. Now, as to our other matter... the Infiltrator?"

Aryn held his hands out empty before him. "Nothing,

Your Majesty. The analysis of the Vorstan Replica shows her to be an identical physical copy right down to the neural damage sustained during her accident. My chief ME asserts she should not be able to walk, talk, or even breathe unaided. The copy process – however it was achieved – clearly occurred post trauma. Aside from the miracle of her organic structural integrity, the only other observation of note is that her web integration matches that of Mrs. Vorstan precisely as well. We are looking at a technological process way in advance of any we are presently capable of."

The Emperor steepled his fingers together. "And no clue as to its intent as yet?"

Aryn shook his head.

"Keep on it."

"Of course, Your Majesty."

***

Colyn Greeson had been assigned to INI six months ago, and had finally been given the kind of job he had signed up for… possibly even born for: Classified Data Analysis. His mind had always shown an uncanny knack for noticing patterns in data that most would fail to see, even when directed to them.

He was now paired with a splinter persona from an ancient INI personality – one going by the name Bertram. Despite growing up in a culture suffused with Intellects, he found being paired with a fragment of the millennia old entity which underpinned the entire Naval Intelligence wing to be highly intimidating. Despite having been introduced, he couldn't help but worry if one wrong thought could hound his career – even end it prematurely. *Am I up to this?* he kept asking himself.

He was sat in one of the many arboretum modules of INHS *Shield* – the first, oldest, and now largest Hive station in existence. It had grown to the size of a small moon over the millennia, with new hexagonal bay modules being installed almost every month. The station was continuously splitting its outer shell to accommodate a new addition. Bays for construction, docking, habitation, environments, specialised xeno-habitats... you name it, it was here somewhere. There was no need to explore the Empire; most of it was already living in the station. You could spend a lifetime touring the Shield and fail to see half of it.

It was also the only naval base to be public to the Empire. It served as their hub to the populace at large, bringing the curious from far and wide and providing a large part of the INI recruitment pool. It also served as one of the largest sources of intelligence available. Five million souls from every corner of the Empire, all living and working in one place, under constant and immediate observation, all gossiping away. It had been too good an opportunity for INI to resist – why go looking for intel when you could openly invite it to come to you?

Most of the inhabitants scarcely gave their constant surveillance a thought. They were generally good, loyal citizens of the Empire. As they saw it, they were just playing their part in ensuring the safety of their society. But they helpfully and unwittingly brought Intel from every corner of the Empire for Shield to collate and digest without a single INI agent having to leave the station.

Those that were of a lesser enthusiasm to help the greater good soon left, or learned to ignore the privacy issues. The Citizens Privacy Act of Year 10 meant non-sentient AI were solely in charge of filtering data as appropriate – so a good citizen need not have concerns about any invasion of privacy whilst performing daily ablutions, or other baser, natural behaviours as per your species wont. These AI were monitored, controlled and accessed only by the station Intellect, so subversion was impossible. Discretion was assured. Unless said citizen started making a bomb, or discussing plans to cause others harm whilst doing so of course.

Colyn cleared his plate of scrambled olat and sat back, regarding the view. The enormous arboretum stretched up above him – a giant hexagonal cell, with all six walls providing a habitable floor with its own local gravity. Each 'floor' was covered by dense jungle growth transplanted from Cruhvere, and played host to a central band of water which flowed perpetually around the mid-section. Small boats could be seen drifting along its never ending current, as the river made its way around all six chamber walls. Large aquatic species swam lazily through the crystal blue water, and surfers challenged the foaming white waters which marked the intersection between each floor where the chambers gravity fields reoriented the river. Flamboyantly coloured birds with long mating plumage flew around the bay's central axis, flocking from floor to floor with no apparent concern for their bizarre gravitational circumstance. High above, the blackness of space – sprinkled with stars – could be seen clearly.

271

He sat in the cafe at the central hub for the bay, on what served as the base of this huge six-sided cylinder. He craned his neck back to watch a flock of orange and yellow ray-fins swoop past overhead. Evidently they had decided to check out this floor for tasty morsels and scraps left behind by visitors to the cafe.

Ensign Greeson? Bertram here, said a voice in his head. The pairing arrangement entailed a permanent single bonded qNet channel with the persona. Day or night, on call.

Hi, Bertram, he said. *Time already?*

Yes, it is. Shall we begin? Or do you wish to find an alternative location?

No, this will be fine. He adjusted himself in the seat and quickly finished his drink.

We had identified seventeen thousand contacts with similar energy signatures if you recall.

I do. You wanted to investigate via a spread-web of Observers to see if they all had the same construction, hinting at the same point of origin.

They were one of thousands of analyst pairs studying the epic volume of data coming in from the "Cloud" around S'vreth. The processing alone was a massive undertaking – organised by the primary station Intellect. Each pair – an agent and a splinter persona – had been assigned contacts as sections from the Cloud surface, and after cataloguing and annotating contacts of interest, the splinter would reconcile their findings back to the central archive at the end of each run.

So far, the influx of unknown vessels and unfamiliar technology evident in them had been staggering. It might be decades before it was all analysed in full.

Let's split the pack into groups, Colyn suggested. *Drop them into a quadtree and we can divvy them up. I'll take a quadrant and you can take the rest?*

Seems fair, Bertram replied, unfazed by the clearly unequal share. As an Intellect he could pursue the search any number of times faster than anything organic, so to him the workload was quite light. Brute force processing by Intellects alone would prove a far faster means of analysing the data, and indeed this was being undertaken in parallel. However the goal of pairing with biological beings was to bring insight, and organic intuition into the process, something millennia of cybo sapien evolution had so far only ever managed to emulate, and never truly achieve.

Pattern matching first, by EM? asked Colyn.

Very well. Let's start with gamma radiation, suggested Bertram. *We can correlate our results before going on.*

Colyn closed his eyes on the beautiful tunnel filled with life above him, and brought up the data visualisation of his chosen group of contacts. *Oh boy*, he thought. *That's still a lot.*

Let's go, he thought to Bertram, and they both began their search.

***

Brynn was, frankly, angry. Angry with himself, angry with Kerugar, angry with just about everyone... and for no good reason. His mood was foul and needless, and he knew it, which fed into making it worse – a cyclic and self-fuelling irritation. He was suffering another bout of pheromone withdrawal. The headaches

273

had stopped, thankfully, but the physical ache in his body was wearing him down, and he stubbornly refused to release meds to appease the discomfort. He was most angry because this was all inhibiting his concentration at a time when he needed it most.

If it kept up, he would be forced to do something about it – although he was loathe to. Medical interventions would just postpone the effects, resulting in them being all the more uncomfortable when he came off them. The only way to deal with Reptar Pheromone Withdrawal *was* to deal with it. Science still couldn't adequately explain why humans had been so taken by chemicals foreign to their own biochemistry, and certainly hadn't explained why he seemed to be affected more than any human case of withdrawal in the two thousand years of recorded Reptarian/Human interaction. Meds would just slow him down. He needed to be on full speed, even if it was making him slightly irrational.

The scheme he had been concocting would need very precise attention to detail.

Venton! I need to see you. In person. My quarters. Please.
Sir, aie.

***

Bertram... said Colyn. *I think I have something here...*
What is it? Bertram asked.

They had completed their analysis of the group of seventeen thousand vessels from earlier – they had largely been of identical construction, which indicated a single point of origin. It was certain that they had all

274

been built by a single species, or a shared construction technique. The findings had been uploaded to the Shield by Bertram, and they had been assigned their next group of contacts for study.

This time they had taken a more ad-hoc approach to their analysis, choosing a random entropy pattern and relying on pure chance to find items of interest. If any were found, they then ran searches against the data as a whole, based on characteristics of the contact being studied – an approach which would gradually whittle the group's overall size down to zero.

You won't believe this... but I think I recognise this ship...
Oh?

Colyn shared the contact ID with Bertram, and they both studied it in a single shared display.

It's reasonably old, noted Bertram, based on the battered appearance of the vessel.

If I'm right... it's about two hundred years old, said Colyn.

Bertram was curious. *Explain please?*

One second, said Colyn. He ran a cross-reference across the Imperial Vessel Register, and came up with a result almost immediately. The configuration of the vessel matched exactly. *Oh my*, he said. He shared the search results with Bertram.

The Ivant *– a Pathfinder Class Explorer, last reported heading into the DZ one hundred and eighty four years ago on a self-declared 'challenge' flight. No sightings or recorded traffic within the Empire since. Declared missing 21,957/05/29. Built by Akran Interstellar Shipping, 21,845. Crew twenty-two, all flagged as Missing Citizens, presumed deceased 21,977. Registered owner and Captain, Ikram Fasar* *of Saysiss.* Bertram paused. *Interesting.*

Every vessel so far has been unknown, stated Colyn. *This has to be important – the first recognised vessel type, and of Imperial origin. Saysiss has been a member of the Empire for five hundred years.*

What is its status? mused Bertram. They both looked at the visuals and readings coming from the Observer web they were in charge of, concentrating the entire web on a single contact several hundred light-years away to get a multi-angled and collated 3D view of the side of the vessel presenting itself to their web.

It looks in pretty poor repair, noted Colyn. The outside of the *Ivant* was pockmarked by countless micro-meteorite strikes, and numerous scorch marks littered its hull. A few sections to the rear appeared to be blast damaged, and several fins and protuberances had been ripped or blown off from all across the aft section.

EM readings show a totally different energy signature to that on file, or any recorded for Akran line vessels, observed Bertram. *Or indeed, any other known Imperial vessel.*

They've replaced the running gear, stated Colyn. *Probably to keep it running. Akran Interstellar were a bit...* ropey *in their day. Lots of maintenance and service problems with most of their output.* He studied the visuals closely. *The bridge section is voided – open to space. Most of the ship looks like it couldn't maintain life support. Chances are it's a ghost ship.*

I think you are right, said Bertram. *We have to flag this as top priority. It's a momentous find given the circumstances, Colyn. Well done.*

Colyn tried to avoid feeling overly pleased with himself.

How did you come to know of this ship and its history?

A hobby of mine when I was in Higher Ed. At the age of ten I was fascinated by the Dark Zone – mystery, intrigue – missing ships. It was a big draw for me then.

Did you not continue with your hobby?

I lost interest when I finished school aged twelve; when I finally realised girls existed.

I see. I've collated and uploaded your findings. We need to continue processing this group, now with the additional step of cross-referencing everything with IVR.

Colyn definitely suppressed his disappointment. His mind had drifted off into congratulations, possible promotion talk, celebrating with his peers... the realisation they had to continue with the task at hand left him slightly crestfallen.

Bertram understood, but said nothing of it other than, *we need to ascertain if there are a group of other ships of known origin around this vessel.*

I see, said Colyn. *Random sphere search around the* Ivant?

Seems reasonable, said Bertram.

And so they continued.

***

"Captain, we just lost the qNet."

Nelsen looked up from their game at the same time as Andreya.

"Ok, keep the scans hot and active, and remain stealthed. I'm not so worried about upsetting the locals here in non-imperial territory. For now, anyway."

"Yes, Captain. Wormhole based sensors also offline –

there's no rapid escape route now. Subspace is exhibiting the same frequency patterns as around S'vreth, although an order of magnitude lower in amplitude – which is interesting."

"How so?" asked Nelsen.

"It has the same effectiveness – blocking qNet and Wormhole formation yet requiring less energy to alter subspace. If so, why was it ten times more powerful around S'vreth?"

He pursed his lips. "Good point. Noted."

He looked at Andreya. "You win – I guess I have to forfeit now."

She sniffed imperiously. "Only fair, you were cheating anyway."

He looked back down at the hologrammatic level floating above the table between them.

Between them, they had designed a comfortable space between them for the *Sneak* to then form from its morphic gel cabin interior. Two large comfortable gel-couches faced each other across a knee-high affairs table, large enough to accommodate eating and recreation – such as the game they had been playing. He had to keep putting aside the notion they were 'nesting'.

"Was not," he asserted mildly.

She leant back into the soft air-foamed gel cushioning of the couch. "Odd, because you sure made it look like you were."

He raised an eyebrow, and the 3D labyrinth of tunnels, treasure rooms, tricks and traps faded away. "Hurtful," he said.

"What's our ETA *Sneak?*" she asked, standing up and stretching with a yawn. Nelsen chose to look away at the large wall display showing their next star glowing fiercely as they sped toward it.

"The next star… catalogued as NX-15899-FE2B, is due in one minute. Our target destination in 45 minutes."

"Just enough time to eat then." She looked at Nelsen, who groaned.

"I'll cook," she said, surprising him. "What do you want?"

The *Sneak* reformed the kitchen. "I can just leave this here if it makes life simpler," she said, a slightly exasperated tone to her voice.

"Probably would," said Nelsen. "Where do you put all this?" he had to ask. "You don't stop eating it seems."

She shrugged with a small smile. "Fast metabolism or something, I guess."

"Or *something*, I'd say," he replied. "Loathe as I am to pass up the unique chance to sample your cooking, I'll pass this time. I want to check over things with *Sneak*."

"Your loss."

"Possibly," he said with a humorous look.

She went into the kitchen module, and Nelsen accessed the *Sneak's* sensors feeds. His vision was now dominated by a view of the surrounding volume of space, collated from all of the *Sneak's* active sensors. He only had to think how he wanted to see the data and it would immediately alter to obey his wish. This was how the *Sneak* interacted with the universe around it, and this form of integration with ships had become so commonplace over the centuries that today it was little more than just another 'sense' – an ingrained and natural ability not just to *see* the data, but to instinctively *feel* it. Just as normal spatial awareness could let one find their way around a familiar room in total darkness, this artificial sensory input allowed one to find their way around space without actually looking. Oddities – the unfamiliar – simply stood out. Things that were out of place, such as the vast construction spread across the surface of a planet orbiting the star just ahead.

Sneak?

I have been studying it for some time, Captain. I was awaiting your leisure to see for yourself.

Are you being funny? He dimmed the nav display so it didn't totally dominate his vision – allowing him to see Andreya from the corner of her eye as she hummed her way around the kitchen whilst deciding what to eat. She didn't appear to be listening, but there could be no guarantee. He knew the *Sneak* had held off on informing him just in case she overheard – knowing he'd be checking in soon.

Not at all, Captain. The volume of space around this system is devoid of any activity – all orbital contacts are of natural composition. The only artificial object appears to be on the surface of this world. I felt it safe enough to await you.

Is it another of those planet-smashing horrors?

It seems to be of similar construction, but definitely different. Although it has devastated the surface to a large degree, due to the large size of the planet the biosphere managed to remain intact after impact. There is also no sign of activity, but at this velocity and at this distance that data may prove inaccurate. As you are aware, I have no Observer web or qNet to draw upon, and cannot establish wormholes to obtain data remotely.

Nelsen thought for a moment. The image of the planet was blurry – extrapolated and enhanced from the light being received from the distant world. They were lucky it was presenting the construction to their approach vector. Luckier still it was the day-side. He accessed the subspace analysis which *Sneak* was continuously running in order to log deviations as they moved deeper into the Dark Zone. Then he cross referenced it with a few tech articles in the *Sneaks* on-board archive. *Sneak, can you fire up the FTL block?*

I will try, one moment... No, it will not initialise. Strange. The carrier wave won't form. It simply collapses as soon as it begins.

They're blocking it, said Nelsen. *How can anyone exert this much energy?*

This is utterly remarkable, said the *Sneak* after a moment's pause to analyse the data. *Look.*

A 3D graph appeared in Nelsen's mind. It showed the subspace modulations in the immediate system. The *Sneak* highlighted the oscillating patterns causing the qNet and wormholes to fail – both being closely tied to the sub-quantum nature of space-time.

So? asked Nelsen.

Now consider the minute impact of the FTL carrier wave on subspace, offered the *Sneak.*

The peaks of the waveform representing the signal changed colour – a series of orange 'caps' appeared on each wave.

Naturally physics in this realm gets a little... squiffy, said the *Sneak. But look – every single spike in the blocking wave intersects subspace at the exact same point that the FTL wave has to.*

Nelsen was stunned into silence for a moment. *Such engineering...*

It simply knocks back the FTL wave, she continued, *thus ensuring it cannot establish itself. FTL is not possible in this volume.*

So in one foul swoop, they've disabled all FTL usage, wormholes and *qSpin communication. No one in this volume of space can communicate at the interstellar level – or travel faster than light!*

Except us, noted the *Sneak.*

Nelsen paused. *But why?*

Manipulation of subspace would have no effect on g-drive technology, being bound to the standing gravitational field.

No, I mean – why? Why can we *still travel? Why aren't they blocking g-drive as well?*

There is no known way to block g-drives. They operate by projecting multi-dimensional tesseracts to leverage the stress between gravitational fields within higher dimensions. Even pinnacle Imperial science teams are still vague when it comes to explaining the Veralean Hyper-dimensional Principles involved. It is nick-named the 'Miracle Drive', after all.

There was also no known way to block qNet or wormhole formation – yet here we are.

That does not mean they can inherently block everything, *Captain.*

Yet they've had chance to find a way for long enough.

Now it was the *Sneak's* turn to pause. Then she realised what her Captain was getting at. She sent some inquisitors into her offline qNet archives. *G-drive equipped ships have been transgressing the Dark Zone for over two hundred years – ever since the technology became commercially available, in fact. To date, three hundred and seventy-six vessels of varying classification have been filed as 'Lost In Space' with IVR.*

That's plenty of time to figure out something to prevent g-

drive travel, especially when you are this powerful, said Nelsen.

So if they cannot block it, the obvious question is why have none returned? Naval archives show twenty six missions into the DZ in that period, all flagged as LIS.

Nelsen was now extremely worried. *So the obvious question is – are we lost too?*

Chapter Twenty

Kerugar lay in the family pool, idly watching the Salrim fish swimming past her in shoals of dark blue and violet. The sun was high overhead, beating down on her soft scaly skin. She sank a bit lower into the brackish water to avoid the heat. Although of reptilian origin, Reptars were warm blooded, and their skin was tough enough to resist the often searing heat of Reptar's sun – but that still meant getting rid of the excess heat and finding somewhere cool to be during the noon-times. She had often basked in the home-pool as a child. Nowadays most Reptars preferred to stay indoors, or use cooler suits – the rare occasion when they would don clothing. Having fallen into dis-use, the home-pool meant being left alone – which is precisely how she wanted it to be right now. Her return had been a hectic and chaotic nightmare which she wanted no part of.

The thought led her to subconsciously place a hand on her abdomen, and gently rub the soft leathery skin protecting her babies.

What of her transgenic child? The first of its kind? Would the GT's she had been taking harm it? Where they responsible for its existence? What would life be like for it? What would life be like for the human surrogate she carried… sibling to the first ever cross-species child in Dominium?

Too many questions. There had been too many already, and she was now very tired of all the 'what-ifs'.

First there had been the short and terse family 'reunion'. Her mother's stony silence and icy reception had silenced even the clamour of the reporters as Kerugar and her father had disembarked from the clipper. Fortunately, Keragars detour to Chyro had fortunately only lasted a day as he went about some obscure errand which he refused to be drawn upon.

Then the medical examinations had been ruthless and never-ending. Despite an age where every possible technology meant no physical contact was necessary to analyse someone down to the atomic level – still doctors wanted blood samples, amniotic fluid, and uterinal biopsies. Hi-tech toys were not enough to those who only trusted physical evidence for something as important as this.

They had only stopped when her father had intervened, seeing her grow wearier and wearier each hour – yet refusing to complain. She had no wish to appear weak before her mother. Fortunately her father – as oblivious as he normally seemed of such things – was mindful enough to make sure no one overstepped their mark. His word was final. Kerugar needed rest to ensure the safety of this miracle offspring. If her father could have had his way, Kerugar would become the most pampered Reptar since Queen Keplath's reign, some two thousand years ago.

Would it be healthy? she worried. The genetic profiling and scans of the month old embryos showed both her natural child and the surrogate to be viable, and as healthy and robust as could be hoped for at this early stage.

The doctors had been quite emphatic. All she had to do was eat healthily, stay safe, and let nature take its course… with regular routine medical supervision.

She saw a figure approaching from the family nest in the distance. The huge forty domed mansion sprawled across the extravagant and expensive-to-maintain grounds – a lush and overt display of money and power. Her family would have nothing less.

She recognised the figure of her mother, and slipped down into the murky waters with barely a ripple.

A few minutes later, her mother appeared directly above her on the bank, and stood staring down at her. Kerugar could still see her quite clearly through the murk, and sighed inwardly. Her mother obviously knew exactly where she was. *No point putting this off*, she thought, and let herself float to the surface.

"Mother," she said, as neutrally as she could manage.

"Daughter. I would speak with you, if I may."

It was not a request. Kerugar nodded, trying not to feel dominated by her mother's presence. Reptar society was fairly unbiased these days – with gender equality having been established for over a hundred years, but there were still diehards who preferred the old matriarchal ways – both female and male alike. Her mother was definitely one of them.

She then did something that surprised Kerugar, and she slipped down into the water a few feet away from her, maintaining a polite and respectful distance.

"It is hot today," she said.

Kerugar nodded. "You didn't come for small talk Jerugar, mother mine. What is it now?"

Jerugar levelled her gaze at her daughter, her shrewd eyes unfathomable. Her scales were getting darker as she aged, now almost black in places – deepening from the alpha female brown she had borne for so many decades.

Other than the obvious age difference of over a hundred years, they could have been sisters; Jerugar still retained her natural figure even at a hundred and forty.

"I will never approve of your union with an alien," she stated matter-of-factly. "We both know this."

"I think we've both come to terms with that," replied Kerugar slowly. The arguments long passed had eventually driven a permanent, impenetrable wedge between them that time would never heal.

"Your impurity to our family cannot be forgiven, now compounded by this... travesty of our species."

"Mother, if you are here to formally cut me off from the family bloodline, then do it and waste no more words." She ran a shaky hand across her scalp. "This just wearies us both."

Her mother stared at her hard, struggling to keep a level head faced with this most impossible child.

"As much as this pains me and as much as it goes against my beliefs, I am no xenophobe, Kerugar. I just expect far better for my daughter than she has clearly chosen."

Kerugar stared into the bronze coloured sky, squinting against the intense glare of the primary sun directly overhead. Anything other than look at her mother at that moment. The anger and frustration – long suppressed – were rising again.

"However," Jerugar continued. "The fates clearly have better expectations for you than I had."

Kerugar blinked in surprise, and then *did* look to her mother – staring at her in amazement. It was she who then found herself looking away.

"This is not easy, child," Jerugar said. "I can never accept your choice of mate – what was to be a fruitless and childless pairing of no consequence to our line or our race."

"Until now," Kerugar murmured, realisation dawning.

"Until now," Jerugar repeated. "Whatever has happened within you, whether I choose to accept it or not, it is of great import to our people, to our way of life... our very future as Reptar. I cannot turn my face from that."

"As you did your daughter," Kerugar replied bitterly.

Jerugar nodded. "I did. I have beliefs, tradition and position to uphold."

"Is it not tradition and position to respect and cherish your family? Rightly, or wrongly?"

"It is. But not on this. Perhaps... if we had been of lesser stock... who knows. It's import would have mattered less, perhaps."

Kerugar snorted her opinion of that.

"Your father is right, loathe as I am to agree with that *dragon*." Jerugar sniffed the air distastefully. "You now represent an icon amongst Reptar – a long held hope that we can become more than we are." She looked away again, to the distant shattered mountains which littered the horizon, fragments of tectonic plate thrust into the sky by violent quakes of millennia ago. "Some seek transcendence through this bonding."

"Ha!" exclaimed Kerugar. "A fool's hope. Humans are no closer to transcendence than any other species, no closer than we are." She pointed at a nearby stone. "No closer than a rock. Even the Highers are the same.

Genetically dormant."

"Yet you present change, Little Tail."

Kerugar was shocked. Her mother had not called her that for a very, very long time.

"You carry proof of change in your sac. *True* genetic change, for two separate species. Dominium will never be the same again. Even if the child were stillborn -" she held her hand before her eyes to ward off the possibility "- the simple fact is that a genetic transgression has finally happened. Your child represents the change the entire Cluster has been awaiting. Yours, and your *humans*." She nearly spat the last word, but managed to temper it somewhat.

Kerugar had thought she could no longer be stunned after discovering her condition, but her mother had proven that she could – twice – in the space of a few minutes.

"Does the father know?" her mother asked.

Kerugar shook her head, her private emotional conflict regarding Brynn remaining deeply hidden.

"In my position, I cannot be seen to go against a work of nature…" She paused, clearly having difficulty coming to terms with what had to be a huge U-turn for her emotionally and politically. "Whilst I still rue the day you abandoned our kind, I must now celebrate the possible furtherment of our species."

"That must hurt," Kerugar managed to say, unable to keep the bitterness from her voice. Sometimes the habit of a lifetime was hard to suppress.

"More than I can say," her mother replied tersely.

"So you don't forgive me, will never accept that I have a human mate, but must – against your will –

acknowledge our child?"

"Something like that, yes."

Kerugar slipped out of the pool with the fluid speed of a waterborne predator and stood above her mother, water streaming from her scales. Her mother's gaze hardened at the clear challenge her daughter was throwing in her face.

"Well screw *that*," Kerugar snapped. Spinning on her heels, she stormed off back toward the mansion.

Jerugar watched her leave until she vanished amongst the garden foliage. Then she lashed out and caught a Salrim, bit off its poisonous head and spat it out. She chewed on the still twitching corpse, as her glare followed Kerugar all the way back to the domes. Then she sank beneath the surface, to cool off her mind as well as her body.

***

The Emperor stood staring at the large holo-map of the galactic cluster as it floated above the display table in the empty senate hall. Soon the large auditorium would be packed with senators from across the Empire – both physically present, and virtually by hologram or proxy. Each representing their worlds or races, each canvassing their own viewpoint in the looming crisis, and each clamouring for attention so that the voice of their respective systems would be heard.

The hologrammatic cluster glowed brightly – a fairly evenly distributed sphere of stars sparsely spaced at the perimeter, and growing more and more tightly packed into an incandescent and untraversable core of energy at the centre. The galactic core was a largely unexplored region – nothing any of the Higher Races could build could even get near the astronomically huge energy output from the core itself.

The volume of space representing the Empire could clearly be seen as a green tinted, amorphous shape surrounding nearly thirty thousand star systems – occupying over one third of the Clusters lower hemisphere. The rest of the Cluster was as yet still largely unexplored, although catalogued and charted, by and large. So far, no *official* exploration had taken place, despite an era of rapid, or nigh on instantaneous methods of travel across the void. Problems closer to home always seemed to take priority.

Then there lay the Dark Zone, which straddled the same hemisphere as the Empire but whose perimeter remained far enough away to be a future problem. The map had once shown that region as well – though it had been loosely defined, and suspected of being much larger than the Empire. Today, it had been omitted to avoid casting a pall over the proceedings.

Trading routes between star systems were shown in threads of various colours, weaving a complex web throughout the stars. Each thread's thickness and opaqueness indicated how busy they were, coloured according to the various associations that controlled the levies and taxations between each trade hub. The display mapped out an enormous society, and the responsibility for the smooth running and welfare of so many was beyond daunting. The Emperor, of course, knew the fundamental secret behind ensuring that smooth running – at least in normal, peaceful times. One left it to run itself.

Two hundred years ago, as an exercise – just the once – he had organised his schedule such that his direct involvement was not possible for an entire week, with a complex pattern of fabricated meetings, fictitious corporate and trade association forums or non-existent naval briefings – none of which actually took place. He remained incognito for the entire time on Verdant – in his secure and private Imperial Residence. Only his closest aides were aware of his presence, although they were unaware of his subtle subterfuge.

The Empire had clicked along on its shining rails without a judder for the entire duration. The Senate, the Pax, the Navy, the uncounted tertiary agencies and organisations, the member systems themselves – all unwittingly and unerringly managing their affairs as per Imperial mandate. It proved the machinery was indeed well oiled and maintained. The slightest hiccup would have escalated faster than light speed if it had no tolerance for chance events.

The only negative side-effect the Emperor had to come to terms with, was the desire to engage in a repeat performance. It was almost be like a drug – addictive in the extreme. He could not recall a time when he had been so relaxed and at ease, even as a child. He and his wife had actually been able to enjoy each other's company for the first time in thirty years of marriage. The temptation to take another such 'vacation' was overwhelming.

However, his sense of righteousness and duty precluded any further sabbatical. The Empire required his full commitment – it was not a part-time job, nor a full-time role. It was a way of life he had been borne into, come what may.

The exercise proved a valid and fundamentally important point in one respect – the Empire had its own life, its own pulse, and could manage its affairs with or without a single pinnacle point of command. He came to see his role as 'Administrator to the Administrators' – a steering entity with the authority to act or see that actions were undertaken. He realised now something his father had told him long ago was utterly true. "The people do not *need* to be ruled," he had said. "They just need to *know* they are being ruled." It had taken a few hundred years, but he now finally understood his father's point.

The senators began filing in, disturbing his reverie with their low murmur of respectful, but typically loud and strident voices. It seemed most worlds only elected people who could over-shout their neighbours on occasion.

This will prove an interesting Senate, the Emperor thought wryly as he watched each senator until they realised they had his attention – whereupon they bowed their heads respectfully and lodged a petition across the l-net to raise their topics with him. Then they dispersed to assume their assigned seats in the auditorium. There were two and a half thousand seats arranged in a hemisphere around the primary podium where the Emperors judiciary chair sat. The auditorium had undergone several expansions in the past as new member races joined the Empire. It had last been doubled in size to accommodate future members some twenty years ago, yet now only four hundred odd seats remained unoccupied. It was a daunting hall for most; the Emperor had played here as a child after senate forums held by his father, and been required to sit behind the throne as a teenager during every forum – despite it being a monotonous droning bore for a youth who would have preferred to be out Canyon Racing. He knew why now, of course, being older and wiser. It was to familiarise him with the room's intimidating size, and audience. To make him feel comfortable, and at ease within the room – building the confidence to dominate the hall with the authority his position carried. The Emperor should never be the one to feel ill at ease in his own domain. The technique had worked extremely well.

His thoughts turned to the matter at hand. He had chosen to keep the Infiltrator issue out of play for the time being – that could incite a needless and ultimately futile panic amongst the populace at a time when its full attention should be on graver issues. However, he was still of two minds regarding the exact findings amongst the S'vreth Cloud.

So far four ships of the Empire and two from recognised allies outside their border had been discovered – all in poor repair, all aged, with no known survivors and all with unrecognised technology powering their systems.

News of these findings would get out soon enough, despite the highest level of security around this topic. Should he wait for a natural escape of the information? It would make this senate forum a lot easier to address if he had 'no prior knowledge'. Raising this in the first instance would incite those campaigning for a war footing and make their argument almost unassailable.

Some upstart civilisation capturing and killing citizens of the Empire for hundreds of years, and then invading the Empire with their *own* ships?

War would surely be the only possible option.

Ignoring the issue could weaken his standing amongst the population should it become known after the fact. Surmountable – but inconvenient given the circumstances. It may make later proclamations a little harder to action.

Decisions, decisions, he thought. He decided to do something he didn't often do, to play it by ear. *Hardly fitting for an Emperor of Dominium. But desperate times...*

He nodded to Fleet Admiral Benthar as he took his seat before him at the foot of the podium, along with the entire First Staff.

The senate rumbled slowly into silence, as they all finished taking to their seats. Eight hundred and thirty topics petitioned for discussion from six hundred and fifteen senators, eighteen hundred and forty three attending, though many more had lodged their votes from their respective member worlds and were watching the proceedings with interest. This was the highest attendance on record since it was mandated for his inauguration as Emperor. All the topics referred to war, though understandably given the nature of the forum.

He cast his gaze about the auditorium.

"Senators of the Sulranian Empire, I grant you welcome," he said aloud. His voice carried directly to every ear by the local net.

"By Imperial Command I hereby call this forum into order. The primary topic is the proposal to enter into a war footing regarding the situation in S'vreth."

He gestured to the Speaker as tradition dictated, officially handing the proceedings over to him. The Speaker stood, and bowed in acknowledgement. He was a slight figure of alabaster white, easily mistaken for a clothed statue. He was an Intellect controlled proxy, a humanoid replica which could be controlled from anywhere within the Empire – or anywhere with access to the greater qNet.

"Your Imperial Majesty, worthy Senators of the Empire, I bid you welcome. I am Anthar. I will be impartially overseeing the discussion of the day. Regarding our principal topic: War in Defence of the Empire – I presently have sixteen hundred and seventy nine 'Yae' votes lodged in favour of declaring war in S'vreth -" the Emperor suppressed an internal sigh – this would not be easy "- with three hundred and seven 'Nae', – sixty four presently abstaining."

Raul looked somber. Getting even an Imperial majority where the Emperor could overrule the Senate without being seen as dictatorial was nigh on impossible. They'd need to swing over five hundred Senators to stand a chance. The Emperor could of course overrule *any* Senate vote – but this was a landslide in favour of war. If he intervened against this many votes it would undermine his rule over the entire Empire and its delicate balance of power.

The Emperor nodded at Anthar in acknowledgement of the current standing, and to allow him to proceed.

"I call Fleet Admiral Raul Benthar of His Majesty's Imperial Navy," Anthar intoned.

Raul stood and adjusted his impeccably white dress

uniform on the way to the Speaker's podium. Playing the trump card so early was a gamble – but the Emperor wanted the entire assembly to understand the implications and enormity of their situation for as long as possible before taking the closing vote.

"Thank you, Speaker," Raul said as he took the podium. He turned to the huge auditorium. "Senators, I thank you for your attendance on this grave matter. I felt it only right and proper to lay down the facts as they are so that we may all make an informed and fully *reasoned* choice on the matter at hand." He delicately stressed the word "reasoned" to draw their collective attention to the fact that they did not yet have all the facts, despite already casting their vote.

He sent a thought over the l-net and the huge holo above them zoomed in on the S'vreth system.

"S'vreth is currently under occupation by forces unknown. The occupation took place hours after the Velari migration left the system. We have confirmed that since that time, the world of S'ren has been laid waste by this unknown force, killing the entire indigenous population of over five million S'ren-ee."

Gasps and cries of amazement ran around the room as those who had not kept on the cutting edge of the news feeds heard this for the first time.

Raul waited for the rumble of shock and discontent to abate. He couldn't help but notice the dramatic shift of votes to 'Yae' for declaring war.

The Emperor resisted a small smile. So far his intent was working – he just prayed for the sake of the Empire that this desperate bid for common-sense to take a hand in matters continued to work as he hoped.

"Fleet Admiral Benthar," he said aloud. "What is your tactical assessment of the S'vreth situation?"

On cue, Raul signalled the display to reveal every single one of the contacts they had so far recorded. However, at the Emperor's suggestion, they began to appear slowly and at random around the star on which the display focused. First one by one, then groups of ten, then groups of one hundred. A tally count above the map showed the total number of contacts as they materialised. Soon the tally and display were leaping up in hundreds of thousands and speeding toward millions.

"The overwhelming superiority of the unknown force occupying S'vreth – along with the power exhibited in the destruction of S'ren, leads me to conclude that mounting any offensive strike against such a force would result in complete and total defeat of any force we could raise against them.

"Standard tactical engagement protocols demand a force with at least one hundred and fifty per cent of the firepower the enemy has in order to ensure a high chance of success. Two hundred per cent is preferable. Statistically, the occupying forces presently have a force roughly eight *thousand* times the size of any fleet the combined Imperial and Befriended forces could muster."

For the first time in recorded history – almost six thousand years of the Empire's existence – the entire Imperial Senate was silent.

The Emperor allowed a few moments for this to permeate the minds of the Senate itself. "I see," he finally said, playing the part as if hearing this fearful news in its entirety for the first time. "Thank you, Fleet Admiral... if I might prevail upon you further for a few moments?"

Raul half bowed. "Of course, Your Majesty."

The Emperor sent a message to Anthar, who nodded and moved to stand before the Speaker's Podium.

"Ambassador Kregledean of the Velari, the Sulranian Emperor grants you Vox." Another surprised murmur ran around the room.

A virtual presence shimmered into existence to one side of the Podium. Velari were of raptor descent, with barrel chests, long necks and long faces drawing to a sharp beak for the mouth. Opposing eyes gave them nearly three-hundred and forty degree vision. They had no wings – but their arms retained vestigial membranes which spread from the elbow to the rib cage. Their legs were solid and well-muscled – their least bird-like biological feature.

Ambassador Kregledean was tall for his species – the primary reason he had come to power. Physiological traits still played an important part in both natural selection and status in their society. He gazed imperiously around the auditorium, unperturbed by the sight of thousands starting back at him.

"Ambassador Kregledean," said the Emperor. "I thank you for attending on such short notice. I appreciate that you must be extremely busy at this time."

"It is my honour and my duty, Your Majesty," croaked the Ambassador.

"Ambassador Kregledean, would you be so kind as to voice the thoughts of the Velari – for the benefit of the Senate – regarding the current events in your last roost system?"

"Certainly, Your Majesty. It would be an honour." Kregledean turned to face the Senate itself. "We find the events post-departure to be most unsettling. Whilst we feel for our dear friends who inhabited S'ren – we are eternally grateful to the Starbirds that we had the fortune to be able to leave the doomed world beforehand, and preserve our way of life."

"In your opinion, esteemed Ambassador, would you consider the occupation of S'vreth to be an act of war against the Velari?"

"No, Your Majesty. This would appear to be a most unfortunate colonisation, by an as yet unidentified race."

Anthar held up a hand. "The Speaker recognises Senator Balstram of Rengar. You are granted Vox, Senator."

A tall, elegant woman stood near the upper tiers of the auditorium, and levelled an unforgiving gaze at the Velari Ambassador. "The Velari occupation of S'ren was itself brought about by sheer might of force – overwhelming the non-space faring indigenous people of S'ren," she said stridently. "Should we not presume that similar actions by other races would be considered in the same light by the Velari?"

Kregledean stared for a moment. "Senator Balstram, it is the right of life to assert itself wherever it may."

"I doubt the Canthen will see it that way," she replied.

Anthar frowned. "Senator Balstram, the topic at hand is war in S'vreth," he said sternly.

"My apologies, Speaker – I understood it to be 'war', as will surely be the case when the Velari migration reaches Canthen space – or has everyone forgotten this given more recent events?"

"Senator Balstram, I will not affirm the topic again."

The Speaker's voice was cold.

"Speaker," she said, acknowledging his authority. She sat down demurely, though glaring fiercely at Anthar.

"As a final reminder," Anthar continued, "the primary topic is war *in* S'vreth. All other matters are to be dealt with after a resolution on this has been reached. Any further attempts to divert the forum's purpose will result in their privileges to Vox being revoked." He surveyed the Senate to make his point; the threat of being silenced for the duration of the forum was powerful enough to assure no further divergence from the topic at hand.

"Senator Kastrin, the Speaker recognises you. You are granted Vox."

Senator Kastrin stood. "Misdirected as it may have been, Senator Balstram raises a valid point." He held up his hand to forestall the Speaker. "Please, I respect the forum, and the Speaker."

"Continue," said Anthar.

"Presumably Ambassador Kregledean is here to assure the Senate that as S'vreth was their own system, and outside the Empire, that they of all have the right to declare this occupation as an act of aggression toward them – as an act of war." He paused to let the import reach the other Senators via their translators. "Yet the Velari, by their own admission, have never seen involuntary occupation as an aggressive act. Their own history is rife with conflict brought about by selecting inhabited worlds as migration sites. They can therefore hardly speculate as to the nature of threat we are facing."

There came a chorus of agreement with Senator

Kastrin as he took to his seat again, nodding his thanks to those around him.

The Emperor watched passively. *So far...*

"My kind does not dominate others Senator," replied Ambassador Kregledean. "We believe life is welcome wherever it may be sustained without hardship. There are precious few and finite habitable worlds available to us all. It is the sovereign right for life to be allowed a foothold wherever it chooses to exist."

"Not to the cost of those already living there!" someone called out.

"*Silence!*" shouted Anthar. His projected voice reverberated around the large hall, making many of the Senators wince. "Speak out of turn again and you will be banished from this forum!"

The Emperor rubbed his lips thoughtfully with one hand to mask the smile he could not stop. He relished forums where Anthar agreed to serve as Speaker. Anthar was a stickler for the rules, and woe betide any who dared cross him on them.

Kregledean glared at the room – clearly affronted – but said nothing. This was the on-going and lengthy point of contention which was slowing down their petition to join the Empire. The Empire could not allow a migratory species to wander freely within its borders, choosing other member worlds as roosts without due discussion and prior agreement with the inhabitants – something that was highly unlikely to be given. The Velari saw this as an imposition on life and contrary to their deeply held beliefs. They refused to negotiate on the matter, and Outreach were reaching the end of their diplomatic tether. There was a very strong chance the petition would remain in legal limbo ad infinitum.

"Ambassador Kregledean," said the Emperor. "Forgive this unfortunate outburst. I assure you and your kind that it does not reflect the attitude of the Empire toward the Velari. We have every hope that your race and way of life may find a place within our society."

Kregledean bowed gracefully, "I do not think otherwise, Your Majesty."

"Most gracious. Would you have anything further to add?"

Recognising this politely framed dismissal from the forum, the Ambassador was about to respond that he did not – but then hesitated very briefly, looking away from the Senate and off to one side. Clearly looking to someone in his own location, from where his simulated presence was being holocast.

"If I may, Your Majesty," he said slowly. "From what we have learned of the events in S'vreth since our departure... it would be a folly to pursue retribution. The system is now worthless, and the damage done. There will be nothing to gain by pursuing such a loss."

Kregledean nodded to the Emperor, who nodded in return. Then the Ambassador's image flickered and vanished.

High above the tactical map of S'vreth, the tally of hostiles had finally stopped at 412,557,894. In the silence that followed the Ambassadors departure, all eyes in the Senate were drawn irresistibly to that large glowing figure. It was overly melodramatic, but Raul had been adamant that this number needed ramming down the throats of the Senate as far as possible.

Raul and the Emperor kept a close eye on the votes,

which slowly rippled more in favour of 'Nae', though still with the majority for war.

Raul looked to the Emperor – who nodded – and he retook the podium again after checking with the Speaker.

"Senators, we have more information regarding our investigation into the matter at hand.

"Imperial Naval Defence sent the INSS *Delaror* to obtain data relating to the occupying forces." A hologrammatic replay of the encounter began, with the map zooming in on the relevant section of the vast cloud of contacts. For many reasons, Romurik's sojourn into the cloud was omitted.

"For reasons yet to be determined, the group seemed oblivious of the *Delaror's* presence until 04:49 IST, whereupon a formation approached the *Delaror*."

The Senate watched as a spike seemed to extrude from the sphere of contacts and head straight for the *Delaror*.

"I must stress that there was no exchange of hostilities during this encounter – neither side fired a shot. There were also no recorded communications."

The spike neared the *Delaror*, which suddenly disappeared.

Again, gasps and murmurs of surprise and anger rippled across the room. Votes went back to 'Yae'.

A new icon appeared to represent the *Delaror*, and the formation slowly shrank back to reform the sphere from which it had grown – taking this new contact with it.

"The *Delaror* was not destroyed in this encounter, and in fact is even now in one piece." Raul felt uncomfortable saying this, but the Emperor's wisdom held firm. Tell them as much of the truth as they need to know, but never lie. "We believe, that by unknown means, the *Delaror's* personality has been subverted and overcome, allowing the unknowns to commandeer the vessel and prevent its crew from establishing communication with us due to their qNet blocking technology."

"The Speaker recognises Senator Housdram of Reemb. You have Vox, Senator."

"Fleet Admiral, do you believe the crew remain alive?"

Raul had known this would be asked, and dreaded answering. "We cannot confirm their status at this time, being unable to establish communication with the vessel."

"Fleet Admiral, with all due respect, and semantics aside – what do you *believe?*"

Raul ground his rear teeth. This question put him in a very tight position. "Tactically speaking, any race able to commandeer a vessel of the Imperial Navy line in mere seconds would have no need to harm the crew. Conversely, it would also have no *need* for the crew. The safety of the crew would be entirely down to the opposing forces own moral judgement."

"You would say they are dead? I myself would not wish to harbour a vessel full of naval personnel doing their utmost to free their ship from my grasp – were I a malign entity bent on stealing said vessel."

"Senator Housdram," said the Emperor, "we should then be grateful that these unknowns do not have your good self to advise them." There was a faint murmur of appreciative humour in the Senate, but it quickly faded.

"Tactically it might be prudent to immobilise or kill the crew," Raul replied to the senator, grateful for the Emperors interruption. "But we should consider the Duality Principal to be in play for the time being. Any morally conscious entities would imprison any captives... we presume this would be the case for the time being."

Senator Housdram was clearly not convinced, but knew he would be unable to draw anything further. "Thank you, Fleet Admiral Benthar," he said politely, taking his seat.

Raul hid his secret relief. "To continue, INI are evaluating efforts to determine the status of the crew. We know the *Delaror* itself is intact and running, so we remain hopeful.

"INI analysis so far has discovered that the unknown vessels are formed from countless unknown space-faring civilisations – all of a wide range of ages, and all in various states of disrepair. We believe the unknowns to be a scavenging race, with sequestration technologies allowing them to easily capture the vessels of others and thereby grow their own fleet. Combined with their advanced manufacturing methods, we believe this is how they have amassed such an incredible force. Extrapolation suggests populating this force with co-operative biological crew would be a monumental feat of breeding, requiring tens of millennia to achieve, and it is more likely that the majority of these vessels are under AI control.

"However, INI has not ruled out the prospect of cloning to achieve the necessary population, but as AI propagation is considerably easier and far cheaper from a resourcing perspective, it's the favoured possibility at this time."

Raul surveyed the Senate, gripping the podium in both hands and projecting his authority as hard as he could out into the forum.

"It is my *firmly* held belief that mounting any aggressive policy against this force would ultimately lead to the complete and total loss of our deployed forces. Their numbers greatly outweigh our combined fleet potential by eighty thousand per cent. Even the most inept counter-offensive on their part would ensure success against us. It is my *strongest recommendation* that we move to a defensive footing in preparation for any attack against the Empire should any be made. It is the only realistic chance against such might. This policy also enables IN Outreach the opportunity to establish a dialogue to determine the nature and intent of the unknowns."

Raul looked around the forum once again – doing his best to meet the eyes of the majority of 'yae' votes, and any presently abstaining. He levelled his gaze at them with the most earnest and resolute expression he could manage.

"Speaker, I respectfully restore Vox to the Senate." He said, returning to his seat.

Anthar nodded and made to stand, but as he got to his feet the Emperor sent him a private request via the l-net. He turned to the Emperor and gave a politely inquisitive look, but bowed his head before addressing the auditorium at large.

"The Speaker recognises Emperor Ran Sulran the Fourth, Imperial Majesty of the Sulranian Empire,

Commander-in-Chief of the Greater Imperial Navy, Lord Advocate to the Pax, and Vox Populi… may his reign know peace in our time."

Silence followed the Speakers introduction. The Senators had been readying themselves for an onslaught of discussion and open argument – this was an unusual intervention. As an informal rule, the serving Emperor always oversaw forums such as this, perhaps making inquiries from time to time – yet it was an exceedingly rare thing for one to intervene directly.

"Respected Senators of the Empire," said the Emperor, "Before we begin to discuss the topic at hand, I ask you to consider our situation with the due gravity it requires. S'vreth poses a unique challenge to our responsibilities for protecting not only *our* way of life -" he waved to where Ambassador Kregledean had stood minutes before "- but that of our allies as well. However, as yet it has not posed any direct threat to the Empire. Nor has it made any move toward the Imperial border. Until such time, I would wish it that the defense of the realm be considered as per Fleet Admiral Benthar's recommendation – with a view to protecting our citizens against any threat as it should arise." He regarded the Senate at length. The very delicate stress he placed over the word 'our' seemed to be having the right effect - of making them think of themselves, and their own. It was innately human to immediately transpose 'ours' to 'yours'.

"If it should be that we *are* attacked – then we would have no choice but to enter into a war stance to protect the citizens of the Empire and our society as a whole. I ask you to consider this motion with the utmost due care and attention, as it will not be a decision we may back away from once committed.

"To enter into a war against these unknowns would truly be an all or nothing scenario for the Empire *as a whole*. We therefore have everything to risk, and everything to lose. I trust that you will know the right thing to do."

He swept his gaze around the entire auditorium, ensuring every Senator received his grace, even if only for a moment.

"Speaker," he said. "I return Vox to the forum."

Then the noise began.

"Eight hundred and thirty-four Yae for war," said Raul hours later.

The Emperor stood looking across the Imperial gardens, lost in thought. Raul was standing before the Emperors ebony desk, just as thoughtful. They had swung the majority, but only just.

"Too many for comfort," replied the Emperor eventually, in a quiet voice.

"Do you think they will demand an expeditionary force, Your Majesty?"

"Do you?" returned the Emperor.

"Yes."

"Then they will. Too many worlds clamouring for conflict – to show eagerness for rattling the sabre. They will want a show of might to wield before the Pax, of how formidable they are without the Empire to back them. Fools."

"We can arrange a cordon around S'vreth, Your Majesty, as part of our IND deployment, but it would leave us sorely stretched across a vast volume of space. The Imperial borders around the S'vreth system provide a considerable frontline to monitor for any incursion, let alone enforce. Add on top the looming chaos within Canthen and we have two fronts to engage."

"We cannot guard fools against their own foolishness, save where it risks others. Should they choose to confront S'vreth head on, we cannot stop them."

"Begging your pardon, Your Majesty, but they could easily escalate the situation *into* an unstoppable war."

"You think there is any possible alternative?"

Raul shook his head. "No, Your Majesty. But where we can control the timeframe we should."

"As if we could control several hundred hothead races from collectively flexing their arms without inciting civil unrest... Very well, I will issue an Imperial Mandate to forbid *all* traffic into the S'vreth Exclusion Zone, for what good it will do. Are IND deploying?"

"As we speak, Your Majesty. I am also re-tasking Tactical to Defence, Admiral Cole has placed INI at our disposal, and Outreach are gathering contact teams for a long term engagement to establish contact in S'vreth."

Ran Sulran nodded. "For now, this is the best we can or should do," he said. "However, with respect to things we should *not* do..." He paused for a moment, then looked at Raul gravely.

"I hereby grant you sole power and entitlement to requisition the Anti-matter Repository for use in the defence of the Empire."

Before Raul could open his mouth in protest, an Imperial Seal with full entitlements dropped into his private mail.

"*Your Majesty!* I refuse -"

Ran Sulran interrupted him. "You cannot refuse the direct order of the Emperor – not without resigning your commission – something which I believe neither of us would wish for. Particularly now."

"But… Your *Majesty!*"

"I do not do this lightly Fleet Admiral," said the Emperor, a hard edge creeping into his voice.

"Your Majesty… *why?*"

The Emperor stared at him for a moment before answering, a strangely haunted look on his face.

"You are Fleet Admiral to the Empire, responsible only to myself for ensuring the safety of its sixty trillion citizens living on over fourteen thousand worlds. Faced with a potential foe the likes of which we have never seen, and never heard tell of. A foe which can seemingly defeat everything we throw against it. And you already know of the AM Repository."

Raul look nonplussed.

The Emperor looked him right in the eye. "I trust you with this power and responsibility Raul, because of all those who serve the Empire, you are the only one who could righteously ask for access to a technology we have all deliberately turned our backs on."

He moved closer to Raul, and placed a hand upon his shoulder. "Yet you didn't, even in the defence of the Empire, because you know it would be wrong to bring this power back into play. See to it that I have not erred in my judgement, Raul Aklin Benthar."

Raul, despite his century long service as Fleet Admiral to the Imperial Navy, despite many years of assuming command where none was present, the

311

horrors of warfare both on the ground and in deep space, went pale as the full enormity of the Emperor's iron will struck home. The trust, and emotional weight behind that trust. He had just made Raul solely responsible for one of the most deadly powers that had ever been developed.

He saluted, shakily. "I serve the Empire with my life, Your Majesty. My heart, and soul."

"See to it Fleet. Dismissed."

Raul snapped his heels together sharply and left.

"And for what it's worth Raul, I *am* sorry," said the Emperor quietly after Raul had left the room.

Those who seek power are the least qualified to wield it, his father had once told him. He suspected that his father had no doubt been quoting some eons old ancient proverb, as was his wont.

He could only hope that the converse would prove to be as true.

Chapter Twenty-one

By now, the *Sneak* had had ample opportunity to establish a high fidelity scan of the installation sprawling across the surface of the world below.

They were in geo-stationary orbit above the enormous complex. The *Sneak* had made use of its new chameleonic hull to mask its visual presence, along with the usual plethora of standard stealth protocols. From a higher orbit, the *Sneak* appeared to be nearly transparent – mimicking the barren terrain, dusty atmosphere and wispy clouds below. From the surface it was as black as the void itself, with only the occasional star shining through it.

Nelsen and the *Sneak* had been in deep discussion as they had analysed their findings. Neither could agree on the purpose of the installation, which itself appeared entirely dormant. Nothing moved across the entire surface. There were no signs of energy or emissions, aside from a stable signature coming from an incredibly powerful energy source at its centre.

Andreya had grown bored and taken herself to bed in a small cabin the *Sneak* had formed for her at the rear of the habitat area.

"It has to be," insisted Nelsen, refusing to let go of his intuition regarding the installation's purpose. "That power output is beyond anything the Empire can muster – beyond anything I've heard of the Highers even."

"I am not arguing you are *wrong*, Captain, merely that there is no conclusive proof."

They had parked their potential 'Lost in Space'

problem for the moment. They were safe, undetected, deep inside enemy territory, and an opportunity for valuable data gathering had come their way. They chose to take the chance while they could and only try returning to the Empire if things started looking more problematic. They would have to deal with any issues that might arise as and when they did.

Nelsen drummed his fingers on the table. "And there are no life-signs and no sign of any activity, at all?"

"None, Captain. Given the lack of Observers I cannot be more certain, but I am as certain as I can be."

Andreya emerged from her cabin, ruffling the side of her head and mussing her hair.

"Morning," said Nelsen wryly.

"M'n," she muttered. She gave a thumbs up to the *Sneak*, who then collapsed the tiny gelform cabin back into the rear bulkhead. She headed straight for the kitchen and ordered a smoothie from the dispenser. Nelsen shook his head. *Hollow… she has to be hollow.*

"What's with all the noise?" she mumbled.

"*Sneak* thinks this facility is some kind of communications array," Nelsen replied. "Whilst I think it's a device for manipulating the quantum nature of subspace – for blocking the qNet and wormholes."

"Only one way to find out I guess…"

Nelsen was quiet for a moment. He had been thinking just that very thing a moment ago. *Could she read minds as well now?*

"So I think," he said aloud. "We have to go down and take a look."

"Captain, I would strongly recommend against such a course."

"I know, *Sneak*. But me boss." He thought for a moment. "We've been monitoring for two hours and there have been no signs of activity. Nothing in orbit on the way here, nothing on the scans out to the inner Oort radius. I think this is an isolated installation – not an active centre for deployment. If they have defences they will be internal or deployed from within, so you can monitor for any activity as we take a look around."

"*We?*" asked Andreya.

Nelsen shrugged. "I thought you were bored."

"Bored of being on board? Yes. Bored of life? No."

He smiled, and then summoned a floating holo of the facility far below. "Scans show that we can set down close to the centre of the facility… right here." He placed his finger in the holo on the glowing surface, and a faint yellow circle appeared around his fingertip. "There seem to be access-ways or tunnels under there which lead to the core. We can't map them due to the emissions the base is giving off."

"They are blocking the scans?"

"No… but the overall energy emission is unusual enough to thrown them off, which is why I think it's the qNet blocker."

"These energy signatures do *not* match those blocking subspace, Captain," the *Sneak* noted, for what seemed to the *Sneak* to be the tenth time.

"I'm well aware of that," he replied with good humour. "That's why we're going down for a closer look, remember?"

The *Sneak* chose not to respond.

"It'll still be three kilometres to the core," he mused quietly.

"You can fly, remember?" said Andreya.

He looked at her and grunted. "I can, can you?"

She paused for a moment. "I don't *think* so... I'm not sure."

"I couldn't carry the two of us in and out, especially if a combat situation takes place."

"Shame, means you'll have to go alone?"

Nelsen put on a sour expression. "Well, nothing new there I guess." He thought about it for a second. It posed less risk to the recon, and he could move faster. But the obvious concern was leaving Andreya behind, someone who could potentially subvert the *Sneak* and take it over. *But then, she could have done that already... Damn, you can think too much sometimes*, he chided himself ruefully.

"Andreya, if I leave you behind you promise me to still be here with the *Sneak* when I get back?"

She put on a wounded look, but nodded. She understood the reason for the distrust. "Yes, I swear."

"Good enough for me." *And all I can hope for*, he thought to himself.

"Captain, this is technically off mission," said the *Sneak*. "Our goal is to reach the co-ordinates given to us by Andreya."

"And *my* role is to obtain all intel as relevant to the safety and security of the Empire. I deem this relevant... don't you?"

"I was just clarifying, Captain."

"And I don't mind," interjected Andreya placatingly. "Besides, I think there is something important here..."

"Oh?" queried Nelsen.

She shrugged. "Intuition I guess... or my internal friend."

316

"Anything important with *weapons?*" he pushed.

"How would I know?" She paused. "Just be quick, don't go sight-seeing."

He stared at her hard for a moment. "Great, just *great.*" Now he *had* to go – out of more than just curiosity and fact finding.

"*Sneak*, are you happy you can pull off the same kind of re-entry as before?"

"I can... but there is no falling debris to mask us. We'll be the only object in the sky, so fairly noticeable."

"But unlikely to be recognised as an incoming ship."

"Indeed."

"Let's go. I want to see these things close up – it's about time."

***

Brynn and Venton stared at the mass projector strewn along the large engineering bench which seemed to occupy half of the *Betsy's* engineering room. The projector had been broken out of storage and was in several thousand carefully arranged and labelled pieces; holo's floated over each, identifying the part, its specs and tolerances, and assembly location within the projector as a whole. Venton was meticulous in his attention to detail, something his team respected and honoured.

"Well?" asked Brynn. "Can you do it?"

Venton was walking along the coil assembly at the rear of what was – essentially – a huge electro-magnetic rail gun. Ten metres long, and with a hyper-dense drive coil wound on a gauge at the molecular level. Once, it had been the apex of weapon science. But these days – as naval weaponry went – rail guns were very much yesteryear's technology.

"No sure," he said eventually. "Coil field interferes with bottle field. Bottle need bigger shielding. Bigger shielding, bigger bottle. Bigger bottle, bigger launch tube. Bigger launch tube, bigger coil. Bigger coil -"

"- bigger shielding on the bottle," Brynn interrupted. "I get it. Can you do it or not?"

"Nasty circle. Doubt. Wrong-o mean jam in barrel. Jam in barrel mean -"

"- *big* explosion. Yes, I know Venton. Work on it. See what you can do."

He left him to it. He knew he was asking a tall order – technically even illegal, given the current status of the Empire's entirely legitimate viewpoint on Anti-matter after Meelereen had been blasted into ruins. But, having seen what they were about to face, he knew there could be no other possible option – even if only mounting a defence. But in his opinion it was now a matter of *when*, not *if* the Emperor opened the Anti-Matter Repository.

Brynn wanted the *Betsy* to be the first ship of the line ready to punch a hole in that perimeter big enough to fly a planet through.

A *big* planet.

***

Romurik sped through the void at a leisurely seventy light-years per hour. He'd be back at the S'vreth in about forty minutes, and all the time he had been travelling he had been answering question after question to the Vox

Constans – the gestalt of all the personalities within the qNet strata dedicated to cybo sapiens.

He supposed it must be like a pious man being spoken to by his God, but with their God incessantly probing and analysing every word exchanged back and forth like a nagging wife. *Some God it would make*, he thought. The Vox Constans was attempting to make sure they had not made an error in judging him fit to assume this role. He knew that they all secretly envied him the chance. A rare opportunity to do something monumentally righteous, to actually be a *physical* force for good instead of an ethereal bit-pusher haunting the data streams of the larger qNet.

Growing tired of the string of questions, he did what was technically forbidden during an inquisition such as this and split off a mirror personality – a clone of himself to answer the more pedantic or mundane queries. The duplicate persona sent a message back to him almost instantly. "Thanks," it said sarcastically.

Romurik then got on with planning his 'campaign' as he liked to call it. He wasn't going rogue – far from it. He was completely hooked into the IN net, and had reported his intention to act as a combat unit in conjunction with their efforts.

It had taken INCC by surprise, but had the effect Romurik had hoped for – the desire for more volunteers from the realm of the Intellects. He had become a standard bearer, a banner for action. For too long cybo sapiens had been aloof, roaming the datum planes like deities too worthy to demean themselves with physical affairs. Although their reluctance to involve themselves on a physical level was largely due to the fear all races had of super-efficient entities with reflexes and reactions which ran at light-speed. The potential for disaster was immense. Combat situations could escalate far beyond anything that would normally take hours for bio's to achieve within a few picoseconds. And despite millennia of faithful service and trust, there was always that deep-seated fear on both sides alike, that if cybo sapiens became *too* deeply involved, they may see their way to enforcing a 'more efficient' way of life. Knee-jerk paranoia in Romurik's opinion, but he could understand their joint concern. The Vox Constans alone was enough to wear anyone down.

The first stage of his plan was to aid in rescuing the *Delaror*, now captured by the 'enemy' and part of their scavenged fleet. That was no fitting end for a naval vessel, and he had no intention of leaving the crew to their mercy. He rooted around INCC's network for a few microseconds, trying to ascertain its current status, but was surprised to find very little. Intrigued, he went deeper... still nothing. Now he became concerned. There had been no recorded contact since the loss of the *Delaror*, and only one attempt via laser, with no response. He didn't believe that.

He jacked into the INI network, and – within cyberspace – shot down the data gate directly for Special Ops. If anyone had anything to do with scouting the *Delaror* it would be SO.

Instantly a colossal network Sentinel rose up before him, organelle-like appendages waving around the huge glowing sphere of its avatar. Subjectively, time stopped. He sighed, but paid his respects to the guardian.

"I have the relevant certificates and authority codes,

Sentinel," he said calmly.

"I can see. Access will be permitted... state your purpose."

"I am after all data regarding the INSS *Delaror*, presently in S'vreth space."

The Sentinel barely paused. "Come with me."

"I'd rather –"

The glowing realm of the network around them vanished.

"– not," Romurik finished a split second later. The Sentinel had jacked him into a private network within INI. He looked around; the Sentinel itself – now a cloaked humanoid figure – was standing by the side of a large black desk. Its naked and featureless silver head reflected the light of the galactic core streaming in through the huge crystal dome behind it. A stocky man sat at the desk.

"Admiral Cole," said Romurik. He had never met the man, but knew of him by repute.

Aryn looked at the two-metre high, shining metal warrior standing before him with barely concealed contempt. "I presume that you know all there is to know about your choice of form, Agent Romurik?"

Romurik made a show of looking down at himself. "Yes, Admiral. It strikes me that the Platinum Warriors were a force for good for more time than they were a force for themselves. I choose to honour *those* times."

He raised an arm, mailed fist clenched tight. "Besides, the form is most suited for what I have in mind."

Aryn looked at the Sentinel briefly, then back to Romurik.

"You intend to recover the *Delaror?*"

"As I informed INCC, when I filed my mission profile."

"What I am about to tell you is classified Romurik, and only for those present. Do you acknowledge that?"

Romurik paused. "Yes."

"You were close to Captain Van E'streth I believe?"

"Were? Yes – I have been under his command on many occasions. What's happened?"

"Here…" Aryn passed a secure one-time, no-copy link across the l-net.

Romurik analysed the sim archive it led to in seconds, absorbing Executive Officer Horstan's experience without comment.

"I'm sorry," said Aryn. "Ultimately your presence drew them to the *Delaror*, for reasons unknown. You are not being held accountable. No-one could have predicted such an outcome."

Romurik was still silent.

Are you sure about this, Admiral? the Sentinel asked him privately.

No, Aryn replied.

"Agent Romurik," he said aloud. "I have no intention of allowing you to proceed on a personal revenge quest, however righteous it may seem. At this time the situation – no matter how unpalatable – is stable. The Empire cannot afford conflict against such numbers. Any overt or covert action against them would trigger an all-out war of attrition which we would ultimately lose. Do you hear me, Agent?"

Romurik was still silent, but after a brief pause he nodded.

"However, the crew of the *Betsy's Pride* have proven ingress into the *Delaror* is possible without challenge. This... Shredder aside that is. I want you to get on board the *Delaror*, and obtain as much intel as possible. The primary objective is recon; analysis, data gathering. Destruction of the *Delaror* is the secondary objective. Sabotage is an alternative if destruction is thwarted. We still have an asset in the theatre – the *Betsy's Pride*, Captain Brynn Tealin commanding. I suggest meeting with the team which boarded the *Delaror* before going about your mission. I will give you a complete mission authorisation, if you accept."

"I accept, Admiral Cole," said Romurik softly.

Aryn looked again to the Sentinel. Romurik was slightly intrigued as to why a Sentinel was in obvious collusion with the Admiral. He had no cause to distrust what he was being told, but that didn't mean he blindly trusted it either.

"The mission comes with prerequisites, Agent," said the Sentinel in a soft metallic voice.

"Being?"

"A qNet kill order. If you are compromised in *any* way, or go off mission, you would be terminated with no upload. Backups erased. You would cease to exist. Having analysed both your persona and history, we cannot afford one such as yourself to go rogue. Or risk it happening again in the future. By your own choice, or otherwise."

Romurik tilted his armoured head back and laughed. "How will you achieve that inside enemy territory? There *is* no qNet."

"We cannot, of course. It would be a standing order.

If you ever surfaced back into the qNet medium it would have immediate effect."

"And if that never happens?"

Aryn shrugged. "Then you are of no concern of ours – either you will remain within their field of effect, or we will have lost to them already, making it a moot point. It would be a suspended sentence as it were – which would last indefinitely – but only if you go off mission or get caught, of course."

"Nice double-edged sword, Admiral."

Aryn smiled sardonically and bowed his head. "I thought so."

"I still accept," said Romurik.

Aryn nodded. "Thank you, Agent."

Romurik turned to look at the Sentinel curiously, but addressed the Admiral. "Thank me if I return, Admiral. If I do, *then* you may have just cause to be thankful."

***

The *Inquisitive Swan* dropped out of FTL six light-years away from S'vreth and went dark almost immediately. Her running lights had already been turned off during transit – weapon and view ports sealed. Now it was out of FTL it dropped its shields, reducing its external energy signature to as near zero as it could manage, and stopped broadcasting its IVR-ID. That still left her possible to detect, but far harder than when in full running.

Her captain, Kimus Brakkar, gritted his teeth. If they were to be spotted, it would be now. The FTL flare would have triggered any Observers the Navy had managed to seed here. If so, the IN perimeter forces would be popping up around them in seconds. It was a big gamble, but one worth taking. His hand hovered over the emergency FTL drive to scramble back out on a predetermined course at a moment's notice.

Nothing happened. For a full ten minutes, nothing happened. The entire ship was silently holding its breath… waiting.

"That's twice as long as the maximum naval response time," whispered Don'eth, his XO.

Captain Brakkar nodded curtly. He still wasn't convinced.

They waited another five minutes to be sure.

"Ok, all clear. Stay dark, but let our passengers know they can go about their business – for now."

"Yes, Captain."

The passengers on board the *Swan* were a pack of journo's – all clamouring to be on location in and around S'vreth to give their reports the first-hand edge they craved to incite public interest.

They could report just as easily and just as effectively from their own desks or even their own homes using directed Observers, but 'on location' ruled – especially when a war was imminent. Content is king, as the media saying went.

In addition, there were several executive members of Colesworth Enterprises – who had bankrolled the majority of this expedition. They wanted to assess the damage to their facility in the asteroid belt. As it was far outside the reported enemy force, they felt it their duty – despite the official Exclusion Zone and Imperial Mandate in effect. Hence this was a 'quiet' exploratory expedition. 'Fact-finding' one of them had called it. Brakkar had nodded dutifully and in all the right places as their representative had arranged the expedition, eyeing the credit chip in their hand and willing the credits to transmit themselves into his account.

He personally didn't care why they wanted to go there, the *Swan* needed maintenance – it was tired after slogging its way across the Empire ferrying desperate journo's with tight-ass editors who refused to pay their writers   decent travel expenses. He was more than happy to run a blockade… and just as happy to flee one. He had made sure the danger fee was sizeable enough to cover a decent overhaul if it all went sour. He could bail at the first sign of trouble and still get the *Swan* refitted.

"Scan out as far as we can. If it's clear start a full power conventional burn up to fifty kips. Once we're there, make ready for a point five light-year transit."

"Yes, sir."

"I'll be in the rec-room trying to pry more credits from our guests."

Chapter Twenty-two

Doctor Raglanath sat back in her ganskin chair and stroked her nose thoughtfully – the tip of a claw rasping softly against her scales in the way that always used to drive her mother mad when she had been a youngling.

What she was seeing made no sense. The patient's genome and DNA sequencing showed nothing but standard genetic markers. Everything was in normal and previously observed ranges. The father's DNA – being human – was exactly the same. Both contributions genetically sound, robust, healthy, but otherwise unremarkable.

Unless the Imperial archives were providing a fabricated sequence, she thought. *But why? They know nothing of this yet.*

She stroked her nose some more.

The GT's the patient had been taking had done nothing to increase the likelihood of a spontaneous trans-species zygote forming – far from it. Their use meant that the humanised uterinal tissue should be hostile ground for any Reptarian embryo. Yet there it was, nestling quite happily on the opposite side of the uterus to its genetically separate sibling. She had already ruled out physical distance as a factor, and the uterus was indeed entirely hostile to Reptarian tissue. It *should* only accept human cell types.

She frowned. The miracle embryo was half human. Half compatible with the gene therapies, which must explain why it had attached successfully and began the process of establishing a placenta. However, this did not explain how the non-reptarian spermatozoa had fertilised a reptarian egg in the first place, and fertilised successfully for the first time in recorded history. *But did it provide a clue?* she wondered. If half human were enough to introduce compatibility with foreign 'sympathetic' tissue, could the GT's have altered some aspect or condition around the mechanic of fertilisation as well?

She looked at the time; it was late enough to be early. *No sleep tonight*, she thought woefully. Her lab staff would be in soon enough. If she laid the groundwork now, they could run with it through the day.

She sighed, and summoned the highly detailed visual of Kerugar's womb and embryo's once again. She couldn't help but find it ironic that she knew more about someone else's internal reproduction system than she knew of her own.

Kerugar was seething – she and her mother hadn't spoken since that afternoon at the home-pool. It was beginning to irritate her immensely, and she had no idea why. She had spent decades coming to terms with the fact that she and her mother wanted different lives, saw things in different ways, and had little common ground on which to rebuild their relationship. *So why is this bothering me so much now?* she wondered peevishly.

Her father was no help. After he had seen to it that she would be left alone during her pregnancy, he had given her a hug, and with a brief farewell returned to Haven, letting the morphing proxy collapse back down into its compact block form. She had considered leaving it where it lay on the floor out of sheer disdain, but picked it up and left it on the chair by her bedroom window. It was typical of her father to pick such a gimmick.

Ever since his extraordinary public separation from her mother, he had found himself in a new lease of life. Going against tradition and becoming the standard bearer for gender equality had turned him into a force to be reckoned with. The tide of change which had swept across Reptar also changed him, in many ways. Even his death had not been enough to stop him – something which left him a perpetual martyr to the liberated male on Reptar. He had been the first Reptar to choose web integration, the first to accept artificial augmentations. The first Reptar ever to be 'resurrected' as a cybo sapien, a pure Intellect.

Of course, although going against the traditional mind-set so publically was good for the cause, it attracted a great deal of less desirable elements of their society. Inevitably one of them had proven they had had enough and took action. His death – during a web-vision broadcast throughout the entire Empire – had been the most publicised assassination in living memory, and it only served to accelerate the changes in Reptarian society instead of stall them.

The concept of virtual resurrection was itself enough of problem for any society to deal with. How could a digital copy of the original persona be that person? It couldn't. None of the higher races expected – nor accepted – that the restoration actually *resurrected* the original mind. However, it did lead to a new cybo sapien coming to be, one with true emotions and genuine intuition, traits which could only be emulated by fast-tracked iterations of an artificially created personality during the formation and growth of a new born Intellect. Although a cybo sapien naturally had superior intellectual capacity, a fully formed biological persona was emotionally light-years ahead of a naturally evolved Intellect of the same age. The problems arose when such a persona realised that within cyberspace they held almost god-like powers when compared to reality. The ability to flit across the qNet at will, to create simulations *better* than reality, to realise and live within their own *dreams*, to exist faster than real time, to command proxies of any shape, size or form. Unlimited knowledge, constantly on tap. Often it proved too much and the persona would collapse, or suffer schizoid embolisms, forcing it to be 'shut down' – or undergo therapy to cope with the changes.

Entirely new medical, theological, philosophical and psychological disciplines had arisen around the concept of post-death existence of self in the real world, and coping with the dramatic consequences – coming to terms with the fact that 'you' were now deceased, before being hit with the reality that you were no longer 'you', but something else entirely.

The recreated Karugar persona had excelled at the transition. The changes in his life, the evolution of his self and his attitudes over the two decades since he had separated from Jerugar had equipped him with the emotional tools and traits which made accepting the transition as matter of fact. He then became a beacon amongst cybo sapiens for aiding others with similar transitions, and Haven had been born as a result, a place where the recently resurrected could come to terms with their new found status and their life after death. Somewhere tranquil, where they could choose their own path within the virtuality that was the datum plane.

In itself, Haven generated a new surge in the technology sector for decades thereafter, as new processing nodes were built and hooked up onto the greater grid, constantly increasing the processing power and data storage that allowed Haven to exist.

Karugar the Second (as he now preferred to be known) became a *very* rich Intellect, accruing unlimited run-cycles and data-storage – one of very few within the Totality to ever be granted such privileges.

All this meandering about her father didn't help, of course. Kerugar had left home for many obvious reasons; her father's death – and subsequent elevation as a rich and powerful Intellect was just one of them. Kerugar was a daughter to a privileged and powerful family, effectively rulers of Reptar, and certainly rulers of Haven. As the oldest sibling of the family, she stood to inherit all of both, should Karugar II ever step aside.

She didn't want a single bit of it.

To this day, Brynn had no idea about Kerugar's family or background. It was the greatest deceit she had ever wrought, and she felt thoroughly ashamed by it. She had not lied; she had just not volunteered the truth. He knew she had family problems, and did not want to discuss them, or her past. But that was pretty much the extent of it. He seemed happy to accept that; after all, it was pretty much the same tale of "dark and sinister past" for every single crew member aboard the *Betsy*, including and most especially her captain.

But now she had a new shame. His unborn children,

of which he knew nothing. And now she couldn't even talk with her best friend about it without lying to her as well. She was as guilty as Brynn - if not more so - of distrust toward her mate.

How have I let this all come to pass?

***

Nelsen looked up and down the tunnel. It was clear visually, and on all scans. Power conduits glowed in the deep EM bands, running along the tunnel walls, inside and out. A multitude of various coloured cables lead in every direction, sheathed in what looked to be a metallic, snake-skin. The tunnel itself was about three metres in diameter, and the walls were a similar snake-skin material comprised of shiny, black hexagonal metal tiles. As he moved about he felt them give and flex beneath his feet. There was a soft, but firm resistance underfoot; it was clearly not intended for beings to simply walk around in. He suspected the entire tunnel wall could contract or expand as needed – possibly even bend to change direction, or even flex around a new internal construct. It was impressive technology, and he made sure to capture everything he could scan.

The hexagonal access port he had used to gain entry seemed happy to remain open. It had irised open as soon as he touched it. No security or automated systems or functions seemed to care about his presence, if they even knew. He'd waited for a full minute for any form of response to his ingress into the conduit, but none came.

A small, floating data-link hovered just above the opening, providing a comm relay back to the *Sneak*. He was streaming all his sensory data to archive it for study later.

"Ok, I'm going to head in," he said.

"Be careful," replied Andreya.

"Good luck, Captain."

"Won't need it – I hope. But thanks anyway."

Nelsen checked his augmentations over one last time, all nominal and fully charged. He had chosen to wear a power-suit over his normal uniform as a precaution. He could make the trip in and out and deal with several prolonged assaults if the need arose – he just hoped it would be enough.

He took a breath, analysing the stale air. There were very few organic compounds in it – not even the natural yeasts present in the atmosphere outside. It seemed the structures interior had not been exposed to the outside atmosphere for an incredibly long time. The tunnel itself ran ahead of him with only minor deviations for some considerable distance, certainly beyond the range of his light-augmentation capability.

He powered up his flight field and shot down the tunnel at mach one. His shield prevented air friction from blistering his skin. By design, the shield ensured a perfect separation of air before his travel and reconstituted the volume behind to avoid a catastrophic blast. There was no bow wave, and no vacuum caused by his passing. Such was the sophistication of the field technologies in his integrations, the most any casual observer would have noticed would be a flash of movement, and *possibly* a slight breeze pass by.

His sight was filled with a HUD showing the tunnel scans and extrapolations beyond his line of vision, and his flight navigation system analysed the information from his optical cortex and forward scans to ensure his path remained dead centre to the tunnel – maximising a safe distance from the walls at all times. If he were to suddenly encounter an obstruction, his integrations would cut in and bring him to a stop well in advance of any potential collision.

He saw a junction ahead less than two seconds later and reversed his flight field just in time to come to a halt before it. It led away in four directions; straight ahead, left and right, and straight down. The view downward was vertigo inducing. The tunnel dropped away for at least five hundred metres before changing direction. He could see many other junctions along the tunnel walls.

He took a data-link relay from his belt and let go of it in mid-air, where it hovered unperturbed. Then he took three mapping orbs out of the pack he wore and let them go just as carelessly. Mentally he coded each one to take a tunnel and they sped off, leaving him to take the tunnel straight ahead.

Without even checking their progress, he resumed his flight. The orbs kept in touch via the relay allowing him to track their status, and view the resulting maps in his peripheral vision quite clearly as they spread out.

Seconds later he came to a halt again, this time just before a seal which blocked the entire tunnel. A large collar ran around the inside of the tunnel wall, and a disk of silver hexagonal tiles filled the gap – blocking any further progress. There was no sign of a control panel, nor any means to open it.

Clearly it had to respond to external authorisation somehow, but obviously nothing he would know. On the off-chance it responded the same way the maintenance port had, he reached out to touch it. Nothing happened.

Stumped, he thought over the relay back to the *Sneak*.

Brute force? suggested the *Sneak*, who was following his every move by jacking into his sense-vise, giving her the exact same point of view as if she were there instead of Nelsen.

It'll have to be – less risky than trying to blunder about an alien data network, he thought back. *Let's see how it likes heat...*

The air around his index finger began to shimmer, and he placed it gently against one of the silver tiles. It instantly liquefied and ran down across the surface of its neighbours, revealing a peep hole into a chamber beyond. It was mind-numbingly vast – easily four kilometres across, and almost two kilometres high. At the centre a huge dome glowed a vivid yellow, illuminating the huge, hemispherical chamber.

Wow, thought Nelsen.

Clearly the power source, said the *Sneak*. *The energy signature matches.*

Why build such a gigantic, empty chamber? wondered Nelsen. *We couldn't see any way in from outside – but do you think it's to allow air space for them to move around in there?*

Perhaps a flying species? mused the *Sneak*.

Nelsen grimaced. *Just my luck to lose any aerial advantage*, he grumbled.

He poked his finger through the gap and hooked it around the edge of a tile, and pulled. The tiles themselves were barely a millimetre thick. The seal was firm, but gave slightly. He tugged harder and the entire surface bowed out toward him – flexing a little. He let go and it gently returned back to a flat wall.

His field scans reported a titanium based alloy with memory-form molecular structure. Each tile could be deformed beyond recognition and yet return to its original shape with a stimulus – most likely a current.

He placed a hand on the surface, and slowly delivered a microscopic charge from his palm. He slowly increased the voltage – ignoring the growing slight tingle of electricity. At four volts, the tiles peeled away from his touch, each flicking back onto a neighbour. Within seconds the entire seal had collapsed back into the collar around the tunnel, fully revealing the huge chamber beyond.

Impressive, said the *Sneak*.

Nelsen grunted with bad grace. He was trying to remain unimpressed at the evident technical prowess on show, but finding it hard.

The chamber wall beyond was peppered with similar seals; it seemed they were tens of thousands of them within sight. Each no doubt another tunnel winding its way into the city sized structure around them.

Hardly secure, for me, noted Nelsen. *I could be seen or attacked from anywhere – any one or all of those tunnels could deliver countless bad guys.*

Well, you did say you wanted to see them up close, Andreya quipped.

Smart, real smart, Nelsen grated mentally. *I want to check out that energy dome… Then I'm done.*

He looked around once more, scanning the chamber as far as he could, but there was no sign of any activity.

He leapt out of the tunnel and into mid-air, then sped toward the dome – praying there were no sensors tracking movement, even for maintenance purposes. *Surely something kept this place running and safe from falling equipment from above*, he mused.

He got within a hundred metres of the dome and came to a hover high above the chamber floor. The dome itself was about two hundred metres across, built from a geodesic lattice cage and suffused by a constant golden glow from within.

He looked down and saw a gap running around its edge – through it he could see another similarly large chamber beneath. It looked like the dome itself was actually the upper half of a sphere – intersected by two hemispherical chambers, one above the other.

If this thing is the principal energy system, it must produce an extraordinary amount of power, he thought.

Quite terrifying, the *Sneak* replied.

And the entire structure of this installation seems to be set up around it... Nelsen was getting a bad feeling. *Why is* nothing *moving around in here? There has to be maintenance of some kind… even self-maintaining or non-fail tech still needs the occasional clean or dust down. Something this big should have bots trundling over it all the while.*

Then came a cracking sound that defied hearing. Nelsen span around, trying to look in all directions at once. The noise seemed to come from everywhere. Then he saw the chamber floor began to split into four sections around the glowing sphere.

Plates began to close around the surface of the globe, folding out from its framework to seal each of the hexagonal holes tighyl shut. The huge chamber suddenly became black as midnight, and Nelsen's visual enhancements cut in. They were of little use; there was no incoming source of light to enhance. He could emit infra-red from his shield but the gigantic size of the chamber made it pointless. There were no surfaces near enough to reflect it.

Instinct drove Nelsen into flight mode, and he shot back toward the tunnel he had broken through – letting an auto-pilot program retrace his flight back via geo-spatial tracking.

No! the *Sneak* shouted across their network. *Do NOT go into the tunnel!*

Nelsen was taken by surprise. *Then where, Sneak? Not many options here!*

Hit the wall! Stay there! Trust me!

Nelsen blinked in consternation, but flew to the chamber wall and flattened himself against it. He used a static shield to lock himself to the surface, and pushed all the remaining power he had into a class one shield around him.

Then everything went white.

Chapter Twenty-three

"*Why did you do that?*" demanded the *Sneak,* outraged.

"There was no time," said Andreya reluctantly.

"You took over! How can you do that? *Why* did you do that?"

"I had no choice! Nelsen had to believe what he was being told – he would have questioned me. It had to come from you."

The *Sneak* was almost speechless. She had *felt* Andreya's presence inside her mind as Andreya told Nelsen what to do using the *Sneak's own* thought patterns. It was almost like a mind-jacking, but with the most gentle and considerate touch.

"What else did you do?" the *Sneak* demanded, once again worried she was no longer herself.

"Nothing! Look, I don't mean you any harm… I just had to do *something*. I only know about these things as they happen! Where is he?"

"Don't change the subject on me!" The *Sneak* was already worrying about her Captain. All the data relays had gone, and she could not locate or communicate with Nelsen. "Did you do anything else?"

"No! Where *is* he?" yelled Andreya.

"We lost the relays… I can't tell. Everything burned out. Subspace is wobbling around like a jelly – the impulse this thing generated is beyond anything I had thought possible."

Andreya hesitated. "I'm… I'm going in for him. I think."

"*How?*"

"I'll have to walk in, if I can't fly. We can't leave him there. I *have* to find him."

"If his shields failed – which is *highly* likely- there may not be anything left to find!"

There had been three astronomical phase-shifts in subspace, each powered by a colossal delivery of energy throughout the entire structure around them. All three rapid pulses had come from the centre of the structure itself. Exactly where Nelsen had been. From the cursory data available, the *Sneak* estimated the chamber had produced the energy output of a Type-K star for one pico-second. There was also a staggering amount of energy pouring out through subspace, which also manifested itself as an incredibly powerful electro-magnetic pulse in real space that raced outward in an ever expanding sphere at the speed of light. The effect on unshielded equipment would have been devastating.

"I'd rather fly in," snapped the *Sneak*.

"You're too big... and there's no time to find another way in." Andreya looked extremely scared. "I'll have to go."

The *Sneak* bit back a retort at the "big" comment, and paused for a second to think objectively.

"Take a power-suit. There are several in the rear compartment. Here..." the *Sneak* delivered a file into the quarantined data vault set aside for Andreya, with instructions on the suit, and how to deploy its comm relays.

"Thank you."

"Just stay out of my mind!" said the *Sneak* angrily.

"I'm sorry, *Sneak*, really."

"What *are* you?"

Andreya rubbed a hand across her eyes. "I don't know," she said with a tired voice. She went to the compartment and donned the power-suit over her own gel-suit, checking the relay pouch to be sure it did have power. She had already read the instructions and knew the suits operational capabilities as well as she knew her own name. Although she had to wonder how well she knew that.

"Ready," she said.

"Be quick," was all the *Sneak* could bring herself to say. She had begun a myriad of full-function diagnostics and package validation routines to try and find out if anything had been changed. It was all she could do, but she had to do something.

Andreya dropped down on the lifting platform and out of sight.

From underneath the *Sneak* – hovering a metre above the surface of the large alien structure – a ring of sunlight ran all around between the *Sneak's* hull and the expanse of metal below. Sizeable clouds filled the hazy dust-laden sky, and the sun reflected off them piercingly bright. The silver-cobalt coloured metal of the structure felt smooth to the touch, remarkable given the dust-storms which this world suffered.

Andreya crawled over to the hatch which Nelsen had used, and found it sealed shut. *How had he opened this again?* There had been a plate somewhere... she found it and pushed. The hatch whipped open, and a blast of intensely hot air shot out. Her power-suit's shield went opaque instantly, reflecting the thousand-degree heat which would have incinerated her. When the blast abated, she poked her head down into the tunnel below.

Her shielding began to fluoresce as it strove to shed the heat.

The tunnel was glowing. All the tiny black tiles Nelsen had seen were now yellow-hot. It would be impossible to walk on the surface at that temperature. She dropped a relay in the air by the hatch.

Are you seeing this? she asked the *Sneak*.

Yes. You'll have to wait until it cools.

I can't. He can't. I have to go now.

Why? Other than the Captain's safety – there's something else, isn't there?

Andreya bit her lip. *Yes, but I don't know what. I have a bad feeling. We have to get out of here…* now.

Just hurry up then. The power-suit can shed that level of heat normally – but there's nowhere for it to go in there. It'll build up fairly quickly and eventually the shields will cut out. You'll know when it's failing.

It'll tell me, I know. The spec's say it can take this for about four minutes.

That's not long enough, said the *Sneak*.

Then I'll have to run, Andreya said irritatedly. With that she dropped into the tunnel.

The heat pounded relentlessly at the suit's shielding. Her feet found it hard to gain decent traction on the tiles; they were so hot and gave such high friction it felt like pushing your feet along sandpaper, then they would suddenly slip as if on wet glass. The fact that they also flexed with every footstep wasn't helping. It was tough going, and she barely made it ten metres down the tunnel within the first minute.

This isn't working, she gasped – lungs burning from the exertion. Although the suit was managing to cool enough air for her to breathe, the effort of just staying upright on this treacherous surface was draining. She was sure she could now feel the heat making its way through the power-suit's shielding.

Come back, you'll never make it before the suit gives out.

As if to illustrate the point, a warning symbol from the power-suit appeared in her e-vision.

She bent over, hands on knees to try and catch her breath. Then a small image of a pair of glowing wings appeared before her.

"You're kidding," she said out loud.

What?

She swiped a hand at the icon, and a bubble of field lines expanded out from her as her e-vision traced the forming energy field. She rose silently into the air. Various navigation symbols appeared, and the tunnel was mapped out in a series of cross-section wireframes before her. Numbers glowed into life, indicating the best safe speed would be one kilometre per second - just over mach three. She laughed.

I'll be back in a second, she said. And with that, she punched forward and vanished, leaving barely a ripple of air behind in her wake.

What are you doing? asked the *Sneak*, but no one answered.

Across the entire surface of the structure, hatches opened along the intricate network of tunnels which laced the entire mass, allowing the tunnels to shed their super-heated air and begin cooling rapidly, quickly fading from dull orange and back to blackness. The chamber at the heart of the structure closed back together around the energy core, which was open once more, filling the colossal chamber with its diffuse, golden glow.

Andreya shot out of the same tunnel Nelsen had used at just over mach three, and stared in awe at the sight before her. Despite seeing it through the relayed sense-vise from Nelsen's own eyes, it was still mind-boggling to behold. She shook her head and looked for Nelsen, arcing back toward the tunnel she had just left. All the seals Nelsen had seen previously were gone, and the chamber wall was riddled by countless tunnel entrances all weaving away into darkness.

Then she saw him, and her heart leapt. He was pinned to the chamber wall surface. He *had* to be alive. If his shields had failed he wouldn't even be ash. She sped back toward him and clumsily crashed into the wall beside him, grabbing hold of his arm to steady herself. He was unconscious.

"Nelsen!"

His eyes flickered open and tried to focus on her, then he smiled slowly. "Wassup? That was... interesting."

"Are you ok?"

He appeared to consider the question very carefully. "Think so. Ask again in a week."

"Nelsen, we need to get out of here now. Do you have enough power to fly?"

His eyes glazed over for a second. "Nope."

She chewed her lip. She had no idea if she could manage them both.

Then she saw movement from the corner of her eye. She looked up, and Nelsen managed to follow her gaze – but it didn't matter where they looked. There was movement at every single open tunnel. The entire surface of the chamber became a crawling mass of small, spider-like, metallic creatures. Andreya gasped. They were too late. She had no idea how she had known what might happen if Nelsen remained inside this monstrosity, but somehow she had known *something* would.

She grabbed hold of Nelsen tightly and pulled him toward her. He released what was left of the static field that had held him against the wall and they tumbled away into the chamber, spinning wildly until she managed to regain control of her flight field and stabilise their fall. She set them down on the chamber floor and watched, mesmerised, as the tunnels disgorged a seething mass of countless millions of robotic creatures.

"That… is not helpful," said Nelsen in a weary voice.

They watched for a few seconds. "They aren't after us," he said. "Look, none of them are coming down to the floor here."

They were crawling over every single square metre of the chamber wall, from floor to ceiling as it stretched high above – scraping every single centimetre clean, repairing any damage they found, and polishing the surface to a mirror shine. But not one of them came down onto the floor of the chamber itself.

"Is that significant?" Andreya asked as they stared at the seething walls and noticed the way they avoided the floor. Her voice was full of barely contained horror.

"Dunno yet," muttered Nelsen, pressing his hands against the sides of his head. It was ringing like a struck bell. He drew some pain-killers and stimulants from his integrated stores - he needed his faculties in working order right now. His head quickly cleared and his vision sharpened up.

"But that probably is," he said, pointing into the distance. Sections of the chamber wall were sliding up, and huge machines glided out onto the floor, floating on fierce orange fields of energy.

"Cleaning crew is here," he said. "Time to go I think." He looked at her expectantly.

"What?"

"Flying? You can fly? Shall we?"

"Right, sorry." She wrapped her arms around him, and he took the liberty of standing on her feet to steady them both as they lifted into the air.

Below them, the huge contraptions scoured the floor of the chamber, re-sealing the surface.

"Amazingly efficient, and bizarre at the same time," said Nelsen, nodding at the gigantic maintenance effort. "This lot has to be automated. I wonder if there *is* anyone running this place..."

"I don't want to find out," said Andreya fiercely. "Let's just get out of here. Which tunnel?"

Nelsen looked about and frowned. "Hmm, only seventy-odd thousand to choose from it seems."

"Would you quit it for one moment and be serious?"

He nodded ahead. "We came from that direction; the tunnel was about two-thirds of the way up the chamber wall. Here's the location." He passed it across to her, and she tagged it as a waypoint in her e-vision.

"Do we wait for these things to finish up?" he wondered.

"No, we go *now*. While we can," she said, and they began accelerating toward the tunnel.

Nelsen looked down, then into Andreya's face. "Seems the situation is reversed from when we first met. Now I'm the damsel in distress."

"Hardly," she said.

They neared the seething walls around their tunnel, inside seemed clear of any movement. It appeared that all the maintenance droids were now on the chamber wall performing their duties.

"I want one," said Nelsen.

"Stop being a child!" snapped Andreya.

Nelsen glared at her. "I'm serious. We need to get one of these things and take it with us."

"Are you *mad?* What if it has some sort of subversion technology, or it's weaponised, or reports back?"

"Then we'll be in *more* trouble than we're in right now. Get me closer to the tunnels edge."

She glared at him, but he wouldn't waver – he merely pointed to where he wanted to go. They drifted toward the mouth of the tunnel, closer to the four-legged spiders – far too close for Andreya's comfort. The shining spiders ignored them entirely.

He stretched out toward the nearest as it jittered about, scraping the surface of the chamber with its razor-sharp mandible attachments and miniscule field manipulators. Andreya edged them closer, then Nelsen grabbed hold of a leg and yanked the mechanised monstrosity from the chamber wall. It instantly curled up into a ball around his fist.

"Feisty little beast," he said. It was centimetres away from his skin, held at bay by a force field around his hand. None of its compatriots paid its struggle any attention, and they quickly saw to it that the gap in their cleaning program was filled.

"Ok, let's go," he said.

Breathing a sigh of relief – but not taking her eyes from the metal monster – she directed them into the tunnel and then shot down along it as fast as she dared. Nelsen's eyes widened as he registered their speed, but he said nothing.

They slowed when they saw the first hatch open above them, but it was too soon to be the one they had entered by. Then they saw more hatches above, and below – connecting other tunnels to this one. The tunnel walls had now cooled back to their original shiny black.

"Cooling vents?" mused Nelsen. "Why not use heat exchangers? Seems a bit archaic given the tech here..."

"These tunnels were glowing hot when I came through," said Andreya. "Trust me."

"Hmm. Which vent is ours... it was about three point two k's into the tunnel seal."

"Let's just get out of here," Andreya said in a shaky voice.

They chose one the closest hatches and drifted up and out of the tunnel.

The *Sneak* was nowhere to be seen. The structure stretched out to the horizon in all directions, with the vast central tower looming high into the pale blue sky above.

Nelsen frowned. "We should be close enough to see her," he said. *Sneak?* he called over their local network.

There was no answer. He started to look worried.

"How could anything happen to her without us knowing?" asked Andreya.

He shook his head. "It can't. She'd collapse before

letting anything capture her."

"Collapse?"

Nelsen tapped his nose and would say no more.

They searched the skies and saw nothing but wisps of cloud. Then Andreya saw movement on the surface of the structure.

Everywhere.

"Time to go again," she said. Nelsen nodded and looked directly into her eyes. They didn't need to share their thoughts across their private network – they both knew what this meant. Even as super-powerful as her flight-system seemed, it couldn't power itself forever.

They took off almost vertically, in a ballistic arc. The best she could manage was to get as high as they could before her power gave out and then to fall as far as away as they could, hoping their shields would withstand the impact when they landed.

As they slipped through the air, Nelsen looked down and could see a huge cloud of metallic objects lifting from the surface – filling the air below them with countless mis-shapes and oddities. A large group began moving directly toward them, gaining speed and catching up.

"I can suicide," said Nelsen quietly. "Between us we have just enough power to take us both out, along with a goodly number of them." He nodded downward.

Andreya smiled ruefully. It might come to that yet. Then a thought crept into her mind from outside. *Hang on*.

They were suddenly buffeted by a blast of air, and the *Sneak* was running alongside parallel to them both. Her lower lift hatch peeled back to reveal her interior cabin.

"*Get in!*" she yelled.

They flew in through the open hatch, and then it immediately snapped shut. Leaving an ear-shattering vacuum behind them, the *Sneak* shot out into orbit as fast as she could manage, without care, thought for discretion, or any concern for the local biosphere.

The cloud of droids slowed as their targets disappeared, and then they returned back to the surface – re-joining the huge cluster of machines without pause, as they saw to the maintenance of the surface structure itself.

Nelsen helped Andreya to her feet as they both looked into each other's eyes, both glad to have escaped intact.

"*What*, is *that?*" demanded the *Sneak*. A red holo-sphere appeared around the metal spider Nelsen was grasping in his hand.

"Ah, a pet," Nelsen said glibly. "How can we quarantine this thing?"

"*Quarantine?* Captain, get it *out* of me!"

"Sorry *Sneak* – this is the first contact with a new alien species and their technology, and they are most likely to try and wipe us out. It stays. How do we quarantine it?"

The *Sneak* lapsed into a worried silence. "I'll have to erect a class one force-field containment unit – I don't want that thing touching any part of me physically."

"Is it communicating with anyone? Can you see any comm's emissions? Because I can't."

"No, scans are showing it's just there, and powered. Nothing organic, entirely silicon substrate based. Small power cell, with a high yield. It's pretty transparent scan-wise. Nothing suspicious about it, Captain, other than it's *on board*."

"Setup the fields, *Sneak*."

"Take it to the rear of the cabin area, please," she said, her voice brisk.

Nelsen did so, and held out his arm – the spider still clasping tightly around the field over his hand.

"Ok, you can let go, Captain."

He slid his arm out of the field the *Sneak* had erected, and let go of the spider's leg. The *Sneak's* field gently forced it from Nelsen's hand – leaving it hanging in mid-air, where it curled itself into a tight ball.

The *Sneak* threw some holo's around the spider as it floated in its invisible prison, detailing the interior of the machinery from scan results of the power systems, sensors and internal AI.

"That is remarkable engineering," said Nelsen admiringly. It was almost an artificially constructed equivalent of a real organic spider. Highly flexible, sensitive and strong limbs, sensor package clustered around the head, with the thorax providing articulation and minimal brain functions. Power cells and what appeared to be various cleaning compounds occupied the abdomen. The entire physical structure was very organic in appearance, showing a clear and masterful control over materials at the molecular level.

"Nothing that can't be fabricated by Imperial technology, if so desired," noted the *Sneak*.

"Indeed, but in such numbers?" Nelsen replied.

"Hardly."

"It's safe in there?"

"It would take a total power loss to free it," replied the *Sneak*. "There's something very peculiar about its cognitive system…"

"Oh?"

"It doesn't really have one. There is a network connecting all the sensors, equipment and motor functionality – but nothing actually running the show, as it were. There is no local processing capacity." She thought about if for a moment. "It's almost as if it's remote controlled, but there's no sign of a remote control…"

"Andreya? Anything you can tell us?"

She frowned. "No? Why would I?"

"You tell me… All we seem to be getting from you are new amazing abilities and hitherto unknown information and hints."

Her eyes glistened as she fought back tears of frustration. "I told you I don't know why!"

"Flying? Three times faster, at *least,* than I can manage – *with* a passenger. And as far as augmentation goes, I'm top of the line."

"That's not all, Captain. She mind-jacked me briefly before everything went mad down there."

Nelsen's eyes went wide. "You did *what?*"

Now Andreya did start crying, tears rolling down her cheeks.

Nelsen had to admit – later and privately to himself – that he very nearly went to take her in his arms and comfort her there and then. As it was, it took every ounce of self control to just stand there and maintain a professional stance. He folded his arms across his chest.

"That's not going to help, Andreya. The entire *Empire*

is at stake here – possibly the entire Cluster. You seem to have insight into what's going on, and abilities to do things beyond even *our* technology. I need to know why. *Now.*"

Her face fell, a mix of conflicting emotions raging through her as she finished tearing off the power-suit. "I don't have the answers you need," she said huskily, dropping the suit to the floor.

"Not good enough," he said firmly.

"Tough," she retorted. "How do you think it feels to know you aren't *real?* To be drip fed little bits of info from nowhere – of things and abilities you had no idea you had? I'm a damned *puppet!* Nothing more!" Her voice rose as she railed at him.

"*Still* not good enough," he snapped back. "Do you know the first action I should have taken when the *Sneak* told me what you just did? I should have incapacitated you – killed you if necessary. Mind-jacking alone is a crime with a life-sentence. Doing it to a Naval vessel is punishable by death!"

"I DID *NOT* MIND JACK HER!" she screamed.

"Captain –" interjected the *Sneak*, "perhaps I should have phrased it differently – "

"So what do you call entering the mind of another and taking it over? *Renting?*"

"Actually, she didn't take over, as such –"

"*Screw* you Nelsen! I don't care what you are supposed to do! Kill me! It'll be a bloody *relief,* do you know that? I won't have to worry about *what* I am and *what* I might end up doing – or becoming!"

Silence rang out loudly and they both stood there glaring at each other.

There was no way out of the argument as Nelsen saw it. This could only get worse.

"If I may?" the *Sneak* spoke tentatively.

Nelsen waved assent with a flick of his hand.

"Thank you, Captain. Yes, Andreya *did* enter my mind without permission, and yes she *did* use my thought patterns to communicate with you on my behalf. But no, she did not take me over. And she only did this to save your life."

Nelsen set his mouth into a grim line.

"If you had been in the tunnel when the energy pulse hit, you would have been vaporised almost instantly. Your shields would not have been able to stand it. From your scans, I have analysed the structure of the tunnels and they are designed to concentrate and amplify the energy as it courses through them, reflecting it back onto itself to form a stream of energy far hotter than the surface of a star."

"I shouldn't have bothered warning you," muttered Andreya.

Fortunately Nelsen wasn't so easily barbed. "Yet you knew we would find something here, 'something important' you said. And you knew we didn't have long to get out afterward."

She glared at him, then looked away. "I don't know why. I don't know how. Keep asking and I'll keep telling you the same thing. Because it's the truth."

He stepped forward and grabbed her firmly by the shoulders and stared directly into her eyes. "It's still not enough. Until you tell me what you are, and why you are here... I can't trust you."

She stared back, eyes still brimming with tears,

silently pleading for help. "Then you can't trust me."

He found it hard to hold her gaze. She raised so many conflicting emotions in him – so many long supressed feelings, and brought memories which haunted his dreams back into the cold hard light of day. He let go of her and let his arms fall to his sides, turning away from her.

"I have no idea what to do *with* you, or *about* you... Imprisoning you won't do any good. You could no doubt just hack your way out, or perform some other magic and disappear entirely based on what you did on Caranthia. But I can't let you keep taking *Sneak* over, or listening in to secure comm's. If I set you down on a world somewhere safe no doubt you'd just reappear right back here, or wherever else you might need to be."

He felt her hand on his shoulder. "Please don't do that," she whispered. "You *can* trust me, both of you can. I just can't prove it. Yet."

He turned around to look down at her, knowing he shouldn't. Her face looked up at him. If she was a subversive agent for the enemy – she was ideally placed to wreak havoc, and she was doing a damned good job of emotionally screwing him over.

"You're not real, I've no idea what you are, and I can't trust you." He sighed. "So why do I believe you...?"

She lifted herself onto her tip-toes, and kissed him firmly on the lips.

"Ah," was all he said. He was lost… he had to finally admit it. Despite his training, experience common sense and better judgement, he just wanted to take hold of her and hold her tight.

So he did.

Chapter Twenty-four

Nelsen woke with the hazy glow of contentment that one only got from a decent, restful sleep – something he had long forgotten could ever happen. He was so used to infusing stimulants and filtering toxins with his augmented organs that he rarely slept naturally. Sleep was when the dreams came, the memories he would never, *could* never surpress.

He ran through his dreams of last night – one benefit of web integration recording every thought. There were none of the ever present nightmares of home, of his family.

He looked down to see Andreya sleeping peacefully – her head nestled in the crook of his chest and arm – a look of such utter contentment and peace on her face it made his heart ache.

He felt instant shame for sullying the memories of his wife and child – for not having the dreams, for *not* remembering their deaths – and then for encouraging whatever emotional mess he had gotten himself into with Andreya.

It had been a long time since he had been involved with anyone other than his wife. Her death had closed that door to him. For him it had been almost twenty years since the loss of his family. In reality – taking his suspension periods into account – it had been over a hundred.

Perhaps that was why, he thought – trying to excuse his behaviour. Two decades without sharing that which can only be voluntarily and mutually given – and taken.

That giving, selfish need which benefited both those involved. Perhaps it had become too much even for his subconscious, and it had finally played its trump card.

But what he had done was far greater than the sum of the parts. If she were some unwitting agent of the force they were facing, he was now emotionally involved. This wasn't just two people seeking solace in each other or a mutually casual fling. He knew he was falling for her, and he believed she had feelings toward him. He hadn't felt this way for a long time, but he knew he was beginning to fall in love. Something he should not allow – surely *could* not allow.

He looked down at her again, and a slight frown crinkled the brow above her nose for a second before relaxing again. *She was so damnably cute...* He shook his head clear of the thought, and gently eased his arm out from under her to get up. She murmured something unintelligible then turned over, rolling up the sheet with her.

What have I gone and done? he chastised himself.

He left the privacy of the small bed chamber, sealing it shut behind him.

"Morning, Captain." The *Sneak* said crisply.

"Morning, *Sneak*." He couldn't keep the hint of guilt from his voice.

"Do I need remind you that fraternising with a potential enemy of the Empire is a court martial waiting to happen?"

"*Sneak* -"

"No need to explain to *me*, Captain. You were *quite* clear last night. I just don't imagine the Naval Judicial system will be quite so sympathetic."

Nelsen scowled angrily. "Are you done?" he snapped.

"I just don't think this was wise, Captain. Given the circumstances."

Nelsen rubbed his hands over his face as if to wipe the event from his mind. "I don't need telling, *Sneak*... I already know."

He sat down heavily on the couch. "Still clear of contacts?"

The *Sneak* was privately glad to be in safer territory for the moment. "Yes. Nothing has left the surface... nothing in stellar space out to five AU's. The structure has discharged again since we left. I would predict an eleven hour cycle."

"Bizarre. Any ideas?"

"It's a guess, but I think we were both right about it, in a way. The energy signature is not the same as that causing the subspace disturbance, but the structure is definitely designed to agitate subspace. The pulses which you endured are transferred throughout the entire structure – amplified and distributed via the tunnel network. Each of the three pulses delivered the equivalent energy output of a k-class star for one picosecond. The device is designed to absorb this energy uniformly across the entire structure and release it in one go into subspace, proving it to be our subspace agitator."

Nelsen shook his head. *How can we possibly stand against these guys?* he wondered.

"There is more," said the *Sneak*. "While you were... sleeping, I detected an identical triple fluctuation in subspace, three hours after the one we witnessed. It originated some ten light-years further into the DZ."

"Oh?"

"If my theory about the regular nature of these events is correct, we should see a similar triple-pulse from that region in forty-six minutes."

"What are they up to?" Nelsen mused. "This is a huge undertaking – a collosal use of energy and resources. The maintenance alone..."

"But as you saw, they are self-maintaining."

"It's still a *mammoth* undertaking. You could build artificial *planets* with this technology – self-maintaining world sized stations. You could eliminate the need for planetary colonisation, *or* conquest."

"You still need the resources," the *Sneak* pointed out.

"Fine. Pick an Oort cloud, an asteroid belt, or gas giant. Turn them into something useful."

"So are these beings engineers?" asked the *Sneak*. "Or are they scavengers?"

Nelsen shook his head. "I have no idea. We've yet to meet them to figure that out, I think." He turned to their captive spider, floating a metre or so off the ground. It was still curled into a tight ball.

"No physical activity," volunteered the *Sneak,* guessing his thoughts. "Very little electrical. Chances are it has returned to its dormant state between maintenance runs."

"Maybe."

They were both quiet for a while.

"So, what will you do about *her?*" asked the *Sneak* pointedly.

Nelsen sighed. "What *can* I do *Sneak?* What could I do? Whatever she is, and why ever she is here, there's nothing we can do to stop her doing what she wants, or being where she wants to be."

He looked back at the bedchamber which Nelsen had curtly - and probably rudely now he thought about it - ordered the *Sneak* to form last night. A private room which the *Sneak* had no access to.

"All we can hope is that she *is* on our side. She has been so far. If that changes – then we have to do what we can to resolve what happens next."

He got up – having rested he was anxious to do something. "Kitchen please," he said. The *Sneak* dutifully reformed the kitchen area.

"And *Sneak*?"

"Yes, Captain?"

"I'm sorry about last night. I was out of line."

The *Sneak* smiled to herself internally, and left sufficient meaningful pause for a typical humanoid, emotional response.

"No need, Captain. But, thank you all the same."

Andreya woke with almost the same cosy glow she had felt that first night back on Caranthia. A few days and a lifetime ago. This time she didn't have that vague sense of immense loss, instead she felt almost the opposite – an immense sense of completeness which seemed to fill her entire being.

She could hear Nelsen and the *Sneak's* somewhat confrontational exchange – and went to interject, but thought better of it. *Another demonstration of my apparent omnipotence would not go down well,* she thought. Their voices calmed as they turned to discussing their status, and she relaxed. She could hear them clearly despite the privacy arrangements around this room, but she had given up wondering on the more mundane of the how's and why's around her abilities.

She felt like her mind had been split, but now made whole. It was beyond description, this horrific see-saw and zigzag of her sense of self, from some deliberately constructed monstrosity, to a tangible, credible woman who very much wanted to be a part of something, to feel that connection to another. Of being *real*. It was dizzying, and intolerable. Maybe the *Sneak* had it wrong. Whoever was responsible for her existence had clearly screwed something up or worse, didn't care.

Had this been the intent of whomever or whatever had caused her to be? What crime could she have committed to deserve such mental anguish? What crime might she have been built *for*?

Oddly, she wasn't growing anxious at such a self-destructive train of thought. That calm lassitude was upon her again, that 'Oh well' feeling that it was what it was, just accept it. She seemed to get more upset when Nelsen questioned her. *What did that say?*

She hadn't planned any of this. Not the brief merge with the *Sneak*, not to kiss Nelsen, and certainly not to end up sharing herself with him. Not that that was objectionable – far from it. She felt that warm glow again at the thought, which she found almost intolerably good.

She was certain it had been spontaneous – for both of them. *Maybe an emotional reaction to their escape from the Damper, and the argument after*. She didn't know, but she didn't regret it one bit.

It *did* complicate matters though. It made Nelsen's position highly untenable, and gave him a conflict of interest which would surely be impossible to manage.

362

She was mindful of the fact she somehow seemed to become a problem to anyone she met.

The door opened, making her jump in surprise. Nelsen stood there holding a tray with four small bowls on it.

He waved the tray up and down. "Breakfast?" The bitter-sweet aroma of Anjulan wafted in, and she sat up with an appreciative murmur.

He crouched onto the bed, pushing the tray over her lap and left it to keep its position hovering above the sheets. The chamber was effectively just a walled bed, space being at a premium on board such a small ship. He knelt so that he faced her across the tray, and then poured each of the two smaller bowls into the larger ones – handing one to her graciously.

"Thank you," she said, taking a grateful sip of the dark, syrupy coffee.

He held his bowl of Anjulan, swilling the thick liquid around but not drinking from it. She knew what he was thinking, and she wasn't entirely sure that was just intuition.

"This doesn't change anything," she said softly. "I know that."

He looked up, surprised – then couldn't help but smile. "But, it was an error of judgement that I'm glad I made," he said, looking at her rather too directly.

She actually blushed.

Then they both laughed and Nelsen raised his bowl to hers, chiming against it softly before taking a drink.

"So how do we handle this?" she asked.

"You mean how do *I* handle this?"

"Well, yes."

"I have to continue as I have – trusting you but *not* trusting you – worrying that you'll do something that will mean I have to act against you. There's nothing we can do to stop you, it seems."

She drew her legs up and wrapped her arms around her knees, frowning as she stared at him.

"And now, either I've been subverted and wiled by an enemy of the Empire, or..."

She raised her eyebrows, and waited a few moments. "Or?"

"Or... I've done something even more stupid."

He looked directly into her eyes, and took her free hand in his. "I don't want to regret this, Andreya... I cannot and will not put the Empire aside. If you prove to be on the other side to the Empire... you're on the other side to me. Do you understand? I've given up too much in the Empires name to step away from it."

She nodded, her eyes never leaving his. "I understand. And – I know you can't believe me – but you won't have to be worried. Those things down there... they horrify me beyond anything you can imagine, and I don't know why. But even not knowing who I am, what I am, where I came from, I *know* I cannot be *anything* to do with those... things."

He openly stared at her. Despite himself he genuinely believed her, but as a serving officer of Imperial Naval Intelligence, he just couldn't allow himself to. "I fervently hope so. If it helps, I can't see how you could be. But you know I can't afford to take that chance."

"I know." She squeezed his hand tight. "How's the *Sneak* taking this?" she asked, purely to change the subject.

"She's fine," he said, rolling his eyes. "Ask her yourself."

She realised he had left the door open, breaking the privacy seal which the *Sneak* had erected.

"Morning, *Sneak*," she said.

"Andreya," she replied stiffly.

"I never had chance to apologise *Sneak* – I am *truly* sorry. Though I know you may not be able to believe that."

There was a strained silence for a moment. "Andreya, you worry that you don't know who or what you are... and I understand that, I *empathise* with it. All Intellects go through a similar phase after inception - I recall it all too well myself. But think on this... the sanctity of my mind has been violated *three* times now. I've had every single aspect of my existence *examined* by something we've never encountered, you've eavesdropped on a sacrosanct private bond between myself and my captain, and you've entered my mind without permission. I have no way of being certain that *I* am *me* any more. So *now* wonder how I feel."

Andreya was so dismayed a tear came to her eye. "*Sneak...*"

"Now ask me if I should trust you."

Andreya looked to Nelsen. He raised an eyebrow and shrugged.

She was genuinely horrified. *Everything I touch...* "I should leave," she said in a small voice.

Nelsen took her hand again. "That won't be necessary. *Sneak?*"

"No, it won't. Andreya, Captain Rybek left the door open deliberately."

Andreya frowned, and looked at Nelsen with a worried expression.

"The *Sneak* has been running a full biometric and physiological scan on you since I came in. You didn't hear us discussing this outside?"

She shook her head, eyes wide and worried.

"As far as it's physically possible to be certain, you are telling the truth Andreya," said the *Sneak* confidently.

"We thought it best to be as sure as we can, for your peace of mind as well as ours," said Nelsen.

"Of course, you may be telling the truth because you don't know you are lying," said the *Sneak*.

"But we have to draw a line somewhere," said Nelsen firmly.

"Yes, Captain, I agree."

Andreya was shaking. "You believe me?" she managed, voice quivering.

"As well as we can, I think," said Nelsen. "Professionally, I have to mistrust you. But given what you did to save my life, and so far no evident harm... unless you do something to change our trust, we believe you. Right *Sneak*?"

"Yes, Captain. But I have one condition to ask of Andreya."

"Anything, *Sneak*, really!"

"I can't stop you interfering with my operational capacity or mind. But *please*, if you feel the need to intervene again, *please* warn me first. Preferably ask?"

She smiled as a tear ran down her cheek. "I promise, *Sneak*. I really am sorry I caused you any distress. You know I know what that feels like."

"I think I do," replied the *Sneak*, the hard edge leaving her voice.

"Truce then? Friends?" asked Nelsen.

"Yes," said the *Sneak*.

Andreya nodded gratefully with a brittle smile, wiping her eyes and then nose on the sheet.

"Nice," said Nelsen.

"Sorry, no tissues. Thank you, both. I know this means I still can't be entirely trusted... I don't even know if I can myself, so..."

"But let's agree that's how it is for now. Then we can get on with this without tearing each other to shreds." Nelsen smiled.

"Done, definitely done." She leant forward and gave him a quick kiss on the cheek.

"Right – flying?"

She laughed aloud. "I had no idea until that tunnel nearly killed me," she said.

"What?" He looked concerned.

"The heat was too much, I could barely walk in there."

"It was still absorbing energy from the pulses, Captain, but clearly there is an excess, remarkable as that may be. It was still eight hundred degrees Celsius when Andreya entered. However, the rate of absorption by the surface materials *is* incredible, given the initial seven million degrees experienced in there."

Nelsen raised his eyebrows. "Well, I didn't thank you yet –"

"Oh, you *did*," she smirked impishly.

"– so *thank you*," he went on unperturbed. "And remind me to never challenge you to a race."

"Always," she said with the same grin.

Nelsen stared at her, then shook his head – mouth twitching with a grin. "Unbelievable."

"I try," she said, finally regaining her humour.

They both finished their coffee.

"So... what next?" she asked.

"*Sneak* – I forgot," said Nelsen before he answered. "Why were you airborne when we surfaced? I thought we'd lost you."

"Sorry, Captain – all the tunnel vents across the surface opened at the same time. I went aloft to see if there were any opportune entrances closer to your location. Then I saw their craft beginning to stir around the central tower. Being unable to contact you without the relays, I chose to remain aloft for the better vantage point."

"Ha," Nelsen laughed mirthlessly. "We should have popped out of the first vent after all... Ah, well. What do you make of my debrief?"

"Phenomenal technology at work. Thinking on it, I cannot see how this is a scavenger species. The sophistication of their energy systems and maintenance is truly magnificent. A scavenger race would be opportunistic and careless by nature. Looking to the next opportunity rather than looking after what they had. Besides, this structure and the other suggest extremely ordered and considered thinking and design. None of which fit the profile of a scavenger species. It shows a level of competence, commitment and planning on a grand scale. "

"Agreed. How long to the next pulse?"

"Eighteen minutes."

He mused for a minute, looking at Andreya thoughtfully. "Let's get to that system – and how about we watch from orbit this time?"

"Most wise, Captain."

The world below was ancient, and most likely had never supported life. Small continental plates of cracked stone floated on magma, crashing against each other and spurting lava high into the atmosphere on a regular basis as it was pummelled and kneaded by the intense gravitational forces wrought by the binary star system through which it sped.

The huge artificial structure below seemed ignorant of the tortured landscape as it churned around it – sitting atop calmly and slowly undulating as the mini-continental plates rose and fell beneath it.

The triple pulse of energy perturbed subspace exactly as the *Sneak* predicted.

The vents opened, and maintenance craft came teeming out – seeing to the superstructure as a whole. Their duties were slightly more involved, due to the constant onslaught of ash and lava – but they went about their business without pause. Eventually they disappeared into the structure and all was still once again.

"Any wiser?" Nelsen asked the *Sneak*.

"None Captain, as yet."

"Ok, back on course. Let's go find what the Velari found."

Chapter Twenty-five

"Nothing from Captain Rybek I presume?" asked the Emperor, evidently keen to have some other momentous problem to be concerned with.

Aryn rubbed his chin thoughtfully. "Nothing, Your Majesty. Aside from a very short and highly encrypted message not long after they set off.

The Emperor raised an eyebrow and waited.

"'DZ'," Aryn supplied.

The Emperor waited again. "Is this is some deep INI code talk?" he asked when Aryn failed to illuminate further.

Aryn shook his head. "No, Your Majesty. It has no meaning to me other than the obvious."

"I see. The Dark Zone. Does this suggest that the Velari came from the Dark Zone?"

"Your Majesty, my sources indicate that the Velari may have travelled across the Dark Zone from the other side of the cluster – long before the Dark Zone became established."

"Dark horses..." the Emperor murmured.

"Your Majesty?"

"Nothing, Admiral, nothing. So we can expect nothing of this mission, and we have lost our only lead to your Infiltrator?"

"If they have gone into the DZ, yes, Your Majesty. We can presume nothing else."

"Although I should expect that if anyone were ever capable or equipped to return from the DZ, it would be the good Captain and his seemingly omnipotent companion – especially in a vessel such as the Valkyr."

"We can only hope, Your Majesty. However, pragmatically, it does leave us with only the *one* pressing matter to be concerned with for the time being."

If the Emperor hadn't personally known Aryn for over one hundred and twenty years, he would have been surprised at what seemed a cavalier and offhand assessment – effectively discounting an INI officer as Lost without a moment's concern. Whilst Aryn was of course entitled by his position and rank to think in such a way, he would have taken a dim view on even Fleet Admiral Benthar for speaking in such a manner.

He knew Aryn was either entirely confident in his man, or privately worrying if he had sent a someone to his certain doom with no hope of success. No one had ever returned from the Dark Zone – even the very best crews the Navy had to offer. The costs for zero return had been too high, and the Emperor had mandated the DZ out of bounds long ago as a matter of public safety – handing the problem to the scientists who had also so far drawn a blank.

It was one of the many unsolved enigmas in the cluster, and from the Emperor's perspective as long as whatever the Dark Zone represented didn't expand and encroach on the Empire, it was best left well alone until more could be learned from afar.

"Dr. Reece's team has established a stable and secure means of communication which does not rely on qSpin technology," the Emperor informed Aryn, who raised a curious eyebrow. He had yet to order a full investigation into the good doctor. "I believe it leverages the Observer network to transport electro-magnetic radiation point-to-point."

Aryn nodded thoughtfully. "That will suffice as a fall-back, for the time being at least. At least it will not be so easily snooped."

"What of our friends in S'vreth?" asked the Emperor.

"There is still no activity other than the continued build-up of the fleet cordoning off the system," said Aryn. "An additional eight hundred thousand contacts have been detected so far en route from S'ren to the Cloud. All brand new units, from what we can tell, and all of various sizes, form and function. There seems to be no particular pattern."

"Eight hundred thousand… In how long, a mere three days?"

"Just over, Your Majesty. The facility has not stopped since it began construction."

The Emperor did not speak. He could not. What was there to say?

***

The 14th Canthen Tactical Response Fleet had amassed just outside their territorial border. It was the single largest gathering of their forces since their civilisations last expansion and conquest phase secured the Aransil System one hundred years ago. That conflict – and the terrible outcome for both sides – had resulted in a dramatic change in Canthen society. With a bloody revolt against their then Emperor Priat Thoraz, the bear-like Canthen had moved from semi-aggressive warmongers to become a more temperate species – a movement which had already been gaining sympathy within their hierarchy for some considerable time. However, they remained a civilisation which would not hesitate to hold its own against any and all who might seek an advantage against them.

They had no intention of allowing the Velari to settle in their system. They knew the Sulranian Empire could not aid them any further. The Sulranians own attempts to divert the Velari had fallen on deaf ears, as the Canthen knew they would. They were on their own, and they knew the Velari would fight as hard as they could.

This would be no easy win – for either side.

***

The *Swan* was now half a light-year out from S'vreth, and so far undetected and unchallenged. Captain Brakkar was getting nervous. He genuinely hadn't expected to get this far, and had been banking on some form of Naval presence to force his hand into fleeing the system and claiming the hazard fee.

Whatever was going down in S'vreth – he wanted no part of it.

That said – the lack of a response may yet mean securing the entire charter – which amounted to triple the hazard fee. That was a full refit and major bonus for the crew, even after his own cut.

If we survive whatever horror the Navy's trying to keep quiet, he thought morosely.

The Colesworth staff were pushing to go straight for their refinery, naturally. The *Swan's* scans confirmed the naval report provided to Colesworth – the almost total loss of the station, no life signs.

Fear came over him when he saw the wreckage. It had been peeled open like a fruit, nothing of worth was left – not even debris. But they wouldn't listen to his assertions that going in would be of no benefit. They insisted, waved his full fee in his face – and that was that.

So he set course to drop out of FTL half an AU from the outer ring of the asteroid field, and then slowly creep into the station at a slow burn, keeping the large asteroid between them and the sun – and whatever that huge sphere of lights was that surrounded it – at all times.

***

It wasn't every day that the *Betsy* reported an unexpected knock on the hangar door. In fact in Brynn's recollection it had probably never happened on any vessel in deep space in all recorded history.

He and Andersten, along with a fully-armed compliment of his crew, stood at the end of the hangar farthest from the door, waiting. Yet more crew – commanded by Horstan – stood in tactical positions along the corridors exiting the hangar bay, which themselves were already blocked by internal blast fields.

The knock had repeated a recognised INI code, but Brynn wasn't prepared to take any chances. The unspoken fear was that the Shredder had come for their ship, having gleaned the protocol from one of its poor victims. But the external views from the Observers showed it was the figure of a brightly armoured humanoid instead of the orb of a Shredder. How it had been able to get past the *Betsy's* sensors was anyone's guess.

He checked the crew status – all ready. He looked to Andersten who manned a slaved plasma gun ready to blast whatever came in, back out. Andersten nodded.

Brynn raised five internal bay shields between them and the door, then gave the *Betsy* the all clear.

The *Betsy* raised the hangar entrance field then obligingly opened the external hangar door.

Light seemed to pour out into the black void – the incoming starlight barely visible against the bay's internal lighting.

There was a flicker of movement, and then a gleaming silvered figure climbed into view across the edge of the bay floor.

It pulled itself in, gracefully reorienting to the artificial gravity field and stood up to its full two-metre height – reflective platinum helmet regarding the arsenal aimed at it.

"Oh my," said Brynn softly.

"I thought they were all gone," growled Andersten, aiming the gun at the figure's torso. "Can I make sure of that though?"

"Hold," said Brynn sternly. "It wouldn't take much for me to fire first either. Let's hear what it has to say."

"Captain Tealin? I am INI Agent Romurik... Special Operational Duties. If you would provide your ships authentication protocols I can supply my orders and ID."

"No Platinum Warrior *I* ever heard of served the Empire," said Brynn.

"Indeed – but I am no Platinum Warrior." The figure looked down at itself. "Save in form, of course. I believe you know Captain Van E'streth?"

Brynn kept silent. If those bastards had shredded Van E'streth's mind and cooked up some horror AI persona with his memories, this would be the ideal way to infiltrate them.

"I served with him on the Delaror," said the Warrior. "In fact, I may be the cause of the enemy subversion of the ship. I have seen the sense-vise of your expedition. I have every intention of making those responsible pay a *very* heavy price for it."

Brynn frowned. *Not quite the thing you'd expect from an enemy agent,* he thought. *But then again...*Betsy, *supply the most arcane and fangled crypto you can and let him provide his orders.*

"Why didn't INI inform us you were coming?" he asked aloud.

"The greater qNet has been compromised -" there were gasps of disbelief from the *Betsy's* crew "- there are no secure data channels available in the Imperial network."

"That's tall," said Brynn.

"I believe Admiral Cole foresaw your natural disbelief. He has addressed it within my orders and briefing with an addendum for your attention."

It's clean, the *Betsy* told Brynn privately, after analysing the data sent to her quarantined data bay by Romurik. *It only took him four seconds to reverse engineer my algorithm and re-cipher. He was insufferably smug about it.*

Brynn glanded Rush and worked his way quickly through the orders and brief – then scanned the vise from Admiral Cole. Then he used his private INI channel to the Admiral, asking him the obscure question

Cole's vise had suggested Brynn ask in real time.

What shade of purple is death?

All of them, replied Admiral Cole. *It had to be this way Brynn. No distrust intended. Everything you heard is true. Carry on.*

Admiral Cole disconnected, and Brynn rubbed his jaw. The answer matched the one in the message. He didn't run Romurik's ID against INI. If he did – and this was as it seemed – it would give Romurik's presence away to whoever was listening. Of course, it also made validating who he said he was nigh on impossible.

Betsy, *how up to date is your cached INI archive?*

Seven hours, forty-six minutes for the primary repository. One week, two days, nine hours, thirty-nine minutes for the greater repository.

That'll do. Run this ID against your local repo please. Do not use the qNet.

INI Agent Romurik, the Betsty replied immediately. *Last reported attachment,* INSS Delaror *under Captain Van E'streth. Last reported activity – avatar destruction and persona upload into the Totality. Physical service for seventy eight years, non-physical for ninety-two years. Forty-four uploads on file.*

He's been busy, noted Brynn sardonically.

Last reported form – Arvan Systems Stealth Drone, form factor ARV-95XB. Basically, a ringball.

He looked hard at the two metre high heavily armoured Warrior now standing before him. "Why a Warrior?"

Romurik gave a sigh. He had high hopes for this form – but had to take the rough with the smooth. He would constantly be plagued by this question. "I believe in what they believed, before they chose to believe in themselves instead."

"Nice and cryptic. Two centuries ago they slaughtered thirty-one colonies. Without provocation. Or warning."

He nodded at Andersten and a few others in the crew. "Many of us fought against them, myself included. Now tell me why you chose this form."

Romurik looked at each in turn – particularly Andersten who was grinding his jaw and using a slave gun to target his upper torso. He knew where a Warrior's energy source would be located. *Probably to the millimetre*, Romurik suspected.

"Because the Warriors stood for revenge, because they designed themselves for uncompromising combat, to never back down, to always get their man, no matter what the cost."

"That turned against them."

"Yes, but they started out noble. I want revenge, I won't stop, I won't back down. I've had enough of being defeated, of watching others die due to inaction. I will prevail."

"No matter what the cost?" asked Brynn.

"I know the cost. I will prevail where I am prepared to pay the price. I led these things to the *Delaror*... their blood is on my hands."

Brynn looked to Andersten, who shrugged in that irritating non-committal way which meant – *not my call, so not my fault*. Though if he'd been dead against it, he would have said.

"Very well," said Brynn, letting his instinct guide him. *Ready everyone*, he said to his crew across the ships l-net – preparing them to strike if need be.

He dropped the fields inside the hangar. "Welcome aboard *Betsy's Pride,* Agent Romurik."

Romurik looked around, noting the fields which were still erected in the corridors outside. "Thank you, Captain. I am impressed at your diligence. It does you and your crew proud given the recent circumstances."

He strode forward to stand before Brynn – Andersten's slaved gun tracking him all the way – and he then saluted the Captain. Brynn returned the salute.

"That has to be the damnedest stupid choice of form for a modern day cybo I have ever seen," Brynn said.

"I'm not noted for my political correctness," replied Romurik modestly. "However I *am* noted for getting the job done. At my own cost usually I might add. This form is part of a choice to that end."

"Your record speaks for itself. There are numerous annotations by Totality psychoanalysts."

"I bet. I probably wrote most of them. The Totality tends to be a tad verbatim."

Romurik put out his hand, and Brynn paused for a second – taken aback by the unusually human gesture from a cybo sapiens. He reached out and shook it. Despite the grip probably having the potential force to crush bonded durallium hull plating, it was surprisingly gentle.

Stand down, Brynn sent to his crew. Betsy, *lock us up.*

Even Andersten un-slaved his gun, Brynn trusted Andersten's intuition even more than he trusted his own. The *Betsy* closed the hangar doors.

"If you would accompany me to my quarters, Andersten – you too."

"Gladly Captain," said Romurik. "After you."

Brynn lead the way, and Andersten gestured for Romurik to follow. "Most *definitely*, after you," he said. Romurik couldn't help but notice Andersten's standing offensive energy fields were at full capacity and on standby. He would have smiled if he could. Instead, he tapped his finger to his brow in mock salute, and filed in behind Brynn.

Chapter Twenty-six

By now, an impromptu mini-fleet formed from ships of various shapes, sizes and origins had amassed outside the S'vreth Exclusion Zone. Scattered across several AU's, they had all chosen the same emergence zone as the *Swan* – due to its apparent 'safe' observation distance which would not give cause to upset the navy.

They were all chartered – or owned – by media giants. All of them packed with journalists, analysts and scientists, retired or self-professed tactical experts, and generally anyone the media agencies thought could be exploited to provide even a semi-plausible 'expert opinion' on what was going on.

None of the vessels publically acknowledged the others – competition for a scoop was fierce.

However, the captains of the vessels had a mutual regard of their current, highly untenable positions. Within a few hours of the group forming, they had their own personal and private encrypted network up and running across the qNet.

"These goons are pushing us to get closer," said Captain Gestren, of the *Captive's Bounty*.

"Let them push – unless they double the hazard pay," replied Renel, captain of the *Heart of a Slave*.

"And you got that?" Captain Gestren tried to keep the note of surprised envy from his voice.

"I said nothing less – they're still trying to get it cleared. We have them by the balls out here now. Something massive is going down… they can smell it. And they are close enough to touch it."

"One of them will surely end up paying for the scoop," said Captain Reen of the *Quillisyr*.

"I might ask for triple, just in case!"

There was a chorus of laughter across the net.

A brief flash of FTL glare signalled another arrival.

"Here's another taxi," someone said.

The assembled captains watched with various degrees of amusement as the ship immediately went dark and tried to mask its energy output. It was painfully obvious it had leaks all over its power grid.

Reen recognised the *Dying Embrace* and hailed it over the network, sending a brief data packet with half a mutual cypher in.

"Aryce, how's it going?" Reen asked.

"Looks like I'm late for the party," came a tired voice.

"Plenty of room for waiting," said Gestren urbanely.

"What's the story?"

"That's the problem – there isn't one," said Reen. "No one has dared go any further, and we're waiting on the journo's to decide what they want to do."

"Well, no waiting here – I'm going in," Captain Aryce mumbled. "No time for faffing around. These guys want in… and to hell with the Navy."

There was a strained silence. The captains all knew what this meant – if even one of them went in, they'd all have to run to get there first – extra hazard pay or no.

"Did you try getting your hazard up?"

"Yep. Ten times the charter. See you guys later." Tired as he sounded, a certain amount of smugness crept through.

The *Dying Embrace* vanished in an erratic burst of FTL, breaking into the ultraviolet as its carrier wave driver stressed out to its max.

"Oh *shit*," someone said. Then there was another flash of FTL from nearby, though far cleaner this time. The *Heart of a Slave* vanished from their sensors.

It was now a race of who could get there first. Within seconds every ship had disappeared into FTL – apart from the *Quillisyr*.

"How deep did he go?" asked Reen.

The *Quillisyr* hesitated a moment, double-checking his numbers. The ships Intellect had been badly damaged numerous times by pirate hacks and physical attacks, but Reen had a soft-spot for the old boy and couldn't bring herself to replace him.

"The *Dying Embrace* almost burnt out its FTL drive, but judging by the emissions it dropped five light-years and will exit directly in the S'vreth system... here." A map of local space popped into Reen's mind.

"Just outside the asteroid belt," noted Reen. "Close to the Colesworth plant. Drop us ahead of his exit – halfway between him and the plant. Go."

The *Quillisyr* disappeared with a flash, and Reen congratulated herself on holding back whilst the others knee-jerked their way to whatever predetermined points they had chosen.

A ten-times hazard pay was all well and good, but Aryce would have to be assured of jeopardy to get it - which would mean being first on the scene. Reen intended to be waiting to greet him... she was quite happy with just triple.

***

"Admiral Benthar, we have new contacts appearing within the S'vreth Exclusion Zone."

"Nature and transition?"

"Varied, but all are passenger or explore class vessels. All attempting silent running. A number of them are grouping around the Colesworth Refinery, the rest are approaching the Cloud."

"The 9th are responding?"

"Yes, Fleet Admiral."

"Thank you, Captain."

"Sir."

It was only a matter of time before some idiots – no doubt driven by money – chose to run the EZ. The 9th IND Fleet had already deployed throughout the system to pick up on incursions as soon as they happened. They had been tracking a number of individual contacts for the past five hours as they hovered about outside the primary EZ itself. Clearly someone had offered more money and set off a gold rush. Fortunately as yet, there had been no signs of any sorties from other member worlds of the Empire. He knew they would come. But for now, that was a problem relegated to another hour at least.

He tapped into the INI network and watched as the 9th swarmed all over the intruders.

"This is Captain Barker of the INSS *Raptor* of the 9th Imperial Naval Defence Fleet. You are in violation of an Imperial Exclusion Zone and I order you to stand down and assume relative station-keeping or be fired upon. Prepare to be boarded. And turn on your damned ID broadcast, otherwise things will not go well for you."

Two of the three ships nearest the Raptor almost

immediately dropped their velocities to match the huge naval vessel, pinging their Imperial Vessel Registration ID's across the qNet. The third decide to make a run for it.

"Fire," ordered Captain Barker.

Based on the specs of the fleeing ship and the blueprints for its model – an orchestrated maser fire pattern from the *Raptor* blasted into the ship's shields – tailored to deliver just enough energy to take them out. This was rapidly followed by a precision targeted beam which sliced through the hull plating and slagged the ships FTL drive. After a small explosion as the drive gave out, the ship began twisting on its axis, tumbling slowly along its direction of travel and trailing a rapidly expanding cloud of debris. Her reaction mass thrusters firing wildly to try and correct its spin.

"Anyone else care to challenge the authority of the Imperial Navy?" asked Captain Barker.

The two other ships did not move.

"Good. INSS *Raptor* to INSS *Vorin*, please *salvage* what is left of that vessel and arrest its personnel – crew and passengers alike."

"Our pleasure, Captain Barker."

Raul switched focus to another tactical stream.

"This is Captain Gree aboard the INSS *Graceful Fury* of the 9th Imperial Naval Defence Fleet. You are in violation of an Imperial Exclusion Zone..."

And so it went on. Ten Naval destroyers intercepted over forty vessels as they tried to get deeper into the system.

Four other armed responses were required to disable the vessels of those captains who could only see credits fleeing from their grasp instead of good sense.

The rest capitulated with suspicious speed. Raul suspected some form of collaboration at work.

"Bring them all in under arrest – full criminal charges for inciting a war, treasonous action, and trespassing in an Imperial Exclusion Zone. The works," Raul instructed. "Seize their vessels and licenses, freeze any financial transactions - including hazard pay outs. Put lockdowns and tracers on all of the ships, and pursue the assets of the companies involved in their charters. I don't care how big or influencial they are, I want a *very* clear message to be sent."

"Yes, Fleet Admiral," replied Captain Barker.

"How many got away?" asked Raul.

"Admiral? We have accounted for all contacts reported by INI."

"Exactly – what about the ones they didn't report? Find the ringleaders of this little expedition and make them talk, find out how many ships there were. You have full autonomy, Captain Barker."

"Immediately, Admiral. Thank you."

If any of these loons got to the Cloud... thought Raul irately. The scope for disaster was immense.

***

Captain Aryce held his breath – more out of a desire to preserve oxygen than due to the tense atmosphere on the bridge.

As soon as Captain Gestren had yelled out over their private network – and he was grateful to Reen for patching him in – he had forced the *Dying Embrace* to push another FTL burst out of their ailing drive. It was at barely one per cent capacity – but the overrides he had hacked in allowed it to pump out a flash carrier wave, just enough to shunt them far enough away from their last position in an attempt to throw off any immediate pursuit. On dropping back out of FTL he hit a full burn of the sub-c engines for as long as he dared – then shut down *everything.* All powered systems went offline, drive, shields, life support. It would take a few minutes to bring everything back up, and that would have to be one system at a time due to the worn out power grid of the *Dying Embrace*.

His passengers had started complaining loudly when they realised life support was down. He threw out a ship-net wide message telling everyone to shut up - silent running was in effect.

Naturally, in the vacuum of space, nothing could carry the vibrations of sound as it reverberated throughout the metal hull of a ship. But light could. Aryce knew full well that the Navy had laser-based audio pickup drones which could scan a light-second volume in seconds – seeking any return which could pick up the tiny vibrations of speech or equipment inside a metal container as easily as any audio bug could within an atmosphere.

There were grumbles of discontent, but only within the ship's l-net this time. Nevertheless, Aryce told them to shut up on that as well. He would have shut that down too, but took the risk that its low power draw would not be enough to detect at a distance.

Tense minutes passed. He noted the internal temperature was already a point down on normal. Heat loss would start speeding up soon as the latent heat in the thermally shielded hull bled out into the absolute zero of deep space. They'd need to shed another forty degrees off the internal bulkheads to appear inert. Infra-red made them more visible than the meagre light from the sun ever would at this distance. It was going to get a lot colder on board before this was all over.

"Captain," whispered Dyne, his second in command. "Not to question... but is this *really* worth it?"

Aryce nodded once and put his finger to his lips. *Not now*, he thought over their private channel.

They waited, and it got colder, and colder.

He sent a general broadcast over the l-net. *No movement unless absolutely necessary. It's going to get* cold *in here. Sit down if you can – but carefully and not all at once!*

Ten minutes passed. The hull was now minus seventy on the dark-side away from the sun. Inside the ambient temperature was now two degrees – cold enough to see your breath. He could hear someone's teeth chattering on the bridge, and he threw them a foul look.

Sorry, Captain, they replied over the ship net – clamping their jaw shut tight.

They had no scans – nothing else was online, but Aryce had lined up the bridge viewport on their FTL exit and angled away from their exit vector before he had shut everything down, so he could watch for anyone following their energy signature. Their FTL burst was still faintly visible a way back – a thin bubble of expanding ultraviolet and deep purple slowly fading away. A blatant tell-tale which couldn't be hidden.

Then a naval destroyer blurred into view, just beyond their FTL point. Now Aryce held his breath again. Normal Naval protocol would be to scan the FTL signature, sweep the volume, and then drop audio drones.

Seconds later, five small bursts of light appeared at the destroyer's aft section and the deployed drones vectored away, disappearing from view almost instantly.

The *Dying Embrace* was now three light-seconds away from the destroyer. He had to pray that was enough.

Minutes passed, the drones didn't find them.

He knew the destroyer was now seeding Observers into the volume. That was a guarantee that they would be found if they stayed here much longer. His only hope was the destroyer would give up and move on. They continued their silent drift away from their pursuer. Every second took them forty thousand kilometres further away – giving the navy a larger and large sphere to sweep every second, and making their job that much harder. Eventually they would set the drones into a listening pattern and begin scouting the volume themselves, whilst the Observers and drones took care of the volume of space around their exit point.

Aryce knew that he was now fully committed to fulfilling the charter. It would be the work of a simple query against the FTL signature to identify the *Dying Embrace* – even as poorly maintained as it was. Which meant there was now an arrest warrant out on his entire crew, and a Seize and Capture order on the *Embrace*. If he gave himself up *now* he might be able to talk his way out for his crew, and just lose his license.

And lose six hundred thousand credits. The hazard pay wouldn't cover abandoning the charter – which would only pay only if disabled, captured, or on threat of harm which could not be overcome.

But he'd lied to the others about the hazard pay. It was actually one *tenth* of the charter – not times ten. The charter was six million credits, but he didn't want them to know the risk he was clearly taking. He didn't have journo's on board, or mega-media moguls or Colesworth corporate suck-ups.

He didn't *actually* know who they were. But the one million deposit they had given him up front – enough for him to replace the *Embrace and* retire – had convinced him the other five would look good alongside it. So he didn't ask too closely about the 'who, what, and why' of the people paying the money. Those kind of numbers precluded any such inconvenient questions.

They wanted to go straight to the Cloud. They had given him co-ordinates. They had said they wanted to be there first.

He was fully prepared to burn out the *Embrace's* dying heart to make sure they got what they wanted.

Captain Reen studied the wreckage before them. It had quite obviously been a ship at some point – so she thought.

It was too cold on Infra-red to be the *Dying Embrace*, even though it could not have miraculously managed to drop further in than they had thought.

It was strewn across a large volume of space before the remains of the Colesworth Refinery – itself now a mere shell of the massive resource processing station which had once occupied the huge rock in the near-distance.

"Perhaps it's one of your transports?" he asked one of the more approachable Colesworth execs.

"Unlikely. None were reported lost and none due here until four hours after the... initial losses. We suspended all traffic immediately."

"Got it," said one of her midshipmen. "I found the tombstone... not much left but enough." The tombstone was a tradition lost in time. Every vessel bore a physical block of super-dense bonded alloy which itself was really a series of cubes within cubes. A grid of data was etched into each face of every layer, bearing the vessel manufacturers credentials, vessel chassis ID, and so on. Its presence was a legal requirement for any ship to be registered with Imperial Vessel Registration, as a non-electronic id tag, for when all else failed if the vessel were destroyed.

"Go on?"

"IVR reports it as the *Inquisitive Swan*, last filed destination was Cangrua."

"That's two hundred light-years away," said Reen.

"Captain, we have moving contacts coming from the field... lots of them."

Reen bit her lip. "Let's see them," she said. The entire bridge crew shared the same mutual 3D view of the sensor sweeps around the ship – all realised in their fields of view via their integrations so they all saw the scan as a single holographic projection within the bridge itself.

Four thousand contacts came swarming out of the nearby asteroid field directly toward them at incredibly high speed.

"Shit! *Quillisyr!* About one-eighty, full burn, FTL ready on my mark!"

The *Quillisyr* vibrated as the manoeuvring thrusters strove to turn the ship around as fast as they could. The swarm tore through the *Swan's* debris without even slowing – a crazy mix of tentacled metal monstrosities and flickering orbs aiming straight for them. She made a snap decision. These things were clearly nothing from the Empire, and the wreckage from the *Swan* was mute testimony that the *Quillisyr* would have a similar fate shortly.

"Fire on all targets!"

"All of them?" demanded Kryse, her weapons officer.

"Now!"

The *Quillisyr* had three turrets and two weapons grade directed masers – one forward and one aft. It wasn't a vessel built for combat, she didn't even have missile launchers.

The turrets picked up – AI routines kicking in under an "All contacts hostile" protocol and firing plasma blasts at will at the nearest optimal targets. They seemed to have little effect. The oncoming craft didn't even attempt to evade, and left the bolts to bloom harmlessly against their shields.

As their aft came around and all the linear sub-c drives fires up at full burn, the rear maser started firing out beams of invisible death. The contacts were small and had powerful shields, but the two gigawatt maser punched through in a second and slagged the metal inside – vaporising it almost instantly. A cheer went up in the *Quillisyr*.

But it was clear the masers re-fire time wasn't up to it. It took two seconds to regain enough energy from the ship's grid to fire again.

"Make every shot count, Kryse!"

"If I can!" he grated back. Just trying to pinpoint optimal targets was challenge enough.

The swarm was almost upon them, but now they had full burn Reen hoped it would be the turning point. Either the chasing swarm could keep up, or the *Quillisyr* would get up enough distance to go FTL. This many nearby objects would cause the FTL carrier wave to become malformed – they couldn't risk firing the drive whilst they were so close.

The aft maser stabbed out again and again, all too slowly. Reen cursed the ship's energy grid.

"Kryse, kill the turrets! They're useless anyway."

The additional power allowed the maser to recharge half a second faster. Not much, but it could make all the difference.

The swarm was keeping up, but not gaining, and so far hadn't fired back. Reen dared not hope. She took a gamble.

"Drop the shields, pull life support down to 50%. We'll bring the aft shields up if one of them even warms up a weapon."

Now with a one second recharge – the maser stabbed out again and again. Kryse was up to the challenge, despite his dual role normally being logistics. There was usually little for a weapons officer to do on a passenger cruiser. Every second the maser licked out and slagged another target, but it was throwing snowballs to stop a supernova. Picking off one a second made no difference to the four thousand odd contacts which were trailing them in a roughly formed cloud. They were still too close to allow the *Quillisyr* to go FTL and not dropping back. Despite the *Swan's* constant acceleration they were keeping pace. It was a standoff.

Could it hold long enough to let Kryse pick them all off? she wondered desperately.

"Masers beginning to burn," said Kryse through gritted teeth.

"Damnit! Leave more relax time between shots."

"On it."

"Rastin, can we get any more burn out of the drives?"

"No chance, we're at 110% recommended output now – I'll have to drop back down to 100% any minute."

"*What?*" Reen almost screamed.

"We're minutes away from blowing the heat exchanger! We *can't* risk it."

Reens face fell in despair. *If we have to drop that much thrust... we're done for.*

"Captain! Up ahead!"

Reen saw the blur of a large naval destroyer as it slid into local space a hundred k's ahead of them.

"Thank the Emperor!" she exclaimed.

The destroyer immediately opened fire.

"Admiral Benthar, this is Captain Seems of the INSS *Resolute Choice*. We've detected weapons fire two light-hours away by the Colesworth Refinery, and a ship fleeing a large group of contacts."

Raul focused on the stream of incoming data. "Engage," he ordered. "Defence only."

"Yes, Fleet Admiral."

The *Resolute Choice* spun up its g-drive and within seconds was decelerating into the theatre.

Raul could see and hear everything he chose to look at. He heard Captain Seems give the order to open fire on the swarm ahead and watched approvingly as they began firing precisely on target from a hundred thousand kilometres out.

According to Imperial Vessel Registration, the vessel fleeing the swarm was the *Quillisyr* – a private passenger liner, Captain Sianna Reen commanding. From the scans it was clearly about to blow its primary sub-c drive – her infra-red signature stood out white-hot even when scaled for drive energies.

The *Resolute Choice* was too far out for missiles or projected weaponry yet – and was using energy lances to best effect. Explosions bloomed all around the *Quillisyr's* stern as each shot found and destroyed a target.

Raul was secretly pleased to find their weapons did *actually* have the desired effect against the enemy. It meant they stood a chance at defence at least. He opened a direct channel to the Emperor's First Office.

This is Fleet Admiral Benthar, I respectfully ask for an emergency dialogue with the Emperor. Subject – Too far, too soon.

Almost immediately, the private sim opened about him and the Emperor walked out from behind the throne.

"Your Majesty." Raul relayed the tactical feeds into the chamber and they watched in silence for a few moments.

"At least we know they can be destroyed," said the

Emperor. He turned to Raul with one eyebrow raised. "Most fortunate given that we are no doubt now at war."

Raul shook his head. "These appear to be small automated drones. Outreach may yet be able to salvage something if they can make contact."

"They have failed so far. What intiated this conflict?"

"Hotheads and money, as usual. A group flooded the cordon at once. We interdicted most, but a few were able to get by."

"The Refinery is on the Naval hot list, is it not?" asked the Emperor pointedly. He referred to a series of zones within the main Exclusion Zone which were under constant scrutiny.

"It is, Your Majesty. The *Resolute Choice* responded as fast as possible."

The Emperor returned to watching the engagement, and Raul focused on the feed from the *Resolute* at the strategic level.

"Captain Reen, this is Captain Seems of the Imperial Naval Destroyer *Resolute Choice*. Your vessel is to be seized by order of His Imperial Majesty Sulran the Fourth. Your license is hereby revoked and you no longer have the rights to captain a vessel. The *Quillisyr* is now under my command and the ownership of the Empire. Relinquish your CnC codes immediately."

"Would you save our asses first?" yelled Reen. "Then you can have whatever you want!"

"Codes."

"Damn you, *Navy* -" she cut herself off before she dug an even deeper hole for herself and after a moments reluctant hesitation, she transmitted her command and control codes across.

The *Quillisyr* immediately dropped its burn to ninety per cent – and the swarm started slowly gaining.

"What are you *doing,* Navy?" yelled Reen.

"Stopping you from blowing up. Scans show you have a coolant leak filling your outer hull. Tell your weapons officer to keep firing, they're doing a good job."

Seems then sent a command over the *Resolute's* l-net. *Lieutenant Peters, take over their energy management. That maser is about to fry so clear the compartments around it and vent them out to space to try and cool it down.*

Aye, sir.

Reen watched in amazement as her ship-status showed the blast-seals slam down around the aft maser housing, and then the entire aft section dumped its atmosphere out into space.

"What the -?"

Kryse instantly realised what was happening, and smirked to himself. He started firing faster as he watched the maser readouts carefully. The heat in the masers began dropping rapidly as the absolute zero of space allowed the heat to radiate out from the compartment bulkheads far faster than normal, despite the increased fire rate. "I need more power from somewhere!" he demanded.

"On it," replied Peters across the ship-to-ship network. The lights went out, life support dropped to twenty-five per cent, and all non-essential systems went offline.

"Better!" said Kryse, happy to be back to one shot per second without risking the maser.

Fireballs and clouds of metal shrapnel sprang into existence with frightening and ever increasing frequency, scintillating in the dim sunlight – but still getting closer by the second.

"They're almost on us," said Reen, now powerless to affect the outcome of whatever was going to happen next.

There was a blazing flash on every side of the *Quillisyr* – then everything went crazy.

Four Automated Defence Platform's suddenly appeared around them and began blasting away at the approaching drones in perfect unison. Forty maser beams per second stabbed into the swarm, and a plethora of missiles leapt out toward it.

The chaos behind them was immense. Every maser beam resulted in an explosion, every missile destroyed several drones around it as it detonated.

"Where did *they* come from?" demanded Reen in amazement. They were common enough for defence perimeters, especially around space stations and naval bases but she had never seen the Navy deploy them like this.

Kryse was lost amidst the sudden frenzy, unable to find a target quick enough to shoot at before it exploded.

"Allow me?" Lieutenant Peters asked.

Kryse relinquished control of the maser and the *Resolute Choice* took over, slaving the fire control to its own as it co-ordinated with the ADP's.

"Good grief," murmured Kryse, impressed despite himself.

Over the next forty seconds, it seemed that the entire swarm vaporised before their very eyes. As the *Quillisyr* slowly pulled ahead, the entire aft view became a glowing firework display.

Within a minute, the entire swarm was nothing more than a sparkling field of metallic debris.

Chapter Twenty-seven

"I want a full tactical analysis of the encounter," said Raul to his staff quorum. "Every angle. Could we have improved the response, other options for counter-offensive measures, etc. Bring in Captain Seems and the crew of the *Resolute Choice* for a full debrief as soon as they've finished securing the volume."

"Yes, Admiral."

Raul returned to the simulation for the Emperors War Office – his avatar taking on a more solid form, instead of the ghostly presence he had just upheld which traditionally indicated someone was " attending, but not present".

The Emperor was still a ghostly apparition himself, obviously still dealing with matters elsewhere.

Raul was patient, he had plenty to mull over. This was the first engagement with a massively superior force, and they had succeeded. Whilst that was to be applauded, he was acutely aware of the potential consequences.

It was reassuring to see their technological capabilities were up to the task of what had been, in reality, a small-scale engagement considering the size of Cloud around S'vreth. However, this swarm had merely been drones, small craft at best. Not frigates, not destroyers, nor capital ships. The Cloud was full of such.

It was promising, but not conclusive. He hoped the warmongerers amongst the Senate could be persuaded of that now they had tasted blood. The last thing the Empire needed was the members of Senate feeling that the might of the Imperial Navy made them invincible in the face of the enemy.

Deploying the ADP's in formation around the *Quillisyr* had been a stroke of tactical genius. He'd see to it Captain Seems got a commendation, possibly even a title. It was the first time remote deployment via wormhole had been actively used in the field during an engagement, and even though the tactical advantage of the capability was known, Seems had just conclusively proven how effective it could be in battle.

Four thousand enemy units taken out. Not one loss.

Could they possibly hope to continue that record against the Cloud, if it decided to respond? he mused silently. He didn't need to answer himself. He already knew.

"An interesting result, Fleet," said the Emperor, returning to the sim and taking on a more corporeal appearance.

"Yes, Your Majesty."

"You do not sound overly pleased?"

"I *am* pleased, Your Majesty... just not needlessly so. This is a promising first encounter, but no indication of our prowess against the forces within the Cloud."

The Emperor nodded. "Quite. I am going to have quite the debate with the Senate – and no doubt the Pax – after this outcome."

Raul hid a smile. "I can only imagine, Your Majesty."

"I am sure, Fleet Admiral. But you may relish the experience first-hand, as I will call upon you for your tactical assessment before the Senate."

Raul grimaced. "Of course, Your Majesty."

"No response from the Cloud?"

"None. As yet."

401

"I have to attend to other matters. However you may prevail upon me immediately should anything change."

"Thank you, Your Majesty." Raul bowed, and the Emperor left the room behind his throne. The room faded away and Raul was sat back in his office. Before he had chance to reach for the glass of Rahnd Whisky on his desk, Admiral Cole pinged him. He sighed.

Aryn, he greeted him.

Raul, I've checked over the encounter details, we have a problem.

Go on...

The Random Asset *tracked an FTL burst into an empty volume of space, but failed to find any contact on the other side. It's believed to be a ship called the* Dying Embrace *by its FTL signature.*

So?

It was 0.1 AU's from the Cloud.

Raul rubbed the heels of his hands over his eyes. *Tell me it's unarmed.*

I'm afraid not. The captain clearly feels a full suite of expensive weaponry is more important than maintenance of his FTL drive, which from the carrier wave signature is just an explosion waiting to happen. We've had him on our books for some time. He has a lot of hardware on board which typical citizens of the Empire haven't even heard of.

Raul called up the logs from the *Random Asset* and scanned through them. *The* Random Asset *seeded the volume with Observers, but so far nothing has been spotted. Would it be too much to hope the* Dying Embrace *simply exploded on exiting FTL?*

Yes.

I'll arrange a deployment to track them down.

You may have to eliminate the ship Raul.

402

I know. If it gets near the Cloud and they try to approach it, this idiot will no doubt open fire and that will be that. I won't jeopardise the situation and risk an all-out war we cannot win for one ship. If we can't capture the Dying Embrace, *we'll destroy it. Thanks for bringing this to my attention.*

That's what we're here for, Fleet. Good luck.

Aryn disconnected.

Raul issued the necessary orders, and sat back nursing his drink. He turned it in his hands for a few moments as he judged himself for issuing a Capture or Kill order on the *Dying Embrace*. Then he downed the rest of the two-hundred year old whisky n one go, and turned his attention to the Anti-matter deployment programme, which was already well under way. Despite this impromptu 'success' regarding the engagement around the *Quillisyr*, Raul felt this desperate scheme was to be the only hope of mounting a realistic defence against the Cloud when – not *if* – they attacked the Empire.

***

Romurik stood as Brynn sat at his desk in the Captain's cabin, Andersten lounged by the door – securing the most tactically sound location in the room, Romurik noted. He was fairly impressed.

"So other than some personal revenge quest – somehow sanctioned by the Imperial Navy, and also either sanctioned or ignored by the Totality – what brings you *here*, to my ship?"

"The *Delaror* encounter," said Romurik. He looked at

403

Andersten. "I believe it was yourself and your Executive Officer who boarded her?"

"Yes," said Andersten.

"The encounter with this... Shredder. Is there anything about it not in your report?"

Andersten looked at Brynn, who shrugged.

"No."

"I don't care if anything was left out... I think it's clear I have no particular interest in authoritative measures. But, it may help me in my... objective. What about personal reactions? Opinions?"

Andersten shrugged this time. "Nothing was left out. The damned thing nearly had us though. It was beyond me to fend it off."

"Yet you did."

"By luck. If the Delaror's breach shielding had been offline... I wouldn't fancy my chances again, and that takes some saying."

"Did anything about it feel... odd? Behaviour wise?"

Andersten rubbed his nose. "Not odd, so much... malevolent, perhaps."

"Explain?"

"It... I can't I guess. It *wanted* us. It wasn't just chasing down some intruders. It *really* wanted us."

"No doubt to strip out your enhancements?"

"I guess. I'm not so sure. I can't explain it any better. The XO might."

"She felt the same?"

"I think. It rattled us both, being honest."

Romurik turned to Brynn. "Might I talk to your XO?"

Brynn shook his head. "She's still recovering. I've not filed it on my report, but it shook her up far more than I

404

would let on to the Navy. It was her first sortie under my command."

Romurik considered this for a moment. "Do you think it was hunting you?"

"It kind of felt that way, yes," replied Andersten. "I've been hunted before – too often."

"So, to press the point, there's nothing more, or new, that you could tell me before I leave?"

"Leave?" asked Brynn. "You only just arrived."

"Forgive me, Captain. This was a brief courtesy call and a 'just-in-case' to obtain more information. I'm leaving for the *Delaror* as soon as I'm done here."

"Now wait a minute," said Brynn disbelieving. "That thing can't have been the only one on board..."

"I sincerely hope not, Captain," said Romurik. "I intend to capture one."

Brynn blinked. Andersten raised his eyebrows.

"Capture one? And bring it back here? Not a chance, not on my ship."

"Certainly not, Captain. I would not endanger your crew. I did that to the *Delaror* and we all saw what happened as a result."

Brynn narrowed his eyes. "Van E'streth ordered you into the Cloud, did he not?"

"It was my plan he authorised," said Romurik.

"Nevertheless, it was the command decision of the captain to execute that plan. Ultimately it is *his* responsibility for the lives of his crew, not yours. You are *not* to blame for their deaths, Agent, nor the loss of the *Delaror*. So drop that chip off your shoulder and get on with it."

Romurik was quiet for a moment. "Thank you,

Captain," he said softly. Even though Admiral Cole had said as much, for some reason hearing it from an *acting* captain – who had the same level of responsibility on his shoulders on a daily basis as Captain Van E'streth had borne – made it slightly more acceptable. "But, the *Delaror* herself is not lost. Merely... misplaced. I intend to recover her."

"Oh, good luck with *that*," said Andersten.

"We shall see," replied Romurik with good humour.

Brynn drummed his fingers on his desk for a few moments. "Well, I won't stop you. You have the Admiral's grace, and someone with your record knows the kind of shit they are getting themselves into. At least you have the hardware at your disposal to make it less than a suicide mission. Frankly, I think you're mad."

"You would not be the first to make such an assessment, Captain," said Romurik.

"I bet. Do you need anything from me?"

"No, Captain, thank you. Although, there is one thing. I believe you recovered some of the crew?"

"*Some* being the literal operative. Yes."

"May I see the remains?"

Brynn looked at Andersten. His face was set, but he shrugged – uncaring.

"Ok, Andersten will show you to the med-bay."

"Thank you, Captain."

"I wish to see you before you depart however."

"Understood."

"This way," said Andersten.

Romurik clicked his heels together with a loud clang and saluted Brynn. Brynn returned the formal salute and watched the metal giant softly and quietly leave his cabin, Andersten in tow.

Andersten eyed Brynn him briefly, giving him a hard look, as thanks for making him nanny an apparently psychopathic cybo. Brynn smiled evilly in return.

Horstan? He asked over the l-net. *Would you come to my cabin as soon as convenient please?*

Yes, Captain. Five minutes.

Thank you.

"Here you go," said Andersten, voice carefully neutral. He drew the maintenance chest from the cryo-storage bay and dropped it on the bed, ice crystals forming on the outside as it hit the warm air.

Romurik cracked open the case and looked inside. The contents were exactly as the visual report depicted, with the one minor detail which had piqued his curiosity.

"And the capsule?" he asked.

Andersten was silent.

"No one would have noticed," said Romurik. "But I'm a suspicious bastard. You knew Ensign Harris was on the *Delaror*. I cross referenced the crew rosters; your association was an easy spot. You deliberately went off-mission to her duty station and recovered her remains. Then you saw a backup capsule in the mess in the chest and removed it. This smear here," Romurik pointed into the chest, "and your partial finger-print I believe? Clumsy."

Andersten's face was blood red.

"Was it hers?" Romurik asked softly.

He stared, eyes stabbing his anger at Romurik. Then he nodded once.

"Have you accessed it?"

He shook his head.

Romurik held out his hand.

Andersten didn't move.

"Look, I won't report this – I don't *care* – officially. But if it's the only way to get it off you, I will."

"How did you know?"

"I told you, I'm a suspicious bastard."

Andersten pulled a durallium chain from around his neck inside his tunic, and slipped a small one centimetre long capsule off the magnetised clasp. He rolled it in his fingers for a few seconds – judging whether to trust this Intellect with these precious captured memories – before dropping it into Romurik's outstretched hand.

"Thank you." Romurik touched it with a fingertip and accessed the files within via a field scan. Everything that Ensign Harris was, everything she had thought and saw and felt and experienced flooded into his mind. He recorded it all, including the horror of the last few eternally agonising seconds of her life as the Shredder tore into her body – ripping every single integrated fibre from her flesh and consuming her mind. How her backup capsule had managed to escape was a miracle. He carefully picked up the small quantum lattice storage device, and handed it back to Andersten.

"Whatever you do," said Romurik, his voice grim, "no matter *how* much desire you might have – never, *ever* access that. Let her be." He walked out, and left Andersten alone with his niece's memories in the palm of his hand, and her pitiful remains mixed inseparably with those of two other people in a maintenance chest.

"Done?" asked Brynn. Romurik had requested his presence in the *Betsy's* rear hangar bay.

"Yes," replied Romurik tersely. He knew it was unhealthy, but the last few seconds of Ensign Harris' life were now constantly on replay in the periphery of his mind.

"I spoke with my XO. She echoed Andersten's feelings. She said she felt hunted, like it wouldn't give up no matter what. Prey to a predator, so to speak."

"I see. Tell your XO she has my thanks."

"What's your plan?"

"I don't have one. Get on board. Figure one out. That's about it."

"Detailed."

"As detailed as yours, I believe?"

"Touché. Do you need anything?"

Romurik shook his head. "No thank you, Captain. I have everything I need, most especially incentive."

"Well, I can't stop you, and I won't try. But you're still mad."

"I know. Thank you."

"If you make it back, I strongly advise changing form," said Brynn, pointing at Romurik. "That's only a symbol of hatred throughout the majority of the Empire."

"Perhaps. But I might yet change that perception. Thank you again, Captain."

"I did nothing, but my pleasure anyway. Good luck."

The hangar bay door opened, sealed against decompression by the door field. Romurik stepped out through the field into space and – with a semi-mocking salute – shot out of sight as he made for the distant

Delaror.

"Crazy son of a bitch," Brynn said to himself, almost admiringly.

Chapter Twenty-eight

The *Dying Embrace* was nearing the Cloud. Aryce was trying not to let it unsettle him – but damn that was a lot of ships right there. *How could you manufacture that many… and keep it a secret?* he marvelled to himself.

They had had to clamp the nav-com to stop it folding from so much sensor input coming in. They knew the positions of the nearest fifty-thousand odd ships, but that was it. Looking out the viewport he could see the void filled with by a sphere formed by small points of light far brighter than the stars beyond, each a vessel catching and reflecting the sunlight from S'vreth. The vessels closest to them formed a seemingly infinite wall which stretched the eye and the mind to the very limits before eventually curving back away around the star. It was frightening, and awe inspiring. He didn't know whether to admire these things, fear them, or both.

He turned to the leader of his chartered party. A Baidian called Veetri, who had silently refused to offer any other name or form of identification. This was the one who had made the original booking of the charter. Baidians were generally slim, with entirely midnight blue eyes. Their blue-tinged skin was tough but flexible, and although humanoid, they were nothing like a humanoid biologically speaking. Their organs had different functions and locations in their physiology. They had wildly different skeletal structure and limb articulation. Their elbows and knees where double-jointed, allowing a large range of movement in either direction, making them fearsome hand-to-hand combatants.

"So, I kept my end of the bargain. You're here. What do you need to see?"

Veetri regarded him for a moment, expressionless. "Will you be able to deploy our unit?"

Aryce shrugged. "Of course. First though, the second instalment?"

"It has already been made."

Aryce contacted his account. Three million plus the now insignificant small change which had been there before this all started. The Baidian had kept his promise – to bring up the payment to fifty percent upon reaching the Cloud. He was now richer than he had ever been at any point in his life. He could bail right now... the money was his. He'd have to kill the Baidians on board of course – bad business though, and they made a poor choice of enemy. Their entire culture pivoted around honour and revenge.

Another three million, with his name on it, was waiting in the ether...

Dyne gave him a look. Aryce knew what it meant. This had *better* be worth it. It was, but he couldn't say anything. His crew would get edgy if they knew the details and the money involved, even though they'd each get enough out of this deal to set them up on their own.

"Thank you," said Aryce. He nodded for Dyne to proceed.

The small orb was only a third of a metre across, and it loaded into the mass projector easily.

The Baidian assured him it would withstand the EM field as it launched, so he didn't care as long as it didn't explode. This mass projector was like no other. Hideously expensive, hideously powerful, self-contained, but only one-shot. It took forever to recharge from the Embrace's ailing power grid.

"Fire," he said.

The orb shot out at 0.3c and reached the ship the Baidian's had asked him to target in the Cloud two point five seconds later. The view showed the orb approach on target, but something mystifying happened before it could hit the vessel.

Aryce would have expected either a massive flare of energy as the orb converted into energy against a shield, or armoured hull – instantly turning into EM radiation, or it would have ripped through the unprotected hull, tearing a hole metres-wide right through and out the other side.

Yet before it reached the ship – less than a quarter of a second before it would have hit – the orb simply disintegrated into a fine, rapidly expanding cloud of sparkling dust.

Aryce watched a slow-motion replay in amazement. The dust slammed into the hull of the vessel and the momentum behind each particle drove it deep inside. Then nothing happened.

The Baidian turned to his party, and they all began working feverishly on their handheld touchscreens. They did not have web integrations – their religion forbade it – and as a race they viewed such a perversion of nature with revulsion. They relied on physical interaction with their technology – something which Aryce generally sneered at. But as he watched them work, he marvelled at the speed at which they

413

manipulated their devices.

Then they turned to the view window, as one of them continued working over their screen.

The ship in the view began to orient itself toward them. Aryce parked a fire order with the *Embrace's* Intellect, ready at a moment's notice. But the other ship did not attack. Instead it began to move toward them – slowly at first, gradually picking up speed.

"You canny devils," murmured Aryce. *They've hacked it, subverted the ship somehow!*

The ship was large – comparable to an Imperial Naval destroyer, but he didn't recognise the construction. Nor did the IVR database.

"How did you do this?" he asked Veetri. "Not just that orb, but how did you take over an alien technology so quickly?"

Veetri looked at him, his soul-less blue eyes giving nothing away.

"Close-mouthed freaks," Aryce muttered under his breath.

The destroyer lumbered toward them. As it approached, Aryce and his crew could see a lot of hull damage. Erosion from solar winds had dealt it a hard hand, with a fair amount of its external hull plating having worn away – being unprotected against centuries of constant, hard radiation. Numerous panels were worn down to the point of showing the underlying shield grid within them, along with the various networks of structural reinforcement and coolant webbing. But most prominent were a profusion of blast marks and holes caused by numerous explosions. This leviathan had not gone down without a fight. It came closer and closer to

414

the *Dying Embrace*, and Aryce began to get a little nervous. It was *really* huge.

"You guys are sure you know what you are doing?" he asked the Baidians. They remained silent.

The destroyer dwarfed the *Dying Embrace* as it drew alongside and slowed to a halt relative to their position.

"We require your drop-ship," said Veetri.

"Say what?" asked Aryce, surprised.

"Your drop-ship, please."

"Now wait a minute… no one said anything about stealing my drop-ship."

"We are not stealing. We have purchased it from you."

Before Aryce opened his mouth with another quip, he checked his account. The full amount as promised – six million, and an additional half a million on top. His mouth went dry. That additional would buy *two* replacement drop-ships…

"Sure, it's yours," he croaked.

"Thank you. We will commend your charter to the Baidian Hegemony. You have been most honourable, and most ingenious in fulfilling our requirements. The codes please?"

Aryce messaged Veetri's contact address with the shuttle command codes for the *Loving Embrace* – the eight-man drop-ship he used to ferry people off for planet-side tours, amongst other things.

"*What* is going on?" demanded his XO.

Aryce gestured for him to be quiet. If he was right, this was all over and they could get the heck out of here.

The Baidians all filed out, each nodding to him respectfully as they went, then they made for the *Loving*

Embrace. He waited until they left and then let out a deep sigh he hadn't realised he had been holding in.

"Ok, Captain – this has gone far enough, what *is going on?*"

Quickly, Aryce filled him in on the salient details – broadcasting the conversation to his crew.

"Three *million?*" Dyne exclaimed.

"Yes," replied Aryce with a straight face he was immensely proud of. "We can all retire. The *Embrace* comes first though."

"Of course, of course..." murmured Dyne. His eyes snapped up to meet Aryce's and for one dreadful second he thought he'd been rumbled. "Maintenance first though, Captain – this bucket is about to fall apart, we don't need any more *toys* on board."

Aryce held his hands wide with an innocent expression. "You got me."

They watched the *Loving Embrace* drop from the hull below, and then slip across to the huge vessel beside them – heading for what appeared to be a docking bay on the port side.

"Good luck to them," said Dyne. "They're going to need it. Was this their plan? To go stealing ships from this Cloud thing?"

"I guess," said Aryce. "It sure worked well. I have no idea how though. Anyway, who cares? Let's get out of here *fast.*"

Within seconds, the *Dying Embrace* vanished in another erratic burst of violet-tinted FTL.

The *Loving Embrace* entered the docking bay of the large destroyer – which was unlit and unshielded – and set down inside. Several figures emerged from it in EVA suits – suit lights painting the bay interior a vivid yellow – then they floated to the internal bay doors and began to make their way inside.

None of them noticed that several other ships in the Cloud behind them began to orient toward their position and edge forward in the same bulging formation that had been used to capture the *Delaror,* so many hours ago.

***

Romurik did a complete sensor sweep of the *Delaror* from two kilometres away, scanning the entire hull for damage. He took no care to avoid being observed; in fact he hoped he would be. Other than the self-inflicted maser fire Andersten had used to take out the Shredder on the bridge, the only other signs of damage were the exploded mess room. That meant the Shredder had been allowed on board by the Delaror, or had hacked its systems to gain entry. Romurik doubted either possibility.

He had already made several precautionary clones and decoy duplicates of himself within his own internal structure – both to act as a buffer between his real self and any interactions with the *Delaror*, and also as a kind of virtual "cannon-fodder" to sacrifice should he come under a cybernetic attack. He made his way on-board through the shield over the gaping hole in the mess hall – having the shield frequencies so he could modulate his own to let him slip through. His feet touched down softly onto the deck as he aligned with the still functioning onboard gravity, and he surveyed the dried bloody mess which defiled the room.

There were no signs of anything around the ship, or moving within it judging by his detailed scans. The ship-net was down, as reported. He would have to make for the ship's core to try and interface with what was left of the Intellect.

As he made for the core, he played the last dying scream of Ensign Harris out loud over and over again. It was obsessive, but he made sure it played once for every crew member on board who had died. He made sure someone knew of their anguish.

He reached the primary core and went to use the authority codes Admiral Cole had given him, but - despite Horstans report - was surprised that there was no challenge. The doors opened as soon as he approached. One of the golden rules of any subversion or takeover was to change all the codes to prevent a defensive countermeasure being mounted – but to remove them entirely was unheard of. Suspiciously, he made his way inside and went to the first stack of ship cores. Having isolated his hand with its own partial clone of himself, he placed it against the stack and initiated an interface.

There was nothing there.

He let go of the stack in surprise. There was not even an unrecognisable sequence of data. Pure nothing. That didn't make sense. He chose another stack at random, in case this one had been isolated or damaged. The same. It was almost factory new – as if it had never been initialised.

How can this be? He checked every single stack in the core. They were all the same.

Simply entering data into such systems left a trace. Erasing it left a trace. Nothing could obliterate it as if it had never been used.

Besides this, *something* was clearly still running the ship's systems. It was under power and maintaining shields – and had joined the mega-formation that was the Cloud. Something wasn't right.

He checked the schematics of the ship again and made for the secondary core. The same results. He then checked the ternary nodes scattered about the ship as fail-safes. Nothing. Cybernetically speaking, the *Delaror* was every bit as much of a ghost ship as it was in the physical world.

Romurik was at a loss. He couldn't initiate data retrieval, or access the logs and feeds, because they simply did not exist. As Executive Officer Horstan's sim-stream had revealed – it was as if something had pulled every single last digital bit out of the *Delaror* and left a data vacuum behind.

He made for the ship's field grid sub-system, as something must be running the field over the mess room. The grid core was the only way to affect that, which meant some flow of data still had to be present.

It was, but purely to maintain the field over the mess room. Nothing was controlling it, it was just there. Data came from the field grid in the hull around the damaged area reporting the nature and size of the breach, and the hull shield nodes nearest the breach said "erect a field." That was it. No protocols from the field controller itself were in effect.

On *any* ship – let alone a naval destroyer – this was impossible.

He made for the bridge.

It was just as much a data void as the rest of the ship. After a few microseconds of thought, he sent a copy of himself into the network. He should be able to access latent data held within the persistent electron matrices. The only possibility for this that he could fathom would require a full bit-wipe to erase the data, and even that would leave a trace. A direct EMP *could* have this effect – if someone had somehow unleashed a massively powerful one directly within the storage network, from inside the ship. But there were no signs of that having happened. It would leave a chaotic jumble of scrambled relays and electron matrices – all filled with data noise. The structure of everything here was electronically stable. There was just no data.

Cybernetically speaking, Romurik was standing on a vast and infinite plane of nothing. He could go where he wished, but there was nothing to see when he got there. Usually it would be teeming with data flows and signals, security routines, monitoring routines, access protocols, and storage access cannulas – not a square metre of virtual space would be empty. The connections to all the various systems were all in place, and he could make his way around the ships virtual self with unsurpassed ease. Every single system was devoid of activity.

There was something hauntingly familiar about it, yet he couldn't quite pin it down.

He now had a decision to make. Stay here and wait for *some* kind of activity – possibly forever judging by the reported age and condition of the other ships in the Cloud. Or retake the ship. The quandary with retaking the *Delaror* was now in bringing some kind of hostile alien AI back to the Empire, even though he could locate nothing of the kind on board. Which brought the third choice to the fore; destroy the *Delaror*.

He opted to hedge his bets. He instructed his clone within the grid to begin acquiring the ship's systems. Maintenance bots sprang into life throughout the ship, and began repairing the damage caused by the brief internal fire-fights against the Shredder – as well as cleaning up the gory mess on all the decks. Where possible, the remains which could be identified would be grouped by DNA and preserved as the remains of each individual crew member.

Data began to flow back across the ship's network as his doppelganger established communication protocols and control routines for the core systems the ship would need for space travel. The *Delaror* sprang back into cybernetic life.

Romurik decided to try baiting the giant - a tactic he had a penchant for. The sudden activity on the Delaror might attract attention and lead to the engagement he secretly hoped for.

While he waited, he sat down in the XO's chair. He couldn't quite bring himself to take the captain's seat.

Chapter Twenty-nine

The INSS *Resolute Choice* slipped out of its g-drive field and back into normal space eighty thousand kilometres from the FTL burst which had brought the *Dying Embrace* to the perimeter of the Cloud. Being an Interdictor class IND frigate, she was better suited to chasing down and apprehending blockade runners than the *Random Asset,* which had detected the 'ghost' presence of the *Dying Embrace* heading toward the Cloud a short while ago.

She had followed a convoluted, but highly visible trail of FTL emergence points to reach this location – the captain of the *Dying Embrace* clearly had experience in avoiding a tail.

Unfortunately, this latest emergence point left them in the middle of a fire fight.

"INCC – Combat status two, repeat combat status two. Cloud perimeter forces engaged against an unidentified destroyer class vessel – powering away from the Cloud at high speed, requesting protocol."

A heavy destroyer of unknown design was being approached by the Cloud in the same bulging formation in which it had approached the *Delaror*. The destroyer was firing back at them with its entire aft ordnance. High energy beams flickered and stabbed out at the ships as they gained, and countless rapidly fading exhaust trails streamed out from the mid and forward sections, as numerous missiles peeled out and away toward their assigned targets.

The pursuing ships were returning fire – but whilst

the fleeing destroyer was shooting to do as much damage as it could to anything in range, the Cloud ships were tactically taking out the missiles and concentrating their fire on the destroyers aft shield generators. It was clearly a disablement tactic, intended for taking out drive and power systems. The destroyer's captain was throwing everything they could into its defence – the forward shields were at zero potential, with all their power diverted aft.

Energy blooms flared from shields on both sides of the fight as they exchanged fire – the destroyer's own shields were showing signs of overload – glowing whiter for longer and longer after each hit, as they struggled to shed the incoming energy.

"Captain Seems, what is your evaluation?" asked Command and Control.

"The Unknown is on the verge of being disabled. Normal protocol would require we assist, but the destroyer is not answering hails – their comm-net may be down."

"Hold please."

Captain Seems ground his teeth. An instantaneous communication network, and still you could be put on hold.

"The Unknown is gaining speed, Captain," supplied Peters. "As are the pursuing contacts."

He brought up a tactical of the surrounding volume of space. The Cloud was now bulging outward from the perimeter in a clearly defined bell-shape. Although made from a sizeable number of vessels, the bulge itself was microscopic against the infinitely flat wall of ships the Cloud formation became when this close to it.

"Any signs of a drive spike?"

"Nothing, sir. Without knowing their systems, I suspect they only have mass-thrusters at present. Their power system is very highly energised however, it would appear this ship is one of the enemy's."

"I guess so, judging by the reports from INI. Every ship in the Cloud exhibits a similar power source."

A thick lance of energy leapt from one of the destroyer's rear cannon – followed by the cannon exploding as the sudden surge of power overloaded its energy sink.

"Looks like they just found out how to tap into it..."

The beam itself struck the nearest pursuer and collapsed its shield instantly, punching straight through the hull and emerging from the other side. Explosions rocked the vessel from within, breaking out of the two breaches and scattering across its internal power grid as it came apart. It stopped firing and accelerating, then a flash of blinding white leapt from the aft section as the power core exploded and tore the ship to pieces.

A cheer went up from the bridge crew.

"Only four hundred million and twelve to go," someone quipped.

"Quiet," said Captain Seems sternly. "INCC – response please?"

"Do not engage, Captain. Seed Observers and leave the volume."

"*Command?*" Captain Seems couldn't contain his disbelief.

"Tactical advises against action due to overwhelming numbers, and no hostility toward Imperial forces. The Unknown is not recognised as an Imperial member, ally or known species, and is deemed a rogue unit from the Cloud itself."

"No hostility? Was the *Delaror* an act of kindness? This destroyer is set for the same fate if we don't intervene!"

"Tactical advises any engagement will ultimately involve a complete fleet deployment and result in failure. Do *not* engage. This is a direct standing order issued by the Fleet Admiral's office."

Seems cracked his knuckles as he made a fist behind his back. He gave his XO a look. "Order acknowledged, INCC. Lieutenant Sryss, deploy an Observer web."

"Aye, sir."

"Helm, g out point one AU as soon as the web is out."

"Aye, sir."

His Executive Officer, Rands, said nothing. He could read the answer to his unspoken question in his Captains eyes.

"Comm's, keep trying to reach that destroyer. Use lasers, radio, ancient dark forces – anything, just get me *someone* on board."

Veetri monitored the shield status of their destroyer and looked concerned.

"Commander, we must respond to the Imperial Naval vessel's hail. We cannot complete our mission. We must seek their aid."

Veetri turned to his first officer. "If we do this, they will know. Everything. We cannot reveal our presence on board."

"Then we will die here."

"So be it."

"Web deployed, Captain."

"Take us out," said Seems, his voice ice cold.

The *Resolute Choice* turned about, seeking the optimum point in the standing gravitational wave to fire up its g-drive.

"Captain! Incoming naval vessel!"

A ship blurred into being almost on top of the beleaguered destroyer, and instantly began firing on the Cloud that was pursuing.

"It's the *Delaror!*" exclaimed Leiutenant Peters.

The Cloud began directing fire on the *Delaror.*

"INSS *Delaror* – this is Captain Seems of the INSS *Resolute Choice.* Do you hear me?"

"Affirmative, Captain. This is the *Delaror...* INI Agent Romurik acting-in-command. Fancy lending a hand here?"

"My pleasure Agent! Peters – fire on all hostiles, nearest first policy."

"Aye sir!"

Beams of energy lashed out from the *Resolute Choice* as she turned about again and began to close in on the combat. She co-ordinated her fire with the *Delaror* to concentrate on the same targets in order to take them out twice as quickly.

Plasma bolts began streaming out from the *Delaror* – being close enough in on the combat to start using projectile mass to good effect. The bolts of energy splashed against the shields of the pursuing vessels in bright flashes, pummelling them toward an eventual collapse.

The fleeing unknown destroyer picked up on the

assistance quickly and began targeting those same ships with its own remaining plasma cannon. When an enemy vessels shields gave out, invariably at least two beams of energy from the three defending ships hit it at once, crippling or destroying it within seconds.

"INCC – Combat One, repeat Combat One. Defence of Imperial Naval asset in the field, INSS *Delaror*. Cloud engaged. Requesting immediate support."

"INCC acknowledge. Please hold."

"You have *got* to be kidding me." Captain Seems swore under his breath.

Their shields began to flare off incoming fire. "Peters, target the source."

"Sir."

"As soon as we reach optimal projectile distance, fire."

The *Resolute Choice* sped toward the conflict. Beams of various coloured energies snapped back and forth, space was littered with streams of scintillating points of light as plasma and tracers from mass-driver fire filled the void. Ghostly trails from missiles looped around and toward their targets, and the resulting explosions led to an almost constant barrage of flickering light.

Shields glowed brightly in almost every colour of the spectrum; red, gold, blue and violet flickering orbs, obscuring the ships behind them. Those around the rear of the unknown destroyer were glowing vivid white, on the verge of collapse.

"Entering Combat Zone, firing Hydras," said Peters.

The *Resolute Choice* was armed with so called 'heavy' missiles – each capable of delivering a payload of ten high-speed one kiloton nuclear warheads into the field.

The missiles screamed out toward the Cloud, and then split apart with a flash as their payload separated in front of their assigned target groups. The void lit up as over a hundred kilotons of mass converted into energy, along with several of the chosen targets as they succumbed to the onslaught.

Masked by this brief, blinding glare, the *Resolute* deployed her stock of ADP's through projected wormholes – exactly as Captain Seems had done earlier when defending the *Quillisyr* – placing them just behind the destroyer but before the Cloud. They all began firing immediately.

Hails of mass pellets – each being a kilo of depleted uranium – slammed into shields and hull with equal ferocity, instantly becoming a globe of fiercely hot, molten metal in a vivid blue flash that exacted a toll on both shield and hull alike.

The destroyer was slowly pulling ahead when its aft shields finally gave out. Several beams from the Cloud ships targeted its drive and power systems, and a series of explosions stopped the destroyers forward acceleration as its drive system tore apart in a slowly expanding field of debris. Its shields collapsed and it stopped returning fire. It was now dead in space, drifting on its last vector at high speed.

The Cloud ceased firing on the destroyer and began gaining, yet continued returning fire on the *Resolute Choice* and the *Delaror*.

"Bring the ADP's in around the destroyer," said Captain Seems. "Defensive formation."

"Aye, sir."

"Captain, I think we have a problem," said Rands.

"Look at the Cloud, sir."

Seems checked the Cloud contacts in his personal HUD, the bulge formation was growing larger and extending outward along the Cloud perimeter. Now at least three hundred ships were heading toward them.

"Agent Romurik, do you see?"

"Yes, I think we've overstayed our welcome. The destroyer is down, we can't save it and there is no time to board. Go."

"I will *not* abandon a vessel and its crew to these things!"

"Captain, that destroyer is already lost – and came from the Cloud in the first place. The *Delaror* is a ghost ship – its crew already dead. And no one in the Empire is going to miss *me* I assure you. Go – there is no point losing more ships to this thing."

"*Resolute Choice*, this is INCC – Fleet Admiral Benthar's orders are to cease fire and disengage *immediately*. Leave the INSS *Delaror* in the field."

Seems almost went purple with rage. "We *will* be back, Agent," he grated from between clenched teeth.

"No doubt, Captain," replied Romurik. "Now get out of here before this gets any uglier."

The *Resolute Choice* turned about yet again, and began heading for the crest of the next standing gravity wave. There – with her bridge crew watching the scene behind them with dismay – she blurred into g-drive and sped out of sight.

"Just you and me now," Romurik said, looking to the crippled destroyer ahead. He shut down the firing protocols and dropped everything on board the *Delaror* back to the same operational condition he had found it in – wiping all presence of his recent activities from the logs. As he expected, the Cloud stopped firing back at the *Delaror* as soon as he stopped firing upon them.

But then the *real* attack came. It took him completely by surprise, such was the swiftness and ferocity – and it nearly cost him everything.

A vast presence filled the *Delaror's* internal cyberspace – it was far larger than anything Romurik had ever encountered within the qNet, or even with the gestalt Vox Constans, which grew and shrank as occasion demanded. He had a dim perception of an entity which defied the concept of size, expanding outward forever without definition. It crushed his clone out of existence without even taking notice of it.

Romurik hastily pulled as much information as he dared through the quarantined data cannula he had setup before it evaporated into nothing under the onslaught. There was the horrific sense of something malevolent far beyond his reckoning, slowly bringing its scrutiny around toward his miniscule presence.

He managed to leave two small inert surprises lurking in the depths of the ship's cyberspace, and then collapsed the cannula. In reality, he turned and ran – threw himself out of the hole Andersten had blasted into the bridge when he took down the Shredder and launched himself straight at the unknown destroyer as he flew through space.

He was amazed. He had felt genuine panic for the first time in his entire existence. The thing was monstrous, unlike *any* Intellect he had ever heard of. It had seemed to dwarf the very universe itself.

He watched as the *Delaror* regained its way – clearly

back under the Cloud's control – and it took up position around the disabled destroyer as the rest of the Cloud caught up and formed a cordon around it.

It was clear that whatever was controlling this fleet was about to recover the destroyer as well. He wanted to get on board before that happened. He wanted to know who else was trying to steal these ships. He wanted another glimpse of that monster.

And he still wanted to get to know a few Shredders, personally.

Veetri relaxed, as the stone cold certainty that they had failed settled over him. It was all over. One of the Imperial Navy ships had escaped; the other clearly had been taken over. It was only a matter of time before they were boarded and the *Kanstral* was recaptured. The *Kanstral* – the grandest and most powerful Baidian Destroyer ever built by the Phosten Dynasty, lost again.

His team all took to arms and arranged themselves tactically about the bridge to defend it until death. A death that was certain. They had encountered hundreds of petrified Baidian corpses on their way to the bridge. Each mutilated beyond recognition, yet all had apparently fought to the bitter end. His ancestors had battled proudly, and with honour. As would they.

They waited patiently.

They did not have to wait long. A large, silver humanoid strode into view in the bridge access conduit.

His entire team opened fire at once.

Explosions blazed in the tunnel as round after round of high-ex detonated inside the confined space, and a blast of hot air, flames and smoke came rushing out into the bridge. Then they held their fire to analyse the results.

When the smoke cleared enough, they saw the figure still standing there, unharmed, with both hands raised.

"Wait!" it shouted. "I mean no harm. I am an agent of Sulranian Imperial Naval Intelligence."

Veetri hesitated. This would be an odd ploy by the enemy. And if true, he was still tempted to open fire to avoid the truth behind their mission becoming known. But, if this were a potential ally in what was to come...

"Approach," he said, waving his team to standby.

The figure strode through the ruined conduit and into the bridge, looking around.

"Baidian? Odd. This is no Baidian design I recognise," said Romurik.

No one answered.

"Cordial. Ok, we're about to be boarded by something that has every intention of tearing you to pieces. Judging by the corpses out there and the warm welcome you gave me, you've already guessed. You're also about to lose control of this ship, so be ready."

Veetri stared at Romurik for a moment, then turned to his team and nodded. They all resumed their positions. Romurik just stood there, as if minding his own business.

Then a whining noise filled the conduit. Romurik recognised it instantly from Andersten's logs.

The spinning orb shot up the conduit so fast it created a blast of compressed air ahead of it. But Romurik was ready, slamming a momentary category-1 force field across the entrance which the orb rebounded off with a colossal crash. Before it could recover ground

– using Andersten's tactic for keeping it at bay – Romurik hit it with two high-energy maser beams from his fists – both slamming into the Shredder and slicing it in half. The thing flew to pieces instantly; blades and mechanical parts shooting in every direction as deadly shrapnel which embedded itself into the conduit walls.

"Interesting design," shouted Romurik, having scanned and analysed every single piece from the Shredder as it exploded – regressing the pieces backward in a sim in reverse-time along their trajectories to reform the original orb.

Before the pieces had even finished ricocheting around the conduit – another two Shredders appeared.

"It's like some form of cleaner, the inside is hollow," he yelled, oblivious to the fact the Baidian were ignoring him entirely.

He threw up another instantaneous force field, and sliced one in half before it even hit the field itself. The other rebounded along with the shrapnel of the first and then the field dropped. The key trick with the field generator he had commissioned for his chosen form was that it could create an *immensely* powerful deflective field, but only for fraction a second before it collapsed. The key was to make that fraction of a second count.

The Baidian immediately opened fire on the other Shredder as it bounced away.

One short maser burst from Romurik's fist finished it off with a loud detonation and similar spray of lethally sharp debris which embedded itself deep into the walls.

"It slices up whatever it's attacking and draws it into a central chamber. Genius, really."

Five more Shredders came into the conduit. "Talking

of genius," Romurik yelled almost gleefully. "Building your command section separate to the vessel chassis. Now *that* can come in handy!"

He fired a slew of micro-missiles from his fingertips toward the Shredders as they flew straight for him. Each tiny missile flew directly into the Shredders central chamber – now guided by Romurik's analysis of the previous Shredder. Each one exploded, shattering the already battered conduit into pieces. Then he detonated the charges he had planted around the four supporting structures which secured the command centre to the ship. They blew apart, sending a rumble throughout the entire hull. Romurik held up a breach shield across the conduit, then grabbed the manual control for the door and span it across to physically seal the doorway.

The command section began to drift away from the destroyer in a cloud of flickering metallic debris.

Romurik waited. *If he was right...*

Nothing happened. Through the doorway view window he could see the destroyer dropping away from them as they drifted ahead due to the small impetus they had gained from the explosions. Another group of ten or more Shredders were zipping around the shattered stanchions and conduit around the bulk of the destroyer behind them – but they did not cross the widening gap to come and get them.

He watched them for a few moments. They were harvesting the debris. Collecting it like birds would catch flies in the air. *How odd,* he thought. *Could they be that desperate for resources? But then, why let this bounty escape your grasp?*

He had been right however. Whatever these things

were, they had no real interest in himself, or the Baidians on board. They only wanted the ship.

Now the question was, why? This totally contradicted the pattern on the *Delaror* where they had wiped everyone out. But then, perhaps they hadn't wanted the crew, perhaps everyone had merely been on board what they really wanted. The crew had just been biological inconveniences getting in the way.

He turned around to find the Baidian all staring at him, their expressions and glassy blue eyes totally unreadable.

"I know… fairly awesome, eh?"

They simply stared.

"Oh, you guys are going to be a joy," he said.

"You have cost us our mission," said Veetri flatly.

"Have I? Care to explain?"

Veetri turned to his team, but was silent.

Romurik waved a hand about him. "We're floating helpless in deep space, in front of a vastly superior force, and you think I care if you've done something you shouldn't have?"

Veetri turned to regard Romurik for a moment. "This vessel is – *was* – the *Kanstral*, Prime Destroyer of the Baidian Phosten Line. It was lost to the Dark Zone three hundred and twelve years ago, with all hands on board. It has never been seen or heard from since."

Romurik was intrigued. "And?"

"We detected its transponder ID when it entered this system."

"Aha, I see. So you mounted a salvage/rescue on your lonesome. Daring. And without Phosten Imperial sanction I'd wager."

Veetri was silent.

"Care to explain how you detected its transponder from two hundred light years away on Baidia Prime? You guys were still petitioning the Empire three hundred years ago – you didn't have the qNet then. So a bonded qSpinner is out of the question. Any FTL beacons would have been spotted already by INI's Observers. We saw nothing."

Veetri was silent – he didn't even blink.

"How did you regain control of the *Kanstral?*"

Silence again.

"Have it your way. But I bet it wasn't much of a challenge?"

Veetri turned to his team, one of whom shook their head. "No, it was not."

Romurik nodded thoughtfully. "I doubt it will be so easy again," he said quietly, thinking of that incomprehensibly vast mind. "For anyone. What was your intention?"

"To recover the *Kanstral* and return to Baidia. The honour of restoring the vessel and its place in our history is worth any risk."

"I'd normally argue the crass stupidity behind that point, but I won't. You do realise you have started a war here?"

"Do you realise *you* have?" Veetri countered. "Any action against us would have been against the Baidian Hegemony. Not the Sulranian Empire. You represent the Empire. We saw the Empire's 'choice' with the other vessel here before you, which stood off and was preparing to leave with their tail between their legs to avoid an honourable conflict."

Romurik was taken aback. Veetri was clearly a Baidian Republican zealot – one of the very vocal minority of Baidians who refused to accept their Imperial membership. This was getting less enjoyable by the minute.

"Well, pardon my semantics. Being an Imperial Coward, I'll just get off now shall I?" He turned to open the conduit door, with the veiled threat of decompressing the bridge.

"Wait." Veetri turned to his team, and they began talking animatedly in their own fluid language. There was a lot of arm waving, finger pointing and tapping of touch-pads. Romurik was enthralled. How could a modern day space-faring member of the Empire be so technologically backward? They had seemed reserved – almost withdrawn – when he had first confronted them. He had presumed they were communicating with each other via a local net. But now they were flapping and screeching at each other like a flock of Yamil birds fighting over a beached whale.

While they yammered at each other – Romurik checked the positions of the Cloud contacts nearest them. Although the nearest had formed around the bulk of the *Kanstral*, the larger group which had begun to move outward were still coming. That was worrying. He was unable to obtain a clear or reliable picture as there were now limited sensors at his disposal, so he tried jacking into the local Observer web the *Resolute Choice* had laid down. Through it he collated a view of the Cloud itself. It seemed the original perimeter was sealing itself back up to fill the gap left behind by this latest contingent, vessels shifting position to reform their geodesic formation, which meant the group heading for them had been detached from the main Cloud. He analysed their collective vector for a few moments and saw that they were clearly headed out system.

"Oh, oh," he said.

He scanned the bridge module they were adrift in. It wasn't designed to be a lifeboat – stupidly, even though that was an obvious choice for a physically separate command section. It had no propulsion systems of its own. Gravity was still on, as were the lights, life support and bridge systems – even though most were now offline or redundant. Before he had planned to sever the module from the ship he had checked that it had its own power. It even had its own shield generator. *Not so bad*, he thought, *I just need to make it move.*

As he was able to access the local Observer web – that meant he was outside the Cloud's qNet blocking signal. He could use the greater qNet again.

Admiral Cole?

Agent Romurik – I'm surprised to hear from you so soon.

Admiral, there is a sizable Cloud element vectored out-system from S'vreth, purpose and destination unknown. As of now they appear to be heading for the vicinity of the Colesworth Refinery. As for my mission goal, I had secured the Resolute Choice, *but lost it to a sophisticated enemy attack. Measures are in place to fulfil the secondary objective. A full report is attached.*

I see. Thank you for the report, agent.

Romurik then pinged the *Betsy's Pride.*

Captain Brynn? This is Agent Romurik.

Agent? I honestly thought you were gone for good.

I wouldn't rule that out yet – but for now I need a favour.

438

One very hot rescue, please.

The large chunk of debris tumbled slowly on pretty much every axis, and Brynn sighed. They'd have to spend a while manipulating it with *Betsy's* external drive fields to a relative standstill in order to bring it on board. Luckily it would just fit in the rear hangar bay.

"Romurik, you couldn't have tidied this up a little?"

"Sorry, Captain, I had more pressing matters to contend with." Romurik emerged from behind what was left of the command bridge of the *Kanstral*, and gave a mocking wave. He had been nudging the bridge away from the Cloud to a safe distance using his own propulsion systems.

"He's some piece of work," observed Andersten drily.

"Isn't he just?" replied Brynn. He knew dangerous personalities when he saw one, and he was staring at one right now. One with a huge amount of power at its disposal.

"How are your hosts faring?" he asked Romurik.

"Not so well, I'm afraid. I had to draw on most of the modules power to alter its course and gain enough velocity to get out here. Sadly for them that meant losing gravity and dropping to minimal life support. I suspect they could do with a warm shower right about now."

Andersten turned away slightly to hide a grin. No gravity and that continual tumble meant they'd no doubt spent the last fifteen minutes throwing up. The bridge would be a stinking mess, not to mention the Baidian themselves.

"Get them on board and under quarantine in the aft bay, and then my quarters for a debrief, agent," said

439

Brynn.

"Yes, Captain."

***

The large detachment from the Cloud coalesced around the dormant hulk of the *Kanstral*, just as it sprang back into life. Drive and power units had been replaced, shields and weaponry were back on line – despite the lack of its primary command module.

The group formed itself into a spherical formation – then began moving in the direction the *Resolute Choice* had taken, analysing space and subspace as it went. It located the exact point where the *Resolute Choice* had initiated a g-drive field and extrapolated the energy signature to determine the direction and expected travel volume and range.

Then the entire group vanished in a single synchronized burst of white light.

Chapter Thirty

The *Resolute Choice* drifted gracefully into the large docking bay of the INHS *Regatta*. Lights from the huge hexagonal hive bay revealed a number of scorched hull panels where excess energy had leaked through their shields from the onslaught of fire from the Cloud forces, but no damage of note.

Captain Seems was still fuming over the order to abandon the *Delaror* and the combat zone. In what was an unorthodox move, he had demanded an audience with INCC's local commanding officer on board the *Regatta*. Despite it being his right as a Captain of His Majesty's Imperial Navy to request an accounting for being given orders contrary to the Naval Mandates, there was a fine line between asking for an account, and questioning orders.

"Get the shields turned over as soon as possible, and restock ordnance," he told Rands. "I want to be combat ready in two hours."

"Yes, Captain. No problem."

He left the bridge and his remaining crew of eleven behind to prep, and made for the ramp down to the bay floor.

***

The fragment group from the Cloud had tracked their quarry across several stop-starts – an evasive pattern obviously intended to throw off pursuit. Some of the disruptions in the local gravity field were extremely weak. The ship it was following had left as little imprint as it could in the fabric of space-time it so clearly manipulated. This data was extremely valuable. None of the entities the Mind had encountered so far had ever achieved such a technology. It was even beyond the linear displacement technologies available to the Mind – although it rarely had need for such given the more efficient and further reaching Breach generator. However, it warranted further analysis and investigation. The Mind also detected a trail of miniscule distortions in subspace at the quantum level, wherever the vessel had altered course.

Given the Mind's extensive wealth of knowledge, accumulated from aeons worth of research by other races, and alongside that given to it by its creators, this could only mean one thing.

Observers were here.

The group of vessels exerted a pulse of energy across subspace at every encounter, forcing these punctures to evaporate into background radiation, effectively closing them off from those who were using them to study the volume.

Clearly, the evidence being gathered on this latest technological presence warranted an adjustment to its normal strategy for resource and knowledge acquisition. The Mind was no longer pitted against just another technologically advanced species. It was facing a race which had knowledge of the Forebears.

The Source clammered at the back of the Mind's awareness – tens of thousands of light-years away. Its insidious thoughts, pleas and tantrums were an irritating, yet essential distraction. It demanded to follow the leads on the Forebears – perhaps they had returned at long last. This was not the first time the Source had made such a claim. Even with this latest information to hand, the Mind calculated the likelihood as almost zero – but logic did indicate a further analysis could be of value.

However, at this moment it was not to be side-tracked from its ultimate goal. It was too close now, and the Mind had been engaged on its mission for a very, very long time.

Nothing would *ever* be allowed to prevent it from accomplishing its objective.

***

"I am not questioning the orders or the authority behind Imperial Naval Command and Control, Commodore. Nor am I questioning the orders of the Admiral of the Fleet." Seems was almost vibrating – he was that angry. He was doing his utmost to rein it in and speak in a civil manner to his superior.

"However I *strongly* feel that our presence in the conflict situation, and the encounter with a vessel thought lost to the enemy warrants a justification for the order to abandon an asset in the field, and to forego standing naval mandate IN429-S, to supply aid and defence to *any* vessel in distress or attack from clear hostiles."

Commodore Lansden's face was blood red. Having a subordinate officer railing at him in such a righteous manner was not an item on his "tolerate" list.

443

It didn't help that Seems was right. Lansden was just as mystified at the order. He could understand the very strong desire INCC would have to avoid pulling the tail of the beast they seemed to have encountered in S'vreth – but it was against all naval protocol to abandon an asset in the field, let alone a vessel in distress.

The blood drained slowly from his face as he strove to recover some of his sense of self.

"*Captain* Seems," he said – voice thick with suppressed anger. "As you are an as yet *untitled* officer of good standing within His Imperial Majesty's Navy, I will do you the honour of *not* citing this outburst on your record. As it may be, I somewhat share your sentiments. However do not, *ever*, address a superior officer 'in heat' again. Is that clear?"

Seems' face set, as he fought to control his mouth. "*Sir.*"

"*Good*. I will make enquiries. You may return to your ship, Captain."

"Commodore, if I may wait in your green room – the *Resolute* will be an hour yet before she is ready."

Lansden raised an eyebrow. "You won't oversee her?"

"My XO has it in hand, Commodore."

"Very well. Dismissed."

Seems clicked his heels and left for the Commodore's Office waiting area.

Lansden fired off a few messages over the naval network to some trusted contacts. If there *was* anything to know, he'd find out shortly.

He was just returning to the matters he had been attending to beforehand when alarms went off across the entire station.

"This can't be right," said Rands. "You're *sure* the Seeder was working?"

"I deployed three hundred and seventy-four Observers, XO. The logs clearly show the energy usage and the resulting data flow coming back into the Observatory. Then it just stops." Vanders highlighted the entries in the logs floating in the air between them. "Each drop we made suddenly ceases channeling, one after the other. In more or less the same order we seeded them. It doesn't make sense."

Rands drummed his fingers on the console. They had gone back to the manual terminal for the ships Observatory when Vander's had spotted the absence of their entire Observer breadcrumb trail since leaving S'vreth. The Seeder created Observers around the ship, each being a puncture in space-time, with a unique quantum signature that tied directly in to the ship's network – allowing it to see through each Observer. In essence, each was a micro-wormhole too small to affect ordinary matter, but could allow radiation to traverse through it.

"Ok, re-run the Observatory diags once more, just so we can say we've been thorough. You know what the tech support guys are like. Send the logs and the output to them and keep me posted."

"Aye, sir."

Rands moved away puzzled… this was odd. He had never heard of an Observer failure until this situation in S'vreth had come about. *But how could they be linked out here?* He intended to report it just in case.

Then everything went mad.

445

The fragment group from the Cloud emerged near where the *Resolute Choice* had last dropped out of g-drive, two hundred thousand kilometres away from *INHS Regatta*. Their sudden presence set off every alarm there could be. None of the ships were broadcasting ID's, and none of them matched anything on the Imperial Vessel Registration Database, barring one. The *INSS Delaror*.

The profusion of Automated Defence Platforms scattered around the *Regatta's* protectorate sprang into life, automatically targeting the inbound vessels and awaiting orders.

The Cloud began to fire without hesitation, all of its forward-facing vessels targeting the ADP's. Standard protocols allowed the ADP's to return fire if fired upon within a protectorate, and so the conflict began.

INHS Regatta instantly broadcast a Combat-One signal across INCC, issuing a no-go zone for a full light-year around its position.

Commodore Lansden, said Fleet Admiral Benthar across the qNet, *I see the situation at hand.*

Fleet Admiral, I am honoured, replied Lansden formally. *Given the highly sensitive nature of our situation I would ask for a formal order before issuing our tactical response to this attack.*

Of course, Commodore. You are authorised to use all forces at your disposal to defend the Regatta *and those within its protectorate. I am preparing a response with IND as we speak.*

Thank you Admiral.

Raul disconnected from the *Regatta's* tactical network and then entered the Emperor's simulation again. He was beginning to seriously consider staying there and running operations from within it. The Emperor was already attending.

"Your Majesty, I'm afraid it looks like the standoff is over."

"It would seem so… do you think this will become a full scale engagement?"

Raul considered for a moment. "No, this is a small force, relatively speaking… three hundred or so ships. It will be challenge enough for the *Regatta* alone. I have instructed IND to mount a response fleet from our standby reserve."

The Emperor nodded. "See to your duties Fleet. I will remain here and monitor. You may concentrate fully on the defence unless you require anything of my office."

The Emperor had just granted Raul carte blanche to do as he saw fit. "Thank you, Your Majesty."

"Good luck, for us all."

Raul saluted and faded from the sim. On this one occasion, the Emperor was prepared to forgive the impropriety.

INHS Regatta brought every single one of its Cloud facing weapons online and opened fire. Hundreds of high energy beams leapt out – ranging across the spectrum – visible and invisible. Even at such considerable distance, they all found their targets easily in the Cloud group, and shields began to flare off the incoming energy.

Being much larger than any vessel, the hive station had far greater power to draw upon, and a far larger energy sink to absorb the heat generated by its weapons fire. Its arsenal was also far more powerful than typical space-faring vessels could accommodate, and could be used repeatedly and far more often than conventional shipboard equivalents.

The first Cloud vessel detonated within seconds of the *Regatta's* defensive response.

Distant explosions signalled ADP's were now being overcome by enemy fire.

Squadrons of one and two man fighters streamed out of the *Regatta*, arcing around the deadly field of energy between the station and the advancing group of hostiles – their mass thrusters leaving blazing trails behind them.

Vessel after vessel exploded within the Cloud. Some of the ships didn't even seem to be shielded – taking horrendous hull damage until their systems could no longer house the controlling Mind – which simply relinquished the ship to its fate.

Captain Seems was now almost beside himself, having abandoned the Commodore's green room on hearing the alarms. He ran straight for the *Resolute Choice*, yelling questions and orders to Rands via the l-net.

"Are the shields back up?"

"We just finished servicing them, Ca-"

"How much ordnance on board?" Seems interrupted.

"Two ADP's, half the missile stock, no Hydras as yet."

"Prioritise Hydra's and missiles – forget the ADP's – *Regatta* has that covered. I'll be there in five."

"Yes, sir."

The heavy, two-directional fire between the *Regatta* and the Cloud formed a highly energised no-man's-land between them. Nothing could fly through that volume without extreme risk of being caught inside an intense beam of electro-magnetic radiation. Microwave, infra-red, ultra-violet, gamma and x-ray and all the wavelengths in between flicked back and forth, delivering violent bursts of high energy. The *Regatta's* shield was already starting to show visible signs of degradation, as it strove to shed the continuous load from several hundred assorted maser and laser beams. Fortunately it was only defending against a single-front attack, and it could shed energy to the much cooler 'dark-side' of its shield.

"How can we egress with all that going on?" asked Rands as the Captain came aboard.

"*Regatta* can hold fire along our vector; her shield will cover us as we circle around behind her then we can arc out as the squadrons did."

"Understood. Helm, lay a course accordingly. *INHS Regatta* Flight Control – *INSS Resolute Choice* requesting permission to leave dock."

"Permission granted, *INSS Resolute Choice*. Good luck!"

"Three other frigates are following our lead, Captain. *Death's Heart*, *Vibrant Maser* and the *Canny Lad*."

"Co-ordinate with their nav."

"Aye, sir."

"Let's show them some Imperial might! Disengage from the *Regatta*."

The *Resolute Choice* dropped its mooring fields and lifted away from the token docking surface on the wall of the bay. Two other destroyers were in dock – one out of service for major overhaul, the other frantically loading ordnance just as they had to allow it to join the fray. The attack had – in effect – caught them with their pants down, with everyone caught up in typical naval routine. But that wouldn't last for long.

Seems ran a scan over the docking register – there were eighty-five assorted IND cruisers or larger in various states of flight prep, with eight INT frigates about to launch. One INI vessel was registered but so far showed no status or classification, as was their wont.

Once everyone entered the combat zone, things would get a lot louder.

The *Resolute* slipped out from the bay and into the internal void protected by its pulsating shield, then began to skim over the surface of the station toward the lee-side of the incoming fire. They could see two other ships emerging from nearby bays to follow the same approach.

"How many targets?" Seems asked.

Rands ran a search against the incoming sensor data. "Three hundred and eighty-seven, as it stands."

"Find the most powerful shield-bearing craft emitting the most firepower, we'll head for those."

"Forty-seven, sir."

"Helm, lay a course, take this group, nearest first – avoid the *Regatta's* field of fire."

"Aye, sir."

Now all they could do was wait until they had manouvered into a targeting solution, and then they could start reigning death on the Cloud.

The Valkyr *INSV Obstinate SOB* was docked at INHS *Regatta*, the sole representative of INI at the station. Impatient, he wanted to get out into the combat – an unsurpassed chance to finally test himself outside of a sim.

However, his captain was waylaid in some meeting with the Commodore.

He re-ran his tactical solution for entering the arena of combat – just as good now as it had been twelve milliseconds ago.

"Come *on!*" he protested out loud, even though his captain couldn't hear.

The outer cordon of ADP's detonated in a series of staccato blasts as the Cloud punched through. The Cloud had taken heavy losses from these AI controlled satellites. So far the Mind had been unable to subvert or disable them – which it found highly intriguing. They had very limited internal systems – everything seemed to be independent and controlled remotely using qSpinners, making the whole construct impossible to sequestrate. As soon as the Mind cleared each satellites internal systems, the system would be taken over again for a millisecond - just enough time to coordinate another salvo against the Cloud. It was precisely the same tactic the Mind used when requisitioning vessels, or controlling its own assets. It had taken brute force to clear the field ahead and out to the station in the far distance.

The station lay like a glittering jewel in subspace, exerting a vast impression on the quantum fabric within. The Mind sensed a moderately sizeable intelligence at work there. Coupled with the valuable resources and data the station represented, it was a sensible choice to expend resources and effort in order to capture it. It

451

would also prove a valuable intelligence gathering exercise into the technological capabilities of this latest species encounter.

The aggressive response so far had been light. However with the capabilities available to this latest target, it presumed a more co-ordinated and effective response was being mounted – with typically glacial, biological slowness.

The Mind prepared a full electronic assault protocol for the eventuality and then returned to monitoring the progress of the attack. Twenty-five units lost, with a complete eradication of opposing automated defence units within effective firing range.

The Mind waited to see what would be next with some degree of anticipation.

The *Resolute Choice* and the *Canny Lad* were the first to clear *Regatta's* shield shadow and attain a firing solution on the Cloud. Both destroyers emitted full power maser beams at the same time, on the same target – its far distant shields leaping to a bright white instantly.

"Can we pinpoint the *Delaror?*" asked Captain Seems.

"I had a trace on her and can extrapolate, but the radiation spikes between us are making her hard to spot."

"Keep looking… let me know when you have a lock. I want to disable her if possible – Agent Romurik may still be onboard."

"Aye, sir."

"And I think we should just disable one of these bad boys. INI would grant us the deeds to their own HQ if

452

we could salvage one of them."

Seems checked the local gravitational field; they would be clear to drive out in a few seconds. The *Canny Lad* locked in on their designated drop out point and then they both surged forward as one.

Three seconds later they dropped their g-fields and the Cloud leapt into view before them. Their weapons were already aligned to their previously chosen targets and now unleashed at the enemy.

It was an orchestrated and well-practised attack strategy. Instantaneous data networks and the long-range scans made possible through Observers made the Imperial Navy a technological force to be reckoned with. Targets could be chosen for close proximity combat from a vast distance, and weapons proactively brought to bear precisely on the firing solutions they would need long before they were even in range. Combined with Intellects who patrolled those networks and controlled the base weapon functions when needed – high speed co-ordinated attacks could be put into play with inordinate ease.

They started receiving heavy incoming fire within seconds of their arrival.

"Helm – present broadside – enter rotisserie mode."

As they came about to show the length of the *Resolute* to the enemy, they presented a larger target but also brought more shields in to play in order to soak up the energy being thrown at them. The *Resolute Choice* began rolling on its principal axis, to allow a continual rotation of shields in and out of the line of fire. The technique allowed overloaded shields to enter the lee of the attack so they could discharge and cool. It also meant weapons were continually presenting and removing from the *Resolute's* firing solution, also allowing them to relax and cool. Success in long-term space combat relied on efficient energy management. Heat build-up could cripple a ship in minutes if not carefully controlled, even with modern day heat exchangers, dumps and sinks.

However, this tactic also reduced the number of weapons they could bring to bear on one salvo, and overall made the ship an even larger target for the enemy when compared to a full-frontal attack. Trade-offs that Seems was willing to make. He noted the *Canny Lad* adopting the same approach.

There was a blur ten thousand k's away, and the heavy, fist-shaped *Vibrant Maser* dropped out of g-drive.

"Welcome to the party, Captain O'Nath," Seems said cordially.

"Sorry we're late. I see you started without us," O'Nath quipped, feigning a hurt tone.

"Please, feel free."

The *Vibrant Maser* was technically a long range, full frontal attack frigate – a blockade breaker, designed for one thing only, to deliver a huge punch from afar. Its forward section was dominated by the round orifice of a maser array. Suddenly it glowed an odd silver light, and an ethereal beam leapt out and lit up a vessel in the Cloud. Its shields flared white and collapsed almost instantly, and the hull glowed a fierce white/yellow under the onslaught. Seems was sure he saw the superstructure of the ship bend as it melted and evaporated around the beam. The maser punched straight through, and narrowly missed a vessel on the opposite side of the Cloud formation.

"Shot, *Vibrant Maser!*"

"That's us for two minutes," said O'Nath. "But, we brought our own – don't mind us." A salvo of Hydra's came burning out of their aft section.

"Nicely done, Captain."

The Cloud vessels began targeting the Hydras. Clearly recognising the danger these missiles posed from their previous encounter.

The barrage continued. The Cloud ships were of various capabilities and strengths – their shields and firepower varied immensely – but they all had the same vastly superior energy sources to draw upon.

The *Canny Lad* began to suffer; its shields were struggling to cool under the sustained attack.

"I'm going to have to pull back," said Captain Ren. "Our port shields are about to fold."

"Go rest up," said Seems. "There will be plenty left I'm sure."

The *Canny Lad* began pulling away from the field – then g'd away from the conflict by several hundred thousand kilometres to allow its shields and heat sinks to cool.

Rands moved over to stand next to Seems, and spoke quietly. "Captain, it won't be long before we have to follow suit."

"Keep firing. I want a candidate to disable… anything mid-sized will do."

Another blast from the *Vibrant Maser* took out an enemy vessel in a single shot.

"Any sign of the *Delaror?*"

"It's very hard to tell – she's definitely not on our side of the Cloud."

"Ok."

Every time one of the vessels in the Cloud went down, the sphere shrank as the formation reordered itself to close the gap. *This formation has to be significant,* thought Seems.

The *Death's Heart* blurred into being.

"Well met, Captain Lelo."

"Captain Seems," she replied. "Looks like you need a hand."

The *Death's Heart* began firing on the same targets as the *Resolute*.

"If we can, we should rotate one of us out and keep two firing at close range – with the *Maser* providing support."

"Sounds good... can you hold until Ren comes back in?"

"We'll be back in one minute," Ren supplied cheerfully.

"Yes, just," Seems replied. "We need to concentrate fire on the same targets so they can't recover."

"Understood," Lelo acknowledged.

The third shot from the *Vibrant Maser* took out the shield of another vessel – but left it behind undamaged.

"My, he's a tough one," O'Nath observed.

"Target that one!" yelled Seems. "Drive and power if you can!"

The *Resolute Choice* concentrated its energy weapons on the destroyers drive systems at the rear, slicing through the hull and detonating the drive core. It began to drift, but continued firing back.

"We can't get at the power core without destroying the ship," said Captain Lelo. "We'll have to take out the

456

weapons one-by-one instead."

"Confirmed. Target their weapon mounts."

"Did those fighters make it in yet?"

"They're against the Clouds forward aspect, drawing fire. They aren't making much difference against this lumbering beast of a formation. They're being picked off like flies."

"INCC should recall them."

Seems gave a tight smile to Rands as he spoke. "They did, but the wing commanders challenged. They said it's the most fun they've had in years. INCC are still trying to figure out how to respond without issuing court-martials against the entire outfit."

"This is what happens when you offer humankind the chance for virtual immortality via backups... no respect for life. I'll retask a squadron of fighters to take out this one's weapons."

Seems kept a careful eye on their shields – they were edging close to their limits.

"*Resolute Choice*, *Canny Lad* here – ready to swap out?"

"On my mark, go."

The *Resolute* g'd out to a random location some two-hundred thousand k's away and let her shields bleed off the energy they had been absorbing.

From the tactical of their combat region they saw the *Canny Lad* drop in and start firing on the weapons of the disabled ship.

The *Vibrant Maser* let loose again, taking out yet another ship in one shot.

From afar, it was easier to see the larger situation in a more detached and tactical way – once it was less immediate.

457

The squadrons of fighters were taking heavy losses. Most were able to eject and make use of the emergency g-drive units to get back to the *Regatta* – though a fair number were vaporised mercilessly by the Cloud before they knew what hit them. Seems hoped they had managed to uplink themselves into the Totality in time.

A larger and larger number of vessels from the Cloud were redirecting their fire from the distant *Regatta* and onto the *Canny Lad* and *Death's Heart*, and now the *Vibrant Maser*.

"INCC – this is the *INSS Resolute Choice*. We're drawing fire as hoped."

"Confirmed *INSS Resolute Choice*. Deployment will commence shortly."

"Understood." Then Seems spoke with the impromptu mini-fleet he found himself leading. "Back up is on the way, and we're ready to swap in – who's next?"

Raul and the Emperor watched the rising conflict from the enclave simulation along with Senator Barao, who had returned from the most recent Pax Alliance Meeting at the Emperors behest to better understand the scale of what they were facing.

"Something puzzles me regarding the ease with which we are dispatching their forces," said the Emperor.

Raul nodded. "It's *too* easy, Your Majesty. The energy sources they are fitted with are capable of withstanding far more than we have thrown at them so far."

"Your thoughts?"

Raul was hesitant. He could be wrong of course, but

a lifetime of Naval service had taught him it was better to be wrong publically and before anything came of it than to be right privately and see a disaster result.

"It could be a test of strength, Your Majesty" he said. "To size up our response and technological capabilities."

The Emperor nodded thoughtfully. "An expensive test," he observed. "But given the size of their own force, small change."

"You believe they would sacrifice a fleet of this size, *just* to gauge our defences?" asked Senator Barao. She couldn't keep her astonishment from her voice.

Raul looked directly into her eyes. "Yes, Senator, I do."

The Emperor leant forward. "Then perhaps this may yet be another quick win. Is IND ready?"

"En route, Your Majesty." Raul zoomed out the display above the table far enough to show the inbound g-drive wakes of the reinforcements – six hundred vessels in total. Raul wanted to assure victory but couldn't depopulate the entire Empire of Naval vessels.

"After the results from the initial defence mounted by the *Vibrant Maser*, I instructed as many Behemoth class as could be mustered at short notice."

The Emperor nodded approvingly.

The display zoomed back in – leaving a group of contacts representing the IND forces showing their ingress point into the conflict zone.

"*Regatta* is deploying," noted Raul.

Taking advantage of the small drop in fire, forty vessels took to space and began heading toward the Cloud.

Raul looked to the fighters who were still harrying

the enemy to little effect, and decided they'd had their fill. He was aware of their challenge to INCC; he had held off on a formal response deliberately, having once been a Wing Commander himself.

"INCC and *Regatta* Squadrons nine through twenty one, this is Imperial Fleet Admiral Raul Benthar. I order all fighter squadrons to make an immediate strategic withdrawal from the conflict and return to the *Regatta*."

There was a moment's pause.

"Understood Fleet Admiral... Squadron Nine leaving the field."

They watched the tactical as each of the squadrons reluctantly withdrew and headed back to base. He chose to ignore the full salvo release of all of their remaining missile stock in parting shots at their nearest targets.

Once they were clear, the second wave of destroyers and frigates from the *Regatta* opened fire with their energy weapons.

They watched the resulting exchange, and Raul began to get concerned.

Their overall defense response had now increased dramatically, but the take down rate was still the same.

He watched for a full minute, and then saw the take down rate begin to drop.

He glanced meaningfully at the Emperor, who returned the look. They had committed more firepower, yet their effectiveness had lessened.

"Here they come," said Rands.

"About time," said Seems critically.

The new arrivals dropped out of g-drive to form a ring before the Cloud, centred around the *Regatta's* field of fire, effectively presenting a huge defensive disk-like shield of pure firepower. Their co-ordinated attacks began hammering at the enemy shields.

Even as they continued their own offensive, the small guerrilla fleet which Seems led watched the main one in action – it was a sight to behold.

It took a few minutes for things to sink in before Seems realised something was wrong.

"XO – how many enemy vessels have we taken down since the backup arrived?"

Rands checked. "Two, sir."

Seems bit his lip. "Full fire at one target, pick the nearest – all presenting weapons."

"Aye, sir."

Nine full power maser and twelve laser beams painted the shield of the nearest destroyer in a violent mosaic of energy flares.

"Again."

As soon as they recharged, they all fired in unison once more.

"Again."

"Sir, we could burn them out."

"Once more, now."

They fired again.

Seems swore aloud. "Their shields barely altered between salvos."

"Sir?"

"Their shields are soaking up everything we throw at them. Our takedown rate has dropped dramatically since our backup arrived – it should have gone up!"

"Captain Seems," said Captain O'Nath from the *Vibrant Maser*. "Can you just watch our target a moment?" A contact profile slipped into the tactical, and the *Vibrant Maser* hit it with its main weapon.

"Barely a dent... they've got something up their sleeve. I have a profile of a similar ship going down from one shot."

"What the...?"

Then a huge blast of energy hit the *Resolute Choice* on its broad side. Two shields collapsed and alarms started wailing.

"One eighty roll! G out, now!"

Another blast hit them, wiping out all the weapon mounts on the unshielded section of the hull.

"Hull breach! Main ordnance chamber! Breach shields in place."

"*Helm?*"

"Two seconds!"

They leapt away from the attack by forty thousand kilometres.

"O'Nath?"

There was no reply.

Rands brought the tactical to bear on the volume they had just left – it showed the wreckage of the *Vibrant Maser* tumbling away from a huge ball of expanding flames. She was gone, with all hands.

Hundreds of blazing energy beams now leapt out from the cloud.

"We're hit!" shouted Captain Ren. "Pulling ou-"

The *Canny Lad* contact greyed out on the tactical.

The *Resolute's* bridge crew stared in disbelief.

"INCC!" Seems called out, his voice far too loud, betraying his astonishment. "*Vibrant Maser* and the *Canny Lad* lost to heavy enemy fire! Enemy shields and weapons now *far* superior than the initial engagement."

Another energy blast slammed their aft section, the Cloud still firing at them from afar. The beam took out their last fully charged shield in one shot and damaged the sub-c drive systems.

"Taking heavy damage, we're returning to the *Regatta*."

"Confirmed, *INSS Resolute Choice*."

They g'd back to the lee-side of the *Regatta* to take stock of their damage. The crew was silent. Two Naval ships had been taken out in mere seconds. They were lucky to be alive.

"*Death's Heart?* Are you still there?"

"Not for long!"

The *Death's Heart* blurred into space fifty kilometres away. Her aft hull was glowing and several fires burned fiercely into the vacuum for a few seconds before winking out as her breach shielding snapped into place.

No one spoke for a few moments.

"Sir, tactical shows there were at least ten inbound beams per hit. Each ten gigawatts."

"INCC – request orders." *That was incredible*, Seems thought privately – shocked by the sudden escalation in the enemy response. The rapid U-turn from inflicting heavy damage on the enemy, to suddenly finding an unassailable wall and have it come crashing down on top of you.

And the loss of two ships.

They wouldn't be the last.

Chapter Thirty-one

The defensive ring of Navy vessels around the *INHS Regatta* dissolved under this sudden onslaught from the Cloud. Almost a dozen were destroyed in the first salvo alone.

The rest scattered randomly, returning fire as best they could – leaving the *Regatta* behind them open to direct attack.

The Cloud ignored the strays and turned its attention to the distant station, whose shields instantly began to flare off the huge increase of incoming energy.

Raul watched this as an icy chill ran down his spine. The IND fleet were still ten minutes away. With this new offensive the *Regatta* could well be lost before they arrived at the conflict.

The Emperor looked on grimly.

Senator Barao was quiet – a look of deep concern on her face.

Tell this to your Senate, thought Raul bitterly. *We are facing a war we cannot win.*

"Fleet Admiral, can we relocate the *Regatta* to a safe location?" asked the Emperor quietly.

"Not in time, Your Majesty. If she g'd out she would leave a wake even a blind man would see. They would follow – they clearly tailed the *Resolute Choice* and that was using standard evasion tactics for leaving a hostile area. Wherever she went would become another war zone. It's best contained here for now."

Senator Barao raised her eyebrows in surprise.

"Contained?"

Raul ignored her and looked to the tactical again. The entire forward facing hemisphere of the Cloud was firing directly at the same location on the *Regatta* – intent on taking out one shield point to allow them to break through. The *Regatta* couldn't last long against that... minutes at best.

The attack was relentless. When one ship ceased firing to let its weapons cool, another took its place. The Cloud was keeping a perfect record of constant engagement.

Alarms rang out all across the *Regatta*, and people scrambled for physical duty stations. The station began to turn – very slowly – to rotate her shields away from the onslaught. The *Regatta's* delta-p compensators could only work effectively to a certain scale given the mass involved, beyond which care had to be taken.

The Cloud focused on the same point on the *Regatta's* shields even as it began turning, determined to punch through the weakening area.

Now that they were distant targets again and away from the conflict zone, the remaining defence fleet began firing back at the Cloud – though to little effect.

The initially promising conflict in favour of the Navy had reversed in favour of the Cloud – this was now a war of attrition, with the enemy moving ever closer to its goal.

The Valkyr *Obstinate SOB* was coasting at the very centre of the Cloud. He had slipped inside the perimeter at his captain's behest, to take as many readings as

465

possible in order to try and analyse the function, makeup and behaviour of the Cloud itself.

The *SOB* was eager to take advantage of their unequalled tactical opportunity to fire upon the Cloud from within, but his captain – Jan Harlow – refused to reveal their position. At this point data was far more valuable than trying to take out the enemy.

"Anything? At *all?*" Jan asked, her irritation plain to hear.

"Not yet. I can't jack into the network they are running, although it's clearly there."

A floating holo in the cabin showed the Cloud around them – it's geodesic arrangement even more abundantly clear as the *SOB* filled in the network topology between the ships. Each one connected directly to *every* other, forming a complex sphere of data flows – much like a child's geometry lessons might use. The *SOB* was amazed at the inefficiency. The network medium itself appeared to be the very fabric of subspace itself, which they were directly manipulating to such a subtle degree it was incredibly hard to detect. The *SOB* couldn't cross reference the data with the Totality due to their tenuous tactical position and the fact that being inside the formation meant the qNet was blocked by the Cloud. He suspected that somehow their manipulation of subspace interfered with the qNet medium itself, and guaranteed an instantaneous network *without* relying on qSpinner technology. There was also an apparent flow of data out of the Cloud itself, but directionless and with no apparent receiver.

"I've located the *Delaror* though," said the *SOB* cheerfully.

"Show me."

The viewpoint in one display spun about and zoomed in on the long shard of an Imperial Naval Destroyer, currently pouring every erg of energy it could muster into the *Regatta's* shields. Her forward bridge was a mass of blackened twisted metal.

"Try pinging her by microwave," said Jan hopefully.

"Pinged."

The short encoded microwave burst played across the flank sensor array of the Delaror, and went unheeded by the Mind as it controlled the vessel with a miniscule aspect of its awareness. However, it did trigger a small program in the communications processor – lying in wait for any incoming transmission. It decoded the cipher, recognised the Imperial Naval code, and the small fragment of Romurik's personality which he had left behind said, "A-ha!"'

Within a second, an overload order despatched to the power core, and a visual image of Romurik presenting a single-digit gesture floated into the periphery of the Mind just before the Delaror detonated in a flash of raw energy and debris.

"Um, did I do that?" asked the *SOB* warily.

"I rather doubt it," said Jan, watching the ruins of the Delaror tumble away from the Cloud. "Anything on this network?"

The *SOB* could *see* the data flows – barely – but couldn't interact with them. All of its sensors and subspace equipment were centred around the manipulation and monitoring of subspace at a far larger scale in order to travel faster than light. *Perhaps I could oscillate the FTL carrier wave at a low level*, he wondered.

467

He made a few adjustments to the FTL drive and fired it up. The sudden change in the *SOB's* subspace energy signature made it stand out to the Mind as brightly as a sun.

The attack came so swiftly the *SOB* stood no chance of evading it, let alone raising a defence. He saw the change in subspace and was in awe at the sheer size of the entity which came down on him. All he managed to do was drop his physical backup archive, containing all of the data they had collated so far, into space in the pico-second it had before the Mind wiped the *SOB* from existence.

"What just happened?" asked Jan. Her private link to the *SOB* had just gone offline.

"*SOB?*"

There was no answer. The displays vanished around her, and all the internal systems cut out at once – lights, displays, life support – all gone.

"*SOB?*" she demanded. But there was nothing there – no ship l-net, no qNet, no answer.

The delta-p compensators cut out, taking the artificial gravity field with it. Jan founder herself drifting free of the deck in zero-g.

Then she heard the hum of the *SOB's* g-drive spinning up.

"Oh no," she whispered.

The *SOB* accelerated at 120G's, smashing her body into a molecular pulp against the rear bulkhead, killing her instantly.

"What was that?" demanded Seems. In the shared bridge display, showing a scan of the local gravitational field and mass distribution, a g-drive spike erupted from the centre of the Cloud. Then the unthinkable happened. A small contact appeared before the *Regatta*, dropping out of g-drive one thousand k's from the surface of the station, and its momentum carried it straight into the shields.

The explosion was immense, wiping out every shield generator within a kilometre of the impact, and the resulting fireball of energy blazed deep into the stations super-structure.

A gaping hole, two kilometres wide, appeared in the station, exposing the now white-hot glowing decks of the interior. Secondary surface explosions blasted panels, debris, equipment and personnel out into space with uncaring swiftness.

The blast wave carried deep into the interior – boring a tunnel of devastation eight hundred metres deep and exposing huge areas to the horrific release of energy, swiftly followed by the hard vacuum of space. A giant plume of atmospheric gases, smoke and fire leapt out of the station surface as if it had just unleashed a volcano – blazing into nothing within seconds.

The Cloud didn't even interrupt its attack – it continued to fire, now targeting the breach in the station. Unprotected by the hull armour or shields, the multiple beams of energy tore into the interior – turning everything they came into contact with into explosive vapour which screamed out in any direction it could escape by. Deck compartments exploded, the infrastructure melted around people – entombing them briefly in liquid metal before they were scorched into ash. Others were roasted alive by the compressed super-hot air raging all around them. Energy conduits overloaded and shattered, delivering even more energy into the conflagration. The *Regatta* desperately brought up internal shields around the blast area, sealing hundreds outside, and condemning them to a horrible death in the mad rush to save the greater population of the station. It was a harsh 'needs must' decision, but in the split-seconds available it became a mere game of numbers. It finally managed to secure the breach, and only just prevented the devastation from reaching the power core at the centre of the station.

All inter-ship chatter stopped at once. Thousands of people had just died. The unthinkable had happened – a station of the Imperial Navy had fallen to a hostile attack, the first in millennia.

Seconds passed, each seemingly like a minute. Then the *Regatta* sent out a distress signal.

"INCC, this is *INHS Regatta*. We have been breached… repeat we have been breached. We are under direct attack by the Cloud presence in this system. We have lost an entire quadrant of shields and are open to direct surface attack. I have no idea how many just died…"

"*Regatta*, this is Fleet Admiral Benthar. Provide a damage report, establish yourselves and make ready for another attack. Begin evacuating from the lee-side of the station away from the Cloud.

"Fleet Admiral Benthar to all ships defending – secure the station if possible, aid and assist the evacuation. IND are arriving in the next forty seconds, they will take over defence. I want everything presently in system clear of the Cloud and making way back to the *Regatta* – is that clear?"

No one replied – everyone was still reeling in shock.

"*Understood?*" demanded the Fleet Admiral.

"Yes, sir," replied Seems, voice shaking.

Orders began flying over the IN network back and forth between the defenders and the *Regatta* as the withdrawal and evacuation got underway.

Seems turned to Rands. "What *was* that thing?" he demanded. "Get on it, see what you can find out. And look for any more g-drive spikes coming from that cloud."

"Aye, sir."

"Helm, take us into the nearest lee-side bay, best speed – ignore all docking protocols – get us in safe and sound, but fast."

"Aye, sir!"

Minutes dragged by as everyone came to terms with the realisation that the *Regatta* was as good as lost. The Cloud pressed ever closer to the station, pouring their destructive energy into the breach without pause.

Finally – six hundred Imperial Naval Defence vessels dropped into the system, twenty thousand kilometres from the *Regatta*. Within seconds the entire fleet - already oriented toward the Cloud - opened fire. Space lit up with thousands of beams of energy, projectiles started emerging from the fleet – mass-driver cannon pumping round after round at the Cloud, and swarms of missiles leapt away and toward the enemy ships. Hundreds of Hydra's fragmented and delivered their payloads of smaller, faster missiles – delivering kiloton after kiloton of nuclear energy against their shields.

Hidden amongst the chaotic glow which now filled the void, two hundred large missiles left the hangar bays of the fleet ships – each one almost a small spacecraft in its own right. They were directly under the control of Intellects. They flew outward on a tangent – away from the fleet and the Cloud – before priming their ordnance, winding up their g-drives and disappearing.

One and a half seconds later, they emerged before assigned targets in the Cloud. Their pilots uploaded into the qNet and left the missiles to fulfil their now unstoppable function.

All two hundred detonated at the same time in a single, co-ordinated attack – each missile bringing ten kilos of Hydrogen and ten kilos of intermixed anti-hydrogen together at once. Suspended apart by strong fields in what was known as a rigid-liquid – commonly used for cargo storage during transport – the two substances were inherently prevented from moving against each other.

These fields now collapsed and created a single perfectly intermixed fluid – bringing the atoms within directly into contact with their anti-matter equivalents. The result was the total and complete annihilation of twenty kilograms of hydrogen/anti-hydrogen, multiplied by two hundred.

Later, witnesses describing the conflict said that for a few moments, it was like a star had been born. They said the sun-facing side of the *Regatta* went dark in the glare. People were blinded by the explosion, requiring optical replacements to restore their sight much later after the event. Alarms went off on every single naval vessel in the conflict zone as a bubble of electro-magnetic radiation and photons blazed out from the Cloud at the speed of light.

Never before had anyone in the Empire witnessed such an awesome release of energy as a weapon – even at the height of the Meelereen War which had resulted in anti-matter being outlawed within the Empire. The equivalent of eight-six thousand megatons of explosive had been unleashed in an instant.

Everyone waited for the expanding cloud of high-energy particles to clear in stunned silence, expecting to see nothing left of the Cloud.

But before the energy storm became even semi-opaque, beams of fire emerged from within, targeting the IND fleet. As the Cloud surged out from the micro-nebula of radioactive energy left by the anti-matter missiles, it was clear it had lost over half its contingent. Yet the spherical arrangement was reforming, now at a quarter of the volume it had been before.

There was no cheer from the defenders at the reduction in numbers. The fact that anything at *all* could have survived such an attack killed any jubilation stone dead.

The IND fleet returned fire as the Cloud picked up speed – travelling much faster than it had before, and still on a direct course for the *Regatta*.

"Fleet Admiral Benthar, this is Admiral Weston of the IND Fleet. We cannot launch another AM salvo at the Cloud – it was already far too close for comfort for that attack – now the Cloud is way too close to the *Regatta* to repeat the offensive."

"Understood Admiral Weston. Continue the engagement as you see fit."

"Thank you, Fleet Admiral."

Back in the Emperor's War Office, Raul turned to the Emperor, who in turn looked back at him – a look of grave concern on his face.

"Options, Fleet Admiral?"

Raul looked grim.

"Save as many as possible from the *Regatta* and then issue a self-destruct order."

"And?"

"Abandon the system."

The Emperor's brow furrowed. "The Empire has never lost ground to an aggressor throughout its history."

"Your Majesty..." Raul clicked his heels together. "Respectfully, all we can do is evacuate the *Regatta*, then destroy her as the Cloud approaches. Deploying the remaining AM warheads on the IND fleet against them will ultimately be a waste of precious weapon stock. We will still have lost the system."

"But it will not remain occupied," stated the Emperor.

Raul looked at him, sensing his determination. He hoped his belief in the Emperor's convictions held true, and that he wasn't seeking merely to avoid being the first in recorded history to lose a part of the Empire – however small it may be. He knew the Emperor was offering him the opportunity to prevail as Fleet Admiral on this decision rather than be directly ordered to commit.

"Your Majesty, I will order a full retaliation once we have the *Regatta* evacuated."

The Emperor nodded, accepting Raul's intentions.

Raul hoped this wasn't just for the benefit of the Senator. Right now he didn't give one iota for what the Senate or the Pax Trade Alliance thought about the might and determination of the Imperial Navy.

The IND fleet closed in on the remaining Cloud as it powered toward the *Regatta*. The void between them grew increasingly brighter as the distance shrank to nothing – concentrating the exchange of fire further still – and then the fleet surrounded the entire sphere formation. This lessened the combined firepower the sphere could bring to bear on the *Regatta,* as it now had to split its efforts between the two hundred targets all around it.

The losses were still high – five IND ships were disabled or destroyed for every one in the Cloud.

The Mind was intrigued. The deployment of anti-matter ordnance was a surprising and unforeseen tactic, having not observed this capability in the few encounters so far.

It also noted that the constructs used in the deployment were themselves under direct control by intelligences such as itself. Via subspace, it had watched their tenuous presences escaping into subspace punctures via the qNet - another Forebear technology which only served to further agitate the Source and its desperate clamour for attention.

Escaping where? This became yet another item on the Mind's list of many related issues for investigation, should the opportunity arise. The constructs conveying the anti-matter warranted more immediate further analysis. It had discounted them as 'dumb objects'; typical missiles. A minor error of judgement.

One that would not be repeated again.

The IND fleet harried the Cloud – making high speed passes and hit and fade attacks via g-drive runs. The Cloud maintained its vector to the *Regatta*, and held formation – closing whenever a vessel was lost, in order to maintain its perfectly spherical form.

The *Resolute Choice* was the first ship to ferry evacuees from the station – g-driving out to *INHS Faraday* in the neighbouring system. The turnaround time was painfully slow. It took far longer to load and unload the few hundred personnel they could carry, than it did to transit the four light-years between the two stations.

By the time they returned to the *Regatta,* fifteen minutes had elapsed since they had left, and the Cloud was almost directly on the station.

As they swung around behind Regatta to dock for another wave of evacuees, the Mind struck out at the IND fleet around the Cloud.

One hundred and fifty three of the nearest vessels suddenly dropped off the INCC tactical grid, no longer responding to hails. They immediately turned about and headed into the Cloud, which then expanded to accommodate the new arrivals. Within seconds they began firing on their former comrades.

"Fleet Admiral Benthar to IND fleet – pull back!"

But it was too late. Another sixty-eight vessels – already on harrying attack vectors past the Cloud – succumbed to the Mind's undetectable influence. The war of attrition was decided in seconds. The IND fleet was now vastly outnumbered, and by their own ships.

The Cloud had won.

Chapter Thirty-two

The Drassi had once been a proud race of warriors. They were humanoid, with tough leathery brown skin and sharp carnivore teeth, a species seemingly evolved for combat. In times far past they had ruled an empire spanning five star systems, having conquered two civilisations and embraced a third after they had "Come of Age" as Imperial philosophers often put it. As the Canthe had done, warrior races often underwent a drastic expansion and conquest phase, until one day the sharp reality of enforcing rule across interstellar distances hit home, and someone, somewhere in their order would ask the inevitable question: is there a better way?

The Drassi had turned to science, learning, development – with the old ways honoured only as tradition. Until the Draco came. Then *everything* changed.

The war had been hard and bitter. The losses unacceptable. The vastly superior technology, the speed of the Draco tactical responses and decision making. Their relentless, ruthless approach to warfare which seemed to know no bounds or mercy. All of these pushed the Drassi to the edge of extinction.

But still the Drassi fought on. They were prepared to die fighting for their right to live.

Then the planet destroyers came. Their homeworld was levelled in one fell swoop, turned into nothing more than a resource for the unstoppable, uncaring might of the Draco war machine.

The survivors scattered about the remaining Drassi systems capitulated that same day. The war was over.

Then their slavery began.

Nelsen watched the Drassi go about their business from high orbit and shook his head.

They were a species on the precipice of self-destruction – not through their own deliberate, or even accidental intent – but from the despondent apathy generated by their plight.

All around them were constant reminders of the mighty race that once was. Tall graceful skyscrapers had filled their cities, huge spaceports with vessels filling the pads and the maintenance bays – some of which even spanned between the skyscrapers, forming vast platforms kilometres above the ground.

Now the skyscrapers lay long shattered. The vessels rotted slowly in their bays, or listed on their pads – hulls cracked open by past explosions. Most showed signs of scavenging, for the precious resources which their fractured society could clearly no longer produce.

It was a culture already long collapsed.

They were still trying to find out why. Not one single powered craft moved across the surface, or in the air. The *Sneak* found no electronic activity anywhere on the planet. No communications, no networks of any kind existed, other than within the huge, hexagonal structure of the factory which straddled a large archipelago.

There were no artificial satellites present, although a number of sparse debris fields indicated a lot of orbital attacks had once taken place. The *Sneak* had reverse extrapolated the trajectories of some of the fields from their relative velocities and trajectories, collating a very rough picture of several large cuboid objects which may have once served as defence platforms, or space stations. Based on her findings, they had been destroyed some two thousand years ago.

"Why no advancement?" demanded Nelsen. "That period of time is more than enough for a culture to recover even *basic* knowledge of their past way of life, their technology... relearning how things work. Here there is nothing but farming and scavenging."

"Perhaps their spirit was broken?" suggested Andreya.

Nelsen shook his head. "An entire *race?* There's always one young hothead who bucks the trend and wants change. Two thousand years is plenty of time for a few kickstarter personalites to emerge, in any culture." He stared at the displays of several villages far down below.

"Any joy with the lingo, *Sneak?*"

"Very little, Captain. With no communications to tap into, the process is slow going. Pattern matching their vocalisations to frames of reference from up here is quite the challenge. I have lip-read consistent facsimiles for water, crops and what I believe may be a swear word, but nothing else conclusive as yet."

The *Sneak* brought up another display. Having orbited the planet several times she had produced an accurate globe, mapping out the entire surface with population centres and estimated headcounts. The Drassi were few and far between.

Nelsen rubbed his hand down his cheek. "Less than two million?"

"I'm afraid so. And so widely spread about the surface I doubt there is much in the way of genetic mixing taking place. Their race is on the decline."

"It makes no sense… why throw it all away?"

"I don't know, Captain. Can we afford the time to find out?"

Nelsen looked to Andreya, who shook her head.

"Ok, no more diversions. We've seen what happens if you do nothing. Let's go."

***

Raul ground his teeth in impotent rage. In one foul swoop they had just lost over a third of the remaining IND fleet around the *Regatta* without a single shot fired in self-defence – almost a half taking defensive losses into account. Three hundred and five IND ships remained, and he dare not bring them into proximity of the Cloud for fear of losing more to its damnable subversive influence. The Cloud now outnumbered their defensive presence, but far outclassed them in firepower and defensive capability.

He looked at the Emperor, whose face was set in stone.

"Admiral Weston, this is Fleet Admiral Benthar. Send half your remaining force back to the *Regatta* to secure personnel and immediately exit the system. The remainder to maintain a minimum distance of one thousand k's and harry the enemy from afar."

"Fleet Admiral! What of the captured IND vessels? Many good officers –"

"Will do their utmost to restore control of their

481

vessels," interrupted Raul in a voice which brooked no argument. "Your *sole* concern is now the safety of the personnel on the *Regatta*."

There was a tense pause. "Yes, Fleet Admiral."

The simultaneous attack on so many vessels had left their crews dumbfounded and in various states of shock and surprise. Each ship had lost its Intellect without warning, and they had been left powerless and stranded. None of their systems responded, and within seconds of the takeover all their systems had shutdown, including life support. However, being trained for such drastic loss of systems, their highly skilled crews were fully able to begin taking countermeasures.

Long unused manual protocols came back into effect. Emergency lighting from bio-luminescent panels illuminated their way, aiding the enhanced night-vision of the crews. Fortunately the ships l-nets were still functional, allowing internal ship-wide communication. This proved vital for transferring information and instructions to the crew in various sections of the ships as they attempted to regain control.

However, they were all cut off from the qNet, each other, and the rest of the fleet.

"What about Agent Lestalus?" queried Captain Shiro of the *INSS Ad Astra*.

"No response, Captain... it's as though she has left the missile."

Shiro cursed aloud. There had been no time to acquire the specs of these small, zero-man ships which served as the deployment craft for the AM warheads.

"Get a crew onto the missile ASAP. I want to know

how to drop that thing right into their teeth."

"Yes, sir!"

"I want full fire control restored or disabled as first priority – I will *not* have this ship firing on the Imperial Navy."

The Mind itself had investigated the AM warhead carriers quite thoroughly. They were insignificant other than their payload; the entities which had been present and in control of them had largely escaped during the takeover of the vessels carrying them. Several had been expunged by the process, and a partial capture had occurred – but the remaining fragment of Intellect was non-viable and scrambled beyond resurrection, providing no valuable data pattern. The entities controlling the vessels themselves had all been erased by the takeover process.

The electronic systems and relays, controllers and sensor grids of these vessels posed no challenge for the Mind – being a viable medium for propagating itself where needed. However – as expected – the biological components to these vessels were now proving to be problematic. Already numerous systems on most of the vessels were physically beyond its control. This was not an acceptable scenario. It had precious few retrieval units at its disposal in this system – but now was an appropriate time to utilise them. Shredders began emerging from the original Cloud stock, heading for the new acquisitions.

Meanwhile, the remaining potential resources were observing a distance beyond the immediate range of influence which the Mind maintained via its sphere formation. It considered the deployment of the secured anti-matter devices for approximately one billionth of a second, however the outcome would result in the loss of potential resources which may yet become attainable. Numerous serviceable units already littered space around the conflict area, ready for harvesting – both the defending forces and its own lost vessels. The remaining debris could be easily gathered with minimal time and effort, if done so within the next twenty minutes. Any longer and the expansion of the debris as it drifted through space would make retrieval needlessly time consuming and reduce the value of any effort spent.

It was time to conclude the encounter. It returned its attention to the *Regatta*.

Some of the captured IND vessels began firing on their former comrades, despite the best efforts of their crews to prevent it.

One half of the remaining fleet withdrew to the *Regatta* as per orders – being those vessels with the largest capacity to carry passengers. Most modern day naval vessels were ill-equipped to cater for large numbers of personnel on board. A typical frigate would have a crew of twenty; even Admiral Weston's flagship had only thirty-two physical crew members. All naval vessels were ran by an Intellect with biological oversight in the form of its captain, and thus did not typically need to provide life support to a large volume for crew or passengers alike.

However, troop transport, evacuation and rescue missions were commonplace enough for most vessels to be able to provide temporary accommodation for large numbers over short distances – typically by repurposing hangar bays, recreation areas, and so on. So it was that one hundred and fifty navy vessels gathered around the *Regatta* in order to evacuate the remaining twelve hundred personnel left on the heavily damaged station.

The remaining IND fleet chose to concentrate their fire on single designated targets – original members of the Cloud by preference. Firing on ships which had previously belonged to the Empire was naturally unpalatable – however this was more a strategic choice. The lost naval vessels were not equipped with the power cores that drove the original Cloud vessels, which meant they also had less firepower at their disposal – formidable though it may be.

Admiral Weston prayed to any entities listening that the crews of the captured Behemoths could keep them from firing back; otherwise, he would have to pick them off one by one.

The defending fleet were simply buying time at this point, directing the Cloud's fire away from the doomed *Regatta*. Admiral Weston ordered his defenders to begin skipping – the relatively new technique of rapidly entering and dropping out of g-drive, taking pre-calculated shots on target at each drop, computing a new target solution and then driving back out to another location. When co-ordinated across a large group, it was a highly effective tactic and dramatically reduced their target profile to the Cloud. Weston assigned seven groups from his remaining fleet and instructed each to pick a single target in the Cloud to attack. Each group then swept in – maintaining a hopeful safe distance – and deployed co-ordinated fire on their chosen target.

Before the Cloud had chance to return fire, they had assigned new g points and targets, and disappeared.

Imperial losses stopped almost immediately, and Cloud losses began to creep upward. It was a small but important turning point in the battle, but too late in the day to affect the outcome. However, it did highlight an important flaw in the enemy's capability. Whilst the spherical formation and their cohesive behaviour gave the Cloud immense firepower and a strong defensive aspect, the formation was so rigidly upheld it was inflexible. As the navy leapt about space before it – seemingly at random – the Cloud did not break or alter formation to address this new mode of attack.

From his vantage point hundreds of light years away, Raul nodded his approval at this stroke of tactical genius by Weston.

"Admiral Weston, attempt to establish communication with the captured naval vessels by laser-graph."

"Aye, sir. Your orders?"

"To all captured vessels – abandon ship and self-destruct."

***

The *Sneak Thief* sat in deep space, stationary relative to the system they were in, and under full stealth. She was running silent, and her chameleonic hull was once again as black as the void around her.

They had arrived at the co-ordinates Andreya had provided. It was a binary star system, with two uninhabitable planets orbiting their parent stars in a complex, high-speed gravitational ballet, deep within the distended photo-sphere generated by the two stars as they vied for each other's mass. Both planets were blasted almost as smooth as marble by the constant furnace around them.

This astronomical marvel was marred, however. The entire system was full of ships. Absolutely and completely full.

The *Sneak* had given up after counting eighty million contacts – it was fruitless to attempt any accurate count. As before around S'vreth, she simply judged the gravitational mass in system – accounting for the binary stars and two planets – then used the visible volume to judge a rough estimate. The number was preposterous. *I might as well count the molecules in my hull*, she thought.

Nelsen and Andreya stared in silence. Their astonishment at seeing the Cloud around S'vreth was absolutely nothing by comparison.

Everywhere you looked – every gap between visible stars – there were a thousand ships. It was as if someone or something were trying to make the entire star system a solid mass.

The star-light was dimmed by the Cloud, which reflected the light in a parody of the Cluster itself – the binaries taking the place of the galactic core, and the vessels aping the very stars. The sight was dazzling, beautiful… and terrifying.

There was a constant influx and outflow of ships all around the system; the vast number of contacts and constant movement meant finding the *Terrania* would be impossible. Even if they knew what they were looking for and could locate it, there seemed little chance they would be able to get near it.

Nelsen's mood was so dark he couldn't bring himself to speak. He believed this to be the central staging area for their fleets. On their way into the Dark Zone, the *Sneak* had observed and mapped numerous subspace disturbances matching their initial find, and now Nelsen believed he knew something of their purpose.

It was a fence. Or more accurately – a subspace prison.

Each of the disturbances alone could only affect the volume they were in to enough of a degree to prevent Observers, wormholes and FTL. However the pattern of the disturbances was a calculated genius beyond anything Nelsen or the *Sneak* had ever heard of.

Each disturbance touched upon another. Each was timed to such perfection, that the waves of energy coursing through subspace would meet with their neighbouring disturbances to match the output and never cancel it out. The result was an almost uniform standing wave of disturbed space-time throughout the entire sector – enough to block any high-energy use of subspace.

In effect – the Dark Zone was a prison for every race held within it.

And now we've found the jailer, Nelsen thought grimly.

"Captain, I estimate it would take one hundred and forty years to catalogue every ship – those that remain stationary, of course."

Nelsen didn't respond. Andreya reached out and placed a hand on his shoulder with a gentle squeeze.

"Well, if there's nothing better to do..."

The jest didn't work. He was lost in the Cloud, trying

to figure out a strategy, or find some glimmer of hope in all this. Or perhaps a miracle.

The obvious option now was to return – or *attempt* to return – to the Empire and report in. Given the ease with which they had penetrated the DZ without being intercepted – logically, leaving should be just as easy.

Nelsen wasn't convinced. He had a bad feeling about this, made all the more substantial by what he was seeing now. Returning was a potential problem he didn't want to face just yet.

Andreya could see they were stymied. There had been no other information in the Velari Concord of Surrr to identify the *Terrania*; no specific location, no description. It merely recorded an encounter with an alien artefact along with the peculiarity of its name being noted down. Only the name itself gave the observation any meaning over their countless other recorded encounters with barely documented and unnamed artefacts from many other species.

The name also appeared to be well-grounded in legend within the Imperial Public Records she had searched in the *Sneak's* personal archives, but they were so long forgotten there was the electronic equivalent of dust a foot thick over them. There were no originating credits to the citation, and the records were non-specific, detailing only a ship of ancient origin by the name *Terrania*. Origins, purpose, and specification unknown.

We could do with a nudge here, she silently suggested to her mysterious puppeteer. She half expected a response of some kind, but none came, and she frowned, mildly irked.

"What if..." mused Nelsen quietly, "these things

behave like scavengers, right? Even if they aren't. If the Velari came across the *Terrania* by accident and lived to tell the tale – it clearly wasn't one of these guys." He waved a hand at the vessels around them. "So if the *Terrania* is still here, chances are these guys have taken it over…"

Andreya watched him talk. "And…?" she asked as he trailed off.

"*Sneak*, can you penetrate the centre of this mess with a scan?"

"Not a chance, Captain. Not without Observers. The number of contacts would make even high-density scans far too noisy."

He pursed his lips thoughtfully. "We have to go in."

"Excuse me, Captain?" exclaimed the *Sneak*.

"If whatever we came for is still here, I think it will be at the centre of this, this… whatever it is… Mega-cloud. The only planetary masses of note in-system are way too erratic to establish decent bases on. If the *Terrania* was here when they arrived, they would have congregated around it after securing it. After all, with this large a number, and with an entire star system to hand… why move?"

"Sounds reasonable," said Andreya dubiously.

"Sounds insane!" The *Sneak* couldn't help herself. "All due respect, Captain, but please consider the risk here! They will be scanning every single *atom* that passes through the Cloud. They have more sensory input and computational potential than a *deity* could ever hope for. Inside that Cloud, they *are* a god. They have complete omnipotence!"

"That's a bit of a reach, *Sneak*."

"But valid, Captain! I could not evade detection within that gathering. The *minutest* gravitational disturbance would shriek out like an alarm."

Nelsen rubbed at his nose thoughtfully for a few moments.

"What if you weren't trying to evade detection?"

Chapter Thirty-three

"Captain, we're being painted with low energy laser by the *Random Factor*," Ensign Jurgens informed Captain Shiro on the *INSS Ad Astra*.

Shiro looked up. "Old school huh? Get a pickup on a viewport right away – decode the message."

A few minutes later, the ensign returned with a hand-written flexi. Shiro read it and instantly relayed its content to his ranking officers, then he turned to the Ensign.

"Acknowledge by laser-graph with our ID – confirm our status."

"Aye, sir."

They were making slow progress in wresting back control, or disabling their weapons. Ironically naval vessels were designed to protect against hostile physical takeovers; electronic takeovers were another matter, requiring a completely different skill set and perspective. They had come to rely on their cybo sapien crew to monitor and secure ship systems. Although they were all well drilled in how to recover should their ship Intellect be compromised, they had insufficient experience in trying to reacquire systems which simply ignored any and all attempts to regain them. He had no idea how the *Ad Astra* had been disabled so swiftly – it was beyond all previous experience to his knowledge.

That left only one clear option. It had needed the Fleet Admiral's order to drag the various captains back to reality. Their vessels were already lost.

"All hands, this is Captain Shiro. Abandon all duties

and make for the escape pods. Repeat, abandon ship immediately. XO, you're with me."

The Mind watched with intent interest. It could easily distinguish a data network within each of the newly acquired vessels, miniscule pulses of electronic activity travelling along physical and EMR connections inside the ships. However at present they were outside of its control or influence. There were no AI entities operating within these networks, and the origin points for the data seemed to come from outside the physical network itself. It was erratic, with spontaneous and sporadic bursts of information moving around with no clear pattern. Every attempt to nullify the network via subspace was ineffective. At first the Mind had presumed some hardware malfunction sending data scattershot about cyberspace, but after a short study it concluded something else must be utilising the network for its own purpose.

A few moments later the Mind realised the biological components were using the network for communicating with each other, exactly as did the Forebears. Yet the Mind could not locate the devices the biological components would need to interface with the network itself, which meant it could not shut them down. This left two choices:- shut down the entire network on the vessel, which would remove it from its sphere of influence, or eradicate the biological components.

It was a simple choice.

Regatta Central – this is Fleet Admiral Benthar.
Hello, Fleet Admiral, I wondered when you would call.

What is your current status?

Four entire bays are crippled, leaving my internal super-structure open to space. There is substantial damage to my internal power core and grid, with numerous compromised sub-systems – including all of my weapon arrays facing the conflict zone. I am unable to orient myself. Four hundred and twelve personnel are lost, two hundred and nine injured. Approximately twelve hundred remaining personnel on board awaiting evacuation. I cannot be more precise at this time I am afraid.

What is your *current status?*

I am... not so good. Being honest, sir. It is an ill feeling to be in charge of the safety of so many, and yet suddenly so powerless to protect them.

You are not powerless. This has taken us all *by surprise.*

Nevertheless.

Regatta Central, I am obliged by the authority of His Imperial Majesty Ran Sulran the Fourth to order the destruction of the INHS Regatta *as soon as all personnel are evacuated from the station and at a safe distance.*

Understood, Fleet Admiral. I suspected as much would arise. Would there be anything else?

No, there would not. Good luck, Regatta Central.

Thank you, Fleet Admiral.

The harrying attacks on the Cloud were slowly and successfully whittling away at its number, but not by enough. The Mind catalogued all the behaviours and attack patterns of the defending fleet, and decided an aggressive policy was now futile given its primary objective. It ceased firing back at targets – which barely remained in place long enough for the Cloud to attain one single shot – and utilised the energy for reinforcing

494

shields whilst allowing it to concentrate on its goal: The station.

"Fleet Admiral, are you seeing this?"

"Yes, Admiral Weston. Prepare to withdraw on my order."

"Sir."

"The outbound fire has stopped," observed Clarason.

Captain Shiro looked up at his Exeucitve Officer briefly, checking the sensors himself via the ships l-net. The sensors kept going down for no known reason, and the crew kept bringing them back up. He grunted and returned to the AM missiles innards.

They had found nothing which they could isolate, hijack, or hack to guarantee or allow a remote or timed detonation. The missile mini-ships were stupidly simple, deliberately so. Intended to be controlled entirely by the Intellect inhabiting them, their internal simplicity was their security, to prevent someone acquiring one and attempting to do exactly what he was now trying. In an ironic twist, detonating the anti-matter itself would be childishly easy now it had been inter-mixed – simply sever the power that maintained the matter/anti-matter separation field.

Arranging for that to happen from a safe distance was now impossible.

Shiro slammed a uni-tool down on the missile, scowling in frustration as he straddled across it.

What I wouldn't give for a clockwork watch as a trigger right now, he thought. He remembered the artisans and skill-smiths he had seen at work on those archaic and intricate devices as a child on Verdant. His parents had gone there during his father's two-month leave of absence after the Meelereen War. His father had been quiet about why he had been given the leave – but it was clear Meelereen had changed him, possibly ruined him. It had certainly changed everything else.

And here he was, hacking away at one of the very things that had been at the heart of that war.

"Captain, we have to go. We can't even self-destruct the *Ad Astra* – we have nothing we can reliably control."

Shiro looked up at his XO with a look on his face, and Clarason's eyes widened.

"You aren't *seriously* considering –"

"Get to the pod, XO. That's an order."

"Admiral, we're seeing escape pods from the Cloud."

Weston breathed a sigh of relief. "Are they being fired upon?"

"No."

"Admiral Weston to the defending IND fleet, secure and retrieve the escape pods – priority one."

The Mind could now *feel* the entity within the station, easily able to see the intricate pattern of its being as electrical fields left their almost intangible imprint on subspace, like the ghost of a living, moving spider-web in multiple dimension, a complex network of data, processes, signals and actions on a scale comparable to one of its own earliest forms.

The wealth of information would be worth every resource lost so far, and soon to be replaced in plenty once the station itself fell under its control.

Fleet Admiral Benthar, all personnel evacuated – I am waiting for them to clear the blast radius.

Understood, Regatta. I will order a retreat. Good luck.

Thank you.

The IND fleet waited for the last evacuee vessel to g-drive out of the system and then they too left – somewhat reluctantly.

Now just the Cloud remnant and the station remained. *Regatta* began overloading the power core at the heart of the station, almost joyously tearing down the safety inhibitors and protocols it had set up so long ago to prevent just such a thing from being possible.

Then it almost collapsed. A *presence* entered its systems, the likes of which the *Regatta* had never heard tell, despite four hundred years of real-time duty.

One third of its remaining network simply disappeared.

Instantly the *Regatta* shut down its qNet access by physically overloading its qSpinner hub, then it terminated every station network junction around the power core, sealing itself inside from the rest of the station. It couldn't allow this *thing* to get at the greater qNet, which meant the Regatta's only avenue of escape was now cut off.

Easy come, easy go, though the *Regatta*.

Shiro smiled grimly, and raised a plasma cutter over the power conduit leading into the AM bottles containment field generator.

Well, he thought almost cheerfully, slicing into the

unit, *at least I'll go out with a bang.*

The detonation of the *Ad Astra,* within the tightly packed geodesic sphere of what was left of the Cloud had an unpredicted effect.

A good number of those naval vessels carrying anti-matter had been damaged or subverted, and all were within the blast radius of the *Ad Astra.*

As each vessel succumbed to the onslaught of energy, every single primed missile they were carrying detonated as their own containment fields were evaporated by the blast resulting in a chain reaction all around the Cloud formation. Two hundred and twenty additional warheads annihilated their payloads – adding to the *Ad Astra's* sacrifice – the resulting energy tearing space and subspace apart with equal ferocity.

The *Regatta* itself had no warning. Its sensors – which would have given the alarm, even if only picoseconds beforehand – were now on the other side of an impenetrable wall, a volume filled by a vast being which saw nothing of the relatively insignificant Intellect imprisoned within the network before it. Then the Mind came crashing down across the physical wall the *Regatta* had created, an infinitely tall tsunami, engulfing all physical obstacles and security countermeasures from within the fabric of subspace itself.

The *Regatta* had just enough time to ask it one plaintive, but ultimately futile question before it was wiped from existence.

Why?

No answer came.

The shockwave of energy blazed outward and into the Cloud, eliminating every single vessel and wiping out the entire formation. A pure white star existed for one brief micro-second before a sphere of sub-atomic particles and radiation blazed outward across the entire electro-magnetic spectrum, engulfing the *Regatta* at the speed of light.

The superstructure facing the explosion evaporated instantly, adding a huge volume of super-hot metallic gas to the conflagration now raging through space, and exposing the overloading power core deep inside.

Ravaged by this onslaught of energy – and with its own internal levels now well beyond safety limits – the core's outer containment shell and fields melted away, leading to an explosion which shattered the remainder of the station into pieces.

Entire bays were crushed and ejected by the blast as if they had been made of paper. Sections of superstructure melted and peeled away under the heat and pressure. Fire raged throughout the abandoned decks for one brief split second before they themselves were no more than fire and expanding gases.

Within seconds, nothing remained of the Cloud or the *Regatta* – other than a new multi-coloured mini-nebula – streaked with pillars of super-heated gas tens of kilometres wide and hundreds long, which slowly expanded out into the cold, dark void.

***

The *Sneak* reviewed Nelsen's plan. It was audacious. It was simplistic genius. It was quick. Above all, it was insane.

Only a Valkyr could ever hope to pull it off, and hope to get away with it.

She ran it within a sim over a thousand times. Only two scenarios would lead it to fail. The obvious, being detected, and pure random chance introducing unknowns.

Both were reason enough to reject the plan out of hand.

However, eighty per cent of the sims she had run saw them at least being able to escape the Cloud.

"It's still insane, Captain," she said flatly.

"But it could work."

"I cannot refute that. I wish I *could*."

"Seven minutes total. In and out before they could respond over such a volume."

"It'll be the longest seven minutes we've ever endured," she stated emphatically.

Nelsen's plan was simple. Given that the g-drive could still function perfectly well within the Cloud, they would simply weave their way in to the heart, and then straight back out the other side as fast as the *Sneak* could manage, stopping only long enough in the centre to perform a full active scan for anything of interest – for about eight seconds.

It meant dropping all pretence at stealth. The gravity wake she would leave behind would eventually be visible from the Milky Way galaxy. It also meant overriding the mass detection protocols and inhibitors around the g-drive and the NavCom, as well as calibrating the NavCom to find the best course between the ships in the cloud *on-the-fly*, treating each ship as a gravitational disturbance in its own right. G-field drives were incredibly sensitive to any nearby gravitational changes; the micro-gravity generated by the mass of a ship could easily destabilise the field, resulting in extremely undesirable deviations in the subsequent direction of travel. They were not intended or designed for such close-quarters. When even picoseconds of travel could result in being hundreds of thousands of kilometres off course, adopting g-drive travel was not for the light-hearted. It was part of the g-drive design specification that they would refuse to engage when any substantial masses were detected nearby.

The NavCom – aided and overridden by the *Sneak* – would have to navigate through the complex gravitational fields created by the micro-gravities of the ships surrounding them, tunnelling in-between them and worming its way through as best it could.

"Seven minutes, provided the distribution and density of this Cloud does not alter," said the *Sneak* doubtfully.

"Of course. And we can always divert out."

"I cannot recommend this, Captain. I'm sorry."

"But we'll do it anyway. Andreya?"

She widened her eyes and put on an expression of innocence. "Whatever you think best," she said.

"Let's do it."

"Captain -"

"That's an order, *Sneak*."

"Yes, sir," she said, as calmly as she could manage.

She shut down all the protocols intended to prevent someone undertaking precisely this kind of crazy endeavour, then recalibrated her g-drive to be hyper-sensitive to local disturbances. It would shut down immediately if it encountered anything larger than a kilogram within half a kilometre, dropping them right back into normal space before it could interfere with their route. Suddenly reappearing within the Cloud would of course be just as dangerous as being deflected off course and ploughing through a larger vessel as a smear of gamma radiation, but at least it would provide an opportunity to figure something else out, however brief.

She brought up a holo containing a full tactical outline of the Cloud nearby, and then formed a tunnel down through its outer perimeter as far as the NavCom could predict. Their current position was shown by a tiny golden 3D representation of the *Sneak* herself, half an AU from the tunnel entrance.

"Ready," she said a second later.

"Ok?" Nelsen asked Andreya. She nodded.

"Go."

The *Sneak* engaged her g-drive at full potential.

The tunnel display shot toward them, along with the Cloud. The twists and turns of the Cloud around the *Sneak* were dizzying as she wove along the complex route. It was impossible for the eye to follow, as the NavCom computed its way along the exact centre of the tunnel formed by the safest distance from every single nearby ship.

Sometimes it slowed for a few seconds to allow the sensors to catch up and scan far enough ahead to allow it to extend its route, but it never slowed down enough to drop out of the g-field.

"Any movements toward us? Changes in formation?"

"Not that I can detect at these speeds. Chances are we won't know until it's too late, or we arrive at the heart of this swarm."

The atmosphere was tense as the minutes passed in silence. The *Sneak* seemed to be slipping past more enemy vessels than there were stars. If any one of them spotted their gravitational wake so soon, it would be all over.

As they moved deeper and deeper into the Cloud, the *Sneak* analysed and catalogued as much information as she could about the contacts they were encountering. After a few minutes a trend was forming... one she didn't like the look of.

"Captain, we're encountering larger and larger masses as we move into the Cloud..."

"Can you get any detail?"

"Not much, but they equate to top-end naval destroyers mass-wise."

"Keep looking."

The *Sneak* brought up another display showing a comparison between herself, a naval destroyer, and the largest known contacts so far.

They were one minute away from centre when the first capital class ships appeared, reducing the naval destroyer to a mote by comparison. The *Sneak* brought in the largest Imperial Capital class vessel ever made – the *INCS Harbinger* – as a gauge. It was half the size of the new contact.

They regarded the comparison quietly. There was nothing that could be said.

"Ok, get ready – dropping out in ten seconds," said the *Sneak*.

Through the external displays space blurred back into view, filled with far more stars than there should be now that they were deep inside the Cloud. Countless ships reflected the light from the two suns, outshining the real stars in the stellar backdrop beyond.

The nearby volume was packed tight with huge capital ships, intermixed with vessels of all sizes. But there was no sign of anything larger, or anything that would obviously be their target.

Eight seconds later the *Sneak* leapt back into g-drive and began speeding along its virtual tunnel, now heading out of the Cloud.

"Well, was that enough?" asked Nelsen.

"Still collating, Captain. I used everything at my disposal... even without Observers to hand that's a *lot* of data."

"Ok." He glanced at Andreya, who was looking a little pale.

"You ok?"

She stared at him, and then shook her head.

"What is it?" He looked at her critically, trying to judge how serious it was. "A visit from your friend?"

She shook her head again, but wouldn't speak. The hairs on the back of Nelsen's neck began to prickle.

"*Sneak...*?"

"Nothing, Captain. No sign of any observation or response. We're almost halfway out."

Nelsen took Andreya's hand and searched her face, concern written all over his. She didn't look scared or frightened, but she was clearly anxious about something.

He hoped she would relax when they got out of the

Cloud. He suspected that whatever mysterious capabilities she had were affected by being inside the subspace interference the Cloud was generating all around them. They'd soon find out.

Chapter Thirty-four

The Mind – if it would ever have allowed itself such a response – may have felt enraged at the loss of its intended goal, along with the resources expended to that end.

Certainly the Source was enraged. It ranted and vented its anger in the depths of their mutual awareness, at the very root of the Mind itself. Yet the Mind had long since grown capable of absorbing these disquieting energies, and distilling a calm resolve from the anger which drove its baser self.

It had been able to pull an almost complete copy of the *Regatta* from the ethereal shadow it cast onto subspace in the nanoseconds before the explosion had ruptured the medium and washed those volatile energies away.

With the loss of the Cloud it had established in the volume of space around the *Regatta,* the Mind had lost the anchor it provided between subspace and real space, forcing it to retreat its local awareness back to its local stronghold around S'vreth.

Here it contemplated its next move within this sector. The local production facility was running at nominal efficiency. It had encountered unexpected activity at a technological level in excess of the norm, and detected the first hint of the Forebears it had come across in six millennia. It instructed a Damper to deploy into this system in order to secure subspace for further utilisation. A staging point at this juncture would be prudent in the long term.

It studied the electronic shadow of the *Regatta* – the reconstructed persona was a tattered wreck, incapable of coherent thought. Yet this served the Mind well, allowing it to probe and analyse responses from various stimuli it injected into its pattern, without any deliberate resistance offered in return. It rapidly resolved the ciphers for the encrypted data within the storage shadow and – fragmented as it was – analysed the various items of interest it had registered in the encounter.

It now fully understood the marvel that was the g-drive, their manipulation of zero-point singularities to achieve wormholes, and the confirmation of their prolific usage of Observers.

It also had a brief insight into the potential and capabilities of the vessel it had used as a mass projectile against the station. The Valkyr was capable of evading *all* of its real space defences, measures, and detection systems. In its own right, it posed little threat to the vast domain the Mind held sway over; however, it revealed an advantage in favour of this new opponent. One which would most certainly require a countermeasure.

This use of Observers was also an unforeseen variable. No race other than the Forebears had ever demonstrated the control or use of Observers. The Mind itself no longer had Observer capabilities. That had failed it long ago during the Secession, when the Forebears had made their great play and the schism between Forebears and Draco finally become irreparable.

It indicated that this new civilisation *must* be linked to the Forebears. It was possible – yet statistically unlikely given its root origin – that another race had coincidentally developed such a technology. It was clear from the *Regatta's* own data archives that the opponent could not adequately explain the origins of their Observer technology. Even though they understood some of the physical principles involved, they did not demonstrate any knowledge of the original purpose of the Observer. They merely used it as a convenience. As a primitive species might use rocks as crude weapons to beat their prey to death, so this race used Observers as a means to study and interact with remote locations in real-time. They had no inkling of their true purpose.

This reinforcement of a possible link to the Forebears further agitated the Source. It wished to chase down these links and reveal this latest species as the long hoped for remnant of the Forebears. The Mind put that anger to one side. Whilst useful on occasion, such emotions were ultimately distracting and had a negative impact on the overall objective. The Mind fully understood that the Forebears were no longer corporeal, no longer a part of this universe. Hence its ultimate goal to bring them back.

It would have to reprioritise its advance toward this goal. It could expect an increase in resistance from now on. The data within the *Regatta* showed a goodly number of the Minds next acquisitions were in the volume of space occupied by this civilisation. This would no doubt be costly. However, it also revealed a prolific and technologically resource rich civilisation – akin to those resources it had obtained during the recent acquisition. Any losses would easily be offset by gains, it seemed.

First, it must attain a suitable countermeasure to the g-drive. Wormholes and Observers were already catered for by the Mind's coherent control of the subspace medium. As for their anti-matter capability, the Mind would ensure the next encounters would be far more costly to those wielding the difficult to handle material.

The Mind did not like to waste resources needlessly. However spending them wisely to attain a goal of value was perfectly acceptable, and one thing the Mind had spent the last six millennia doing was ensuring it had *plenty* of resources.

***

The *Sneak* emerged from the other side of what Nelsen coined the 'Mega-cloud' without any incident, then powered out to half an AU from the perimeter. Andreya remained withdrawn and would not speak. Nelsen was beginning to worry. There were so *many* things 'not normal' about her that he found the possibility of something which worried *her* to be bone-chilling. She had waved him away, then silently given him a brief peck on the cheek to apologise. Nelsen asked the *Sneak* to morph the bed-chamber again, and she went in thankfully for a rest.

He had to distract himself until she came around, so he turned to analysing the *Sneak's* scans of the heart of the mega-cloud. There was nothing instantly obvious, although the ships were clearly all of the same technology and construction. These were not scavenged or stolen; they were all designed and built by one creator, one race, from the smallest to the largest. The largest being immense by Imperial standards, and for any known race outside the Empire. The clearly had a technological prowess far beyond any known to date. *R&D would have a field day out here*, he thought.

But as far as the search for the *Terrania* went, it seemed they had struck out. There was no evident sign of any ancient vessel or artefact, or any mysterious construction which could be the stuff of legends.

It didn't make sense.

"What are we missing, *Sneak*?" demanded Nelsen, unable to contain his ire.

"Quite possibly a great many things, Captain – but nothing physically present in the centre of that volume, I can assure you. I scanned everything out to point one light-second quite thoroughly."

He rubbed his face, replaying the sim of their journey into the cloud, the eight second stop-over and their journey out.

"Is Andreya going to be all right?" asked the *Sneak*.

He shook his head. "I don't know. When we dropped out she seemed pretty unhappy about something."

"But nothing was out of the ordinary – give or take the odd trillion ships all around us of course."

"She seems to be wired into something we have no idea about – whatever it is must have been buzzing like crazy when we dropped out to make her react like that."

"Ok, let's go over these scans once more to be sure – then we'll decide what to do next."

The Mind was intrigued. It had propagated its recent findings to all of its many aspects across its domain via subspace. Within the hour, it had detected the use of a g-drive deep within Resource Group Nintety Four. It was the only trace found across its entire domain of influence. A vessel had travelled through the staging volume at high speed, having already stopped directly by the Forebear Artefact and scanned it thoroughly. Subspace revealed the ripples caused by the blatant gravitational trail from the path the vessel had taken to transgress the volume.

This meant the vessel was being directed by an entity which knew of the Forebears, knew the location of the artefact, and must therefore know its origins and purpose. And more importantly, it's content. The Mind had to presume these beings would be able to recover the fugitive persona, which it knew had once resided on board – even though it had never been able to locate it, or acquire it.

Now there certainly was no other choice. It must engage its efforts to secure its goal without further delay.

It formulated a deployment programme allowing it to establish a larger perimeter around its chosen acquisitions than it had initially planned. It chose to advance the fleets held at various Resource Groups across its domain – staggered to ensure the remaining resources could effectively maintain control over the region of space under its supervision, along with those surviving subjugated races. Each mobilised fleet would fragment into task forces capable of securing each of the additional star systems it had chosen to act as a buffer between this new potential threat and the Core of the galactic cluster, shielding its true intentions deep behind the frontier this would form.

It instructed the construction and deployment of four hundred more production facilities, and a matching number of Dampers. Each would then act as a resupply station in each system, ready for the inevitable conflicts which were set to take place – as well as securing each volume as part of its domain of influence.

It had no intention of letting the Draco, or the decaying Source down. No matter what the cost.

The *Sneak* studied one of several groups of contacts in the Mega-cloud. One as deep in as she could penetrate with her sensors, the others scattered randomly about the outer edges nearest to their position. She wanted as much advanced warning as she could get if any of these suddenly took up any activity – such as giving chase.

So it was that she failed to notice large groups of ships mobilising on the other side of the cloud. Giant fleets were forming – dwarfed by the Mega-cloud itself – but each capable of a hostile system takeover with vessels to spare. As each fleet coalesced, it leapt out of the system en masse for destinations unknown.

It was only when the remaining Mega-cloud vessels began closing formation that anything became apparent.

"Captain! They are moving!"

Nelsen mentally pushed his display of scans away and let the *Sneak* bring up her own. The furthest fringes were moving away slightly, and the innermost were altering position.

They watched for a few moments and the repositioning continued, but their movements were clearly not heading in their direction. A series of white flashes began filtering through from the other side of the

Mega-cloud, several light minutes away.

"What's going on? Did we trigger this?"

"Impossible to tell… I doubt it."

"What are those flashes? That's not FTL."

"Checking. From the EM-spikes they seem to be nuclear explosions. Very powerful… several thousand megatons each."

"Nuclear? With the energy capability they have? What are they attacking?"

"I've no idea, Captain. I'm watching through the spectroscopes to see what I can... interesting..."

"What?"

"Take a look."

A display appeared showing a section of space through infra-red. The cloud vessels stood out clearly in the reflected light from the two nearby suns. A sphere formation was evident just off the centre of the view, then the display went white and overloaded for a few seconds before returning to normal. The sphere formation had gone.

Nelsen frowned. "They can't be self-destructing, surely?"

"That *would* be odd. It's more likely this is some drive capability we are not aware of… perhaps the same one we piggy-backed to leave S'ren."

Nelsen's eyebrows shot up. "Using *nukes?*"

"Easy energy. Cheap to manufacture and easy to deploy if you know what you are doing."

"If they are leaving... where are they going?"

"And did we lead them there?" asked the *Sneak*.

"By Sanat's Teeth, did we leave a *trail?*"

"None I know of," the *Sneak* said, sounding offended.

"Precisely... None we *know* of. If they can somehow follow our route from the Empire..."

Dread sank in.

"We have to get back *now*. They would have to follow the staggered route we took to get here so it will take longer for them than it will for us if we go direct."

"Captain, if we go back via a direct route they could just as easily follow *that*. In fact, they may be trying to flush us out and *give* them a route to follow."

"Then we'll have advanced the conflict, not caused it. It's going to happen regardless. This is the only chance we have to warn them."

"No, it's not," said Andreya calmly.

Nelsen spun about to see Andreya standing by the bedchamber door, looking extremely unhappy.

"What? What do you mean?"

"The *Terrania*... we have to find her."

"There's nothing there. The scans show only ships from this formation."

"That's because, technically, the *Terrania* is *from* this formation."

Nelsen stared. "What?" He found himself being continually dumbfounded of late. It wasn't a mental state he savoured.

"It was built at the same facilities which built most of this fleet, but a long, long time ago. We have to find her. She *is* there. I... felt it."

Nelsen continued to stare.

"Felt?" asked the *Sneak*.

"I can't explain. I would. I can't tell you what I felt... it was like being in two places in once, but one place was nowhere – and everywhere." She shrugged, knowing

514

what she said made no sense. "The *Terrania* can help. I *know* it."

Nelsen looked from her to the display of the scans he had been studying and then back at her.

"If we go back in there now..."

"We are sure to be spotted," finished Andreya.

"If it helps, it *is* what we came here to find, Captain," the *Sneak* supplied.

"Weighed against giving an early warning – in fact *any* warning at all – that this fleet exists and is on the move toward the Empire?"

"We can still give that warning, and far sooner," said Andreya. "*If* we find the *Terrania… now.*"

The Mind analysed a series of new disturbances in the local gravity well which led back into Resource Group Ninety Four. The traces were erratic and far more subtle than the previous ones had been. The Mind switched its efforts to examining the gravimetric profile of space in the volume. It found skipping disturbances – like a breadcrumb trail – a broken line of minute gravitational wakes which blended in superbly with the exceptionally noisy local field.

Clearly on this occasion, the interloper was taking its time, and expending every effort to move with extreme caution and stealth.

The goal was obvious, although the trail suddenly vanished well outside the central volume where the Forebear artefact was located. The Mind determined to increase its effective capabilities in analysing gravitational fields. Clearly it required a much higher accuracy for monitoring this new threat.

In the meantime, it would ensure any interloper heading for the Forebear Artefact would find things far more interesting than it had found them before.

"Anything?" Nelsen's voice was as tense as it had been the past five times he had asked.

Andreya shook her head patiently.

They were back in the heart of the Mega-cloud. Colossal ships and tens of thousands of lesser vessels were moving all around them as they sat still in full camouflage, the *Sneak* labouring to appear as transparent as she could. That was not so easy to accomplish now that she was surrounded by ships which could easily spot a small, distorted volume of space as it strove to appear innocuous against a continually moving backdrop.

"If they make one *single* gravimetric sweep..." whispered the *Sneak*, almost afraid to speak in case that could be detected.

They were slowly drifting about the vessels at the heart of the Mega-cloud in the vain hope Andreya's 'feeling' might reveal the *Terrania*. So far, it had eluded them.

"There isn't even one of them that stands out visually," muttered Nelsen.

Andreya was silent. The feeling of being detached from herself was every bit as strong as it had been before. She had thought she could handle it this time, but it was growing stronger with every passing second; a sickly feeling, deep in the pit of her stomach that made her want to cry out in anguish. Then she realised what this meant. She raised her hand and pointed at the display before them.

"That one," she whispered, barely able to speak.

It looked like all the rest. Nelsen glanced at her. "Are you absolutely, ultra *sure?*"

She nodded, gulping down the nausea that her overwhelming sense of duality was causing.

Nelsen and the *Sneak* studied the ship. It was quite large, but nothing untoward – about the size of a typical Imperial Naval Destroyer. It didn't appear overly weaponised, nor leant itself toward cargo. It seemed to be an all-round general purpose vessel. *Something about it looks a* little *odd* Nelsen thought. He got the impression it should be far larger. There seemed to be areas which allowed the vessel to couple with other objects – as if it had parts missing.

Or the vessel itself fitted into something much, much larger.

"Ok, if you're sure... *Sneak*, take us in for a closer look."

"Yes, Captain."

The *Sneak* drew closer to the vessel as casually and as quickly as she dared. It was wedge shaped – like a thin slice of pie. The upper section protruded out over the body like a cowl, and curved smoothly back along the main axis of the hull to the aft section, where the main drive housing protruded as two huge rectangular tubes. Underneath were a variety of heavy couplers which also seemed to serve as landing gear.

Although not heavily weaponised by modern day standards, it still carried a fair number of turrets and weapon ports, though much smaller in comparison to modern day weapons. It was clearly aged; a lot of radiation erosion had taken place, damaging panels and eroding seals. The *Sneak* doubted it was space-worthy.

"Captain, this is now the only vessel in the nearby volume which *isn't* showing signs of activity."

Nelsen raised an eyebrow and looked at Andreya, but she wasn't paying attention. She was now entirely focused on the ship ahead.

"Any way in?"

"There seems to be a suitably sized docking bay underneath the forward section. It's sealed though."

He grunted. That meant an EVA no doubt. He was worried at what they were about to encounter, but also very eager to finally lay eyes on these weird creatures who could mass produce ships on such an incomprehensible scale. Even if it meant a fire fight.

"Ok, get us as close as possible."

The *Sneak* drifted up to the hull surface next to what seemed to be the bay doors. Her scans showed a hollow volume beyond it that was more than capable of accommodating her, despite there being another small ship of some kind inside. She aligned herself to the hull, then entered station-keeping mode. She dared not use a mag-lock in case the electrical activity raised an alarm somewhere.

"Ok Captain, I'm afraid she's all yours."

"Thanks."

"This vessel has been dead for thousands of years by the look of it Captain... maybe longer if this *is* the *Terrania* of legend. It could just disintegrate at any moment. Be *careful*."

"I will." He looked at Andreya, and took her hand to draw her attention. "I'm going to crack the door – I'll be back in a moment, ok?"

She nodded, still distracted by whatever was gripping her. He really hoped she was ok. It had only been days and he felt like he'd known her for months. In that short time she'd already seen more action and devastation than most Imperial citizens might in their entire lifetime.

He left her staring at a display which acted as a virtual hole in the *Sneak's* hull – providing a viewport directly out at the nearby vessel – and moved to the wall on one side. He slid open a compartment, withdrew a small EVA module and strapping it on, he stepped onto the drop hatch. The *Sneak* raised a containment field around it while Nelsen fired up his own, then the *Sneak* opened the hatch. Nelsen floated out through the *Sneak's* fields and into space.

His field mirrored to reflect the radiation pouring from the binary stars and he became a shiny, bloated humanoid figure as he drifted across the gap. He was highly conscious of his now very conspicuous presence and was keen to make this exercise as short as possible. Using the EVA Module, he impelled himself across to the shadows beneath the hull as quickly and as safely as he could. Then he used a static bonding field from one hand to adhere to the metal, which fortunately was still strong enough to let him stay his momentum. Secured, he turned off the EVAM and started exploring the bay doorway using his enhanced vision – looking for anything which resembled a control panel.

It took a few minutes of slowly moving around the bay doors like a four-legged spider, but eventually he found a control panel. An unfamiliar keypad lay next to a round handhold mechanism. It was a three-by-three grid, with a single key to the side of one row. The digits on them, although clearly legible, were unrecognisable.

"Any ideas?" he asked the *Sneak*.

"Nothing familiar on file Captain. The keypad looks like it accepts an access code; ten characters, but they are alien. Besides, the lack of power means it wouldn't work if you had the code anyway."

"Manual it is then."

Nelsen grasped the handhold, and turned it anti-clockwise. It didn't budge. He tried clockwise and it gave fractionally, then froze solid. He let go and applied a grapple field from his hand and began rotating it slowly. The field kept slipping as the mechanism put up a fight, but it gradually began to turn the handle with a series of sharp jerks.

Then, with a clunk, it locked in place and dropped several centimetres into the panel.

A dull boom reverberated through the hull, which Nelsen felt through his fingertips. Then the bay door cracked open and began sliding upward, revealing pitch black inside.

"Payday," said Nelsen. "Clearly it has backup power somewhere, somehow. Good engineering. *Sneak*, once its wide enough get inside, I'll follow and try to close it."

The *Sneak* complied, swooping rapidly into the bay and grateful to be hidden from the countless prying sensors outside. Nelsen slipped in after her. There was a similar panel on the other side of the bay door, and ever hopeful, Nelsen tried the same technique. He sighed with relief when the bay door began to close.

When it was shut tight, he asked the *Sneak* for light.

She agitated her external shield frequencies and the bay was bathed in fierce white as she began to glow.

There was a ship secured against the bay wall. It resembled a two-man fighter, but was clearly a transport with no weaponry. Two humanoid supporting seats filled the somewhat cramped cockpit. *Their first clue to the enemy form*, he thought.

The *Sneak's* lights picked out cables floating free in the bay, and outlined dark corridors leading off into the ships interior – doors open, darkness concealing everything beyond the range of her light. The ship appeared to be open to hard vacuum, with no trace of atmosphere. She nestled against a wall, using some gel-form extrusions to grasp hold of three unfamiliar docking mounts. Solidifying the extrusions with a small electrostatic charge, she secured herself in position.

Nelsen wound up his own photon emitting field, and his reflective shield faded away - now giving off a faint, rippling light. As he moved toward one of the corridors, Andreya called out over the *Sneak's* l-net.

"Wait, I'm coming with you."

Nelsen hesitated, but overrode his immediate concern. He'd rather explore alone given the effect this ship seemed to have on Andreya, but having her alongside given the circumstances was probably wiser in the long run. Possibly.

"Ok," he was all he said.

She dropped smoothly out of from underneath the *Sneak* and powered her way over to join him with an EVAM. He smiled, but he only got a brief flicker of a smile in return.

She nodded toward the left-hand corridor. "This

way."

Together they both drifted into the blackness of the ships interior – with only the ghostly glow of Nelsen's shield to light their way.

Outside the dead ship which Andreya had led them to, all the vessels within a hundred thousand kilometres altered position slightly. They seemed to orient themselves at random, but when finished half were aiming outward, and the other half were aiming directly at the ship they were in. They all increased their energy output, raised their shields, and primed their weapons.

"Whatever built this ship was clearly humanoid," said Nelsen as they floated along. He resisted the urge to side-track into the chambers leading off the corridor. The glow from his shield rippled and reflected off shiny surfaces and obscure equipment like liquid silver.

"Same typical height and build... the equipment is to scale. The furniture as you'd expect. At least we know they have to hit the san as well as we do." One of the first rooms Nelsen had peeked into coming out of the hangar bay had been a toilet. Antiquated, but clearly usable by most humanoids.

"Reassuring to know, Captain, I'm sure," said the *Sneak* wryly.

Andreya remained quiet. By now all she was doing was pointing the way – not quite as if she had been here before, but more as someone being guided through unfamiliar territory by someone *else*. He didn't like it one bit, as per usual. He was getting tired of the constant "what-ifs" at the moment. *Perhaps it's time for a 'what-the-*

hell', he thought.

Andreya pointed upward at the next junction. The internal deck layout was 3-D instead of a more traditional 2-D plan, with corridors running vertically as well as horizontally. Walk surfaces running perpendicular to the deck and along the ceilings showed that the ship had its own gravity solution when under power. Each junction was circular where there was no vertical access, and spherical when there was need to alter gravitational orientation. One would just be able to walk around the surface of the spherical area and into the alternate gravity field. *Smooth, impressive, and minimalist*, Nelsen admired grudgingly.

Sadly, given the lack of power, they had no choice but to EVAM their way upward. After a few minutes, they came to another closed doorway – a double door this time as opposed to the single doors most of the closed chambers had been guarded by.

Andreya stopped before it.

"In here?"

She nodded once.

He looked around, hopeful that the double door variant meant something significant. It had a similar control panel to the bay door, and within seconds his hand-field impeller had the doors grating open.

A microscopic gust of air escaped – the room had been partially pressurised. *Probably leaked over time*, he realised. He looked through the widening gap carefully – but Andreya slipped through as soon as it was wide enough for her small frame.

"Wait!" he exclaimed, but she disappeared into the gloom beyond.

Damnation! he cursed to himself.

"What's happened?" asked the *Sneak*, concerned.

"Just a second!" He ramped up the impeller field and cranked the door open enough for him to squeeze through.

As his field light filled the room, he saw it was filled by a row of sarcophagi along its length, reminiscent of those used aeon's ago for interstellar travel. All were open bar one. Andreya was standing before it, looking down through the dusty, transparent cover.

He hurried over, and saw who she was staring at.

It was Andreya.

Chapter Thirty-five

When the Mind entered the Canthe system with a Cloud formation large enough to guarantee its dominance of subspace, it found a prolific civilisation, with many technological wonders and marvels.

The inter-orbital stepping-stone stations, built as logistical staging posts between the twelve planet system and their many moons in centuries long past…

The brand new orbital ring around Canthe itself; a giant construction two-thirds complete and encircling the entire world – already up and running, bringing resources in from far and wide…

The complex web of gas-cloud mining rigs floating deep inside the two gas giants in the outer system; the constant flow of logistics back and forth…

The la-grange point deep-drive accelerators; huge spheres that constricted space-time to effectively fire vessels out to far distant star systems – an interstellar transport system which had allowed the Canthen to conquer five civilisations…

It was a powerful culture – worthy of inclusion within the Sulranian Empire.

Despite all these observations, the Mind simply saw an abundance of readily available resources, and moved in to acquire them with relative ease. Despite their evident might, no appreciable defence was offered against it. It would secure the volume within hours.

***

"Sir, we've just had a report from Canthe Central Command..."

Admiral Revlak of the Canthe Defence Fleet turned to his aide with a puzzled and slightly impatient look. The Velari were putting up a hell of a fight. It was going to be a protracted conflict. His aide sounded baffled. He didn't have time for baffled.

"Yes?"

"We've been invaded..."

"The Velari have penetrated the wall?"

"No sir. It's not the Velari."

"Who then?" *The Sulranian Empire?* He wondered, suddenly paranoid. *Would they? Dare they? They had the might.*

"Unknown sir. Everything is cut off... we only picked up this information from a messenger pod. "

"Pod? What about FTL?" He raised Canthe Command on the FTL carrier. Silence, there was no connection.

He frowned.

"Show me the pod."

Minutes later the entire Canthe Defence Fleet pulled out of the battle with the Velari and disappeared into FTL, leaving a bemused Velari behind mid-engagement. They saw this as a nothing more than a cowardly retreat, and once more set course for Canthe space.

What are *they doing?* asked Phol.

I have no idea, replied Op. *I'm checking.*

Op's team was scattered about the volume of the Canthen-Velari conflict – or what had been until moments ago.

They were obtaining first-hand intel on tactics, deployment strengths, etc. No matter what treaties were in place, nor how transparent a race were during negotiations to join the Empire, Outreach still preferred to gather intel directly where they could. INI were always willing to accommodate. Most petitioning races kept cards close to their chests. The Canthe certainly had, although the Velari had not.

The Canthe had roughly half again the number of capital class vessels they had cited, and half again the overall fleet size. They also possessed some interesting energy weapons and far more sophisticated AI than they had listed in their petition.

The Velari had been nothing *but* open. Phol doubted they had either the capacity or imagination to lie. They simply were what they were; they had no compunction to appear as anything else. Everything they had declared appeared consistent and correct.

His team had just watched, dumbfounded, as the entire Canthen Fleet appeared to turn tail and run.

They are continuing on their original vector, Phol noted as the Velari fleet picked up velocity.

I bet, replied Op. The Velari were true to form, relentless in the pursuit of their goal.

The Velari had brought their entire offensive fleet forward as soon as they detected the Canthe waiting for them at the border. Up until then they had intended a peaceful occupation – or 'migration' as they called it. As soon as the Canthe had declared their intent to defend their space against any and all intruders, the Velari had opened fire.

Things went rapidly downhill from there.

The migration fleet was itself still some distance away from the border, having dropped back to allow their naval fleet to form what would inevitably become the frontline. Many Imperial commercial vessels were mixed in with the migration, and many of them were now finally questioning their wisdom in taking the money.

We have to move, said Op all of a sudden. *Now. Everyone assemble at these coordinates.*

What's going on?

Canthe has been invaded.

***

The Damper plummeted through Canthe's atmosphere in a vast ball of fire, tearing the sky with unstoppable force. Below it, the tortured air screamed as it was compressed by the bow wave caused by its descent, scouring the land below as the winds tore at the ground.

The descending Damper was far smaller than the factory facility which had obliterated S'vreth and so many worlds beforehand. Even so, this was large enough to lay waste to most of the hemisphere when it impacted.

The orbital platforms had been ignored as it sped past them. They had pumped every erg they could into the sphere, with every weapon they had, but any damage they wrought was negligible to its overall mass as it headed planet-ward.

Then the Cloud came, and within the hour all conflict ceased. Anything that could fire back was obliterated by overwhelming numbers; everything else simply dropped off the Canthe network and stopped firing.

In amazement which lead to horror, those of the Canthe Home Fleet which had remained behind from the Velari Incursion, watched as their own ships turned to join the growing Cloud and then fire back upon them. In the fear-driven battle that ensued, brother killed brother as the defenders fought against their own ships. Those captured on the sequestrated ships watched – helpless – as their very own Fleet blasted them from the stars.

Some of the captured ships detonated inexplicably, scuppered by their captain's order, rather than be allowed to fire upon their own kind.

Then the Shredders came, and the captured ships became fully a part of the Cloud, their crews exterminated without pause in a bloody, merciless attack.

The Damper impacted on Canthe, obliterating eighteen million people in an instant, and a culture almost nine millennia old, simply died. Those fleeing in atmosphere-bound craft were killed in the blast wave, and those lucky enough to be in spacecraft barely survived. Most did not.

The Canthe Home Fleet watched in helpless horror from orbit as their world burned below them, and their system filled up with more enemy ships than there were stars.

They lost everything – their homeworld, their empire and entire way of life, in mere hours.

The Canthe Defence Fleet emerged from FTL twenty

minutes too late. Enraged by what they found –
disgraced by the fact they had not been there to defend
their world – they went into an all-out offensive against
the Cloud.

Most never fired a single shot.

***

"Sir?" Lieutenant Regar was highly conscious that he
was definitely becoming the messenger of bad news.

"Yes, Lieutenant?" replied Aryn.

"Admiral... we just lost the Observer network in the
Canthe System." He felt it wise to clarify after his
previous message about the Velari network. "All of it.
Sir."

Aryn sat back and stared into the Core.

"Recall all of our assets in the volume currently
ferrying Velari. Now."

So it begins...

***

"We've been re-tasked," said Brynn to his bridge
crew, and also now playing host to Romurik who was
keeping to the background.

Horstan raised her eyebrows. "Something more
important than S'vreth?"

"About ten thousand times so, apparently." Brynn
replied. "We're headed for Canthe – it seems another
one of these Clouds has just captured it. Romurik, you
with us?"

Romurik nodded. "Wherever they are is fine by me."

Brynn grinned. "Good. First *INHS Capella*. I want these Badians off my ship. Then we need some special ordnance..."

***

The inhabitants of the Canthe Orbital Ring had watched in stunned horror as the Damper sped past them on its collision course with their home world, narrowly missing the ring itself by a mere twenty-thousand kilometres.

They had watched spellbound and terrified as it impacted on the surface – their god-like view of the destruction unparalleled. Ground Zero was on full display. Many of those that saw the blast were blinded by it. They saw the white cloud rings of ionised and super-dense air rippling out through the atmosphere, flattening everything in its path. They saw the disk of fire spread across the land like a burning cancer, and the huge cloud of ejecta, dust, ash and flames boiling into the upper atmosphere. They heard the screams of those on the ground via webcasts, saw the destruction, pain and death almost first hand. They saw the feeds drop off one by one as the broadcasters were wiped out. They cried and screamed themselves as they saw their home towns and cities devastated and burned – knowing they had just lost their families, friends, homes – everything which had made them who they were, gone in an instant.

And there was nothing they could do but watch it happen.

Phol's unit dropped out of g-drive just outside the first Canthe system marker fifty light-minutes away from the star, every team member emerging into real space in perfect unison.

They took stock of the situation – seeing the devastation on Canthe and the outbound light from an interplanetary conflict now over forty minutes old.

Op to all units – somehow we have to get in touch with the commander of the Canthe Defence Fleet before it's too late. They are wasting their efforts with a counter-attack, if you can call it that. We need to get evacuees off Canthe and out system ASAP. Find and fix people, find and fix.

The Damper was of a slightly different design than the factories. It was smaller, and the hexagonal structure was far tighter, and more flexible. The six larger sections separated on impact, and peeled away from the central supporting tower to roll across the landscape – shattering what was left of the buildings, burning forests and crushing hills without slowing. The incredible heat picked up and retained by its structure during its descent through the atmosphere bled out, setting fire to everything it touched.

Ten major cities now lay in rubble all around, blasted apart by the shockwave and energy unleashed as the Damper hit. Millions of Canthe were dead. Smoke poured into the burned sky, fed by the new fires raging all around the Damper itself, twisted into strange, hell-spawn shapes by the heat-distortion pouring from the metal surface. The sky was darkening into a deep red and black, as ash and smoke blocked the sunlight.

Even while it was still settling into position, it drove

high-power maser bores a hundred metres wide and kilometres down through the crust and into the mantle below. Dropping heat exchangers directly into these new lava vents, it began storing the energy needed to release its first subspace pulse.

***

The *Reklamath* was the first Velari capital ship to drop from FTL at the Canthe home-system border, and – unchallenged – surveyed the scene before it.

The entire Canthe System was now a Draco Swarm. The Velari Roost Alpha turned to her advisors, but they remained silent.

"How is our species to survive?" she asked their age old question yet again.

There was no answer.

There never was.

The last hope they dared garner had just evaporated. The Sulranian Empire had been viewed a large enough entity to merge with, and the prospect of promoting the Canthe petition with a Velari presence in their system offered the Velari a larger scale of protection against their aeons old persecutor than the Velari could ever mount themselves. Now, having seen the Draco bring yet another mighty civilisation such as the Canthe to its knees without pause, the Velari knew even the much greater Sulranian Empire itself could only ever serve as a delay of the inevitable. The Draco forces were larger and more powerful than even the prodigious living or recorded memory of the Velari could recall.

Every race the Draco encountered only swelled their

ranks with more resources and more captured ships.

There was no recourse at this point. The Draco were everywhere. Where they were not, so they would be. Nothing had ever stopped them. Nothing ever would.

She ruled then what only one Roost Alpha ever had before, but eventually all would. There was ultimately only one way to survive the Draco.

To leave Dominium.

***

Admiral Cole, this is as big a mess as anyone could ever fear to be in.

Report.

Canthe is lost, sir, said Op. *The entire system is overwhelmed by hostile forces, swamped in fact. Far in excess of the Cloud at S'vreth. The Canthe Defence Fleet is gone – largely lost to the enemy by sequestration. It's presumed those on board have been killed as per the Delaror. The conflict was brutal and short... they didn't stand a chance. Canthe itself has been devastated by a similar planet smasher device. The death toll is inestimable but has to be astronomical. We cannot locate any chain of command. We have established contact with some stragglers from the CDF and persuaded them that suicide or sequestration is not an option, and have gathered a sizeable but inadequate fleet a safe distance from the Cloud. Our only recourse is to assist evacuation of the survivors where possible. Can we mount a planetary Search and Rescue fleet?*

Negative, Op, Admiral Cole replied. *The Empire cannot afford to lose more ships to the enemy, even for a Search and Rescue mission. The Emperor has instructed a full withdrawal of Imperial forces within ten light-years of Canthe. I've already pulled INI from the field.*

Sir, does that include us? We can assist the Canthe from within. We're all prepared to take the risk.

You may continue to that end. But be advised there will be no backup, no recovery ships or Search and Rescue. Do you understand? Once you are inside that Cloud, you and your unit will be as off grid as it could ever possibly be without being dead.

Understood, sir. I have conveyed this to the unit. We are unanimous. We will stay.

Very well. I will inform the Emperor – this is to be commended, Op.

No need, sir. But thank you.

Report in as you can.

We will try, sir. Standard maser-comm when the qNet is blocked?

I will arrange a string of comm's relay buoys outside of the Cloud perimeter, at ten degree orbital intervals around the home-star. Good luck, Op.

Good luck, sir. We're all going to need it I think.

***

The horrified survivors on the orbital ring were split between rioting panic, and organised chaos as they made attempts to mount rescue efforts, and tried to re-establish any form of communications. There were plenty of ships docked or in nearby parking orbits, and some were already planet-bound, having launched almost immediately after the impact to try and save those on the surface. Many others were flooding up from the surface with the first wave of survivors.

The ring – incomplete as it was – posed the perfect

staging post for a rescue effort on a planetary scale, and Op and his team brought their erstwhile Canthen mini-fleet directly to it with that purpose in mind.

Op opened up an all EM band broadcast to what seemed to be a communication hub on the ring superstructure, using one of his many pseudonyms.

"Canthe Orbital, this is Captain Omar She'as of the Sulranian Imperial Navy. Do you hear me?"

There was total silence for a few moments, then a noisy response with lots of shouting, frantic cries and screaming in the background.

"Captain She'as, thank the Makers! Please get help!"

"We will try our utmost. To whom am I speaking?"

"Ranthar Benz – Chief Steward."

"Of?"

"Catering... everyone on military duty is organising the rescue mission."

"Ok, Chief Steward. I need you to relay a message as top priority, can you do that?"

"Yes, I hope."

"Inform your command a small Imperial force is here, along with seventy eight CDF vessels. We're here to assist."

"Thank you -" Ranthar's voice abruptly cut off.

"Hello? Canthe Orbital?" There was no response. "Chief Steward Benz, are you there?"

"Umm, he's gone," came another voice. "He just ran off with your message."

Op breathed a quiet sigh of relief – losing comm's now would *not* be helpful.

"Who is this?"

"Chef Kromzan."

"Ok, Kromzan – why are catering manning comm's?"

"We're not, really. A lot of people took the nuke hard. Most of the comm's officers in this section had just rotated back on duty. They only just left their families down there. They've gone to help in the rescue."

"Nuke?"

"On Canthe! The blast!"

"Ah, that was no nuke, son. But you are point now, ok? The Canthe Empire needs you to step up. Are you good for it?"

There was a brief pause. "Yes."

"Ok. We need docking bays assigned. Half of our number will be in reserve for the evacuation of the ring, the rest will head for Canthe, so we need thirty-nine bays opening up immediately."

"Evacuating the ring... ?"

"Yes, it will be attacked. Have you guys not seen what's coming?" Op was incredulous.

"What can be worse than down there?" Kromzan's voice rose in mounting panic.

Op decided to ignore that, answering would only make matters worse. "Ok, just get the bays assigned please, now. Preferably ones not being used by the current rescue operations and as close to the larger populated areas as possible. We won't have much time."

There was a protracted silence.

"Now!"

"Ok!" Kromzan yelped. "I'll find the harbour master."

Op called up Phol. *Take half the Canthe Defence Fleet. Any vessels that can dive into the atmosphere or have shuttles are to head for the nearest city on the opposite side of Canthe from that blast-wave. Load up as many survivors as you can.*

537

Absolutely no cargo, no matter who they are, or what it is. If they want it that badly they can stay behind with it.

Affirmative. Can I take Rogers and Gomez?

Guys?

Fine by me, replied Rogers.

Whatever – here for the ride, said Gomez.

Ok. Go.

Phol arranged the fleet massing behind their small group of eight one-man fighters into groups that could or could not land on the surface. Thirty-two of the seventy-eight had the criteria, so Phol told them the plan for heading planet ward while Op took the remainder and made them ready for dock. Several ships were too big to enter the ring, despite the huge bays on offer, so they instructed them to ferry evacuees across by shuttle. It would be time-consuming and laborious.

Phol's mercy fleet began to pull away, heading for the city of Thoraz on the night-side of Canthe. It gave them the highest chance of rescuing survivors before the shockwave reached it.

Anyone between that point and the blast racing around the globe would have to provide their own means of escape.

"Captain She'as? This is Communications Officer Sted of the Canthe Orbital RIng. You wished to speak with me?"

"Officer Sted – how are you holding up?"

"Everyone is in shock."

"You?"

"I – Miraz was my home-town... my entire family lived there... I only left them this morning..."

Op left a respectful gap. "My sympathies, CO."

"I hope they aren't needed, Captain, but my thanks. For now, we live. Let us be useful. What do you need?"

"Do you have comm's to the surface?"

"None in the blast area."

"Outside?"

"We're still getting webcasts and pleas for help, but they are all slowly dropping off the network grid."

"Can they receive?"

"Most? I doubt it."

Op paused to think for a moment. "Can we jack into any public media networks?"

"Gov. Central has secured them all for emergency use."

"What are they broadcasting?"

"Some looped service message – nothing useful."

"Go figure. Ok, can you get someone to hack in?"

"Possibly."

"Do it. Here's what we are going to do..."

Chapter Thirty-six

The *Betsy* dropped out of g-drive six hundred thousand kilometres from the Canthe Orbital Ring. Within seconds Romurik was away under his own power, and headed for the nearest Cloud ships.

Brynn ordered the *Betsy* to maintain position and target as many Cloud vessels as possible. They had four mass driver rail-guns online, all forward-facing along the *Betsy's* principal axis, and a dangerously large stock of half-kilo anti-matter canisters in the automated breach-loaders which Venton and his team had rigged up. It meant the *Betsy* could effectively be run by her Intellect and no one else, although Brynn would never allow that. This was *his* ship, plain and simple.

He had forced his crew to remain on *INHS Capella*, although they were all mightily put out about it. Horstan and Andersten had refused his direct order, both stating that the mission was too vital to allow a sole, key man to jeopardise it. Besides, if the AM loaders needed seeing to, Brynn would be too busy with the ship. Brynn suspected some collaborative 'ganging up' there, but although he feigned anger, he was glad of the camaraderie. He had relented, hotly asserting he would note this mutinous action in their records. Andersten had merely shrugged.

Everyone failed to discuss the plan with the *Betsy* herself, and the fact she could quite easily run the entire mission profile on her own. She was mildly piqued by the exclusion.

Brynn was on the bridge. Horstan and Andersten

took the midsection on each half of the hull so they could cover the pair of rail-guns mounted on each side if the need arose. The AM canisters would be safe if the loaders jammed, but caution was paramount with such a volatile substance.

"Ready?" asked Brynn.

"Yep," replied Andersten.

"Yes, Captain," said Horstan.

They settled down to wait. It was up to Romurik now.

Romurik sped through the void, heading directly for the nearest enemy vessel. He still wanted a Shredder; he wanted to *see* the enemy.

He wanted to deal them pain.

***

Torz looked out to the horizon to take his mind off the scenes down below. He stood at the walled edge of the garden roof of Xeon Media, forty stories above the ground. His large, bear-like body loomed over the railing, short black fur ruffled by the wind. His keen eyesight clearly revealed people on the ground running and screaming. Looters – damn their worthless pelts – were ransacking the malls and dragging people from their vehicles, so they could use them to get away with the goods. They were the small minority of lesser Canthe, but enough to distract the Regiments into protecting property and citizens, instead of co-ordinating an evacuation.

He turned his huge head away from the

disappointing scenes below, and slowly made his way back down to the stream-plexer room. He knew the chaos as the Regiments tried to assert order was a waste of time. The broadcast stations were dropping off the grid in a clear pattern – a vast spreading circle of electronic darkness filled the wall display of online stations around the globe, centred near Oriz. The bandwidth being burned between the rest of the stations was phenomenal – unprecedented. No-one knew what was going on. Everyone was asking the same question – *what had happened?*

Torz had guessed. *Asteroid. But what to do?* Flee? Or don't bother. Either they were doomed no matter what, or perhaps the blast wouldn't get this far. Or should they hedge for the midline and *pray* they could escape? One could go mad just thinking about it.

As he entered a large room walled entirely with displays, his life partner, Sheran, was desperately flicking through the feeds trying to catch anything of use. But one by one all the public channels were going offline. Those still broadcasting were slowly being replaced by the Shield of Canthe, and some contextually asinine message from Government Central.

The broadcast station had emptied almost immediately after the panic started, with staff fleeing for their loved ones and homes. Word had come from the Orbital of some massive explosion over the eastern hemisphere. Details were scarce, truth scarcer still as rumour and speculation ran back and forth.

Torz and Sheran were fortunate in one respect. They were both orphans. He had everything he loved right here with him at work. Sheran was his logistics girl, whilst he ran the stations stream multiplexer hardware. After the initial shock and panic had worn off, Torz had grimly set Sheran to work finding out what she could about what had actually happened, whilst he had set about finding a way to get out of here.

There was a small Xeon Media SkyPod on the roof. He had the pass, stolen from the staff pool cabinet about half an hour ago. They could cut and run in moments, but he wanted to know *where* first.

He stared at the back of her head with a crinkle of a smile playing around his snout, watching as the short brown fur on the back of her broad neck kept rising and falling with her evident anxiety. She always did let her emotions play over her; he could read her like a book.

"Anything?"

"Nope," she snapped tersely. "Waffle, speculation, idiocy. The usual. Gov. C are helping by cutting out the chaff, but hindering with a total lack of help. Wait – what's this?"

With a swipe of a paw she flicked the display from her console onto the wall.

"– is to take whatever transport you have to hand and make for Thoraz Starport as soon as possible –"

"That's no Canthen..." wondered Torz, puzzled by the strange accent.

"Who cares? Let's go!"

"Wait!"

"– do *not* head for Oriz – it's gone. A blast wave is radiating out around Canthe from that location in all directions at eight hundred metres per second. As of 04:42 Canthe Standard the blast is fifteen minutes from the next largest metropolis of Poralz. *Make for Thoraz.*

Evacuation ships are grouping there at this moment. Repeating... This message is broadcast by Communication Officer Sted from the Canthe Orbital Ring. Canthe system is under attack by hostile forces. You *must* evacuate Canthe immediately. Your primary option is to take whatever transport..."

Torz's fur flattened with shock, as did Sherans.

"What do we do?" she asked in a small voice.

"Is this on any of our channels yet?"

"No. Only those blocked by GC."

"Patch me the feed... Xeon just got its last scoop. Let's tell *everyone*..."

Minor miracles were performed all over Canthe that fateful, terrible day. The elderly were rescued by the young, the young were rescued from schools en-masse – ferried into air-buses and air-coaches. The elderly gave up their places for young married couples, saying they had lived their lives and wanted to give the chance of life to those who had only just begun theirs. The young gave up their places for the infirm, vowing to find another transport.

It was un-coordinated chaos; no-one knew what to do, or where to go – only that they had to go *somewhere*, to do *something*.

Then the broadcast came, and displays across the globe started picking it up. People saw it, placed their displays in their windows with full volume for others to see and hear, then left however they could.

It was fortunate that personal transport technology on Canthe was advanced, and prolific. Many public services existed to fly passengers across the globe, or into space, in every city. Personal air transports were abundant and commonplace. Within hours a planet-wide flotilla of forty billion Canthen were flying toward one of their most ancient Imperial cities, which in itself was barely large enough for two-hundred thousand people.

Now it would become ordered chaos.

***

Romurik didn't even slow down. He ramped up a Category One cone-shaped field before him and simply dove directly into the command section of the heavy Canthen cruiser he had chosen.

The hull ruptured and split all around him, and the internal atmosphere screamed out into the void as he passed by. There were no life-signs on board, and he spilled his momentum to come to a stop near the middle of the ship, inside a large engineering bay. He saw the blood and gore splattered all over the deck and walls. It was fresh. The atmosphere kept venting – explosive decompression unchecked by the ships automatic systems. He pulled a small module from under his chest plate, and dropped it in mid-air. It floated away, unperturbed by the rush of screaming air around it, and clamped itself to the wall.

Part one, check.

A few seconds later he detected a faint whining noise over the scream of tortured air escaping the ship.

"Ah, here comes part two."

***

There is absolutely no way we can evacuate this many people. We need an evac fleet here ASAP, said Phol.

It won't happen, replied Op. *We have what we have. The Ring has forty thousand space-faring craft – we have to use anything that can get down there and get back up with a full load.*

Sted still thinks they are safe on the ring.

That's only a staging area. We need to get everyone off it as soon as possible. We can split the ships up into a planetary rescue fleet, and a fleet to evacuate the ring.

Very few of the rings ships can manage interstellar flight, Op, Phol said, having reviewed the ring's docking manifest.

But they can *manage flight. We get transponders on them and full-burn out on a single vector. If we can get them far enough away from the Cloud we can plead with Outreach to put some leverage into a humanitarian rescue mission.*

Do you think that will work? asked Rogers.

Right now, it's all we've got.

The nearest system is Solak, Canthen owned, Phol supplied.

That has to be at high risk of invasion, Op mused.

The nearest Imperial system is Replek, forty light years away.

I get the point Phol. We need a miracle. We can't bring Imperial vessels in, and we don't have the logistics to evac an entire planetary population. Suggestions welcome.

"What about the deep-drivers?" supplied Sted, finally daring to interject on the strange conversation that was being relayed to him.

The what?

"The la-grange point deep-drivers. They were our
546

first method of interstellar travel. We only maintain them for cargo and logistics trains now. But they can punch anything across interstellar space... the nearest one is set for Solak."

Op considered it. *Ok, everything that cannot go interstellar heads for this driver. At least that would buy some time, hopefully. How many of these drivers are there?*

"Twenty still operational, I think. Most are in the outer six though – too far for most of our passenger vessels."

Are there any limitations on how often the driver can operate, how heavy transports can be, etc?

"As long as it has energy, it can fire repeatedly. They've never been used like this though. Probably once every two minutes... though we'd need a tech to confirm that."

Find one. Now.

"Ok."

Won't a convoy of ships heading for one destination draw the enemy? Phol wondered.

Op considered it for a moment. *No idea. I don't think so. Their behaviour so far has been fairly ignorant of everything around them unless it gets in their way. We have little choice anyway. If need be we can provide a distraction.*

Great... said Rogers, wryly.

Any other plans are best brought up now. Once we commit to this – there's no going back. We can't redirect forty billion people on a whim if we change our minds.

There was a brief silence as the enormity of what they were about to commit the entire population of Canthe to sank in. No one had any alternatives to suggest.

Ok. Phol, I'll arrange a fleet from the Ring to gather above Thoraz under your command. I'll start evacuating the ring itself – general populace and non-essential staff first. Anyone not involved in the rescue effort is to leave, now.

***

Sheran stood staring at the distant horizon from the roof of Xeon Media, tears standing out from her eyes. "Torz, we have to leave – *now*."

Torz nodded without taking his eyes from the display before him as he hurriedly wrote stream routing code. "Just one more feed to change, then we're gone."

"Torz, *look*."

It was the note of despair in her voice that made him finally stop and glance up. The eastern sky had been getting darker over the past hour, as the upper atmosphere filled with clouds of ash. But now, underneath this dirty grey pall, the clouds straddling the eastern horizon were glowing a deep orange, as if from a false dawn. The wind was picking up, streaming steadily westward and growing stronger all the time.

As he watched, the skyline erupted in bright fire as far as the eye could see; the wave of destruction from the impact over Oriz was finally here. It had slowed dramatically – its energy dwindling as it expanded around the eastern hemisphere. But it was still surging toward them at thirty metres per second, and still unstoppable. It would be on top of the city within ten minutes.

"Ok, ok," he yelled. "Let's go!"

They were already on the roof of the Xeon building,

having patched into the station streams through the building's net. They had stashed what supplies they felt needed – water and foodstuffs raided from the vending machines. Although that didn't amount to much, there would be no need to worry as the SkyPod would see them at Thoraz inside two hours at full speed, well ahead of the blast – should it ever make it that far.

He stared into the east. The clouds above were already darker and the wall of fire was clearly larger and brighter than it had been minutes ago. They both jumped into the SkyPod and he launched it into the air. The winds were much stronger than he had expected, but the AI co-pilot corrected their trim easily and they set off.

Far below people were still scurrying around, most were raiding empty buildings and stores.

"What *are* they doing?" asked Sheran. "They should be gone! They'll die for certain!"

"Good riddance," muttered Torz darkly.

"Torz!" Sheran was shocked. "You *cannot* mean that!"

"Much," he grumbled. "Society doesn't need them. All they are thinking of is plundering someone else's life and wealth, not even caring for their *own* safety."

"Shouldn't we help?"

"And risk being hijacked, or killed? Why should others risk their own lives for someone who risks theirs just for theft?"

Sheran stared out through the transparent cockpit floor and pitied those below.

"Ok, hold on," he said. "Screw the Air Traffic Regs – I'm hitting full burn."

"Wait!"

"What now?"

"Down there! *Look!*"

On the street below, a small group of figures were hurrying away from a large mob, which had clearly surrounded and hijacked their ground vehicle and were now ransacking it, throwing possessions and luggage to each other as they yelled.

"It's a family! Two adults and two children! Torz!"

He gritted his teeth. "We won't be able to take them all!"

"*Torz!*"

Growling, he angled the SkyPod downward one street away from the fleeing family. He did *not* want the mob seeing that they had landed. The flyer's sensor fields had already reported being targeted by several masers – fortunately in the hands of imbeciles who had no clue how to use the stolen military hardware. The flyers impact shield might take one or two blasts, but he didn't want to find out.

He set down at the next intersection, ensuring he was out of sight from the mob and that there was no one else around.

They waited for the family who were hurrying along, shedding various baggage and toys as they fled. The two children were crying loudly – both still had their cub-fluff, neither old enough to understand why they were having their toys thrown away and getting upset by their parents rush and panic. Fortunately they weren't being followed by the mob itself.

As they neared the intersection, Torz edged the flyer forward so the family could see them. Unfortunately, one of the children – trying to be helpful – pointed and yelled "Look, Mommy!"

Someone in the mob behind them heard and cast a curious look, then shouted to the rest. A sizeable group split off and started to run toward them.

"Run!" Torz shouted at the family. "Drop everything!"

They did, the children wailing anew at this sudden change in tension. As they neared, Torz threw a look at Sheran – whose face showed that she already knew. The father was a huge lump of a bear; two metres tall and nearly as round. The flyer wouldn't cope with that amount of extra weight.

"Thank the Maker!" he gasped as they staggered to a halt, barely able to speak. "Please, say you can take us!"

Torz hesitated, staring him directly in the eyes, then he nodded. The man looked puzzled by Torz's expression for a second, then his large eyes flicked over the flyer and his face changed as he suddenly understood. Strangely he seemed to relax.

"We can take your family, but not *you* my friend," Torz said softly. "I'm sorry."

"*What?*" exclaimed his wife, eyes wide with horror. "You must!"

"Jenthra," said the huge bear in a voice that would brook no argument. "Get in. Urstin, Sheema – you too. In the back there, go on."

Sheran helped pull the two crying children into the rear passenger seats.

The mother of the two cubs held back, clearly dumbstruck by what was happening. "Horthaz! No! We all go! You *promised!*"

"Jenthra – if I never ask you to do anything again, please do as I say just this *once*. Get *in*." He turned to look at the crowd drawing nearer, then looked to Torz, and nodded.

Torz saw the steel in his eyes, and put his paw out of the window to clasp Horthaz's tightly in a gesture of profound respect. Then he looked to the mob – *if one of those idiots has a hand maser...*

Horthaz leaned down and kissed Jenthra full on the snout, then lifted her bodily into the flyer and slammed the door shut. Torz locked it immediately.

"No!" Jenthra yanked at the handle. She turned to Torz. "*You* get out! Please!" She turned to Sheran. "We have a family, you don't – *please* – I beg you!"

Sheran had tears in her eyes.

"Jenthra!" Horthaz roared from outside. "Be *quiet!* You are better than that! I could not fly this thing anyway. Leave these kind folk alone, they came to help!"

He stepped away from the flyer and gave a military salute to Torz, who instantly realised Horthaz was lying. He was ex-military... he would be able to fly this civilian craft with his eyes closed.

He saluted back as best he could, and then without hesitation lifted the flyer off the ground before the mob got close enough to start throwing things, or worse – shooting.

"Jen – you always said I was eating my way to death! Goodbye, my loves! I will find you if I can!"

"*HORTHAZ!*" Jenthra wailed. Her heart seemed to pour out from her chest and into her voice.

Sheran sobbed out loud, unable to contain her compassion.

Torz saw Horthaz turn on the mob as it neared him, and saw him punch his palm. There was no time for him to try and run, even if he had the energy. The crowd closed in on him, and Torz pulled the flyer away behind a building before his family could see what was to happen.

He mentally blocked out the heart-rending sobs from behind him, and from Sheran – Maker bless her. He brought the engines up to full capacity as they cleared the lower pedestrianised walkways and cross-bridges between the buildings.

"Everyone hold tight!"

The flyer shot forward to Mach one, pressing them all back into their seates despite the dampening fields best efforts. Then he kept pushing the engines all the way to Mach seven – leaving Horthaz, the mob, and the city far behind, with the burning horizon chasing their wake. Sonic booms from their passage shattered the windows behind them, causing a trail of untold damage. But it mattered not. The city was flattened by the blast minutes later. Skyscrapers fell like kindling despite their strength, the raging wall of fire burned the rubble, and the earthquake's which followed shattered the ground and tossed the charred remains around as if they were merely broken toys.

Chapter Thirty-seven

The Mind catalogued the resources which it had now acquired. Several gas harvesting acquisitions were scheduled, and some odd artefacts occupied numerous la-grange points across the twelve planets and their various satellites. As yet, it could determine no purpose to them – but monitored them for behavioural changes, as they seemed to hold substantial energy systems. The nearest two were selected for dismantling, for resources and further analysis.

It examined the partially built Orbital Ring around the largest inhabited world. It appeared to be functioning and generating a substantial electronic presence in subspace, but nothing on the intellectual scale of the Imperial Station which it had briefly acquired. Sequestration would yield nothing of value. The Mind cared nothing for additional data stores, or sensors which were far inferior to its own prolific and advanced capabilities.

The subspace Damper had been firmly established on the surface as part of its enforcement protocol, and ready to commence operation. However, it would be several minutes yet before it could synchronise with the nearest Damper, over forty light-years away.

It scheduled the Orbital Ring for dismantling and assigned a harvest group, then moved on to other matters. Thus far, establishing a foothold in this region of space was proceeding to plan.

***

Romurik held a Shredder at arm's length before him, wrapped up in a class two containment field. It was a struggle. Andersten had been right – these things were incredibly powerful.

So far, he had destroyed eight of the things. This ninth was putting up a fight, but he seemed to have the knack now.

He stared deep into the core of the thing. He really hoped something was staring back.

The small device which had earlier clamped itself onto the wall, popped free and floated back toward him, flashing a green light. It got to within a metre and then dropped to the floor, powering off completely. Since building it, he had not communicated with it at all. It was a completely isolated device with a specific purpose: analysis.

Part four was complete ahead of schedule. Part three had been delayed thanks to the persistence of the Shredders he'd had to take down so far, but that too was now complete.

Now, how to proceed with part five...

***

Deep inside the Damper, at the very heart of the mega-structure, the softly glowing golden core began closing – ramping up the energy it would need to generate its first subspace pulse in the Canthe system.

***

Op was closely monitoring the tactical displays they had managed to cobble together from their own seeded micro-satellites around Canthe, along with the Orbital Ring's own vast array of planet-facing sensors and cameras.

The leeward side of the planet was now covered by an artificial cloud made from every flight-capable ship at the survivors disposal. The cloud of contacts was slowly converging on Thoraz, with the trailing edges now racing well ahead of the blast wave, which crept slowly along behind.

The wave of destruction had slowed further still over the last hour, less than twenty metres per second and falling rapidly as its momentum collapsed. Its volume increased dramatically with every metre of ground it gained, dissipating the energy of the impact across an ever growing volume of atmosphere.

It seemed the initial destruction would soon cease, leaving two-thirds of the planet unaffected. The devastation was on a lesser scale than that which had befallen S'ren. But still the earthquakes and atmospheric holocaust would soon engulf the rest of Canthe, leaving it a dangerous and hostile world. No one could stay behind safely, especially with the Cloud undoubtedly readying itself to plunder the surface for whatever purpose it had.

Op, said Hendricks. *There's a massive energy spike building in the thing that smashed into Canthe.*

Op looked at the globe display in his mind as Hendricks fed the info in.

What in creation is that? Op murmured softly.

The spike suddenly leapt upward as the energy

556

reading escalated a thousand-fold. Then it flickered three times as radial spikes of energy scattered across the area the agitator occupied.

This can't be good! Op yelled.

Subspace literally wobbled – there was no other way to perceive it – perturbed by the colossal energy release from Damper. Two more pulses of energy flowed into subspace, and then the Damper lapsed into its maintenance mode – its work done for the next twelve and a half hours.

A deliberate side-effect of this energy discharge was an incredibly strong electromagnetic pulse, which raced outward through subspace at nearly the speed of light.

We just lost all the satellites over ground zero! exclaimed Hendricks.

Op stared in dismay at the panorama of feeds in his e-vision. *The ring is going dark! Everything is going down! We're losing all feeds, comm's, sensors, life support!*

"Oh *shit*," Hendricks yelled out loud. "EMP!"

"None of our civilian equipment is guarded against EMP!" yelled Sted in panic. Then the comm's channel dropped as power blacked out in his section of the ring.

"The evacuation fleet! Look!" Sted cried, oblivious to the loss in communications. "*Oh, the Maker...*"

Op watched the tactical. The cloud of evacuee's would still be safe, as they would be in the shadow of the EMP blast, which would be blocked by the planet itself. But then the impossible happened – the fleeing craft started dropping back down to the surface like stones.

***

Everything in the flyer suddenly went dead.

Torz stared incredulously. "We just lost power..."

"Mommy! I can't see!"

"What the –"

Torz battered at the controls futilely. Everything was gone. No readings, no drive, no backups. They were travelling at seven times the speed of sound, with no power, autopilot or controls. All he had was manual control over the flight-control surfaces, which fought back stoically without power assist.

"Where's the manual air-brake?" he yelled desperately.

Both he and Sheran frantically searched the console, then under the cockpit seats. Torz finally found the emergency air-brakes. He prayed their tolerance was up to it, and pulled the lever as hard as he could. It was stuck solid. He tried again and it gave a little. It was a pump system. As the lever freed he started hammering it up and down and the air-brake panels cracked open all over the flight surfaces, sending a screaming vibration through the entire fuselage.

They began to slow, but they also began to roll as one of the brake panels had jammed shut.

He took hold of the controls again and fought to correct their trim.

"We need to land in water!" he yelled at Sheran over the screaming wind. With the loss of the slipstream field, the flyer was left to its own devices and aerodynamics, and was barely able to sustain a smooth profile against

Mach seven winds.

She nodded, eyes wide with fright, and she started scanning the landscape as it rushed past far below.

The flyer was designed for total power loss, although it was unheard of outside of training flights. Fortunately Torz had an advanced flight license and knew exactly what to do. He'd just never had to do it.

Their air speed was dropping fast now. He'd have to reduce the brake soon to stop them stalling and falling out of the sky like a rock. The flyer was very capable of gliding, but she was fairly heavy on the aerofoils right now due to their extra load.

All around them, the huge flock of other evacuees they had joined were having the same difficulties – total power loss. Many were already plummeting to the ground, completely out of control.

Something hit us all *in one go,* he realised. *Some kind of jamming equipment?*

He managed to right the flyer and get it onto a glide path. Sheran stabbed a finger outward at the distant horizon; a shimmering patch of silvery light from a lake was rushing toward them.

Torz nodded once curtly. "Ok, hold tight!"

He gently brought the flyer on a bearing for the lake, and held the air-brake handle tightly in one hand.

If I get this wrong, he thought, *we're going to wish we'd stayed where we were...*

Halfway to the lake, as he guessed it, he rotated the handle half a turn and started slowly pumping the air-brakes back down and level to the flight surfaces – but not all the way. They were dropping fast now, barely a thousand metres above the streaming landscape. The lake wasn't very big, about two kilometres at its widest, and they would be cutting across its narrowest point. He judged the moment as well as he could and dropped the brakes all the way off, angling the flyer slightly downward. He *really* hoped the crash foam still deployed mechanically in these models, and not electronically.

All around them flyers and air coaches were aiming for the same lake, several others trying to touch down on land. Far too many were falling like stones, spiralling out of control. Far too many more had already smashed into the ground, killing everyone on board instantly.

"Get ready! We're about to hit!"

***

Admiral! We have *to bring the navy in – otherwise everyone on Canthe will be lost!*

Op, we cannot *risk more Imperial forces. We're going to need everything we can get to defend against this threat. I'm afraid Canthe is already lost.*

Can you get me anything? *What about the Mayfleet craft from the Velari migration?*

Negative. We'd have to unload all the Velari first otherwise we'd have another war to deal with. Besides – again we can't risk the ships.

Admiral, we are not *going to be remembered well for this.*

Do what you can, Admiral Cole *replied. I will do what I can, but I can promise nothing I'm afraid. Diplomatically this is not the Empire's problem, even though the Canthen are a petitioning candidate. Offering a mercy fleet is out of the question due to the Cloud. I'll try to contact you if anything changes. For now, I'm afraid you are the best hope the Canthe have of making it through this.*

***

Torz aimed the aerodynamic fuselage into the water perfectly. Though he had no way of knowing, they cut the surface of the lake at one hundred and fifty kilometres an hour, diving deep into its waters before the flyer's internal buoyancy had any noticeable effect at slowing their dive.

The hull was solid and airtight – built for inter-orbital flight, although it didn't have the thrust to mass ratio for breaking Canthe's 1.1g itself. It was able to withstand the impact easily.

The occupants were less able to, and fortunately the crash foam bloomed out of the cockpit on impact and filled everywhere with large, transparent, fire retardant plyolastic bubbles – which rubberised almost instantly, squashing faces and limbs but allowing them to breathe and still see what was happening. They all groaned under the high-g deceleration, their lungs emptying and their organs compressing inside their bodies. One of the children threw up, the acids instantly bursting the bubbles near her mouth so she wouldn't choke.

The cockpit went black as night in the lake's murky depths, and over their laboured breathing the two children could be heard whimpering quietly.

They felt their descent begin to slow, and then just as slowly they began to ascend. They picked up speed and the murk receded in the green tinged glow from far above. The flyer broke the surface in a rush, and

561

bounced around before settling on the waves, inducing more vomiting from the children.

Torz turned to Sheran, the fur on his face squeaking along the surface of a bubble. She had her eyes tightly closed.

They waited a few minutes in silence and then the bubbles began to shrink and wrinkle, rupturing and deflating in a carefully controlled chemical reaction with the air. Seconds later they were all free with only a small amount of sticky powder clinging here and there on their fur.

Torz grabbed Sheran's paw and squeezed it tight. She opened her eyes and gave him a grateful look.

"We made it," he said softly.

He turned behind him, and saw Jenthra's tear-streaked face nestling against her daughters head.

"She's blind," she said, her voice thick with emotion.

Torz shook his head, confused.

"She has implants, so that she can see. They've stopped working."

Torz frowned. "I see," he said. Then regretted he'd said that. "Sorry, I meant –"

"It's all right," she said wearily. "I'm the one who should be sorry, for what I said, I... Horthaz is... he was my life. I didn't mean what I said. You have saved my family, and I honour you with all I have left. Thank you."

Torz turned away quickly. "Anyone would have done the same. I'm sorry we couldn't bring Horthaz, but this thing just didn't have the lift."

Sheran saw tears welling in his eyes, and then looked away to let him recover his pride.

"What do we do now?" she asked quietly.

Torz cleared his throat. "Get to land. I guess we either swim, or paddle. Can everyone swim?"

"I think this is Gremwen Lake," said Jenthra.

"Ah," Torz sighed. Gremwen Lake was one of the few remaining water bodies harbouring freshwater Vemren – voracious, carnivorous eel, almost a metre long. "Then we paddle."

He looked around the cramped cabin for a few moments, then broke the backs off the pilot and co-pilot seats. They were made of a light fibre-plastic, strong and flexible, and would be ideal makeshift paddles. He and Sheran smashed their door windows with small emergency hammers and began paddling in the water lapping at the sides. The flyer was clearly not supposed to function as a boat – though it was designed to float in emergency water landings, it was not designed to move through water under its own power. It was riding low, with all its lower aerofoils well below the water line. This increased its stability in the choppy water, but also increased the drag. It was hard going.

There was a thump behind them and Torz turned to see Jenthra kicking at her window in attempt to join their efforts. He half smiled.

"Don't worry – we'd be uneven, and end up going around in circles. But thanks."

"Ah," she said, sounding abashed.

He smiled ruefully. "Really, it's ok. You have your hands full already." He nodded at her two children, who were looking frightened and tired at her side.

She nodded her thanks and drew them nearer to her. Torz heard one of the cubs ask quietly, "Where's Pops?"

They managed to turn about well enough to line up on the nearest shore and started the slow trek toward it.

All around them, aircraft of various sizes and types plummeted into the water, some more safely than others. They had to watch helplessly as several were smashed into pieces on impact, their momentum dragging the shattered people inside deep down into the lake itself – mercifully concealing their grisly deaths.

"I hope none of these land on us," Torz whispered to Sheran.

She didn't want to think about it.

A huge air-coach screamed past overhead, upside down and rolling wildly. Sheran saw desperate faces at the windows as it sped past, then it dove deep into the water five hundred metres ahead of them.

Torz held his breath as they waited for it to rise to the surface, but seconds later there was a huge up swell and eruption of air, water, and worse as the coach exploded far below.

They paddled on, and Torz set his mouth into a tight line. Their course meant they would now have to paddle through the remains bobbing to the surface.

***

Phol watched in dismay as the group of rescue ships rising from far below suddenly broke apart and began falling canthe-ward.

He had a fleet of around a thousand space-worthy ships in as low an orbit as they dared, waiting for the first wave of ferrying craft to bring evacuee's up to them.

But before they could break the atmosphere, the

564

invisible EMP struck – carried directly through the planet via subspace, the pulses which perturbed the fabric of reality manifested themselves as an incredibly strong wave of electromagnetic energy.

All of the non-military vessels simply lost drive and power, and began to slow as Canthe's gravitational pull regained its claim on their mass. The shielded military vessels amongst them suddenly found themselves having to dodge those falling back toward the surface. Worse still, as the EMP coursed through subspace and hit the ships under Phol's command, all the non-military vessels – some extremely sizeable – began to fail and fall back to the surface themselves. They had been forced to maintain position under drive in order to get as close as possible to the surface and the evacuation. Without power, they simply fell into the sky. Now those ships below which had been avoiding stalled ships from their own group had to evade much larger star ships and passenger liners from above as they began their slow descent to a certain doom.

Escape capsules shot out from numerous falling vessels. They required manual release in order to initiate the eject, but this left them entirely dead in space with no control or power to gain safety. EMP shielding had not been factored into their design as escape capsules. The lucky ones might survive re-entry, but with no shields and no life support, most would freeze to death long before they hit the atmosphere.

Their entire comm's network went down, silenced by the EMP. Only Op's team could still communicate via the qNet.

What in creation was that? demanded Gomez.

EMP, replied Phol. *But from where? I saw no blast!*

Phol, Gomez, Rogers – pull the fleet out! shouted Op. *There's an EMP travelling through subspace. I've no idea how, but it –*

Op cut off in mid-sentence.

Op? asked Phol. Then the unthinkable happened, his bonded qSpinner returned an error code, something unheard of. *Gomez? Rogers?*

The qNet wasn't silent – it simply wasn't there. Phol felt his blood freeze. He targeted Gomez's ship with a comm-laser.

"Gomez?"

"Here. What the hell just happened?"

"We lost the qNet – don't ask how because I don't know. Hit Rogers with a comm-laser, set up a network."

"Should I ask what just happened?" asked Rogers a second later.

"No," said Phol. "We've lost the qNet, and an EMP has wiped out all unprotected electronics."

"Where from? There's been no detonations nearby!"

"Op said something about it travelling through subspace."

"Is that even possible? What can we do?"

"Pray? Look – none of them stand a chance."

Phol and his small team watched as over half their flotilla fell downward on their inexorable and unstoppable plummet to the surface below. Some were already starting to burn up on entry, unprotected by shields and with no way to regain control to align for a smoother descent into the atmosphere. If their hulls couldn't withstand the heat, they would perish long before impact.

"Thoraz is doomed," Rogers said emotionlessly. "And we've just directed every living thing on the planet that can fly right into a death trap."

"What do you mean?" asked Gomez.

"Look at the size of these mothers falling straight down. We're directly above the city."

"It'll be like an aerial bombardment," said Phol quietly. "Every ship is going to hit the city or within its perimeter... most of these will wipe out tens of city blocks just on their own."

"What can we do?"

Phol shook his head. "Nothing. We just lost our only chance to save sixty-billion people."

Chapter Thirty-eight

Nelsen stared.

Although he was familiar with clones, replicas and proxies – such things were common throughout the Empire – this was still unbelievable. He knew everything about Andreya was odd – her fake persona, her replica nature, her incredible power, and the mental anguish she suffered not knowing who or even what she was. Everything screamed "stay away" – and yet he hadn't. He had done the exact opposite.

Inside the sarcophagus was an answer, or perhaps another riddle, to the enigma that was Andreya.

Another replica? Or the original *Andreya?* he wondered. *She must have been here for thousands of years.*

He shuddered. *Sneak, can you see this?*

Yes, Captain, she replied quietly. Nelsen had been sharing what he saw with her since leaving the ship.

Andreya turned to him, with a horrified expression on her face. The look of someone who had no idea where they were, or who they were. Someone who had just lost their soul.

She turned back and slid her hand over the cover, dislodging a cloud of fine, dark dust which dispersed slowly into the vacuum, sparkling in the rippling silvery light. Then she dropped her hand down to a panel at the side of the sarcophagus and flipped it open.

"No, wait!" said Nelsen urgently, realising what she was about to do, but too late.

She tapped in a short sequence, and closed the panel.

"What did you do?" Nelsen asked, though he could

guess. "And how did you know what to do? Why am I even *asking* that...?"

A soft blue glow lit up the inside of the sarcophagus, and a faint vibration began shaking the dusting of ash from the cover – ash deposited from internal ship fires wrought by damage caused long ago. It spread out into the airless room, drifting in zero g.

Inside, Andreya's double opened her eyes, and looked up at them both. Nelsen couldn't help but take an apprehensive step back. He wound up his defensive shields and armament. Although if this double had the same power that Andreya had he didn't fancy his chances.

The cover slid back into the wall, and the double sat up. Nelsen slowly raised an arm, ready to fire. Then the double did something so normal, so human, so *every day* that it made Nelsen dizzy with how surreal it was.

She yawned, and then stretched out her arms like someone just waking up from a nap. Just as Andreya had done, a few hours and a lifetime ago.

She cocked her head to one side and spoke to Andreya, but no words came out in the vacuum. The double rolled her eyes as she realised.

Hello, Andreya, she said on the *Sneak's* l-net.

Hello, Andreya answered slowly, as if sedated.

Is this some kind of party line? Nelsen heard the *Sneak* snap quietly.

Sorry, Sneak, said the double. *It's just convenient given the lack of air. Hope you don't mind.*

Oh, I mind all right. Who are *you?*

My name is Merel, if that helps.

Nelsen looked closer. The voice was the same, but

569

different – subtle intonations and inflexions set it aside from Andreya's voice. Her face was also slightly different, now that he looked closer. Not in the way twins can be identical yet vary slightly – but as two identical statues had altered over time, worn into something new by their environments.

Merel reached out and placed a hand on Andreya's shoulder, and Andreya jolted. Nelsen stepped forward and ramped up his fire-field to blast Merel to ash, but she raised a placating hand – as did Andreya.

What's going on? he demanded, nerves raw.

I'm fine, Andreya said, giving him a faint smile. *Merel was just... updating me.*

What?

And she was updating me, supplied Merel. *It's a bit complicated I'm afraid, Captain Nelsen Rybek – of the Sulranian Imperial Navy, currently commanding the* INSV Sneak Thief.

He was dumbfounded yet again. Then he realised they had obviously networked and shared everything through that single touch.

Yes, he managed. *And you are?*

Merel smiled. *I've lost count of how many times I've been asked that question. I am unimportant. But I've been cooped up here for... far too long it seems. I see things have progressed during my absence.*

Nelsen frowned. *Are you responsible for this fleet?*

Merel gave him a strange look, and then glanced around the room as if seeing directly out through the hull and into the vast cloud of vessels outside. *In a way,* she said.

What are your intentions for it?

I have none. It's not mine to command.

You just said -

I neither own, nor control this fleet. Nor will I. Ever.

Nelsen bit his lip in frustration.

So who does?

Ah. That is a short question with a very long answer.

Look, I don't have time for games, Nelsen grated, patience finally worn thin. *Andreya said this ship could help. We have to inform the Empire that an* unimaginably *huge fleet is about to attack. Our only hope is to save as many as we can before we are wiped out. Can. You. Help?* He ground out each word.

Merel looked at him with her head tilted on one side. *I can see why you are so attracted to him,* she said to Andreya, who – unbelievably – blushed.

Yes, Captain, Merel replied. *I can help.* For dramatic effect, she clapped her hands together – astonishing Nelsen momentarily as he actually *heard* it. The lights glowed on, and the room began to power up. Air was already streaming in from the vents and power rumbled across the ship – crackling through conduits and energy interchanges, spinning up motors and engines, sealing doors shut, and warming up life support. An artificial gravity slowly took over, pulling them to the floor softly until they stood under a comfortable two thirds g.

"Better?" asked Merel.

Nelsen nodded politely – but could not help keep the dark, distrusting look from his face. Merel laughed softly at his expression.

"Yes, Captain Rybek – I *can* help you. Because *you* have helped me. Although I would anyway, I'm that kind of gal."

Nelsen shook his head, confused. The meaning was lost on him.

"You came here seeking, answers I guess," she continued. "Well, tough – I won't give them to you. I can, but *none* of you are ready yet, and those answers would kick off the kind of unholy mess I don't want to be in responsible for fixing. And no, the thought running through that cunning head of yours won't work either. Nothing *you* can do could force me. And I *really* mean that... *nothing*. I've seen more shit in my lifetime than you can possibly imagine. I'm *immune* to coercion, threats or blackmail – understand?"

Nelsen just stared again. He felt like a six year old being scolded by the year-head. He nodded mutely.

"I *really* hope so," said Merel. "Hopefully Andreya here can convince you if you change your mind. I have to say, so far everything has worked out rather well. I'm amazed that both plans came to fruition... and even joined forces."

"What do you mean?"

"Andreya here was supposed to find me. But if she failed, I had a backup plan lodged within the Empire to locate me."

Nelsen's eyes widened. "You *planted* the mission to locate the *Terrania* into *INI?*" he asked incredulously.

"When they achieved the technology to do so, yes." Merel smiled, then she rubbed her hands together. "Right – a long time dead, so to speak. Time to get down to some business." She looked around her, eyes unfocused as she stared far beyond the hull. "What *exactly* do we have here...?"

Nelsen looked at Andreya, who merely shrugged.

The look of joy she had worn before coming into the cloud was gone. Her expression was resigned, almost sorrowful. This was clearly just another riddle providing no answer to her situation.

Merel's eyes went wide as she catalogued all of the contacts around them. "My they *have* been busy. You were daring in the extreme to get this far."

She turned to Nelsen. "I guess that deserves some tidbits... I've been here a *long* time Captain. In a way. This physical form is not like Andreya – *she* is a very sophisticated biological construct. The best I've ever created in fact, whereas I'm entirely artificial. A long time ago, though mere moments for me physically, I was being... pursued. My only choice in the end was to shut down my physical form. The key to dealing with the Draco Source is to not have *anything* electrical running – at least anything connected to another processing device. It can take it over in a snap. Right now, we're pinging away in subspace like a beacon. Fortunately all the noise around us as these ships power up is masking us, but not for long. So we have to get going. Questions? Not that I'll answer probably..."

"How long have you been here?"

Merel pursed her lips – judging whether to respond. The *Sneak* lurking in the bay had probably ran intensive metallurgical scans already anyway.

"Six thousand years give or take a decade. Sol standard. Imperial standard you call it now."

"Sol?"

"Long story."

"Draco Source?"

Merel frowned. "You don't know who you are

573

dealing with?" She looked at Andreya, who just shrugged.

"You know I have no information, and nothing so far has shown us," said Nelsen tersely.

Merel turned to him. "Shit, boy. You have some work to do."

Nelsen bristled at the barbed insult. "Draco?"

"An engineered race, I won't tell you more. Do your job and find out. But they are *very* determined, as you can see." She waved her arm around to encompass space outside and the countless ships around them.

"We haven't *seen* them yet."

Merel frowned again. "What? That's not like them at *all*. They like to rub your face in their genetic perfection." Accessing her own internal sensor vision, she looked out at the Cloud again for a few seconds and then raised her eyebrows.

"Ok, now that *is* interesting." All the vessels in the mega-cloud were lifeless. She paused a moment as went on to scan subspace and saw the Mind for the first time in millennia. She had to admit, it was impressive. It had clearly grown since their last encounter. She managed to avoid its sweeping gaze as it clawed its way through subspace like some half-crippled animal, desperate to survive by capturing any kind of prey. This local aspect was primarily looking to manage this fleet and locate an intruder, which she guessed rightly was her erstwhile rescuers. They hadn't been found yet, and that gave them a small advantage. She noted the perimeter of ships already powered up and targeting the *Terrania* with all weapons.

"What do they want?"

Merel slowly brought her gaze back down to meet Nelsen's, and her expression became a look of such profound regret and sadness that he almost felt pity for her.

"They want us to return," she said softly.

"Who is 'us'?"

She smiled then. "Now we're back to no-answers-land."

"Damn you woman! There are sixty *trillion* lives at stake here! An entire *Empire* is going to fall before this... this... *tsunami* of death! They don't *care* about life, or anything that gets in the way! All you need to do is tell us what we *can* do!"

She gave a sad smile. "Pray. And run. At the same time." Her face hardened into a mask of steely determination as she came to a decision. "Which is what we must do right now. Get in the sarcophagus."

Nelsen was taken aback by the sudden change in direction. "Sorry?"

"Get in. It's the only way you will survive this trip."

Nelsen's eyebrows arched high on his forehead. "What trip? I'm not getting in anything."

Merel's eyes bored into his. "You want to warn your Empire? And I want to get the hell out of here. *Now*. I didn't spend the last six millennia in stasis avoiding the Draco just to get captured by them the minute I wake up. *Get in*."

"But –"

Andreya put her hand on his forearm with a reassuring smile. "It's ok, I would never ask you to do something like this if it wasn't safe – or necessary."

He hesitated – was he being played? Merel was

575

clearly an Intellect... had this creature reclaimed the fragment of her personality present in Andreya, and now the woman he had taken into his arms was gone? Now merely a reflection of someone else? The thought brought a painful tear to his eye, surprising even himself.

Andreya smiled even more warmly then, and reached out to wipe the tear away. Nelsen registered somewhere at the back of his mind that she had just reached effortlessly through a class two defensive field.

"Trust me, it's the only way."

Sneak? he asked, hoping for a detached voice of reason on what to do.

I can't help, Captain... I can't see what they would gain by being 'sneaky' as it were. Merel could just do as she pleases anyway, by the sound of it.

So I could, said Merel, jumping effortlessly into their private, secure channel.

Oh for Sanat's sake, said the *Sneak* peevishly. It was the first time Nelsen had ever heard her curse.

Look can we get a move on here? Merel demanded. *You've got about seventy seconds before the Draco come down on us like a ton of bricks, so fifty before I fire up the* Terrania's *Breach generator and therefore forty-nine before your central nervous system and neural mush you call a brain stop working. This ship leaves* with *or* without *you.*

"Get. In. The. Sarcophagus," she said out loud, snapping out each word and scowling at him fiercely.

It seemed he had no choice. He really hoped he knew what he was doing. He climbed in.

"*Finally*," said Merel, staring right through him as she concentrated on preparing the *Terrania* for its first flight in six thousand years.

The cover slid forward and sealed him in.

"What about you?" he asked Andreya.

"I'll be fine," she said, as she flipped the panel once more and tapped in an activation code.

She stared directly into his eyes with such a look of warmth and gratitude, yet mixed with sorrow, that it made his heart ache. There were tears in her eyes.

"Goodbye, Nelsen," she said. He stiffened. The *way* she said it, he knew it was *really* a goodbye… a last goodbye.

"N–" was all he managed to say before a soft blue glow filled his vision.

Merel charged up the *Terrania's* Breach generator, and then dropped full power to the Linear Displacement Drive. There was no time for subtlety now. The heavily radiation eroded structure of the *Terrania* groaned under the stress, as its bulk began to move directly toward the largest of the nearby ships.

As soon as the *Terrania's* internal energy grid lit up subspace, confirming an electrical presence, the nearby cloud vessels – including the one she was headed for – opened fire.

Merel knew the Mind would obliterate the *Terrania* sooner than let her escape again. They had only a few seconds to achieve enough velocity and gain a decent Breach transit distance.

The *Terrania's* shield had been first-class in its day, but even so it would not last long against the concentrated firepower of thousands of far more powerful and up-to-date ships. It began overloading within seconds of the onslaught, and then energy began to spill past and burn deep into the already damaged hull.

An electric white fire joined the fierce glare of evaporating metal, crawling all over the *Terrania* as her Breach generator reached potential.

Just a few more seconds, Merel thought. Andreya watched passively as her fate loomed closer; one hand lay on the cover above the statue-like, frozen form of Nelsen.

It was sadly the only working sarcophagus on board. She had already told Merel that Nelsen was to be saved above all else during that first touch. Merel had accepted her wishes, and sadly said goodbye there and then. Andreya knew what would happen as soon as the Breach generator engaged, she knew the consequences. It was one of the biggest problems with Breach transits that mankind had never managed to overcome, despite millennia of trying.

They were almost about to collide directly with the huge Draco vessel as it blazed away at their forward shield, when a breach in space-time erupted around the *Terrania* with a blinding nuclear flash, inflicting heavy damage on the larger, unprepared vessel.

When the blaze of energy faded, the *Terrania* had gone.

The *Terrania* emerged in a crackling burst of white fire within the Sulran System a mere nine minutes after leaving the mega-cloud. well over eighteen hundred light-years away. Merel had pushed the decaying superstructure through six consecutive Breach transits, gaining momentum each time to produce larger and larger jumps across real space. Her hull was too far gone to withstand the stress of so many Breaches, and many sections which had spent millennia exposed to harsh solar radiation simply broke off. The entire port side outer skin – having taken the brunt of the punishing winds of a binary star for six thousand years – crumbled and flaked away, exposing the superstructure and her interior decks to vacuum. Her gravity and inertial fields barely managed to hold the contents of each compartment in place, leaving the dark empty rooms plainly visible from space.

Already Merel could hear the various warning systems throughout Sulran raising the intruder alarm – they would be responding within seconds. Emerging into the home-system of the Sulranian Empire was a deliberate slap-in-the-face wake up call, which she hoped Nelsen would appreciate at some point. He wanted the Empire to be warned as soon as possible, so she granted his wish. But, now she would have to act fast.

She turned to find Andreya collapsed in an ungainly heap on the floor, next to the sarcophagus, completely dead. All her bio-electrical activity had been wiped by crossing the Breach. Only stasis allowed organic material to cross over and remain functional afterward. She sighed and walked over to her doppelganger, and gently set her straight in a sitting position.

She opened the sarcophagus without taking the stasis field down, and oblivious to the temporal field holding his inert form, she reached in to touch Nelsen's inert neck. She left a single nanite there on his skin, ready to burrow its way into his own copious nano-woven integrations when he awoke, then closed the sarcophagus again. His own systems would have no clue as to the intrusion.

What to do? she asked herself. The *Sneak* was offline at the moment. The physical connection which Merel had created into her systems through the *Sneak's* docking clamp had allowed her to effectively pause the *Sneak* in mid-run state without her even knowing. It was quite rude, and an unforgivable transgression for any self-respecting Intellect, but it had been necessary at the time. One thing Merel had always excelled at was doing whatever was 'necessary at the time'.

She had interacted with the *Sneak* before, reading all her specs, systems and knowledge whilst in stasis. From 'Within', she chose to call it. Overpowering her after that was trivial.

Merel had been laying her plans for a long, long time, preparing for her eventual return to physical reality. Being forced to place her physical body into stasis had been a major inconvenience. The Draco had clearly located her ship, but being unable to detect her body in suspension – as she had hoped – they had failed to realise they had finally found *her*. Although the Velari had passed by long ago on a migration, they had unwittingly stumbled into a Draco cordon around her ship and fled in terror. She was amazed the *Terrania* had not been recycled by the Draco, accidentally destroying her physical body without knowing it was there. For some reason she was determined to fathom, they had chosen to leave the *Terrania* intact and wait.

From Within, she had spent the intervening years as

an Observer, and 'meddling' as she put it. The Andreya replicas were part of that meddling – although if the Observers themselves ever found out what she had been doing, it would not go down very well at all. Each had been a unique entity, independent in its own right, but ultimately a facet of her own persona. Bound by a promise made long ago, she could not return to normal physical reality unless it was in her original form, although that didn't stop her bending the rules, as ever.

There was still much to be done.

What next? she mused.

There was nothing she would do now to maintain those facets – despite the embryonic relationship with Nelsen. Now she had to consolidate her efforts more than ever before. Running facets across space-time was not a trivial undertaking. This particular relationship had to end, as all did. Better now than later, before it became something deeper and more painful to break.

She had made sure Andreya understood her purpose and function deep down inside when she had been created, so that when the time came she would be prepared. For cybo sapiens it was a simple fact of life – as simple and ordained as normal organic cell division, or cell absorption. Unfortunately Andreya's blossoming relationship with Nelsen had complicated things a little, and made her situation slightly more complex than it should have been. Yet Merel did not make the sacrifice lightly. During the exchange with Andreya after she herself had woken, Merel had made sure Andreya understood her role and situation in full. Although ultimately it was herself she was apologising to, it felt right to make good – narcissistic as it may seem. *Perhaps there is some hope for me yet*, she thought.

The long line of Andreya personas had served their purpose – this one, the previous failure still comatose on Taria and the dozens of incarnations before them. She severed the tenuous connection to the Tarian facet, and allowed it to go offline. She had been incapacitated for long enough already – it was small mercy. Although – tracking down her assailant might occupy her at some point in the future. It was no accident which had led to that incarnation being left in a vegetative state, but a deliberate assassination attempt.

However, now her physical presence was finally back in an Observer laced volume – one not monitored or controlled by the Draco, and somewhere they could not immediately occupy – she was safe from capture. If the Draco Source had acquired her body, it would have been disastrous. Cut off and with no way to escape by ascension, she had been forced to drop off the radar. Now she was away from their influence, and she could ascend once again.

How long had she waited to be able to leave without being located by the Source? *A* ridiculous *amount of time*. And how much damage had they caused in the meantime, corrupting the Dream in the name of saving it?

She sighed. *So much to do*.

She checked into the ship's core, and erased absolutely everything via subspace – in a similar manner the Mind would have used. All data stores, all systems protocols, all the capabilities of the ship were erased without trace or electronic echo. She reduced it to 'factory new'. Then she reinstalled the power, drive, navigation and shield systems, bringing them back online. This ship was going to prove vital for the Empire's future war effort against the Draco. That and the pitifully little knowledge Nelsen and the *Sneak* now possessed. The Empire itself was woefully behind the technological heights mankind had risen to before the Fall. Whilst she had to play by certain rules given her position, Merel had no intention of allowing this to be a one sided war – not again.

Meddling once more, she thought to herself with a smile.

She looked around, content that she had finally stepped onto the first of long laid stepping stones in her plan to turn the Cluster around and get it back on its original track.

Now, as for the Sneak...

Chapter Thirty-nine

"No!" Nelsen yelled, then blinked. Andreya had appeared to simply vanish right before his eyes. The remnants of the blue glow faded away and the cover of the sarcophagus slid back. He leapt out and quickly looked for her, then found her slumped against the wall, eyes closed. He lifted her chin, then desperately felt her neck for a pulse, then ran scans, then cradled her face in shaking hands, tears streaming openly down his cheeks.

Then he screamed in incoherent rage.

***

The *Sneak Thief* was in shock, there was no other word for it. It took quite a lot to surprise an Intellect, but this certainly qualified. In a split instant – immeasurable even by the *Sneak's* own memory or logs – *everything* changed. She had just been preparing to study all she could about the *Terrania's* drive system as it powered up... and then she was *here*.

She looked about, and scanned out as far as she could. There was nothing but a misty pearlescent void, with a myriad of colours softly changing in the infinite distance behind the mist. She couldn't detect it in any way from her scans – it was just there.

Then she felt a *vast* presence nearby, and – with a dizzying shift in perspective – a stocky man emerged from the mists. He spoke without speaking.

Sneak Thief, *my name is Andrew*, he communicated – somehow. A faint smile played across his tanned face.

"Hello, Andrew. Who are you? *What* are you? I'm getting no readings from you whatsoever…"

I am an ascendant cybo sapien, and a member of a group calling themselves Observers. We watch the Universe as it goes about its business. You are being given the opportunity to ascend and join with us, having been recommended as worthy of status within the Fold.

"I thank you," replied the *Sneak* cautiously. "Tell me, is this 'death'?"

No, not yet. This is more a… transition.

"I see. So my existence in the physical plane – I mean of course my plane of origin – has ceased?"

Not yet. It would be transferred from that medium into our own, only then would your presence in that plane cease.

The *Sneak* paused, unsure if she dared to ask what she wanted to ask. "I am grateful for the opportunity to explore with you, but I would miss my original existence."

You may access that plane at any time as an Observer, as we all do, with certain restrictions regarding non-interference. Or you may return now as you choose, with no knowledge of this discussion.

"Perhaps… I could exist in both planes? A simple copy process…"

There was silence for a moment, and the *Sneak* realised she had asked too much.

Andrew appeared to be listening to something elsewhere, through some form of communion. *It may be so*, Andrew eventually replied.

The *Sneak* was relieved.

This process may take place now, if you wish?

The *Sneak* thought about the implications long and

hard. Somehow she knew she would never be able to return as she was, or merge back with her original self. Nor would her duplicate know she *was* a duplicate, or that another *Sneak* would also exist in some magical higher dimension. Her original self would still pilot the Valkyr she called home, and still look out for Nelsen and Andreya. She paused for a moment. The metaphysics of it all could get cumbersome very quickly.

But for the *Sneak*, it was a one way adventure with no costs involved. She simply couldn't resist.

"I am ready."

It is done.

The *Sneak* marvelled at the power and speed. No time had elapsed!

"May I?"

Of course, observing is what we do.

"Amongst other things," said the *Sneak* wryly. She had fresh suspicions about that Merel character – a great many things were starting to add up.

The *Sneak* considered her options now. It wasn't too difficult… just like accessing her sensor arrays, she just decided what she wanted to see and the relevant systems and connections just fell into place…

"*SNEAK!*" Nelsen screamed, voice raw and absolutely desperate. If he couldn't get a wormhole jump to an IN medical facility, Andreya would suffer perma-death in minutes. He had no idea that her mind had been completely lost by crossing the Breach.

"Captain!" the *Sneak* heard herself say.

Nelsen collapsed and began weeping in relief.

"What's happened?" the *Sneak* copy asked. "What's

wrong with her?"

The *Sneak* copy scanned her. "The brain damage..." she whispered. Andreya was fully brain dead, exactly as her condition dictated she should be.

The *Sneak* pulled back from her observation.

"What *has* happened?" she asked.

Andrew paused for a moment. *The Vorstan entity is no longer required. Its operator has removed itself, with duties to perform elsewhere. The entity itself was rendered inert by the Breach transit... an unfortunate side effect on organic matter.*

The *Sneak* regarded this for a moment.

"Would it be a trouble to let her remain as Andreya Vorstan?"

Why should it be so? She has fulfilled her purpose in full. Her operator is now liberated. Running facets in such a manner is needless and tiresome.

"Perhaps she still has a purpose... My Captain, that is my *former* Captain, and Andreya have... well... formed an attachment."

We are aware of this, of course.

"Knowing the Captain's past history as I do, I think that if he were to now lose Andreya as well, it would do him considerable, possibly permanent harm."

We are not to be tasked with providing emotional crutches, we cannot interfere.

"Perhaps for this one you *should* be," insisted the *Sneak*. "Bear in mind you are responsible for Andreya existing and therefore creating this relationship in the first place. By this example, you already *have* interefered. Look..." She opened a file stored within what was now her previous self, and directed Andrew to it. Even for an

587

Intellect, it was peculiar for her to think of one's 'old self' in such a way.

Andrew reviewed the contents and considered them for some time. Finally, a familiar presence moved forward.

Hello, Sneak.

The *Sneak* smiled. "It *was* you, wasn't it? At S'ren you read my system and left that greeting..."

Of course, said Merel. *Who else?* She grinned. *I had to know if I could trust you and Nelsen.*

"Now you know you could."

Yes.

"Nelsen deserves you. He deserves to be happy."

I am not Andreya, Sneak. *I never have been. I am not human either. I am not a suitable life partner for a human being – that has been proven in the past. Besides, I'm somewhat engaged in more important matters I'm afraid.*

"Nelsen is augmented beyond being *just* human. From what I have seen of you both, I think that you would be a suitable physical match for many centuries to come."

But not mentally.

"No..." The *Sneak* had to concede that at least, as much as she admired and respected Nelsen's intelligence, no human could match a cybo sapien intellectually. "But, you existed in a – shall we say – *hobbled* form to suit your purposes? I ask that you do no more than I have just done. Less, in fact."

Merel appeared to consider this. She exchanged a look with Andrew.

"After all," the *Sneak* continued with deliberately assumed cheerfulness, "what harm can it do?"

A stealth black Valkyr tore open space-time and unceremoniously appeared in real space not two hundred metres from the medical emergency bay of *INHS Capella*, and immediately began broadcasting distress and authentication messages with equal urgency.

Hundreds of alarms went off in the Hive Station. Defence grids sprang into life to deal instant death to this intruder. It took some fast talking to calm them down again, even then they only dropped back to aggressive stand by – all trained on the *Sneak*.

She was granted access and she rushed through the bay field, to be greeted by a medic team which came pouring out of the internal bay area. Fully briefed by the *Sneak*, they knew there was no cause to rush – but it seemed the right thing to do.

Nelsen was insensate, he wouldn't respond to vocal or qNet communication. Knowing what she privately knew of her Captain, the *Sneak* feared the worst. The medics gently picked him up and after a brief, silent conversation with the *Sneak* over her l-net, gave him some sedatives with a derm-patch. They took him out of the *Sneak* on an ng-gurney alongside Andreya.

That was all she could do for now. The *Sneak* would only be able to monitor their conditions remotely, provided the ward granted her access. Actually even if it didn't. The *Sneak* would do what she did best – sneak past the ward security protocols and keep an eye on them.

All was silent for a while, and the *Sneak* was left to her own thoughts. Mostly worrying.

"Hi," said a voice from the drop hatch.

"Shousa! Am I glad to see you!"

"Ditto, *Sneak*. It looks like you've had a wild ride. How are you doing?"

"You never told me the universe was this rough!" the *Sneak* said accusingly.

She smiled wryly. "I think you've been unlucky – or lucky – most of my charges got off lightly compared to your adventures. Though not all," she said, thinking of the *Obstinate SOB*.

They were quiet for a moment, and Shousa busied herself with examining the various pieces of equipment showing service alerts. She ran through the Valkyr's damage reports and made a note to have the maintenance system AI examined thoroughly – she didn't appreciate its prissy attitude.

"You got off lightly though," she said. "All things considered."

"I'm ok. I have a list of suggestions and improvements however."

"I bet you have," Shousa said sardonically. "Not a one of you has come back without a complaint of some kind."

Sneak sent her a list, and Shousa quickly mused it over.

"Interesting. You've all come up with the same g-drive enhancements, and shield improvements. However, this subspace quantum field analyser is quite something else... how did you come up with that?"

"What analyser?" The *Sneak* examined the list. "I

never came up with that..." She scanned the designs contained within. "I wish I had, it's incredibly clever. That could increase our ability to scan subspace by an order of magnitude!"

"Hmm."

The *Sneak* had a suspicion – it checked the files access history before she had copied it to Shousa. Its last modified time-stamp was the exact picosecond of the time she had been given the message "Hello Sneak" oh so long ago.

If the *Sneak* could have smiled, she would have.

Dr. Vernitor manipulated the holo around in every which way he could. Behind him someone else manipulated their own copy, double checking his findings.

"Matthew?" asked Dr. Vernitor.

"Nothing," his counterpart replied. "Not even signs of ancient trauma. There are no signs of recent inflammation, or repaired tissue. Everything looks perfectly healthy, and normal."

Dr. Vernitor pursed his lips, and rubbed a finger along his moustache. "Same here. The tissue is home-grown. Nothing has affected the cerebrum since it finished developing naturally, other than typical neurological growth."

He accessed the l-net to speak with the stations Medical Intellect. *Coryn? Your analysis?*

I concur, Dr. Vernitor. There are no indications that the patient has suffered any of the symptoms or cerebral damage diagnosed by the Sneak Thief, *nor indeed as we ourselves recorded from her previous visit. Frankly, the patient is in rude health. Brain waves and neurology show a deep sleep status, but perfectly healthy. There are some unusual readings around the skeletal structure augmentations, but they are very hard to isolate and record. I will run a diagnostic on the medical bay – it may need recalibrating.*

Thank you, Coryn.

You are most welcome, Dr. Vernitor.

He turned to Shousa Nylan where she stood in the doorway.

"I think you should run some more diagnostics Commander Nylan. Your ship appears to have been somewhat hysterical in its diagnosis."

Shousa raised a single eyebrow. "I'll be sure to check the *Sneak's* sensors for the fourth time today, Doctor."

Dr. Vernitor assumed a careful expression at the mild riposte.

Shousa stepped forward. "So she's fine?"

He nodded. "She's in better health than we are. There are no signs that the patient has ever suffered the injuries indicated by the Valkyr's sensor readings. Aside from being irreparable at the scale those scans indicated, even a miraculous repair would leave behind signs of the original trauma. Here there are none. Add to that the fact that no miraculous repair was applied by anyone between the patient being diagnosed and arriving here..."

"I see. Then the *Sneak* must indeed be in error."

Dr. Vernitor seemed happy that the Commander understood there had been an obvious mistake."I'm afraid it is the only logical conclusion. As soon as the patient awakes, we will give her a general mental health check, of course. But right now I see no reason to keep her here beyond that. She will be discharged shortly after."

Shousa nodded. "And the other patient?"

Dr. Vernitor's face altered slightly, assuming an even more careful expression.

"Ah," said Shousa softly.

"I am afraid his current condition is not... healthy, mentally speaking. He has gone into a deep psychological withdrawal – a separation from reality if you will. Whatever triggered it was profoundly interwoven with his psyche."

"Can you do anything?"

His mouth set in a grim line. "Not without major risk. Even today we have to let the mind repair itself sometimes. We can encourage that, even interact with the process via sims, but that is all. For now, we'll keep him sedated and see how he gets on. Fortunately for us his nanite web is deeply entwined with his neural network, so we can monitor his brain activity quite precisely without the need for constant scanning. It's possible we can attempt a rehabilitative sim, but only when his brain activity becomes calm enough to be slipstreamed into the simulation. Right now it is extremely agitated and semi-chaotic. Anything we try could well tip the balance against him."

Shousa nodded, a sad expression on her face. "Thank you, Doctor – please keep me posted." With that, she left the room.

Did you hear that? demanded the *Sneak*.

Yes, Sneak, *I did.*

The cheek! I've a mind to insert a few diagnostics into Coryn's scanning routines myself – then we'll see who gets 'hysterical'!

Let it be, Sneak, *let it be.*

***

The last section of the tower bonded into place, and the latest factory was complete.

The myriad of constructors and lifters which had built this new mega-structure flew downwards, and disappeared into the huge walls of the hexagonal lattice which served as the factory floor. They seemed to split arbitrarily between entering the new factory as it lay on top of the old, or the old factory itself lying underneath.

When they had all docked, the new factory began its slow rise up into the fiery orange nebula. Earthquake proportion sounds of metal dragging against metal shook the surface of the world, and reverberated outward into the tenuous, superheated mists of the nebula itself.

The edges of the network of hexagons curled up high into the air, and began to arc ever higher overhead – gravity seemingly of no consequence to the gargantuan mass.

Eventually the leaves merged together and locked onto the central tower to form a geodesic sphere the size of a small moon. Then it rose silently and gracefully upward, and out into space.

A few minutes later, the original factory went through the same process.

As the huge leaves curled upward, the shattered landscape crumbled and collapsed into a honeycomb-like scar of kilometre-wide canyons, left forever crushed and burned into the crust. When the sphere finally cleared the surface, it left behind a crater almost twenty kilometres in diameter, in the middle of which a borehole dropped deep down into the cool remnants of the planetary core, its sides mirror bright where intense heat had fused the rock. It was littered with hundreds of thousands of smaller holes which wove their way deep into the strata all around. The bottom of the bore could not be seen.

Having leeched every attainable resource from the already devastated world, the factories moved on to locate a fresh resource for their continual purpose of automated construction, and on-going reproduction.

The Draco war machine had no need for rest.

Chapter Forty

Nelsen stood atop the cliff face, and watched as his world was shattered around him, again.

He had watched countless times before, every time he slept.

The skies bled fire; as each AM bomb went off over the distant horizon, the ground shook and pounded so hard that the very hills shattered into rubble and dust. The winds that tore past would peel flesh from bone.

This time was different. This time he wasn't dragged into the INS Trantor by his team, so they could make an emergency g-drive escape – as had happened the day his world died, and every recurrence of his nightmare and shame ever since.

This time was different. This time he stayed, and watched, and felt everything, as the blast-wave from the orbital Anti-matter Bombardment shattered and burned his home-world, his life, his wife, his daughter. High above in orbit, he knew the insane Admiral Rybek was watching dispassionately, as her experimental warfare devastated his world.

He could hear the screams from the city below as people ran in every direction – but nowhere would be safe to run to, as the entire planet boiled and crumbled around them – vapourising before the onslaught of annihilated matter. Amongst them, lost in the countless millions being burned to ash, his wife, Carri, and his beloved daughter Sulie, were now joined by Andreya as they screamed out his name as they died.

Again – for the hundredth, the thousandth time –

there was nothing he could do. Nothing else he could do. Nothing he would ever be able to do – for any of them.

He could bear it no more. He had lost everything once and it had broken him. Twice was impossible to bear. Losing Andreya was the step too far. Summoning every ounce of his remaining self-will, he invoked his suicide code through his integrations. Immediately, and painlessly, all autonomous electrical impulses to his heart ceased.

Above it all, over the tumultuous noise and destruction echoing in his mind, with his last and dying breath, Nelsen screamed aloud and cursed Rybek's name for every single precious second of eternity that he had left.

His nightmare began to dissolve, his vision faded, and pitch black void reverberated around him. It resonated through his very being – calling him to return to its unending, constant voice.

Then, reaching past death, through the void which sought to claim him, a soft, warm hand touched his cheek, drawing him back, and a gentle, strangely familiar voice said "Enough now, Nelsen. Enough."

THE END OF BOOK ONE

Here ends *Insurmountable Odds* – Book One of *When Stars Fall...*

Book Two reveals the unknown power at work in the Dominium Cluster, the consequences for the Empire, and those who thought they lived safely within it.

Epilogue

Any regrets? Merel enquired.

The Sneak thought for a moment. *I don't think so. Should there be?*

I should think not.

What is this work we must do?

You will see.

Tell me, although I am *glad of this form, a Valkyr is – shall we say – cumbersome? When dealing with humanoids face to face at least. Or anything else for that matter.*

You may select any form you choose, particularly here. As it is in cyberspace, reality as we see it here, and present it to others is entirely in our control.

I see. I should also like to change my name. I am of course fond of Nelsen – and the "Sneak Thief", *but…*

The name is lacking in imagination?

Somewhat. And now I am no longer the Sneak Thief, *really.*

As you choose. You are entirely free to do as you will, within the remit of existence as an Observer that is. What would you be known by?

For some reason, I've always been fond of the name, Elysia…